# *The Half of It*

## Also by Juliette Fay

*Catch Us When We Fall*
*City of Flickering Light*
*The Tumbling Turner Sisters*
*The Shortest Way Home*
*Deep Down True*
*Shelter Me*

# Praise for Juliette Fay's *Catch Us When We Fall*

"A novel about resilience and the power of human connection, *Catch Us When We Fall* is perfect for fans of emotionally honest women's fiction."

—Brenda Janowitz, author of *The Grace Kelly Dress*

"Suffused with compassion, wry humor, and the unexpected grace of healing, it's a story not of angels or demons, but of two people struggling to find a safe harbor in the broken landscape of addiction."

—Randy Susan Meyers, bestselling author of *Waisted* and *The Widow of Wall Street*

"A hopeful, poignant novel about the tenacity of the human spirit, our capacity for forgiveness, and all the ways a heart can grow when we least expect it. You'll want to curl up in bed with this heartwarming story."

—Allison Winn Scotch, *New York Times* bestselling author

"*Catch Us When We Fall* is full of hope and heart and genuine love. I already miss checking in with these beautiful people who are trying their hardest to heal and connect."

—Allie Larkin, bestselling author of *Stay, Why Can't I Be You*, and *Swimming for Sunlight*

"*Catch Us When We Fall* is a beautiful story about life's darkest demons—grief, addiction, and broken promises—but Juliette Fay's characters are so lovable and emotionally complex the book left me suffused with light and hope. I read this in a gulp, alternately crying, laughing, and cheering."

—Ann Mah, bestselling author of *The Lost Vintage*

# The Half of It

*A Novel*

## JULIETTE FAY

*wm*
WILLIAM MORROW
*An Imprint of* HarperCollins*Publishers*

FIRST EDITION

*Designed by Diahann Sturge*
*Leaf illustration © Nadezhda Molkentin / Shutterstock, Inc.*

Library of Congress Cataloging-in-Publication Data has been applied for.

ISBN 978-0-06-323596-0

23 24 25 26 27 LBC 5 4 3 2 1

*For Linda Dacey, my beloved stepmother*

## A Continual Autumn

*Inside each of us, there's a continual autumn. Our leaves
fall and are blown out*

*over the water. A crow sits in the blackened limbs and talks
about what's gone. Then*

*your generosity returns: spring, moisture, intelligence,
the scent of hyacinth and rose*
*. . . . . . . . . . . . . . . . . . . .*
*Very little grows on jagged*

*rock. Be ground. Be crumbled so wildflowers will come up
where you are.*

—Jalāl al-Dīn Muḥammad Rūmī,
thirteenth-century Persian poet, Islamic scholar, and Sufi mystic

# *Chapter 1*

*2021*

Helen sits on her favorite bench in the woods by the river, boot heels dug into the stony New England earth, body hitched forward slightly to accommodate the baby backpack. Limp, fleece-swaddled legs dangle by her hips.

Fall is in full profusion here in Belham, Massachusetts. Yellow leaves glint like gold off the surface of the water as they glide by; afternoon sun casts bright but diminishing rays that bounce against the ripples.

Helen doesn't see the beauty. Her blank stare conjures only the wrong turns; regret is a thing with teeth. There's movement out of the corner of her eye, and for the briefest moment she's sure it's an animal that will chew her to bits.

But it isn't.

A small child—maybe two and a half or three years old—running. His little-boy legs paddle at the dirt path with the delightful inefficiency of limbs that have only recently learned to accomplish this feat of anatomical engineering. Chubby fists clench as his body concentrates on propelling him forward. Grinning to himself.

The sight of her catches him unawares and he stops smiling, eyes suddenly round in fear. His gaze is locked on hers when his foot hits a root in the path, and he spills forward onto his belly, his neck not yet strong enough to keep his lovely little face from smacking into the dirt.

Helen is up and running to him as he lets out a wail of pain, the sleeping one-year-old on her back jostling against her so that she almost falls right on top of the little boy.

"Hey," she coos, squatting down next to him, "hey there." She doesn't want to touch him—children are so well-versed in stranger danger these days, and she doesn't want to fuel his panic. But he can't seem to lift himself out of the dirt, and still crying hard, he only manages to roll over onto his back like a baby turtle.

"Can I help you up?" she asks.

"Yessssss!" he wails and reaches up to her. She slides her hands into his little armpits and lifts him, intending only to right him onto his feet, but he clamps his arms behind her neck and wraps his legs around her waist like a baby monkey, nearly destabilizing her. She gets a better grip on him and stands up.

"Where's your grown-up?" Helen gently wipes at the dirt on his cheeks with the sleeve of her sweatshirt.

"I runned away!" he says, and this precipitates a whole new round of sobs.

"You ran away? From who?"

"My grandpa!"

Helen immediately pictures an evil old man hitting the boy—or worse—but she warns herself against jumping to conclusions. "Why did you run away from him?" she asks mildly so as not to further inflame the situation.

"I played a triiiiick!" He wails with remorse. "Grandpaaaaa!"

"Okay, okay," Helen croons, trying not to laugh. Her daughter, Barbara, was emotional and dramatic like this as a child, and

Helen had often marveled at the girl's ability to allow feelings (any feelings, good, bad, or indifferent—the girl could make indifference dramatic) to erupt like flames from an unpredictable volcano.

Jim was always so perplexed by Barb's emotional outbursts, as if she were an alien species with whom, try as he might, he couldn't quite communicate. Helen had told him countless times, "She's young. She just feels what she feels." And he would chuckle and say, "Apparently." But to this day, Barb still felt what she felt. It was a wonder.

Helen pats the little boy's back and says, "Don't worry, we'll find Grandpa."

She's just turning to head up the path when she hears a man's voice in the distance booming, "Logan! Logan, where are you? Logan!" The panic in that voice makes Helen's heart hurt. She's occasionally lost track of a child and knows there is nothing more terrifying.

"He's here!" she calls back. "Logan's here! He's okay!"

"I'm okay!" the little boy echoes in his high, sweet voice. "I'm okay, Grandpa!"

Helen feels the man's thumping footsteps coming toward her before she catches sight of him rounding a turn in the path. His face is ashen with worry—either that or he has alarmingly bad circulation. His shoulders hunch forward as he jogs toward them in a strange, ungainly lope. As he gets closer, Helen sees the reason for his galumphing gait: he, too, has a baby on his back, a little pink-capped head bobbing up and down, in and out of view from the oversize pack.

"Hi, Grandpa!" Logan sings out, suddenly happy and excited, as if this is a pleasant surprise rather than a mildly traumatic event that he himself set in motion. He leaps to his grandfather's arms before the man is quite close enough to get a good hand on him, and the guy stumbles forward, gripping the kid and pressing him into his chest a little too tightly.

His face somehow sets off a ping of memory, a long-buried familiarity, but before Helen can study it further, tears form in the man's eyes, and his face contorts into a barely controlled sob. Helen is a bit taken aback. Jim never cried. She's only seen men cry at funerals. Except for Barb's father-in-law, who cried at their wedding.

"Jesus, Logan," he chokes out. "You scared the shit out of me."

"Dat's a bad word," says Logan from inside the man's nearly smothering embrace.

"Sorry." The man shifts the child into one arm and puts a hand up to pinch the tears out of his eyes. "Don't tell Mommy, okay?"

"Dat's okay. Jesus is good."

A laugh bursts out of the man then, and he catches Helen's eye, and they both start to laugh. Helen puts a hand up to her mouth. She wants to keep this feeling.

With his face relaxed and smiling, the memory comes clear. Cal Crosby.

Cal fucking Crosby.

With no sign of recognition, eyes still twinkling with humor, he pulls the child back to look at him. The little boy puts his hand up to his grandfather's cheek, finger pressing on an errant tear. "Is it raining?"

"A little," he says, though the sky is a cloudless crayon blue, "but it'll pass."

Helen continues to stare. How does he not recognize her? But he's focused on Logan, and she can almost feel the ebbing panic of his pounding heart pulsing through the crisp air against her own body. Fear can blind you. She knows that.

There's a squawk from the pink cap behind him, and he kisses the boy and attempts to lower him to the ground. But Logan isn't having it.

"Hold me!" he begs.

"McKenzie needs her bottle, buddy."

"My legs hurt," he whines.

It's Helen's escape hatch. Let him deal with the bruised toddler and hungry baby. No one wants other adults bearing witness to the inept handling of unhappy children. Because it's always inept. Child wrangling is rarely elegant, and by the looks of him Logan is summoning the demons of a five-alarm tantrum.

Barb and Danny had loved to throw fits in public. A two-year-old Danny once howled like he'd been hit with a hammer because Helen wouldn't let him hold the steak knives in her shopping cart at Target. On a trip to Ben & Jerry's, Barb had hurled her ice cream to the ground, convinced that someone had licked it (And who would that have been—the bespectacled scooper? Helen? Aliens?) and wailed for another. Sam was the gentle bookish child. He never complained on his own behalf. But he could become utterly distraught if he thought a passerby was holding a dog too tightly on its leash, and no amount of explaining about puppy training could console him.

Helen has a brief vindictive wish for Logan to throw a good fist-and-foot-flailing thrasher. Something to make Cal fucking Crosby *really* cry . . .

But honestly, does she even care anymore? It was all so long ago. Oceans of water have passed under countless bridges. She's brought three humans into the world. Buried a husband in the enforced emptiness of a pandemic. Moved to a little town where she knows no one except her daughter and son-in-law, who are utterly engrossed in the endless blessing of this baby, and the endless exhaustion of new parenthood. At fifty-eight, Helen Spencer somehow finds herself relegated to solitude at the edge of other people's lives.

Maybe she's due for a good fist-and-foot-flailing thrasher herself.

*Oh, grow up*, she tells herself. It's for the best that he doesn't recognize her. Who wants to revisit that mess? Better to move on. Put one foot in front of the other. She has always been a good little marcher.

But before she heads down the path, Helen takes one last look at the boy's smudged, angelic face and feels a duty to say, "He hit the dirt pretty hard. Tripped over that root there."

"I tripped," confirms Logan, nodding solemnly. His lower lip begins to quiver at the memory of his rather impressive fall.

The baby is crying in earnest now, sobs coming in little jags between gulps of air. The man, oversize presence though he is, is physically trapped between two small children and their oversize needs. He looks around as if hoping to MacGyver a solution out of twigs and moss. He's an Eagle Scout, Helen remembers, but fire building won't help him now.

She actually feels bad for him. In forty years, she's had not one moment of pity for Cal fucking Crosby, so it's kind of interesting. Also, how does the bastard not recognize her? Honestly, this is the most interesting thing that's happened to her in months.

"Hey, Logan," she says, "how about if I hold you while your grandpa feeds the baby. We can sit on this bench over here."

The boy leans out to her, and she collects him into her arms again, but when she walks toward the bench he whimpers, "I don't want to sit!"

"It's my favorite bench," she says. "You'll love it." And without waiting for further approval, she lowers herself. She's done a few rounds of puppy training herself and found it far more helpful than any parenting book. She snuggles him onto her lap and gives him a teasing little poke. "See, isn't this fun?"

Logan is confused by this. What's so fun about sitting on a bench, after all? Only moments ago, she was sitting on this very bench having zero fun. Negative fun. But now she's enjoying herself. It's like reading a plot-twisty book and wondering when the truth will reveal itself. Her enthusiasm quells his peevishness, and the little boy says only, "Shh, your baby is sleeping."

Cal slides one shoulder out of the backpack, pulls out the stabilizing arm, and gently sets it on the ground. He roots around in the attached pouch for a moment as the baby shrieks in despair. He pulls out a bottle, hauls the little banshee out of the carrier, quickly cradles her in one arm while he rubs the nipple over her bottom lip trying to get her to settle down enough to realize that he's giving her the very thing she's demanding at such a high decibel.

Logan puts his hands over his ears. "Too loud." This is despite the fact that his own cries were scaring woodland creatures in all directions only a few minutes before. Now he's the noise police.

Cal bounces on his knees a little. "Okay, Kenz, come on now, it's right here," he murmurs, still dabbing the nipple at her wide-open mouth. Finally, she latches on and slurps hungrily. Her little fingers wrap around the bottle, and she holds it herself. Cal puts a finger against the bottom, adjusting it to the proper angle.

*A pro*, thinks Helen, and remembers how easily he picked things up, the bastard. But then she wonders how he lost Logan. Maybe he's slipping. She slides over on the bench. "Want to sit?"

He gives her a quick smile as he sinks down and shifts the baby into a more comfortable hold on his lap. She notices the sheen of anxiety-induced sweat on his upper lip. He wipes it self-consciously against the shoulder of his chamois shirt and reaches up to tug off his wool cap. His short-cropped hair is a little more auburn now. It was bright red back then, and he'd kept it long even for 1981. All that flowing beauty. It had felt like silk against her fingers.

His eyes are bookended by matching deltas of creases at the corners, but they're still that soft blue she remembers a little too well. There's a scar on his upper lip that wasn't there forty years ago. He hasn't shaved today, and his whiskers are sprinkled with white.

*So that's how you turned out*, she thinks.

"I'm hungry, too!" Logan suddenly announces, and Cal leans down toward the backpack again, hand emerging with a fairly smushed sandwich. He peels off the sticky plastic wrap and hands over a half.

"It's all ick," whines Logan.

"Sorry, kiddo, that's what we got."

Helen says, "I'll eat it."

Logan jams the sandwich into his mouth.

"Another satisfied customer," says Helen. It's a phrase her father often used, and the words unexpectedly make her chest tighten, even after all these years. To dispel the sadness, she focuses back on Cal Crosby and his potential incompetence. "How'd you lose him?"

Cal shakes his head. "The little . . ."—*shit*, Helen can almost hear him say, but he pivots to—"snip. I was changing the baby, and I was just getting her into the pack, and I look around and he's gone." He shakes his head again. "His mother would've killed me six different ways. I just got back in her good graces, and if anything happens to him . . ."

*Good graces*, Helen thinks. *That's a slip he didn't mean to make.*

"My youngest would take off every chance he got," she says. "I had to hang on to him so often, I was afraid his wrists would have permanent indentations."

"Youngest?" His perplexed gaze shifts to the baby still asleep in the backpack.

Helen doesn't know what to say for a moment. Jesus, he really doesn't know who she is. "She's not . . . She's my granddaughter."

Cal's eyebrows shoot up. "Oh. I just assumed—"

"You can't possibly have thought I was her mother." True, Helen is still coloring her hair, unlike several of her friends who "embraced" their gray under cover of Covid. Hers is perhaps a little more glossy chestnut than her natural mousy brown was back in high school. And she is fairly fit for her age, though the time required for her daily three-milers has gradually increased like the size of her ass. Still, she is clearly not of childbearing age.

"Well, I figured maybe late in life . . ."

Helen lets out a snort. "Not this late."

He frowns at her. "You could be midforties. It's not that far-fetched."

"Look at me."

He's on the defensive now. "Seriously, you have great skin and—"

"Cal, look at me."

# Chapter 2

## 1976

Helen Iannucci was not a good sitter. Girls were supposed to be better at keeping still and paying attention than boys, and she was probably better than most of the boys in her class, but this required a concerted effort on her part. It was okay to jitter and tap if you were a boy. It just made a girl look nutty.

She liked being outside. She had been a Girl Scout, with high hopes that there would be hiking and campouts. But her den mother, Mrs. Galudet, did not like bugs. The troop stayed indoors and did a lot of so-called Indian crafts. Helen wasn't so sure that Indians made sit-upons, which the girls wove out of construction paper because Mrs. Galudet couldn't find the kind of frondy stuff that would have been slightly more authentic-looking. And Girl Scout cookie sales put Helen over the edge. Countless hours sitting outside the post office and accosting people to place their orders. She quit in fourth grade.

"Those cookies," her mother scoffed in her piquant Italian accent. "Taste like the box they come in."

Annabella Iannucci had not one ounce of patience for food in boxes. Cake mixes made her apoplectic. "Why!" she would rail. "Why not use the flour and salt and sugar from your own cupboard!"

Helen's father, Lou, had encouraged her to stay in the troop. "Aren't a lot of your friends in the troop? Isn't that what nine-year-old girls do? If you quit, and all your friends are in it, won't you be lonely?"

It was true, most of the girls in her class did go to Mrs. Galudet's and make dream catchers out of acrylic yarn and wire hangers. But Helen wasn't especially friendly with those kinds of sitting-still girls. Her best friend, Francie Hydecker, was horse crazy. They spent a lot of time cantering on imaginary steeds around Francie's vast, expertly mowed backyard. Helen didn't really think horses were kinder and smarter than humans, like Francie did, but the horse thing wasn't so bad. Sometimes they'd gallop for a while and then Francie would say, "Now it's time to go in your stall." She liked to practice her brushing and currying on Helen's back, which Helen found very relaxing.

The transition to Hestia Junior High in seventh grade was hard on Francie and Helen. Francie's obsession with horses did not morph into an obsession with boys as it did for most girls. If anything, Francie's love of horses only became more extreme. The horses at Hotchkiss's barn were nice to her; twelve-year-old boys were not.

Helen, on the other hand, was not obsessed, exactly, but she was suddenly very *aware* of boys.

"That's because you're the same height," said Francie once, when they were discussing how all the dumb girls in their dumb school were so into boys, and they weren't. "Everywhere you turn you have to look at boys' dumb eyes."

This wasn't true. Helen was actually taller than most boys her age. But she would rather have sat still for a week than call more attention to that. Some of the really mean boys called her the Wop Giraffe.

Helen got the idea about joining the Hestia Junior High track team mostly because Francie was so busy with Hotchkiss's horses. At first Helen had gone along with Francie to see if maybe she, too, might want to earn a dollar an hour shoveling shit after school but found that she did not. Francie talked to the horses more than Helen, so the whole thing was just tedious and bad-smelling.

By spring, she was bored and irritable and sort of itchy in a weird way she couldn't really explain, but she was on the fence about the track team. She liked the idea of being outside and running around like she'd done with Francie since she was six. But the team was coed. There was both an upside and a downside to this: upside, it wouldn't be weird to look at boys' bodies in motion, which she very much liked to do; downside, this could call attention to her long legs and cause an uptick in Wop Giraffe references.

Boredom and boys tipped the scales. And she figured if she got good at it and won races, they'd stop calling her embarrassing names and respect her. At least maybe a little.

Getting her parents to sign the forms for the track team required strategy. She came into the kitchen precisely as Annabella was sliding her signature anise cookies into the oven.

"Mama, I'm joining a team at school."

"The math team?" Annabella valued well-prepared food, well-behaved daughters, and well-paying jobs, in that order. Also, she kept the books and dealt with distributors at Lou's auto shop.

"Um, no, not the math team."

"Not the French team. Such an ugly language." Annabella made a series of gasping noises in her throat to imitate her impression of French. She had never wanted Helen to learn Italian because they were Americans, they spoke English, end of discussion. But

Helen knew her mother was a little miffed that the administration of Hestia Junior High had, in its dubious wisdom, chosen to offer the "ugly" languages of French and German, and not her own lyrical Italian. Which she no longer spoke.

"The track team," said Helen.

Annabella wiped a salt-and-pepper lock of hair off her forehead, leaned against the chipped but spotless Formica counter, and crossed her arms under her bosoms. "What—running? You run around in a circle? That's the team you want to join?"

"Yes."

Annabella frowned. "Luigi!"

There was no answer. Annabella continued to frown. "You go like this?" She pumped her fists up and down in front of her. "With all-a you pieces flying around?"

"Mama, my pieces don't fly very far." Helen had not yet acquired her mother's voluptuous figure. Nor would she ever, but at twelve she still held out hope.

Annabella gave a little smirk, then twisted toward the open window and yelled, "Luigi, get your head out from under that hood and come in the house, please! Important business!"

Luigi Iannucci, who went by Lou ("With an *o*," Annabella would occasionally say with an eye roll when she was annoyed with him), loved restoring cars almost as much as he worshipped his wife and daughter. He'd had his own auto body shop for five years now and had wanted to call it Iannucci's, but Annabella had put a stop to that.

"You got no accent, you got the light hair, why do attention to your name?" Lou had immigrated with his Northern Italian parents in 1938 when he was fifteen.

"Call attention," Lou had gently corrected.

"Call attention? That doesn't sound right." She looked to Helen, the true American, whom they had given a nice, inspiring

American name. No one could deny the all-American ingeniousness of Helen Keller. (It was, however, a lot to live up to.)

"Call attention is correct," seven-year-old Helen had said.

Annabella had grinned and sang out, "Attention! Attention! I'm calling you!" and this had made them all laugh. It was okay to be not-quite-so-American when it was just the three of them. They quickly settled on Eagle Auto Body for the name of the shop.

Now Luigi came in the back door of their small but sufficient house on Kisco Avenue, wiping the grease off his permanently darkened fingers with a rag, and humming "I've Got You Under My Skin."

"Luigi," said Annabella, interrupting him. "She wants to join the track team. Running around for no good reason."

For No Good Reason was an ever-expanding list of things that included eating at restaurants ("My food's better"), camping ("You want to sleep on the ground like an animal?"), and board games ("Take too long"). Annabella did love playing cards, but not bridge because "take too long."

Luigi blinked his hazel eyes, assessing the situation. The first love of his life was opposed, and the second was apparently in favor. He turned to Helen. "Why do you want to run track, sweetheart? Is Francie joining? Are there nice girls on the team? Are you worried about your weight?"

Her father liked to get all his concerns right out on the table from the get-go. In terms of Helen, they often revolved around her friendships and self-esteem. Luigi himself had many friends. He was generous, easy to get along with, and never had a bad word to say about anyone except politicians and racecar drivers, a breed of men who clearly did not respect the delicate beauty of a truly great automobile. And he felt good about himself. He owned his own business, was tall and reasonably attractive, and he was married to a smart, sassy beauty who cooked him a gourmet meal every night and would personally debone anyone who looked at him sideways.

Unwittingly, he often made clear that he worried his only child—the one he and Annabella had prayed and waited so long for—did not enjoy the same critical life assets of friendships and self-regard.

*He thinks I'm fat and friendless*, thought Helen.

"I like running," she said.

"It's good exercise," Luigi conceded, though she'd never seen either of her parents engage in anything that could be considered exercise. They were both in motion all day; who needed a gym? "But you know you're fine just the way you are, right?"

"Yes, I know," said Helen. But now she wondered, was her butt getting big? Because being too tall and skinny with no boobs was hard enough, but add a fat ass onto that package and things were going to get freakish. To her father she said, "I just like running, and it might be good to make friends other than Francie."

"Why? What did she do?" asked Annabella suspiciously.

"No, nothing. We're still best friends. It's just that she's always at Hotchkiss's—"

"Madonn', with the horses," muttered Annabella.

"I just need something to do."

This was not going well. Just needing something to do was No Good Reason territory. She had to get back on message with her strategy. "Actually, I was thinking that if I run track in the afternoon, I'll probably be extra hungry when I get home, and maybe you'll have to make a little more food, Mama. I could help with that. I could cook with you on the weekends, and you could show me how to do it, and then we'll have plenty."

Annabella had been bugging Helen to learn to cook for years. Helen never had the heart to tell her mother that cooking just didn't hold the same kind of alchemical fascination for her. Annabella was creating masterful works of art. To Helen it was just something you had to do so your stomach wouldn't growl.

A sly smile arose on Annabella's face. The woman had an unerring nose for attempts at manipulation, which played no small part in her husband's business success. She wagged her finger at Helen, a *well-played* gesture. "Okay, smarty," she said. "You run and then you cook. I'll show you everything, and we'll make so much, we'll fill the freezer!" Annabella had a freezer the size of an AMC Gremlin in the basement, and it was generally filled to the gasket at all times. She had lived through World War II in Italy as a teenager; she came by her minor food hoarding honestly.

"Another satisfied customer!" said Luigi, relieved and happy that his two great loves now agreed, and he was spared from having to King Solomon his way to a peaceable solution. "Maybe you can invite your new friends over for dinner sometime, too."

It was settled. Helen would run track. But she no longer felt as enthusiastic as she had before her parents agreed to it.

THE JUNIOR HIGH track team turned out to be good for Helen. And she turned out to be very good for the team. After three seasons, at the end of ninth grade, she had achieved her full and final height of five feet, nine and a half inches. Her coach, Mr. Grost, rounded up to five foot ten. Helen rounded down. Either way, she had the longest legs of any girl and most of the boys on the team.

"Like a stork," Annabella would say when the subject of Helen's stature came up. (She was not nearly as concerned as Luigi about Helen's self-esteem.)

Mr. Grost helped her to streamline her gait and strategize about when to lay off and give her muscles a little extra oxygen, and when to "blow the doors off," as he liked to say, and all this improved her times. But more than anything, Helen was good at running because the very act felt like her natural state, as instinctual as flight to a bird. The only person who called her Wop Giraffe anymore was Ricky Zugravescu, and he was often too busy smoking unfiltered Marlboros and giving his friends artistic but inappropriate tattoos behind the cafeteria dumpster to make it to class.

Helen had become a star in the little world of little Hestia's very small track team. Then in tenth grade she hit Corden County Regional High School, and everything changed.

# Chapter 3

**2021**

W hat? Wait a minute . . ." says Cal Crosby, fumbling around in the breast pocket of his chamois shirt. He pulls out a pair of cheap readers—possibly women's, it looks like, with the fake gold trim at the hinges—and pushes them onto his face.

Helen waits, suddenly regretful that she's outed herself. It was fun to watch him muddle through with the kids and reveal little tidbits, like an apparent falling-out with his daughter (Daughter? Cal fucking Crosby is someone's *dad*?), without the greasy wad of past events clogging up the works. She was the proverbial fly on the wall. Now she's a fly on flypaper.

Cal studies her for only a second before his face freezes in a sort of controlled panic: shock sprinkled liberally with fear and . . . something else, like his face can't make up its mind . . . It almost looks like relief.

"Helen," he says.

"Hi," she says.

"Wow."

"Yeah."

"Holy shit."

They both turn toward Logan, anticipating his censure, but he gazes up into the trees with what Helen calls the No-Nap Stare. A slow blink. Then another. He'll be asleep in her arms any second now.

Cal cuts his eyes warily back to Helen. "How've you been?"

If that isn't the stupidest question she's ever heard.

"Good," she says. "You?"

He smiles, shaking his head in wonder. "Um . . . good?"

Damn those soft blue eyes. She can't help but give a little smile (a cool one, she hopes, or at least not warm). "Great."

"Hold on. When did you know it was me?"

*When you stopped crying*, she wants to say. But what is she, a playground bully? A scorned teenage girl? *Grow up*, she tells herself. *Be you now, not you then.*

"After things settled down a little."

"But you didn't say anything."

"It was kind of fun to wait and see if you'd figure it out."

"Which I didn't because I'm half blind."

"Nice glasses, by the way."

He reaches up and pulls the readers off to look at them. "Ah, Jesus, they're my wife's."

Cal Crosby's wife. Well, what did she expect.

"Will she be upset that you took them?"

"Nah, she's got a million of them." He puts them back on and gazes at her. "You look great, by the way. I think that's what really threw me off. You do not look my age."

"Yeah, I do. And I am."

*It happened*, she suddenly has an urge to say. *I am that girl.*

"Helen Iannucci," he murmurs.

And then it's too real. Him, her. That time, and all that came after.

She was tougher once. A couple of years ago, before the pandemic, maybe, she could have swept it back under the very thick, very dusty rug where it belonged. But she was laid bare by the virus's unrelenting grind. Losing her mother, then Jim. So much time spent alone, reviewing. It was the reviewing that had gotten to her. And suddenly there isn't a rug big enough. For any of it.

"I . . . um . . ." Logan is sleeping now, and Helen begins to slowly, gently shift him onto the bench between them. "I should get back. She'll be up any minute, starving, and I didn't bring any food. I don't usually stay out this long."

That isn't true. On beautiful days like this, sometimes she stays out for hours, hiking through the woods, the baby happily babbling on her back. But Helen woke up in a funk—this is becoming more and more common—and forgot everything, even a spare diaper. She just put the baby in the pack and walked out.

Cal watches her do this. "Oh . . . sure . . . okay, thanks for your help. Don't know what I would have done if you hadn't been here."

"You would have worked it out. You seem pretty good with them."

"I'm learning."

She smiles. "Aren't we all."

She stands to go, and he says, "Helen. It was . . . I mean, it's really good to see you. I'm glad I know how you turned out."

*You don't know*, she thinks. *Not the half of it.*

"Same," she says, and lights one last brief smile before she turns and walks back down the path.

# Chapter 4

## 1978

"Cal fucking Crosby's on the team?" said Marybeth Guchel. "Gag me."

"Such a spaz," Wendy Moriarty, Marybeth's very best friend of the moment, responded. They were in Helen's algebra section. Based on their answers in class, Helen was pretty sure Marybeth was doing Wendy's homework for her.

The two girls stood a few feet away from Helen, fingering their ponytails and surveying the crowd. They were from Velmont, one of four towns that offered up their mostly virginal sons and daughters to the active volcano of Corden County Regional High School.

Helen followed their contemptuous gazes to a diminutive creature, all pale skin and sharp elbows, with the most amazing mane of red hair. He stood on the edge of the milling flock of hormones and acne, shifting back and forth on his feet like a boxer.

"Don't try so hard," Wendy told the boy. "It's just cross-country. You're not Rocky."

"And get a haircut, for godsake," said Marybeth.

"I'm not joining," he said. "I'm just checking it out."

"Jesus, don't *talk* to us," said Marybeth.

They both had long, silky light brown hair, the sides blown back in feathered wings so impressive that Helen thought they might take flight at any moment. And she really wouldn't have minded if the two of them lifted off from the CCRHS track and sailed off to parts unknown, or like teenage Icarettes, flew too close to the sun and got singed. They were scary. Helen was not prepared for this new level of teen girl aggression.

It was but one of many things she was not prepared for at Corden County Regional High School. Hestia contributed the fewest students to this mosh pit; Velmont the most. The Velmont kids lived closest to the "big city" of Schenectady, New York, which was about a half hour to the east, and thus generally considered themselves more urbane. Ottandaga and Odenkill (the *O*s) were stacked in the middle, with Hestia hanging off the far end to the west like a vestigial limb.

"Gather up, runners, gather up!" shouted Coach Costarellis, ringlets of black hair bouncing against his shoulders as he spoke. He seemed youngish, although most adults who were not ancient looked younger than Luigi and Annabella, who, in their mid-fifties, were the oldest parents of any Helen knew. And he was "groovy," which, far from the pinnacle of cool it had been a decade earlier, was now used as a pejorative by the teenagers.

"Here's the deal," said Coach Costarellis. "Running is an all-inclusive sport. You want to run, you run. No one is going to exclude you from partaking of the greatest physical activity—well, *one* of the greatest physical activities—known to man."

Marybeth Guchel made a surreptitious peace sign and murmured, "Make love, not war."

"He's kind of cute," whispered Wendy.

"If you like aging hippies."

"Oh, go kiss your Andy Gibb poster."

Coach went on. "Seven boys and seven girls will make varsity, the rest are JV, which is super, right? No cuts. Everyone's in."

"Blah, blah, kumbaya," muttered Marybeth.

"Mr. C Row the Boat Ashore," tittered Wendy.

"We're going to start off with an easy three-mile jog, just to get those glorious muscles warmed up," said Coach. "Seniors, take the front and show them the route. Anyone who still needs to hand in registration forms, come see me first."

Helen glanced at a girl standing next to her, mustered up her courage, and said, "So, um, want to run together?"

"Sure! But I have to do the paperwork first."

"I can wait," offered Helen, thinking how great it would be to tell her parents that she'd made a new friend. She was on reasonably friendly terms with a lot of people. Kids didn't seem to mind her. But they didn't seem to go out of their way to invite her over, either.

There was always Francie. Their friendship had withstood the tests of Francie going off to horse camp every summer; Helen studying all hours to "make America proud of her," as her parents insisted; and Francie blowing off schoolwork to make macramé hanging planters and scoring a solid A-minus average anyway.

Francie was into ceramics now and spent most of her free periods in the art room babysitting the cantankerous kiln. Helen ate lunch with her there when she wasn't studying. This further diminished Helen's prospects for making other friends, but it was just so . . . easy. The rest of her schoolmates generally behaved like a flock of seagulls, swooping around, screeching for no apparent reason, and taking things that didn't belong to them. Like her attention and focus and peace of mind. Francie was a dove (albeit with clay-spattered clogs) by comparison.

Helen's parents worried about her penchant for solitude and lack of an inner circle. They liked Francie and had hung their only houseplant (a spider plant that had not been watered in months) in one of her macramé hangers. But her wealthy-enough-to-go-to-horse-camp-yet-couldn't-be-bothered-to-wipe-off-her-clogs lifestyle was confounding to them.

"You got something on you face," Annabella would say on a remarkably regular basis, licking her thumb and swiping a smudge of dirt / ceramic glaze / God knew what off Francie's cheek or forehead.

"Thanks, Mama A," Francie would respond, holding still while she was groomed like a kitten by a mother cat. She had come up with that moniker at the age of six when "Mrs. Iannucci" was a mouthful, and Annabella had allowed it. Helen suspected she even liked it. If Francie had been her real daughter, there would have been a fight every damn day. As it stood, Annabella could shake her head and smile at Francie's eccentricities from the safety of no familial connection.

Now at the first meeting of the track team, Helen hoped that this girl might be a reasonable friend prospect. But these hopes were dimmed when she responded to Helen's offer with "Ugh, look at that line. Don't wait for me, it'll be years."

"Oh, okay," said Helen, trying not to act like she cared. "I'll catch you next time."

"For sure!"

Helen took off at an easy lope after the others, across the field and onto one of the side streets that rambled along near the river. As her body warmed to its very favorite pastime (no matter what the coach implied about other pleasurable activities), there was a little part of her that was glad she wasn't running with anyone else. She could glide at her own pace, undistracted by the off-tempo gait of others. The road was wide with almost no traffic, and she was soon passing people—not on purpose, but only because her body could move to its own internal percussion section, which happened to favor a vivace beat.

"Show-off," huffed Marybeth as Helen passed her.

"She's faster than us," wheezed Wendy.

"She doesn't have to act like it."

*I'm not* acting *like it*, thought Helen. *I just am.*

The captains in front turned down another road that curved away from the river and up Stanley Hill Road. She'd heard about Stanley Hill. The kids called it Heartbreak Hill after the six-mile incline in the Boston Marathon. This uphill wasn't nearly as long, but it was a challenge, and she'd been excited to try it. Everyone's pace slowed, including Helen's, but one by one she continued to pass other runners until she came up behind Cal Crosby, battling madly, arms pumping in random arcs out from his body. From the back, with all that red hair flying, he seemed like he might actually be on fire.

"Hey," he panted as she came up beside him.

"Hi," she said.

"This is hard."

"Stanley Hill," she said, the incline getting steeper, her own pace downshifting slightly.

"It's beating . . . the crap . . . out of me," he rasped.

She laughed and that slowed her even further. Cal was a couple of inches shorter than she, and hunched forward as he was, his head came up to about her chin. He was more or less flinging himself up the hill.

"I'm just . . . giving it a try," he insisted.

"You're not bad."

"I suck."

"You run like a lit match." She had no idea where that came from. Probably just an image conjured by his stick figure body and flaming red hair.

He looked over at her. His eyes were baby boy blue. "Yeah?"

"Uh-huh."

He smiled. "I'm going to take that . . . in a good way."

The slope of the hill flattened slightly for a couple of blocks, and it was easier to talk.

"I meant it in a good way," she said. "Why would I say it to your face if I was being mean?"

"People do that all the time. Shit-talk to your face."

"Well, I don't."

"You just do it behind their backs."

"Not really," said Helen. "I mean only if they really deserve it, and people need to be, like, warned or something."

Stanley Hill was not quite done with them; it got steeper just before the top. She thought he might be having a mild asthma attack, but then he wheezed out, "What's your name?"

"Helen."

"Helen what?"

"Iannucci."

"Helen Iannucci . . . you are not . . . a bad . . . person."

"I'll take that . . . in a good way."

"Do," he said. And for all his poor form, he was keeping up with her.

"Tuck your elbows in," she said, her own breath getting ragged now, too. "And don't . . . hunch your shoulders."

"Like this?" His flapping subsided a little, and his torso lengthened, but he still looked like he was actively in pain.

"Just enjoy it," said Helen.

He let out an incredulous snort. "*Enjoy* it?"

And just like that she went from being the kind, encouraging girl to the weird girl who liked running uphill. Why was she bothering to help this strange, skinny pelican, anyway?

"Or don't." She pulled away from him.

He just ran harder.

As they crested the hilltop together, spent and panting, slowing to suck in oxygen, he grinned and choked out, "I enjoyed it!"

She smiled. He really was a funny little thing.

# Chapter 5

## 2021

Helen's strides get longer as she approaches her daughter's small house. She can feel baby Lana waking and shifting in the backpack. The little girl is not a wailer. She is strangely patient with the flaws of her caretakers. This only serves to make Helen feel worse about failing to bring a sippy cup or snack.

She feels bad about everything these days, even choices that are decades old and have no bearing on anything anymore. Moving to North Carolina to be near Jim's work, instead of back to Upstate New York to be near her parents. Jim's golf course design and maintenance firm was based in Raleigh, and it seemed silly to make him commute. Except that Jim's work took him all over the country and he had a study over the garage for when he wasn't strolling around some former tobacco field with an eager investor or crunching numbers with a general manager above the pro shop somewhere. As it turned out, Jim could have based himself anywhere. And Annabella could have been a full-time grandmother instead of a three-times-a-year visitor.

Lana's beautiful face is puckering with unhappiness as Helen races to pour milk into a sippy. They learned during the adoption process that the name Lana means "calm as still waters" in

Hawaiian. Barb and Cormac had no idea how apt it was when they met her six months ago.

Helen hands her the sippy, and the little girl's face smooths into a beatific smile as she lifts it to her lips. Fourteen months old now. How lucky they were to get her. Helen scoops her up and they sit together at the kitchen table. Helen gazes down into Lana's face and Lana stops sucking long enough to give her nonna a wide smile.

*This*, thinks Helen. She feels her galloping pulse slow to a trot.

LATER THAT AFTERNOON, when Lana is down for her second nap (God bless her, none of Helen's children napped at all), Helen goes to Barb's desktop computer and googles Francine Hydecker. And there she is.

Fran Hydecker, Seven Meadows Farm, Plymouth, Vermont.

Helen clicks the link and finds that it's not just a horse farm. It has equine therapy for kids with special needs and an art studio with a gallery and shop. The pictures are rich with color and bucolic serenity.

"Good for her," Helen murmurs, clicking through the descriptions of textile classes and the next kiln firing. But deep in her solar plexus she feels brittle, as she remembers the last time she saw Francie.

IN 2018, AT the age of ninety-five, Annabella Iannucci finally admitted that it was no longer easy to haul grocery bags up the flagstone path from the single-car driveway into the house. She also had to confess she had no clue what to do when her new laptop gave her error messages. "You come live with me," she told Helen. "The kids are gone. Jim does his Jim stuff." But Helen did not want to go back to Hestia, New York. The whole point had been to leave.

"Mama, it's so nice down here. The winters are mild—you don't have to yell at the plow guy to be careful around your boxwoods, because there *is* no plow guy."

Annabella had given a little snort of disinterest and said, "If I move down there, I'm gonna bring the plow guy with me, just for spite."

Eventually she acquiesced, the little house on Kisco Avenue was sold, and most of the well-worn furniture was dropped off at the local Goodwill. Luigi's garage full of tools, carefully dusted of cobwebs every month or so, were donated to a vocational school. Annabella's near century of life was reduced to a couple of boxes of mementos that immediately went up into Helen's attic and were never looked at again and one enormous suitcase of clothes. ("No rollers," Jim muttered as he hauled it to the car. "Hernia city.")

By the time the pandemic picked up speed in the end of March 2020, Annabella had been living in North Carolina with them for almost two years, wits still fully present and accounted for as she held court from her comfy chair in the kitchen. She resumed her cooking lessons with Helen, offering tips, correcting missteps, alerting Helen when the eggplant had baked a little too long. "The cheese is getting crusty. I can smell it."

She had strong feelings about things being burned. "Do not cremate me," she'd told Helen any number of times over the years. "How will your father know it's me if I'm scorched?"

But Covid had everyone terrified that spring. The funeral home would not agree to transport Annabella's body all the way to Hestia, New York, a twenty-hour round-trip journey. With no one sure exactly how the virus was passed—how long did it stay on surfaces, how long in the air?—the driver's safety could not be assured.

They cremated her. Helen cried for days about that decision.

"I'm sorry, Mama." She whispered her atonement into the possibly infected air. "I'm so sorry."

"We had to," Jim kept telling her. "It would have been un-hygienic."

"Grandpa will know her," Sam assured Helen from the solitude of his apartment in Seattle. "Trust me, Mom. Grandma is recognizable in any form." This had made Helen laugh, then cry even harder.

In the end, Helen drove to Hestia alone with Annabella's urn tucked behind the seat belt in the front seat. Jim was feeling "off."

"*Will you please take your goddamned medicine!*" Helen screamed at him the day before she left. Bereft, already exhausted and stressed at the idea of the long trip, Helen was in no mood for Jim's fantasy that his arteries would magically unclog themselves if he just got some fresh air. That is to say, *more* fresh air. He was in the backyard practicing his putts every day as it was.

"Okay, fine," he muttered petulantly. But she was fairly certain he wouldn't.

On the drive, she played Annabella's favorite Frank Sinatra CDs and sang along to keep herself alert, surprised at how many of the words she still knew. She spoke out loud to her mother all the stories she could remember. All the good times. "Remember when we went to Niagara Falls, and Papa made us do that *Maid of the Mist* boat, and you said, 'Why you want to pay to get wet? Let's go home and I'll spray you with the hose for free.' But then you loved it. You laughed and said, 'Next I'm gonna do the barrel!'"

And the not-so-good times. "I'm sorry we moved away. I'm sorry you were alone so long. I'm sorry we couldn't keep the house. I'm so sorry, Mama."

The funeral home had made all the arrangements. At Precious Blood cemetery, by the double plot where Luigi was waiting, there was a graveside service, albeit brief. An elderly priest Helen didn't recognize had been sent over to say the prayers. The hole seemed far too deep.

*You're together now, right?* Helen wondered as the priest tucked his Bible under his arm and headed for his aging sedan. *You found each other?*

When she turned around, there was a woman standing some distance away, the wind putting knots in her long salt-and-pepper hair. Her mask was a batik print of blue and green. Helen was still wiping a tear out of her eye and wondering who it was when the woman said, "I always wished she was my real mother, not just Mama A."

It was all Helen could do not to rush into Francie's arms and hug her breathless.

"How did you know?" was all she could think to say.

"The obit was in the Hestia paper. My brother told me about it. I'm in Vermont now."

"You came all this way!"

"It's not that far," said Francie. "Not for her."

They spoke for a few moments more, trading the standard information that seemed strangely beside the point. Helen was still married to Jim (Francie's face remained diplomatically blank), three kids, North Carolina. Francie finally got her farm. She only had a few minutes, had to get back to help with evening chores. Several of her workers had stopped showing up for fear of infection.

"If it's too fresh," Francie said, "don't answer, but . . . how did she go? Covid?"

"No. I quarantined us so hard we were practically on the Space Station. She just wouldn't get out of bed one day."

"Wow." Francie shook her head. "Annabella Iannucci not getting out of bed."

"I know. So unlike her."

"What did you do?"

"Well, she . . . um." Helen could feel the prickle of more tears behind her eyes. "She wanted me to get in with her. She wanted . . . she wanted a snuggle." *Snuggle* was one of those Americanisms Annabella had learned and hung on to.

Francie's eyes filled. "She was the best snuggler."

"Yeah, um, so I did. And we talked."

"What did she say?"

"She said . . ." The tears fell now. "She said she was a . . . a satisfied customer of life. And she said I was a good daughter. She was so happy to be my mother, and I had made her proud. *Vita mia*, she called me."

"She spoke Italian? Oh, Helen."

Helen looked at her old friend, and even through a Niagara Falls of tears, she could see that familiar face, so kind, so honest. A little too honest at times, but that was Helen's problem, not Francie's.

From six feet apart, the two women looked at each other and wept.

Then Francie inhaled a sniffle and reached across the distance to hand Helen a card. "Please call, Hellie. Really. It's time."

WHEN SHE GOT home, Jim said his arm hurt. But maybe it was more of a shoulder thing. Or his chest. Helen took him to the emergency room. She wasn't allowed in because the world was up in flames with Covid, of course, and she was too anxious to sit in the car, so she walked around the vast parking lot, and got hot and tore off her coat, dropping it on the curb somewhere.

Then the triage nurse called.

Helen never went back for that coat, the one with Francie's card in the pocket.

In the year and a half since, Helen thinks of that coat at strange times. When she buried Jim. When Barb and Cormac adopted Lana. When Sam went back to Seattle. When Danny fell off that damn cliff he was climbing and busted his wrist, and he called her from the hospital and said, "I'm fine, Mom. Don't worry so much," and she wanted to scream, *I didn't used to be like this before you three came along! You are my child! You are a worry pill I take every day!*

But she just said, "Jesus, Danny."

Then for some reason the coat pops into her head, and she wonders where it is. Did the hospital maintenance crew throw it in a dumpster and now it's in some landfill buried under empty paint cans and spent coffee grounds and plastic milk jugs? Probably.

But she likes to think a homeless person found it, and it's keeping that person warm somewhere. And she wishes he or she would pull the card out of the pocket and call Francie and tell her where they got the coat.

"Don't think she just threw your card away," the person would tell Francie. "She left her coat outside an emergency department. Something terrible must have happened. She's probably just beside herself, and is maybe questioning who she is anymore, and can't quite bring herself to reach out to her very best friend, who was like a sister to her, and whom she's only spoken to once in thirty-five years."

# Chapter 6

## 1978

The other guys on the team gave Cal Crosby a hard time about the way he ran. "Headless chicken" was a favorite taunt, and "Octopus" for the way his arms waggled around. After a week or two, they settled on "Spazby."

"I'm not even really on the team," Cal would mutter. "I'm just checking it out."

But he kept showing up.

There was no way he was making varsity, Helen knew, but for all his inefficiency, he really wasn't too bad. He could keep up with her, which was saying something.

Helen dangled from the bottom rung of the girls' varsity roster. The six-footers, like Felicity Manning, just had more leg going for them. (Felicity was the only real six-footer, but Janine Franka and Gwen Sobeleski liked to put themselves on par with Felicity, and who wouldn't? The girl was getting scouted by colleges already and she was only sixteen.) Nancy Munsie had the lungs of an opera singer. And the other girls above Helen on varsity were not taller or better oxygenated, but somehow they always had a millisecond or twenty on her.

On training runs, Cal would straggle along beside her and make her laugh.

"This is really good for me, all this running," he told her one day, "because when I'm a rock star, I'm going to be bouncing around the stage for hours like Mick Jagger."

"Yeah, you and Mick." Helen smirked. "I definitely see it."

"He's a runner, you know. He has to keep fit so he can be all 'Jumpin' Jack Flash is a gas, gas, ga—!'" Cal crooned the line with his head thrown back until an autumn leaf fell into his mouth. He sputtered and spat, and Helen laughed so hard she doubled over, and six of their team members passed them, no doubt wondering why Cal Spazby was hocking up a hairball and Helen Last-name-with-all-the-vowels was in stitches over it.

"WHY DON'T YOU show up to practice on Fridays?" Helen asked Cal in the end of September as they did a warm-up jog by the river.

"That's my Baskin-Robbins shift," he said.

"Can't you get a weekend shift?"

"Oh, I work weekends, too. Gotta save up for college."

"How come you do Fridays then?"

"Nobody wants Friday afternoon. It's prime hangout time. I take it because I'm trying to stay on the manager's good side."

"Are you ever on his bad side?"

"No, it's just that . . . well, to be honest, I'm not actually that great."

"At scooping ice cream?"

"Yeah, I don't know. It's just not a natural thing for me."

Helen thought for a moment. How was ice-cream scooping natural? Or unnatural? Wasn't it just . . . scooping ice cream? "Is there some special trick to it?"

"Oh, sure. It's physics, getting that scoop in tight, but not, like, too tight so the cone cracks. A lot of my scoops fall off."

Helen tried not to laugh, but she couldn't help it.

Cal chuckled. "I actually got an award at the end of the summer."

"An award?"

"Yeah, the manager does superlatives, and I got one."

Helen couldn't wait to hear it. "What did you get?"

He grinned and puffed his chest out, feigning pride. "Most Likely to Make a Kid Cry."

ONE DAY CAL was uncharacteristically quiet. "What's up?" Helen finally asked him.

"No, nothing. Just, you know, fucking everything."

"Like?"

"Dumb stuff. It doesn't matter."

"Okay," she said, but she wondered.

Then he smiled.

"What?" she said.

"I was just thinking about how you kick my ass every day because you run like hell on wheels, and some days I wish you would just slow down. But you can't because you're"—he sucked in a lungful of air and belted out a line from a Paul McCartney and Wings song—"*Helen! Hell on wheels!*"

Oh, she liked that. She liked it a lot. Nobody thought she was hell on anything. She was that quiet girl who studied hard, and ran all the time, and hung around with that weird girl with the clay on her jeans.

He grinned at her. "You like that one!"

She shrugged and tried to stop smiling.

"Yeah, don't give me that," he teased. "You do."

"I THINK CAL Crosby might have a crush on me," Helen said one day as Francie was unloading the kiln. Mrs. Sullivan, the ceramics teacher, was only part-time, and by October Francie had proven herself a devoted and competent acolyte. She had not yet been allowed to unload a glaze firing without supervision, but she was gunning for it.

"Oh, he definitely does," said Francie, reaching in to pull a wobbly-looking pot thing out of the kiln, thick white asbestos mitts up to her elbows.

"What? How do you know?"

"Because I see him in the smoking area sometimes, and he always mentions you."

"What does he say? And what are you doing in the smoking area? You don't smoke."

"I just hang around with some of the art kids there, and occasionally I take a puff, so I don't seem like I'm hanging around because of them."

"Which you are."

"Well, duh."

Helen thought about this for a minute. "Do you have your own pack?"

"No, I bum them off Ricky."

"Zugravescu? Jesus, Francie!"

"He's not that bad."

"He's already done a stint in juvie! His badness is documented!"

"Yeah, but he can be nice. I know he used to call you Wop Giraffe and everything, but that was last year."

This was all a lot to take in. Francie smoking. With Ricky Zugravescu, who was apparently "not that bad." And Cal's crush confirmed.

"That hair," said Francie.

"It's practically taking over the planet," said Helen.

"Apparently you said he runs like a lit match. He mentions that a lot."

"I said it once."

"He must really like it."

"I'm not going out with him."

"Why not?"

"He's like a foot shorter than me! How would we slow dance? He'd have to be on stilts or something."

Francie affected a suave tone. "Or he could just lay his head on your heavenly bosoms."

"Oh, yes," cooed Helen, smoothing her hands down the front of her almost flat chest. "So heavenly!" And they cackled like teen-age witches.

THE NEXT DAY at practice, Helen told Cal, "Francie Hydecker says she sees you in the smoking area sometimes."

"Oh, yeah, Francie. With the clay . . ." He motioned vaguely around his body.

"Yeah, well, what are you doing smoking?"

"I don't know. It's just a habit."

"It's a bad one. You'll never be a good runner if you smoke."

So he quit.

# Chapter 7

## 2021

The number is right there in front of her, but Helen hesitates.

*Hi, Francie; it's me, Helen. Oh sorry, I guess you go by Fran now. Well, I know I should've called you last year after my mother died, but I lost your card when Jim died, and then, well, I just didn't. But I bumped into Cal fucking Crosby today, and now I really need to talk to you. There's not much to tell. But you are the only person on God's green earth who would understand that even though there's nothing to say, it's just . . . well, it happened. And you would get that.*

*Nope, that doesn't sound self-serving and needy,* thinks Helen. *Not at all.*

If only she had picked up the damn phone anytime between her mother's funeral a year and a half ago and this morning when she flew out of the house with the baby on her back. If only. But now it seems so immature. And if there's one thing she wants Francie Hydecker to know it's that she's not the same stupid girl she was when she was twenty-three. She's been around the block a few times. And yet, even if that's true—and it is definitely true—Helen's not sure if she's actually any smarter than she was back then. In fact, her greatest fear is that she isn't. Has she actually learned anything? Anything at all, other than that she ended up in a place she wasn't supposed to? That all the decisions that seemed like the right thing to do at the time maybe weren't? And she should have sat herself down and had a real hard think about them.

Helen is pretty sure Francie would get it. But she's not entirely sure. So she clicks out of the Seven Meadows Farm website, goes into the kitchen, and spreads some almond butter on a banana while she waits for Lana to wake up.

AT SIX THIRTY, Barb flies in the door with things hanging off her like a bellhop at an old-time hotel. Purse, camera bag, a sack of food, umbrella, the mail, a crushed paper bag from her husband's bakery. Helen and Lana are sitting on the rug in the tiny living room stacking blocks, and Lana is startled at first. Then she bestows one of her signature drooly grins, and Barb drops everything with a *whoosh* and says, "Hi, baby!"

"Mama!" says Lana. Helen and Barb laugh and clap, and Barb sits down on the floor next to them and rolls Lana into a big hug.

"Crazy day?" says Helen.

"Guh," sighs Barb. "But whatever, who cares. I'm home now."

Helen doesn't believe this for a minute. Barb is a relentless engager. Things happen to her. She happens to other people. Life is some sort of messy, muddy, joyful, infuriating scrum, and when the day is done, she needs to debrief so that she can go back out tomorrow and engage some more. Helen waits.

"Well, as you know," says Barb, "Roy has no social skills."

Barb's boss's inability to keep from pissing people off (especially Barb) is a song that Helen knows well, and it seems that every day brings a new verse. "Oh, no, what this time?"

A group of older women, friends from childhood, had come into Roy's photography studio for a sitting. "They wanted to commemorate the fact that, despite Covid, they were all still alive! It was beautiful! They were so gray-haired and wrinkled and just *gorgeous*!" But they got too chatty, still so grateful to hug and pat hands and kiss one another's cheeks. "They wouldn't sit still and stop cracking jokes, and Roy got annoyed and told them this wasn't a tea party."

"Wow," says Helen. The guy really is so clueless.

"Of course the room goes quiet, and they just stare at him in horror, and he starts shooting! And I'm behind him because he can never let me be more than seven inches away, in case he needs to switch out a lens or something." Barb smiles impishly.

Helen loves this part of her daughter. The pot stirrer. "What did you do?"

"I just rolled my eyes and—" She holds one hand palm up; with the other she tips up an imaginary teacup, pinky extended. "They all crack up, and Roy's still snapping, none the wiser."

Helen beams at her daughter, this funny, brave, loving soul.

"What?" says Barb, as if she doesn't know. As if she can't feel the warmth of her mother's admiration radiating through the room.

"You remind me of Grandma," says Helen.

BARB'S HUSBAND, CORMAC McGRATH, is the sort of happy-go-lucky-yet-hardworking guy that you want your only daughter to marry. He seems to know instinctively that a person's life can go awry in any number of ways, and somehow his hasn't. He doesn't take credit for this—he's not the type to give unwanted advice or judge others—he just seems grateful. One of those things that has gone particularly well is his marriage.

Helen and Jim sometimes worried that Barb might have a hard time finding someone who could build the kind of nest in which their flighty little chickadee might want to roost. She had her "tortured artist years," as Jim called them, when she seemed to cast about from job to job, friend group to friend group, never quite finding her stride or feeling completely comfortable. Helen secretly worried that Barb had inherited her own jitteriness and hesitance to land. (Of course, when Helen had been suddenly grounded by pregnancy and marriage, she'd made the best of it. That was Helen's way; it wasn't necessarily Barb's.)

And then about five years ago, Barb got a job at Cormac's Confectionery just to make the rent while trying to get her batik fabric business off the ground. It never did take off; in fact, the dye seeping into the floorboards of her apartment had gotten her evicted. But suddenly she was very enthusiastic about serving half-caf skinny extra-foam lattes.

"He's no spring chicken," Jim would comment when the fact that Cormac was ten years older than Barb came up. "But maybe that's what she needs."

*Every kite needs her string*, Helen often thought. Then she would look at Jim and think, *Maybe we're both kites. Or both strings.*

CORMAC'S GENERALLY SMOOTH brow has been wrinkled for a year and a half now as he struggles to make up for the battering his bakery took during the first twelve months of the pandemic. But he's a man who knows how to put the day behind him, and when he comes in later that night, after Barb and Helen have eaten dinner and bathed the baby, he calls out, "Helen, where's the dance party? Crank up Mom's Playlist!"

Helen started the after-dinner dance party tradition when her kids were little. She'd fire up some Aretha Franklin or Beach Boys, and they'd dance around the living room until they were exhausted and sweaty. Bath and bedtime went a lot more smoothly once they'd wiggled out those final ya-yas of the day.

A few years ago, Barb walked Helen through the steps of setting up a Spotify account and adding songs to her library, in which there was one—and only one—playlist. Now Helen taps at her phone, linking to a speaker in the tiny living room. Suddenly the walls are vibrating with sound.

"It might seem crazy what I'm 'bout to say," sings Pharrell Williams.

Barb hands pajama-clad Lana to Cormac, and then they're all dancing, Barb clapping her hands, Cormac swinging the baby around, her face bright with excitement. And Helen is bouncing like a kid who can't sit still.

"Because I'm HAPPY!" they all sing along with the chorus. And they are.

THAT NIGHT, AS she lies in bed and listens to the wind blow and the fallen leaves skitter around the tiny yard of her little ranch house a mile away, Helen thinks about those women in Barb's studio, just grateful to be alive and together.

The next morning, before she can ruminate to the point of inaction, she places the call.

A man answers the phone, his voice low and gravelly. "Seven Meadows Farm."

*Ricky*, thinks Helen. The unmistakably abraded growl of blackened lungs. And she almost hangs up. Because what can she say to Ricky? *I'm sorry I may have underestimated you, except I'm pretty sure I didn't, but still I shouldn't have said anything to Francie about it, even though she said Jim was "unimaginative," which we both know for Francie is like saying he's a hunk of asphalt, and why was I dating that instead of a person?*

*Chicken*, Helen goads herself.

"Hi, can I speak to Fran, please?"

"Sorry, she's not here."

*She doesn't own the farm anymore. She moved away, left no forwarding address. You'll never find her*, Helen's rising panic whispers.

"I think she went into town to—" He stops suddenly and speaks away from the receiver. "Oh, hey, you *are* here. It's for you."

"Hello?" says Francie breathily, as if she hasn't had a minute to take off her coat.

"Francie, it's Helen."

She thought it through that morning while her coffee slowly went cold. Helen Spencer, Helen Iannucci, Helen from Hestia, Helen your dumb friend who lost your card and couldn't put on her big-girl pants and simply google you.

There's a beat of silence. "Helen," Francie says evenly.

Now Helen knows exactly what she's up against.

"I'm sorry it's taken me so long."

"I'm sure you were busy."

"No, it's not . . . I mean, yes, but . . ."

This is exactly what Helen was afraid of. She wants to hang up, but she can't give up on Francie. Not again. Not yet. "Francie, I . . ."

"Yes?"

"It's just been . . . a lot."

"It's been a lot for everyone, Helen."

"Yes, of course you're right."

Helen wants to say, *My husband died!* But that feels like a cop-out. Because Jim being dead didn't keep her from calling for a year and a half.

"I came to Hestia," said Francie. "I came for her, but I also came for you. And you couldn't even—"

"I should have. I've thought of you so many times, and . . . I've missed you. I've missed you so much, and I am *so sorry*."

Regret seems to ooze from her pores these days.

Then Francie says, "Me too."

"No, you have nothing to—"

"I'll decide if I do or not. That's up to me."

"Oh. Okay."

The silence on the phone goes on for a while, as if they have to reacquaint themselves with the very fact of the other's existence. Helen finds herself strangely comforted by Francie just being there in her ear, alive in her Francie-ness.

"Helen." She says it just as quietly this time, but now it's more of a sigh.

"Yes?"

"How the hell are you?"

"Um . . ." Helen laughs.

Francie laughs, too, and this fills Helen with more hope than she's felt in a long time. Francie Hydecker's laugh is one of her favorite sounds. It just took thirty-five years for her to remember.

They only talk for a few minutes, as if hesitant to say the wrong thing, another gaffe that could separate them again. But Helen musters up her courage and asks, "Could I come up and see the farm sometime? It looks like you're doing great things."

"I'd love that."

"Really?"

"Yes, really! When?"

"Well, I babysit my granddaughter Tuesday through Thursday, and I do the books for my son-in-law's business, but that's pretty flexible. I'm in Massachusetts now, so it's an easy drive."

They decide on Monday the following week. When they hang up, Helen realizes her heart is pounding. *It's okay now*, she tells her heart. *Maybe we'll even have a tea party.*

# Chapter 8

## 1978

Wendy Moriarty was improving. Coach Costarellis was helping her. A lot. He spent extra time making sure her stride was "integrated" and her hips "supported her spine." He didn't seem overly worried about Helen's spine or anything else about her. As a result (and, okay, admittedly Wendy's natural coordination and athleticism, but whatever), Wendy was now a credible threat to Helen for last place on the varsity roster.

Cal was outraged on Helen's behalf. "She is not as good as you, Wheels." He had taken to calling Helen Wheels. "You're just getting psyched out by her whole *Wendy* thing."

Wendy definitely had a thing, which included long, silky hair. ("Used to be frizzy," Cal insisted. "Believe me, I've known her since kindergarten, and there is definitely some sort of petrochemical involvement going on.") Also, she was tall and thin like Helen, but she had breasts that were just a little too big for her frame, which was to say, perfect. And a tiny, adorable nose. ("That nose belongs on a baby," Cal scoffed. "No way she's getting a teenage amount of oxygen through that thing.") But apparently she was, because she ran like a gazelle.

Helen reported all this to Francie after a dinner of veal scaloppine, Caesar salad, homemade bread, and individual fruit tarts still warm from the oven. Annabella and Luigi were sitting in the parlor drinking coffee strong enough to revive the dead, as they usually did in the evenings. They would discuss the latest happenings at Eagle Auto Body, the neighborhood, Hestia, and the United States of America.

In the fall of 1978, they were worried about Jimmy Carter, for whom they had voted because he owned his own business, not like that Gerry Ford, who was only ever a politician. Annabella was skeptical about peanuts ("Not real food," she would say. "You ever see a recipe with peanuts?") but Carter had a kind face and an accent, as she did. Jimmy, as they called him, was getting some flak about having signed off on the Susan B. Anthony dollar. "Chauvinist pig" was a phrase Annabella had taken to. For the rest of their marriage, anytime Luigi made a mildly unsupportive comment about a woman, which was rare, she would hiss "Chauvinist!" and that would be the end of it.

Up in Helen's room, the girls discussed the goings-on with the cross-country team.

"Okay, I get that you're worried about your place on the list," said Francie, who was embroidering a yin and yang symbol on a pair of jeans that were so beat-up they must have belonged to one of her older brothers. "But who cares about that other shit."

"No, I don't care at all. It's just . . . I don't know. Why do some people always have it easy? Like *always*. I mean, has Wendy Moriarty ever had a pimple?"

"She probably never even had diaper rash," said Francie.

"She probably poops Oil of Olay!" said Helen.

Francie snorted with laughter and accidentally stuck herself with the needle.

IT TURNED OUT that cross-country running at the high school level involved an impressive vomit-to-student ratio. Some runners puked from nerves before a meet. Others puked afterward from running so hard. Cal Crosby was the only one on the team who did both.

"Jesus, Spazby," said one of the older boys. "How does that parking meter body of yours hold so much fucking food?"

If puking and winning had any correlation whatsoever, Cal would have been an Olympian. Unfortunately for Cal, and for the team, this was not the case.

"I'm the worst," he muttered to Helen, wiping his mouth on the hem of his running tank after straggling across the finish line and upchucking in a rhododendron.

"Jerry Klimper is way worse," said Helen.

"Jerry Klimper is a clown who doesn't give a shit. He only joined the team so he doesn't have to work in his dad's septic-pumping business after school."

"Why did you join?"

"I just wanted to check it out."

"Well, it's the end of October and we're six meets in. You've checked it out pretty thoroughly."

"You think I should quit?" Oh, the look on his face. Honestly, quitting was not a terrible option. But that look.

"No, of course not. I just think you should . . ." What? What exactly should this poor kid who ran like a drunken mallard, heaved up a third of his body weight at every meet, and was relentlessly teased by the other kids do?

"*Enjoy* it?" said Cal sarcastically.

Helen shrugged and gave what she hoped was an encouraging smile. "Don't quit," she said. "It sets a bad life precedent."

A WEEK LATER they had a meet with Hackford High School. Unlike Corden County Regional, Hackford did not receive a substantial number of its team tank tops from the basketball cast-off pile. Also unlike CCRHS, Hackford had separate girls' and boys' coaches, assistant coaches, and a mascot (a kid in a tiger costume who was only available when both the Hackford football and soccer teams were not playing, of course, but still).

"I don't have to tell you this is big," said Coach Costarellis, standing near the driver, the motion of the bus causing him to sway like a willow. "If we can beat Hackford, we have a shot at the league title."

"He's dreaming," Cal murmured to Helen. "That's like saying if the CCRHS football team can beat the Giants, we have a chance at winning the Super Bowl."

"Yeah, okay, but don't be negative before a meet."

"Personally, I don't have a lot to be positive about."

"First of all, it's not just about you. And second—"

"I didn't say it was all about me, I just made the point that me personally, I'm not likely to do very well. I'm all in for everyone else on the team. Well, at least the ones who aren't complete assholes. Which isn't many."

"And *second*—"

"If you say 'Enjoy it,' so help me—"

"If you interrupt me one more time, I'm changing seats."

Cal clamped his lips. Helen laughed. "Yeah, that shut you up all right. Listen, here's the thing. You are not actually a bad runner."

"I su—"

Helen turned her body toward the aisle and began to stand.

"No, hold on," he said. "I'm sorry." She didn't turn back for a moment, and he put a hand on her arm. "Wheels, I'm truly sorry. I will keep my yap shut from now till the end of time."

"If only," she said with a snort.

Cal smiled a sort of sheepish, smitten smile, and she was reminded that she had some power over him. Power she had to wield carefully and not abuse.

"You've improved a lot."

He raised his hand.

Helen rolled her eyes. "What."

"I just want to interject at this time that you are the only one who gave me any pointers or anything." She had taken it as a personal challenge to get him to improve and often gave him feedback, tips, and encouragement.

"Come on. Coach C didn't help you at all, ever?"

"Yeah, right. That groovy douchebag. He was too busy with Wendy."

Helen sighed. Coach Costarellis's favoritism had hurt them both.

"Okay, well, you're probably right about that, but here's where we are now. You are going to run your race, right? And you can run it thinking about Coach C and Wendy and all the guys on the team who said mean things. Or . . . you could just run. And"— she almost said *enjoy it* but stopped herself—"see what happens. Appreciate what your body can do. Just run."

A tiny grin rose on his face. "Like a lit match?"

"Like a lit match."

CAL THREW UP twice before the race—once in the baseball dugout, and once by the driver's-side door of what turned out to be the Hackford boys' coach's car. And he threw up after the race in front of the timers' table. But in between he actually looked strong, Helen thought. Not quite like he was enjoying it, but not like he hated every minute, either. And he came in a very respectable twelfth— just enough to edge out Mark O'Malley for the last varsity spot.

The older guys slapped him around some in that way that boys have of saying congratulations with hematomas (except for Mark

O'Malley, who was trying very hard not to cry). And Coach Costarellis dubbed him Scrappy Crosby on the bus ride home. (This naturally mutated into Crapsby by the time they pulled into the CCRHS parking lot.) They hadn't won the meet, but they hadn't been completely humiliated—in part because of Cal's performance.

"Okay, be honest," he said when most of the howling and cheering and Hackford trash talking had slid into a sweat-infused exhaustion on the long ride home. "Did you really think I could do it or was that just a pep talk?"

"I thought you could do it," said Helen. "But I also thought you needed a pep talk. More of a butt-kicking, actually. But, yeah, I was pretty sure you could do it if you put your mind to it."

Cal looked out the window for a while, then he mumbled something.

"Sorry?" said Helen.

"I said, that's what my dad always tells me. That I just need to put my mind to it."

"To what."

"You know. Anything. Like football."

"*Foot*ball?" The thought of pale, bony Cal playing such a brute-force sport was frankly hard to imagine.

"Yeah. He played in high school. He always says it was the best years of his life. Kind of tragic, really."

*Not to mention mean*, thought Helen. How do you tell your own child that your happiest days were before he was born?

"Wait, is that why you joined cross-country? So you didn't have to do football?"

"Sort of. It was between that and scooping ice cream every day, which would have been more, you know, lucrative, but I also might have lost the will to live."

"Wow," said Helen.

"Yup," said Cal.

"Well, I'm glad you picked running."

"Yeah," he sighed. "That definitely turned out to be a good decision on my part." A little blush tinted his cheeks, and Helen got worried.

*Don't do it*, she thought at him. *Don't ruin everything and ask me out.*

"It's funny how when you make a decision like that, you just don't know how it will go," he said. "Like cross-country seemed less bad than football or working more, but honestly only slightly less bad. I wasn't psyched about any of my options. But now here I am, *enjoying* it." He rolled his eyes, but he was smiling a smile so warm and sweet that if he'd asked her out in that moment, Helen didn't know what she would've done.

She might even have said yes.

# *Chapter 9*

*2021*

On Fridays, Helen takes the back table at Cormac's Confectionery and goes over the books. The pandemic hasn't been good to her gentle giant of a son-in-law, and they're only recently back in the black. Of course, it was brutal for almost any brick-and-mortar business, but it was especially hard on eating establishments.

"You have to pivot!" Barb said when Belham storefronts began to go dark in the summer of 2020.

"You've said the word *pivot* to me so many times, it's beginning to lose meaning in my brain," said Cormac.

This was where Helen came in.

Holed up in her echoing house in Pinehurst, North Carolina, having recently buried her mother and then her husband, she felt the ripple of shoulda-coulda-woulda slowly begin to surge into a tidal wave.

*Shoulda moved closer to the kids.* This, of course, meant Massachusetts near Barb or Washington State near Sam. "Moving close" to Danny meant riding along in his camper and eating out of a cooler.

*Coulda downsized and bought that little cottage on Oak Island Jim was always fantasizing about.* At least there'd be less house to manage and an ocean to look at.

*Woulda done so many things differently if I'd known I would end up alone at fifty-eight, rattling around in too much space, with only that voice in my head saying,* You blew it. You had a strong lead, and you still lost the race.

Barb checked in daily in that relentless way she had.

"You don't have to call me every day," Helen told her in September 2020, as Covid cases began to rise like a nationwide fever. "I'm fine. I'm safe. I'm Zooming with Megan and Julie and Karen. I take my runs. I'm working from home." She'd been doing the bookkeeping for a couple of Jim's golf club clients for years. "The whole world is digitized now. It's easy."

"You are not Zooming with Megan and Julie and Karen."

"Well, not daily."

"Weekly?"

"Biweekly. Ish."

"Yeah, okay. So you basically have no human contact."

"Well, it's kind of like Grandma, I guess."

"No, you are not like Grandma! She had an auto body shop to run, and she was down there every damn day, interacting with suppliers and mechanics and anyone who had so much as a nick in their chrome within a twenty-mile radius. You are a hermit."

"It's a pandemic! Any single person who is not acting like a hermit is being irresponsible!"

"There's responsible, and then there's hermit, and then there's you."

Helen burst into tears.

"Mom," Barb soothed. "Mom, I love you, and you're depressed. Everyone's depressed, but you just lost your two closest people. I call you every day because you need me to do this thing that you don't want me to do."

"Stop being the grown-up," sniffled Helen. "I'm the grown-up in this relationship."

"This just in, I'm thirty-four."

One week and seven phone calls later, Barb sang out, "I have THE BEST NEWS!"

*You're pregnant*, thought Helen. Barb's infertility had nearly undone her a couple of years before. They'd been deep in the adoption pipeline when the pandemic stalled placements. On some days, Barb lost hope of ever having a child. *Oh, dear God, please let her be pregnant.*

"I found you a house in Belham! It's tiny and gorgeous and well-maintained. It has woods out the back and trails for you to run. YOU WILL BE SO HAPPY THERE!"

"Um, what?" said Helen.

Barb's friend Emma's elderly father had died of Covid, and the family was bereft and exhausted. Helen would be doing the family a kindness by taking it so they wouldn't have to slog through the painting-staging-listing-negotiating process, and she could have it for a song. It was a mile away.

"No, honey. I love you, and I love what you're trying to do for me and your friend. But I can't just pick up and move in the middle of all this mayhem."

Barb huffed an annoyed sigh. "You're going to make me break a promise, aren't you?"

"Well, I'm sorry if you promised Emma that I'd buy her dad's house without even asking me, but—"

"A promise to Grandma."

Helen rolled her eyes. Those two were always in cahoots. The Drama Sisters, Jim used to call them. "What are Zsa Zsa and Eva up to now?" he'd ask with a smirk.

"Okay, I'll bite. What promise to Grandma."

"She made me promise not to tell you something."

Helen shook her head in irritation, remembering how she used to have to tell Annabella on a fairly regular basis not to side with Barb all the time. "You're a mother!" Helen would say. "You're on my team!"

"Spit it out."

"She said she should have moved to North Carolina with you and dad a lot sooner, but she didn't want to admit she was wrong." Barb affected her grandmother's accent. "'Too stubborn,' she'd say. 'Don't be stubborn like me. Like a cat, I'm stubborn.'"

*Oh*, thought Helen. *Oh, Mom.* Her throat tightened and she coughed and said, "She meant like a mule."

Barb laughed. "I asked her about that, and she gave me that face, you know, the whaddayou-talking-about face." Helen knew that face like she knew her own. "She said, 'Mule? A mule takes orders all the day long! A cat listens to no one, drinks you cream, and tells you to shove it.'"

Helen laughed. Barb had her grandmother down cold.

"I'm offering you some cream, Mom. Don't be stubborn like a cat."

OH, WHAT THE HELL.

This was a phrase Helen Iannucci Spencer rarely even thought, much less uttered aloud. Barb sent pictures. The house was a little three-bedroom ranch. Emma had had it taken down to the studs and updated it two years before when her father had gotten too frail for his sprawling colonial in New Hampshire. Clean and open, with new fixtures and appliances, it didn't even need to be painted.

"If you hate it, you can flip it in a nanosecond," said Barb. "But you have to tell me this week, because Emma's gutted, and she needs this thing off her list."

"Oh, what the hell."

OF COURSE HELEN regretted it immediately. The thought of emptying and selling her own house had her fretful by day and sleepless by night.

"And I'll have to find a seller and hope for a decent price," she told her friends during their monthly Zoom happy hour. "Who wants to move now?"

"Are you kidding me?" said Megan. "Do you have any idea what houses with pools are going for, with no one sending their kids to camp this summer? A pool that big is like an Ivy admission."

"I'm texting someone right now who's looking," said Julie. "You'll have an offer before you pour another glass of pinot."

"Hey, I'm texting someone!" said Karen.

"Well, text fast, sweetie," said Julie, waving her phone in her Zoom window. "I'm already getting kiss and prayer emojis."

HELEN HAD NOT wanted that pool or that house. After the crash in 2008 when jobs were being lost like loose buttons, Jim suddenly wanted to upgrade. "Home prices have dropped like a stone," he told her gleefully. "And Pinehurst is a golfer's paradise."

"You just got laid off—we'll be lucky to pay the mortgage we have!" Sometimes she really didn't understand him. Actually most of the time.

But he wasn't worried. In fact, he was excited to leave his golf club management and design company and go out on his own as a consultant.

Helen was apoplectic. "The first thing rich people will cut is their country club memberships! No general manager is paying for consulting services at a time like this."

"It's not like people are going to *stop playing golf*, Helen," he said as if this were the most preposterous thing he'd ever heard. "They'll make their kids take a semester off from college, but they'll play, believe me. They'll just play at cheaper courses. And the cheaper courses will need help adjusting to the influx and higher expectations. I'll be in more demand than I've ever been."

He was right about that. He quickly developed a niche for being the reasonably priced consultant who knew how to get your little, slightly shabby course to the next level. Demand for his services had him traveling the country, often gone for most of the week to places like Boise and Tulsa. He'd been right about something else, too.

When they first looked at the house, he'd loved it, but Helen was not sold. "We don't need a house this big. Barb is already gone; Sam and Danny will be out soon enough. And the pool. My God, we could host the Olympics."

"You and I both know that Danny"—he gave her a pointed look—"needs a lot of room."

Daniel Luigi Spencer was a "spirited," "high energy," "active" child, so said every last one of his teachers. "And loud," Jim would add. "That kid could get a job warning ships away from rocks."

But it was Jim who got in the pool with Danny on the mornings he was home to burn off some of that "high energy" before school. And Jim who encouraged Danny to join the swim team, and got him into martial arts, and eventually rock climbing.

"Go for a run with me?" Helen would ask Danny from time to time.

He'd make his grandmother's whaddayou-talking-about face and say, "Why?"

"It's too boring for him," Jim explained. "He needs a full-sensory experience."

And when Danny rewarded all Jim's efforts by taking up golf, Helen did not try to hide her jealousy, at least not behind closed doors with Jim.

"I spend all week keeping that kid from getting kicked out of school, and you waltz in and win the prize!"

Jim smiled. "Occasionally I do get some things right."

Unfortunately, one of the things he got wrong was forgoing his blood pressure medication.

FOR A YEAR that was so disastrous in so many ways for so many people, Helen's move to Belham, Massachusetts, went off without a hitch. In fact, its hitchlessness was terrifying.

Karen's friend (not Julie's, much to her chagrin) bought the house for a ridiculous amount before it even went on the market; they wanted most of the furniture and a dizzyingly soon move-in date. Helen frantically emptied closets and drawers and cupboards, giving away as much as she could. Emma couldn't bear the thought of having to sell off her father's mostly new furniture and housewares and begged Helen to keep everything.

By mid-November, she found herself driving north with her clothes, Annabella's still-unopened boxes of memorabilia and several boxes of her own, a few pictures she liked, her pillow, and ten bars of her favorite salted caramel dark chocolate, polishing off four during the twelve-hour trip. She pulled into her new driveway, wheels crunching on the remnants of a recent snowstorm.

*I'm going to need a plow guy*, she realized. *How did this happen?*

"DAT'S MY FRIEND!"

Helen looks up from inputting this week's receipts just in time to see Cal's grandson barreling toward her.

"Hey!" she says as Logan reaches the table and throws himself at her. She laughs and lets him climb into her lap. "Where did you come from?" She looks up and scans the bakery for Cal. She can't help it.

"Logan, no! Oh my gosh, I'm so sorry!" A young woman with strawberry blond hair pulled into a slightly askew ponytail hurries over, jostling the baby in a car seat hanging from one hand while trying to keep her purse strap on her shoulder with the other. Cal Crosby's blue eyes look out from delicately pale skin. Her nose and mouth are covered by a mask printed with a graphic of the Earth in neon blues and greens.

"It's okay," said Helen.

"Logan, come down from there, honey. You can't climb into strangers' laps."

Helen hesitates. Does she explain how she knows the boy? It might get back to Cal, and Helen doesn't want that to happen. She really would rather eradicate the whole concept of Cal Crosby from her life.

"You picked me up," says Logan, gazing up at Helen with concern. It was a big event in his little life. Why does she need reminding?

Well, she's not going to gaslight a toddler. Besides, Helen is reasonably sure Cal never told his daughter that he'd lost her precious son, and that a girl he'd had a crush on in high school had come in for the save. Helen could toss it off as a brief and unremarkable encounter.

"Yes, I did, didn't I? Yesterday in Jansen Woods."

The woman stops being a harried young mother for a moment and takes Helen in from top to toe. "You're . . . um—" She pauses.

Everything is in that pause.

"You're my dad's friend from high school. He told me he ran into you."

*So much for Cal keeping his mouth shut*, Helen thinks. The woman's assessing gaze suggests he said more than *friend from high school*.

"It was quite a surprise," Helen says with forced nonchalance.

"I'm Janel Crosby." She hitches up her purse strap and holds out her hand to shake, still studying Helen.

"Helen Spencer. Your dad knew me as Helen Iannucci." *It was a long time ago*, she wants to say. *I was another person then.*

Janel scans the laptop and spreadsheets on the table. "Getting some work done?"

"Yes, it's a nice sunny spot with all the coffee I can slurp." She resists the urge to put her hands over the time sheets printed with *Cormac's Confectionery – Believe in the power of baked goods* circling the logo of a muffin.

"Oh, you work here," says Janel.

"My son-in-law is Cormac," Helen concedes. "I'm the book-keeper."

Janel nods as if this is a clue to some as-yet-unsolved mystery. "So you're here a lot."

"Not that often," says Helen. "Unless someone calls out sick and he's desperate for a sub."

After she moved to Belham last November in the middle of the pandemic, Helen and Barb were the only staff for a while. Cormac had limped through the summer, but with the spike in cases in the fall, fewer and fewer people were going out to eat. He couldn't make payroll and had to lay off the entire staff. In fact, Helen delivered the bad news herself because Cormac felt so bad, he couldn't bring himself to do it.

"How come *you're* still getting paid?" asked one of the snottier high school kids at the staff meeting.

"Actually I'm working for free so Cormac can save his business and offer you your job back someday. If you want to work for free, you're more than welcome to stay."

After the meeting she heard Cormac murmur to Barb, "Your mom's a bit of a badass."

Barb chuckled. "Yeah, but don't tell her."

Logan wiggles down from Helen's lap. "Donuts!" he says.

"Really nice to meet you," says Janel. "I'll let my dad know where to find you."

*Shit*, thinks Helen.

# Chapter 10

## 1978

Ricky Zugravescu was in Helen's American Literature class. *In* was a relative term, given that he was often absent; on those days the room was relatively on-leash, or at least less like the headquarters for some unspecified revolution. He was far from popular, and most kids avoided him, his sullen black eyes boring into anyone who looked at him a second too long. Nonetheless he seemed to have a natural-born talent to rabble-rouse, and when he did deign to grace Am Lit with his presence, strolling in unapologetically late, elderly Mrs. Gilcrest would visibly brace herself.

The other kids took this as a cue to whisper things like "Shoulda retired sooner, Mrs. G.," or, "Hello, 911, we have an intruder."

One day in early November, Ricky galumphed in ten minutes after class had started and circled around behind the students, thumping Mark O'Malley hard on the shoulder as he passed.

"Z," murmured Mark in cowed acknowledgment.

"Mal," said Ricky.

He collapsed into a seat, pulled out the empty chair next to him, and put his feet up. That's when Helen, sitting at the next desk, saw Francie's embroidered yin-yang sign on the thigh of his jeans.

Helen gasped in horror, outraged on her friend's behalf.

"What," he said, glaring at her.

"Where'd you get those jeans?" she whispered at him.

He didn't answer, only looked away and smiled to himself. *Smiled* at the memory of stealing her friend's handiwork!

"You have to give those back!" she hissed.

"Fuck off, Giraffe."

"All right, now," Mrs. Gilcrest warbled in a vain effort to gain control. "Let's resume our analysis of Jay Gatsby."

"Greedy, self-pitying bastard," replied Ricky. "Discuss."

"RICKY STOLE YOUR jeans!" Helen said, hurrying into the ceramics room and letting her overstuffed backpack thump onto one of the art tables.

"What?" said Francie, confused.

"He was wearing them! The ones with the black-and-white thing!"

"They're his," said Francie.

"Are you sure? Because they look just like the ones you were—"

Francie chuckled. "His jeans, my embroidery."

Helen dropped into a chair and shook her head. "What the hell is happening."

"We're, ummmmmm . . ."

"Don't hum at me, Francie. What is the actual deal?"

"Kind of . . ."

"Oh my God, *are you going out with him*?"

"Li'l bit."

"WHY?"

"Don't be such a snob, Hellie."

"I am not a snob! I am concerned for your life!"

"You don't need to be concerned. He's very sweet to me."

"*Sweet Ricky Zugravescu* is an oxymoron."

Francie shrugged and smiled to herself.

"You kissed him!"

Francie's smile turned sly.

"Oh my God." Helen shook her head. "You kissed the school thug."

Francie's gaze came up and leveled at Helen. "You're jealous."

A direct hit. Helen felt her neck flush. But she had to fight her corner. "Of locking lips with a walking ashtray?"

"You're jealous that I kissed someone before you. Even though I'm me."

"What is that supposed to mean?"

"I'm not Wendy Moriarty or Beth Harriman." Beth was a mediocre cheerleader, laughed entirely too much, and her social power came from not claiming too much social power. "And I'm not you."

"What is *that* supposed to mean?"

"You have excellent judgment."

"Francie, you have good judgment!"

"I have okay judgment. And that's fine. It gives me a lot of room to . . . I don't know. Be me. You just need less room."

Helen blinked, trying to absorb this. There was something about it that rang completely true, and yet also implied that having excellent judgment—which she did, it was generally acknowledged—might not be as good a thing as it sounded. How much "room" did one person need? How much was allowed?

"How was the kiss?" she asked.

Francie squinched her nose. "Kinda gross!"

Helen laughed. "Really?"

Francie wagged her tongue around her mouth.

"Ew!" said Helen.

"Yeah, I'm pretty sure it was his first time, too. He didn't have a clue what he was doing."

THE CORDEN COUNTY Regional High School cross-country team had one meet left, and though it was not likely to be a nail-biter—only Felicity Manning had made states, and no one else was expected to—Coach Costarellis loaded everyone onto the bus and drove to Paddow Mountain State Park. "For inspiration," he said.

"*I'm* inspired to find a nice meadow to lie down in and get some sun," said Cal as the bus bumped along toward Paddow. "Except I burn like a marshmallow, so you have to keep an eye on me."

"I'm not keeping an eye on you, Match." She had taken to calling him Match, mostly because he liked it, but also because as nicknames went, it seemed more household-item-y than romantic. She hoped he got the message. "I'm running."

He sighed dramatically. "Can't you just stay still sometimes?"

"I have a hard time with that. It makes me feel weird." She'd never said this out loud before. (Francie, of course, just knew.) But it was Cal. Yes, okay, he had his little crush, but he also seemed interested in knowing her as a person. And he was kind of a weird kid, too, so she felt less odd by comparison.

He gazed at Helen a moment. "That makes a whole lot of sense."

"It does?" She had hoped for exactly the opposite, that people would be surprised to hear it. But whatever. It was just Cal.

"Absolutely." He nodded. "What about school?"

"I guess I'd like it better if classes were outside and we could move around." She'd also never before considered how school could bend to meet her needs. It was school. It bended for no one.

"How long have you been this way?"

She shrugged. "Whole life. My parents had to fence in the back-yard."

"Do you like to dance?"

"I love to dance. But not, you know, as a career or anything. I took ballet for about twenty minutes when I was six."

"Too much holding poses."

"Exactly!"

"So just . . ." He moved his shoulders around.

"Yeah, nothing special."

"And you love school dances."

"No! I mean they're okay, but not because of the dancing."

"But you love it."

"Yeah, but *school* dances . . . Everyone's watching everyone else, and you have to be cool and not . . . like . . ." She could feel herself blushing.

"Like what?"

"At home, I'm kind of . . ." Helen could barely look at him.

Cal's face went wide with understanding. "You're like this!" He flung his arms around and bobbed his head, attracting glances from other kids.

"Stop!" she said. "Don't!"

"You let loose," he whispered.

"Shut up," she hissed.

"I'd like to see that sometime."

"Absolutely not."

"Maybe someday."

"Never."

WHEN THEY GOT off the bus at Paddow Mountain State Park, Coach Costarellis said, "Okay, gather up, runners! The point is to get inspiration from the beauty of nature, and to challenge yourself to run hard in unfamiliar terrain. Now, who's got a watch? Raise your hands." He glanced around at the arms in the air. "Groups of four. You." He motioned to various clumps of kids. "You, you, you, and you."

Helen had a watch, and she was grouped with Cal, Mark O'Malley, and Jerry Klimper. Mark's attitude had changed dramatically since Cal had stolen away his spot on the varsity roster. Suddenly he didn't care at all anymore; he ran with Jerry (who had never cared) and ambled across the finish line whenever he felt like it.

Coach C continued, "Go in different directions when the trails split so you don't trip one another. Then turn around in twenty minutes and run back down. Everyone back at four thirty!"

There was a lot of shuffling and bumping at first, but after a few minutes the runners spread out. Helen led their little group up the main trail, then turned down a side path. She looked back to make sure Mark and Jerry were still with her. She never worried about Cal. He was always with her.

The other two boys were walking. "Hey, keep up, you guys!" she called out.

Mark said, "Shove it, Helen," and Jerry flipped her off.

"Screw them," said Cal and took off past her.

"We're supposed to—" But what was she going to do, babysit Mark and Jerry?

Helen followed Cal up the hill, accelerating to catch him, focusing hard to avoid roots and rocks. He sped down another side trail, and for the first time she realized that at maximum capacity she still couldn't keep up. How had this happened? Watching his back recede, she saw that he wasn't as gawky as when they'd started. He looked almost . . . graceful.

Her quads were ablaze, and her lungs were drowning, all in a desperate bid to keep from allowing any more distance between them. She lost sight of him when the path turned, and she almost called out, *Wait, don't leave me!*

When she came around the turn, he was nowhere in sight. There was a path off to the left. Had he taken it? She slowed, jogging in place for a moment, trying to decide what to do (and keep from passing out).

"Wheels!"

She spun around. "Where are you?"

Cal's head popped up out of the grass in a clearing to her right. His face was bright pink, and he was panting, but also laughing. "Did you think I ditched you?"

She had. She thought he'd ditched her. And it had brought on a mild panic that she could never have anticipated at the beginning of the season, or even last week.

Helen walked over, hands on hips, ready to tell him to get his butt up and finish the run. But he smiled up at her and said, "I'd never ditch you, Wheels."

She flopped down in the grass a few feet away, arms and legs splayed out like his, and gazed up at the sky. It was so clear and blue it hurt to look at it, so she focused on one of the few cottony clouds drifting by and let her oxygen-starved body replenish itself and her heart stop knocking around like a bumper car.

For once it felt good to be still.

# Chapter 11

## 2021

As Helen turns down yet another side road off a side road, she starts to suspect Google Maps is having a little app-y fun at her expense. But then she sees the wooden sign that hangs from an oak tree so big it must have been a sapling during the Revolutionary War.

SEVEN MEADOWS FARM. And in slightly smaller type below: HORSES AND ART.

*She did it*, thinks Helen. All Francie's dreams come true in that one slightly crooked, weather-beaten piece of wood.

The driveway is long; she passes huge abstract metal sculptures planted amid the maples and underbrush. Lichen-dotted stone walls rim the potholed road; her RAV4 will definitely need a realignment when she gets home to Belham.

At its end, the road descends gently toward farm buildings growing out of the landscape like fairy-tale mushrooms: a two-story stone house on the right, enormous umber-colored barn on the left with a shaded paddock in front and a sunny corral behind. Several smaller buildings are sprinkled in between the two, the largest of these with a painted sign that says, OFFICE AND GALLERY. Helen glides into the small parking area on the left.

She's spent most of the drive to Vermont ruminating on what to say. How to encapsulate her life for Francie, and probably Ricky, too. He'll be disgusted with her, of course. Always was, and now the only tales she has to tell are from lifestyles of the bougie and vapid. At least that's how he'll see it. At least that's how she *thinks* he'll see it.

But maybe not. Maybe Ricky Zugravescu has found a way to be less angry. Maybe Francie's kindness has softened him. Change is possible. Helen has seen her own children grow and change, after all. Barb from a girl whose emotions dictated her every waking moment to a woman who's learned how to keep herself on an even keel (mostly), even when life gets legitimately hard. Sam from family peacekeeper (Barb and Danny were often at war, and occasionally Helen and Jim let the tension between them leak out, too) to an environmental lawyer who wades into battle with eco-villains. And Danny from a loud, hyperactive kid who never met a high place he didn't want to dangle from to a man who craves the quiet beauty of nature, supporting himself (except for the occasional cash infusion from Helen) as an extreme-sports cameraman, a livelihood based on careful planning, risk assessment, and patience.

Change is always possible. But in Helen's experience, it's not probable. People tend to go on being who they are, or who they're forced—by the random distribution of genetics, situation, or just dumb luck—to be. So much can hinge on a single factor. Or a decision. Or a moment. Doesn't she know that all too well.

She hopes Ricky's moments of the last thirty-five years have led him to peace and contentment. To being a kind and loving partner. To not holding an insurmountable grudge against Helen. Soon she'll know if any of that has happened. Or if, conversely, his baked-in rage has been fueled to an all-consuming wildfire.

*I bet there are some great running trails around here,* thinks Helen as she walks the gravel path from the parking lot to the office. It just seems like there's room for a person to breathe and move and be who she was meant to be before all those other things got in the way. Room for two old friends to reunite and put the past behind them.

She opens the door and a bell jingles on the back as she enters. The room is framed in unfinished beams and wood-panel walls. Shelves and display cases feature jewelry, ceramic pieces, cards, and knitwear. Colorful (and occasionally incomprehensible) paintings cover the walls. There's a desk with a cash register to the right, and signage on the wall behind it about horse-riding fees and equine therapy schedules.

Near the desk is a door with a small, smudged sign that says, PLEASE DON'T COME IN UNLESS YOU WORK HERE, AND IF YOU WORK HERE, YOU SHOULD BE OUT WORKING.

The *please* sounds like Francie. The rest sounds like Ricky.

The door opens and out steps Francie, her wild gray locks pinned up in a messy bun behind her head. Her face—previously obscured by the mask and tears at Annabella's graveside—bears a dusting of sunspots and filigreed wrinkles. Her eyes are just as big and brown. And her jeans are speckled with some sort of earthy material. The jeans are exactly the same.

"Hellie," she says, and reaches out.

The hug goes on for a long time.

"AND HOW'S JIM?" Francie asks.

After a tour of the farm, they're sitting at a picnic table in the sun behind the office/gallery, drinking tea, and eating grain-free, dairy-free, sugar-free muffins that have no right to taste nearly as good as they do. They've gone through Helen's kids and Francie's art shows and have moved on to the dicier subject of the men in their lives.

"He died," says Helen.

Usually she says he "passed." It feels so much more normal-course-of-life than that he expired far too young from a potentially preventable thing. "Heart attack."

Francie's face drops, and she reaches out to clasp Helen's arm. "Oh my God, Helen."

"A year ago April. Right after I got home from Hestia."

"Ohhhhh," says Francie, realizing the significance of the timing.

"Yeah. He had a heart condition."

She wants to add, *He also had an aversion to lifesaving medicine. Or any medicine, really. Also sunscreen, bug spray, calamine lotion, antibiotic salve, ACE bandages, and cough drops. He was morally opposed to aloe. That's what I was dealing with.* She wants to say this, but she doesn't because she still has a corner to fight on the subject of marrying this man. At least she feels like she does.

Instead she says, "We really miss him. He was a wonderful father." This is true. He was great when he was home, which wasn't a lot, but when he was, he was very "present," as the parenting articles say. Helen feels her throat tighten and her voice gets a little chokey when she says, "I don't think the kids will ever really get over it." And this is absolutely true. Danny has a surprisingly beautiful tattoo of a golf ball sitting on a tee with his father's initials on the shaft. It's on the inside of his forearm; she sees him run a hand over it sometimes on the rare occasions when he's home.

"I got so many notes from his friends and clients about how much he meant to them," Helen adds, still building her case. "People I didn't even know. He worked with struggling golf clubs in less affluent areas, and they really came to rely on him.

There was one general manager in Georgia, Kesia Neep, who just sobbed—" Whoa, why is she bringing this up? "Well, anyway . . ."

Francie nods and gazes off into the trees, as if she needs a moment to incorporate these unexpected details into the old, pixilated image she's had in her mind all these years. She's also probably noticing that Helen didn't say *she* will never really get over it. Helen's not over it, but she sees a day in the not-too-distant future when the thought of it won't completely piss her off.

A truck's engine hums in the distance, growing steadily louder until it cuts off somewhere in front of the barn. "Oh, good," says Francie.

*Let's get this over with*, thinks Helen.

A tall man with thick gray hair heads toward them, barn jacket hanging off a wiry frame, work boots clumping across the grass. *He shrunk*, thinks Helen. Ricky was built like a bookcase.

As the man gets closer, it becomes clear that he's not Ricky. At all. His limbs hang comfortably from his body in a way that Ricky's never did. Ricky's limbs were always spoiling for a fight. This guy reminds Helen of Sam Elliott without the mustache.

He leans down for a quick kiss from Francie, and Francie smiles a sweet little smile, and Helen knows this is good. This guy is good.

"Helen, this is my business partner, Vernon Shields. Also my—" She gazes up at him, searching for the right term.

"Bitch?" he says, and Francie bursts out laughing. He turns to Helen. "Really nice to meet you," he growls with a smile. The gravelly voice that was apparently also not Ricky's.

"Very nice to meet you, too. I'm Helen, Francie's old friend from Hestia."

His grin goes wide as he turns to his partner. "*Francie?* You were *Francie* back then?"

"Oh, shut up," says Francie.

"She's still Francie," says Helen. "You don't think I'm switching to Fran after fifty years, do you?"

Vernon sits, and the two women employ him as the needle they need to begin stitching up the gaping hole in their friendship. They regale him with the funny stories and half-forgotten memories of a childhood they galloped through side by side.

They brag about each other. "Francie was the queen of the ceramics room. Mrs. Sullivan was always forgetting to turn off the kiln. Honest to God, that school would've burned to the ground if Francie hadn't been there to keep an eye on things."

"Senior year, Helen was the fastest girl in the whole school, sprinting *and* cross-country. No one could catch her."

"Not even any of the guys?" asks Vernon.

Francie and Helen look at each other. "A few," says Helen.

"Cal fucking Crosby," says Francie.

Helen laughs. It was Francie, after all, who'd dubbed him that. Francie shakes her head and mutters, "That asshole."

"I saw him."

"Cal? When?"

"Last week."

"*Last week?* You saw Cal fucking Crosby *last week*? You should have led with that!"

"He's not anywhere near the most important part of this visit, Francie."

Francie grins. "Yeah, screw him."

Vernon seems instinctively to know that his work here is done. He says something nonspecific about a lesson and clumps back across the yard toward the barn.

Francie says, "So?" and Helen tells her all about Logan falling, and how Cal didn't recognize her, and that was fun for a minute, but then it got weird, and she hauled out of there. She also tells Francie about his daughter finding her at Cormac's.

"So he lives in your town."

"I guess. Or maybe he was visiting his daughter? No idea." Helen gets a funny look on her face.

"What?"

"No, it's just . . . I don't think of Belham as my town. It's my daughter's town. I'm only living there because she does."

"How long ago did you move in?"

"About a year."

"Sounds like it's your town now, Hellie."

"Maybe. I'll have to think about that."

"His daughter saying, 'I'll let him know where to find you'— that's the crux of the matter right there."

Helen snorts. "He sure wasn't trying to find me forty years ago, was he? Maybe he finally has something to say about it."

"Maybe *you* have something to say about it."

"I don't. I'm over it. Really, Francie, who actually gives a shit about high school anymore?"

"Helen Elizabeth Iannucci! Is that a swear I hear?"

Helen laughs. "Yeah, well, you were doing all the swearing for me back then. Jim never swore. I had to pick up the slack."

"It's a dirty job, but somebody's gotta do it."

They giggle about this, and then a quiet descends between them.

*Now*, thinks Helen. *Now or never.*

"Where's Ricky these days?"

Francie takes a breath and says softly, "He died. It's ten years ago now."

"Oh, Francie," Helen whispers. "I'm so sorry."

It's clear to Helen in this moment that she's sorrier for Francie than she ever was for herself. She reaches out and puts a hand on Francie's shoulder, and Francie lays her cheek against it. She says, "I know you never understood what I saw in him . . ."

"That doesn't matter."

"There was more to him than you knew—than most people knew."

"Of course there was," says Helen. "I'm just sorry I can't apologize to him now."

That night rises up in their memories. Helen drove to Francie's apartment in Bennington, Vermont, to tell her she was pregnant, and Jim wanted to marry her. Francie tried to talk her out of the latter, telling Helen she was putting herself in a box she would never escape from. Things escalated until she called Jim "stiff and unimaginative," an accusation so loaded coming from Francie that Helen felt as if she'd been slapped across the face.

"Well, at least I'm not wasting my life and talent propping up a violent druggie!"

Francie blanched. "Jesus, he's—"

"He's a criminal. You'll be visiting him in jail before long. And you're lecturing me?"

"He's right in—" Francie pointed to her bedroom just as the door opened.

Ricky leaned in the doorway, eclipsing it with his size and his fury. And something else. Something unfathomably dark and sad. He'd always seemed like a poorly trained rottweiler to Helen, but now she could see the kicked puppy, too.

"Hi, Helen." His voice was so calm it was terrifying.

And before either of them could say another word, Francie screamed at Helen, "Get out! Right now! Get the fuck out and do not come back!"

Over the next few days, Helen perseverated on how to fix this and go back to being best friends. She wanted so desperately for Francie to be at her wedding, by her side as she had been for all the important moments of her life. She apologized to Francie by mail. (Francie wasn't taking her calls.) Looking back, she realizes it was more of an *I'm sorry, but* kind of apology—*Sorry, but you said horrible things about my boyfriend, too.* Francie responded with her own unapologetic apology and agreed that she and Ricky would attend the wedding.

Helen hadn't invited him. And she was damned if he was going to be there, with his abysmal black eyes boring into her. The day would be hard enough with her father's grave so fresh the grass had barely grown over it. With a baby hiding beneath her empire waist wedding dress. And Jim.

You could do worse than Jim. Way worse. But marrying a man because there were worse men (like Ricky!) did not counterbalance all the other things. Not by a long shot.

"I invited you. I'd prefer if Ricky didn't come." It was a deal breaker for both of them. And it broke them.

"I WASN'T WITH him when he died," says Francie. "I mean, I was there in the room when he passed, but we weren't together."

"Oh?" says Helen, treading so lightly she's almost levitating.

"Yeah, we broke up years before, in our thirties. We broke up a lot over the years, but that last one was a doozy."

Francie seems to want to talk about it, so Helen asks, "What happened?"

"He raised a hand to me."

"Jesus."

"He'd never done that before, and he didn't actually hit me. But he wound up."

"How did you handle it?"

"I screamed at him to get the hell away from me and told him to stop being such an asshole. He said he came from a long line of assholes, and then he left and never came back." Francie looked out over the garden and the corral beyond, where Vernon was slowly leading a horse with a little girl in the saddle. "It was just so sad, Helen. He hated himself. That was what I'd been fighting with all those years—not him. His self-loathing. And it's a losing battle if the person can't give it up."

Francie's honesty was such a raw, unfiltered thing. Helen hoped she could be that honest one day. "You said you were with him when he died?"

"He came to me years later. I always held out hope that he could somehow find his way back to me. When he did, he had cancer."

"Oh, Francie."

"Yeah. Lung cancer. The first thing he said was 'I had it coming.'"

"Because he smoked so much?"

"Because of everything. Never being the person he hoped he could be. Never overcoming his shitty family, and his anger, and his bad decisions." Francie sighed. "He was calmer than I'd ever seen him. Relieved, I think. He'd finally gotten what he thought he deserved."

They sat there with the scent of hay swirling in the breeze, and the sound of the horse's hooves patiently treading the corral, Vernon's low voice murmuring assurances to the girl.

"I called him terrible things," said Helen.

"Nothing he hadn't already called himself many times."

"Still. I would do anything to take it back. I didn't even mean it. I just wanted your blessing about marrying Jim, and I was mad that you wouldn't give it. I took it out on him."

"Thanks." Francie patted Helen's hand. "I forgive you on his behalf."

"It's not the same."

"It means a lot to me, though. And I meant a lot to him. So let's let it go."

Helen feels the weight of that particular burden lifting and realizes it never got lighter over the years, only heavier. "Okay." She exhales. "Thank you."

"He gave me this farm."

Helen is speechless for a moment. "But I thought"—she looks around—"didn't your family . . ."

Francie's face loses its warmth. "My parents finally got divorced about thirty years ago. Mom got a lump sum she spent mostly on rehab stints, and the rest of it went to the nursing home when she was diagnosed with Alzheimer's. Dad married the much younger woman he'd been seeing since before I was born, they had a couple of kids, he died, and they got all his money. So no, the Hydecker fortune did not fund so much as a bale of hay."

Helen's jaw drops. "Francie."

"Yeahhhhh." She strings out the word like the slow wilting of a flower.

"Was all this going on when . . . ?"

"The adultery and the booze."

"Yeah, that."

"I knew my mother drank too much and my father didn't love her. That's why I practically lived at your house." She smiles briefly at Helen. "I didn't know about my father's secret life. Apparently, he'd always planned to leave my mother when the boys graduated from college, but then I came along and adjusted his timeline."

Helen shakes her head. It's amazing how much of other people's unhappiness has been loaded onto Francie's shoulders over the years. "I should have been there for you."

"We should have been there for each other. It was a mistake we both made."

Helen gazes at her friend's beautiful fifty-eight-year-old face. Thirty-five years of wrinkles and sunspots she didn't get to see the arrival of. "Let's not make it again," she says, and Francie smiles. "But wait," says Helen, "how did Ricky . . . ?"

"He sold some pieces for pretty good dough before he died. Sculptures. Those are his out along the road. Also, he had a trust fund."

"A *trust fund*? His family had money?"

"His family didn't, but his grandfather did, and he left it to Rick because of some insane, decades-long feud with Rick's father. When the old man died, the father contested the will and Rick had to pay a lawyer to defend it, which really pissed him off. He decided the best revenge was just to let it sit there collecting interest. He'd send photocopies of the statements to his dad every once in a while. Apparently, it drove the guy completely mental."

"Did you know about all this?"

"No, he didn't tell me about it till he was sick. He said it was just another example of how messed up his family was, and I didn't need any more evidence of that. I got a letter from his attorney after he died. He left me everything."

"God, Francie, wouldn't he be thrilled to see you here in this amazing place knowing he made it all possible!"

"He is." Francie sighs softly. "I feel him here a lot. He's happy now."

# Chapter 12

## 1978

Helen and Cal lay there in the grass on Paddow Mountain. It was going brown and thin, and when she turned her head she could see right through to his face, which was turned toward hers.

"How Italian are your parents?" he asked.

She bristled. She'd been teased by those with fewer vowels in their names for most of her life. She'd been called "Anthony!" like the little boy in the Prince Spaghetti ad. And though no one called her Wop Giraffe anymore (even Ricky had switched to just "Giraffe," which was bad enough but didn't impugn her ethnicity along with her height), the lingering sting was still there.

"A normal amount of Italian," she said.

"No, I mean were they actually born there?"

"Yes."

"How old were they when they came over?"

"He was fifteen and she was twenty-five."

"Wow."

"What, 'wow.' There's nothing 'wow' about it."

"Are you kidding? Imagine coming here from another country, where they speak a whole other language and have a totally different way of doing things, and you have to start all over, learning like a baby. That's pretty wow."

"My father doesn't even have an accent."

"I'm fifteen, and I'm pretty sure if someone dropped me in the middle of Italy and said, *This is where you live now. Deal with it,* I'd piss myself."

Helen laughed. "When I get home, I'll ask him if he wet his pants when he came over."

"What? No, don't say that."

"Why not? He'll think it's funny."

Cal raised his eyebrows. "Your old man must have a better sense of humor than mine does."

"What's your dad like?"

"Well, he's not a guy who moved halfway around the world and learned a second language with no accent, let's put it that way."

"Do you get along with him?"

He didn't answer for a moment, then he said, "Do you get along with yours?"

"Yeah. I mean, they expect a lot of me and drive me crazy sometimes. But you know . . . they're okay."

"I bet they're really proud of you."

Helen thought about that. They were. Really proud. "I guess."

"Guess, nothing," he said. "They're crazy about you."

She laughed. "How do you know?"

"From your face. You like them, right? As people?"

"Yeah, so?"

"Well, if you like your parents, then they love the crap out of you."

"Is that a rule?"

"Pretty much."

She thought about this. It made sense, actually. Most parents loved their kids, she figured. But most kids complained about their parents. If they actually liked their parents, as she did, then it was a surprisingly happy situation.

"Do you like your parents?" she asked.

"Um, well. I love them. They gave me life. And they're not, like, abusive or anything. But I probably wouldn't have picked them." Cal gazed up at the trees. "Nope, I definitely would not have picked them."

"Why not?"

"They're just not . . . We don't . . . I don't know. Like, my dad works at the lumberyard, which he complains about, but he doesn't look for other jobs. He just bitches about the splinters and cracks another beer. He's not a dumb guy. He's actually pretty smart about some things. He could probably build a house single-handedly. But he has no idea why I would want to go to college, and he sure as hell isn't going to pay for it, even if he could afford it, which he can't."

Helen was surprised by this. "I thought Velmont was pretty . . ."

"Rich?"

"Well, yeah."

"Maybe there's more rich people than average, but there's poor people, too. We're not poor, but we're not the Moriartys, either." He studied her. "I thought Hestia was kinda . . ."

"It's no Velmont, but there are a few wealthy families." She thought of Francie's house with the stone pillars on either side of the driveway.

"What about your family?" he asked.

"My dad owns an auto body shop. It's not fancy, but he does okay. My mom does the books, and she says it's a cash goat." Helen laughed.

"A what?"

"She means cash cow, but she doesn't always get American sayings on the first try. Or the fifth."

Cal smiled. "She sounds hilarious."

*She is*, thought Helen. *I'm lucky.*

"What about your mom?" she asked.

Cal's face softened. "Bonnie Crosby is . . . She's tired a lot. You know, six kids, never enough time to get it all done."

"Six kids! I didn't know you had that many brothers and sisters. Where are you in the lineup?"

"Oldest."

He got quiet then. The guy who always had commentary on everything.

Helen picked a long stalk of grass and tapped his arm with it. "You are definitely going to college."

"Yeah? How do you know."

"Because you're smart and you work hard."

He grinned. "Maybe I'll get a cross-country scholarship."

"Yeah, um, like I said. You're smart and you work hard."

He laughed and pulled up some grass and threw it at her.

THEY WERE LATE getting back to the bus, but not as late as Mark and Jerry, so no one really noticed. They were mostly quiet on the ride home. Once, Cal glanced over at Helen and smiled. And she smiled back.

She had made a friend. A real friend, almost as good as Francie. Not a friend she would likely bring home, because her parents would have a hard time understanding that there was nothing fishy going on. (*Fishy* was a word her mother had learned on the first try.) In fact, Cal himself might take it the wrong way.

So she wouldn't invite him home to hang out. And it sounded like he wouldn't invite her over to his house, either. But they could be friends at school and at cross-country.

"You're going to do indoor track for your winter sport, right?" she asked.

"Absolutely," he said. "Gunning for that scholarship. I gotta keep up my skills."

They tittered over this. Cal and his scholarship.

"Good. Because you are definitely going to college," she said. "Don't forget to study."

THE LAST MEET of the season was two days later, and as expected it was fairly inconsequential, except for Helen and Cal, who beat Wendy Moriarty and Mark O'Malley, respectively.

"A moral victory," Cal murmured to her on the bus ride home.

"Especially for me," Helen murmured back.

"Geez, you are so competitive. Why is yours better than mine?"

"Because Wendy is the queen of the grade. She gets everything. Except this. I, Helen Iannucci, little Miss Nobody, get *this*."

"There are so many things wrong with that statement, I don't even know where to begin."

"Come on, you know she's ridiculously popular, and then she suddenly becomes a sports star, too, without even breaking a sweat? That is just cosmically unfair."

"Okay, but that's not what I'm talking about. I'm talking about you being a nobody, which is not true, you are very much somebody, which I am well aware of by the ass-kicking you give me every day." Cal lowered his voice to a whisper. "Also, Wendy's older brother is in jail for getting bombed and driving his car into the lobby of the Velmont Country Club and nearly killing a couple of people last summer, and her parents turned on each other and almost got divorced. So bad shit happens to her, too."

"Oh," said Helen. "That's pretty awful."

"Yeah. And why does you beating her outrank my beating Mark, who is, might I add, a douchebag?"

"He's not really a jerk. He's just jerk adjacent."

"Jerk *adjacent*?"

"Yeah, he goes along with whoever he's with. So he starts hanging out with Jerry and suddenly he doesn't care about running anymore, even though he's pretty good. Or Ricky Zugravescu, who is grand theft auto waiting to happen."

"Z's not that bad. He just looks bad. And he kind of cultivates that, so it's not even a real thing."

"How do you know?"

"I know him."

"From where? You didn't grow up with him like I did."

"From around."

"The smoking area!"

"Yeah, but I quit."

"But you still go there."

"Purely social."

She narrowed her eyes at him. "Not even a puff?"

He held up three fingers. "Wheels, I'm tobacco-free, I swear."

"What's the three for?"

He quickly put his hand in his lap and shrugged.

"Is that a Boy Scout thing? Are you a Boy Scout?"

"No!" He looked around quickly. "Well, yes, but we try to be cool about it."

She laughed. "*Cool Boy Scout* is an oxymoron."

He stuck his chin out. "It's actually *super*cool. We just act like nerds so guys don't swamp the troop."

Helen snorted with laughter. "Yeah, it'd be like a run on the bank!"

"Okay, can you shut up now, snorty? You learn a lot of great things in Scouts, and you camp out in the woods and use knives and shit, and if you make Eagle, it helps you get into college."

"Are you going to make Eagle?"

"Hell, yeah! I'm slaying it! I'm building a bridge over this little stream up at Paddow, and my dad's getting me the lumber at cost."

She grinned at him. He was such an adorable little nerd.

"What? It's awesome."

"No, it is," she said. "Hikers will really appreciate it."

JUST BEFORE THE bus pulled into the CCRHS parking lot, Helen realized she was really going to miss Cal during the three weeks before indoor track started up. Almost a month without his wry observations, and goofy, hilarious stories, and his . . . well, his love for her. She felt loved just for being herself. It was so easy. And she loved him, too. He was a good person and a loyal friend, and he got her. The only other person who really got her was Francie.

As they were filing off the bus into the darkened parking area, and everyone was starting to disperse, Helen was ruminating on how the two of them could hang out—maybe just once, or even twice—before indoor track, when Cal said, "Hey, Wheels, can I ask you something?"

A prickle went up her neck. It was coming.

*No*, she wanted to say. *Please. I love you. I need you in my life! Please don't make me hurt your feelings.*

She kept walking down the sidewalk, as if pretending she hadn't heard him might stop this runaway train that was about to derail and kill all the passengers.

"Wheels?"

She turned around. "Yeah, what's up?"

"So, um . . ." He pulled himself to his full height, which was still a couple of inches shy of hers, and took a deep breath. "Can I take you to the Homecoming Dance?"

"As friends?" Helen said in a desperate, last-ditch effort to avert catastrophe.

He locked his blue eyes onto hers, and forever afterward—even despite everything that happened later—she would credit his bravery in that moment, because he did not veer off course, despite the fact that he could surely see that this would not end as he hoped. He understood her so well; he could read her like a book. He knew.

And yet he said, "No, not as friends. As a date."

"Cal."

"Yes."

"Cal, I really like you."

"Good."

"You've become one of my best friends."

"Ditto," he said.

"But I just don't . . ."

"What."

He needed her to say it. And that was fair. If he could muster the courage to ask, she could bring herself to answer truthfully. For his sake. In the hope that if she hurt him a little bit now, they could get past it sooner.

"I don't feel that way about you."

She watched that land like a punch to the solar plexus. He looked as if he'd forgotten how to breathe for a moment. Like oxygen was a tricky concept and he couldn't quite recall how it worked. And then he nodded. "Okay," he said, as if it might not be that surprising after all. That he'd seen it for the long shot that it was for a guy like him. He nodded again, and smiled a no-hard-feelings smile, and walked away.

"How's he doing?" Helen asked Francie a week later.

"Ummmmm," Francie hummed to buy herself time. "He's fine."

"No, seriously."

"Well, he's not exactly the Lucky Charms leprechaun these days, but I don't think we have a jumper on our hands."

"Ugh, Francie, what am I going to do?"

"Not make it worse."

"How do I do that?"

"By not trying to make it better and making it even worse."

"How are the kids at the smoking area treating him?"

"They pretty much leave him be."

"Well, that's good at least."

"Except Ricky. He started calling him Archie, you know, from the comics. Because of the . . ." Francie pointed at her hair.

"God, that guy is such an asshole!"

"Helen Elizabeth Iannucci! We do not swear!"

"You swear all the time."

"Then I didn't mean me, did I?"

"Seriously, why does he have to be such a frickin' jerk?"

"He's not being a jerk, Hellie. He's actually being nice. Everyone feels so sorry for Cal, they're not even calling him names anymore. At least Ricky shows some respect."

"By taunting him?"

"Of course. It's actually kinda brilliant. Archie's dopey, but Betty and Veronica think he's hot."

"They're *cartoon characters*, Francie! That is not respect!"

"Except in Guy Land. You don't have brothers. You have no idea how fucked-up their worldview is."

HELEN DIDN'T GO to Homecoming. She had wanted to before Cal asked her. She had thought maybe they might have a dance or two (fast ones, not slow!) and she might let loose a little. A very little. But he would get it, and he would crack up. She had really wanted to make him laugh.

But after he asked her, she felt so sad and awful, she couldn't bring herself to go. Francie didn't go either, but rabid emus couldn't have dragged her there. "Not my cup of Darjeeling," Francie said. "I might probably hang out with Ricky."

"You might probably?"

"You could join us."

"I'd be a third wheel and I'd stick out like a sore thumb."

"You wouldn't."

"I would. A third thumb."

"He'll be okay," Francie said.

"Ricky?"

"Oh, Ricky'll be fine. I meant Cal."

"Yeah, I know. But still."

Helen did not go to the dance, and she did not hang out with Francie and Ricky. She went for the longest run of her life, got a little bit lost, sat down behind a mailbox, and had herself a good hard cry. Then she asked directions and made it home just in time to keep Annabella and Luigi from activating the National Guard.

"That's it! No more running!" said Annabella.

"Sweetheart, you scared us," said Luigi.

She was sorry, she told them. So very sorry. That seemed to be her permanent state.

OCCASIONALLY HELEN SAW Cal passing in the hallways, and he'd give her a little head bob, but he kept on walking. She wanted to say, *Come on. Enough now. Let's go back to being Match and Wheels.* Francie told her to give him some time, he'd come around when he was ready. But that had barely held her back.

It was that awful Ricky Zugravescu muttering "Heartbreaker" at her in Am Lit one day that had stopped Helen in her tracks. She had broken sweet little Cal's sweet little heart. Who was the criminal now?

Indoor track started the week after Thanksgiving. Helen couldn't wait. She went out shopping for a T-shirt to wear that might make Cal laugh and break the ice. She picked one that said, WE DON'T CARE HOW THEY DO IT IN NEW YORK CITY, with a drunken worm hanging out of an apple.

That Monday afternoon, she stood in the field house with the rest of the runners. There were many more of them than turned out for cross-country. Indoor track was known to be pretty casual, and a lot of kids did it just for social opportunities. Coach Walker was in his sixties, about fifty pounds overweight, and clearly biding his time till retirement. His welcome speech to the team included no inspirational material; however, he was quite passionate about everyone getting picked up on time. "I am not hanging around while you kids vandalize the property and make out."

Helen suspected it was hard to do both at the same time. It seemed like an either-or proposition. She planned to laugh with Cal about it when he showed up.

But he never did.

# *Chapter 13*

*2021*

On Thursdays, Cormac has a standing date with his friend Sean, who grew up with him in Belham. Sean is a pediatric nurse at Boston Medical Center, though he spent most of his career in third-world countries, tending to the victims of wars and natural disasters. He's an interesting guy, and Helen likes him, though there is a bit of a feral quality to him. Sean doesn't always seem to fully understand how things work in the first world. He was a long time coming to email. And don't get him started about texting.

He comes over after dinner on Thursdays, and he and Cormac hang out in the throw-rug-size backyard, sitting in beach chairs and tossing logs into the firepit, drinking one beer too many (about four), and "solving the problems of the world," Sean likes to say. Which means he's not revealing what they talk about, and neither is Cormac.

Sean comes in this Thursday night like always, saying "Picture taker!" when he sees Barb, and wrapping her in a hug that always goes on a beat or two longer than Helen expects it to. Or thinks it should. Sometimes Cormac says, "Dude," or punches him in the arm. Sean always gives Helen a warm greeting and a hug, too, though the hug lasts an appropriate duration.

Then the two men grab their beers and head out back. They used to go to a decrepit little lakeside bar called the Dudley Palace, but during Covid they switched to Cormac's house. Cormac even rigged up a tarp to unfurl between tree limbs on wet days. As far as Helen is aware, they have never missed a Thursday for any reason.

After Monday's visit with Francie, Helen finds herself wondering about all the things that have happened (and continue to happen!) to the people around her of which she has no idea.

*I had no idea*, she thinks as she ponders Francie's life and Ricky's. Helen is starting to suspect that she doesn't ask enough questions. She's never wanted to pry. But now it becomes a strange sort of self-improvement goal: *Pry more*.

"How come Sean always gives you those long hugs?"

Barb looks up from pitching a vast array of brightly colored, jingly baby toys into a basket in the living room. "Oh, that," she says.

"Yeah," says Helen. "What's that about?"

Barb laughs. "I just have a high huggability factor, I guess."

"True . . ."

"Okay, remember when I was going through all the—" Barb waves her hand around.

*Infertility*, thinks Helen. She knows Barb doesn't even like to say the word.

"Sean was so kind. And he was a really good friend to Cormac, because I was pretty . . ."

*Despairing*, thinks Helen. *Angry. And hard on your husband.*

"Sean just started hugging me. And it felt weirdly good. Also, he's been through some stuff, too. Like, serious stuff. So now we just hug each other."

"Cormac doesn't mind?"

"Nope."

"And you don't mind that your husband spends every Thursday night with someone else?"

"Why would I?"

"Some wives would."

"You never minded when Dad was gone most of the week working or playing golf with his friends, right? So why should I mind Cormac having a few hours to hang out with Sean?"

Helen doesn't say anything for a moment, and Barb says, "Did you mind?"

"Not really. I mean, I would've liked it if he'd been around to help out a little more, but . . . Dad and I weren't always . . ."

"In sync?"

"That's a good way to put it. We weren't always in sync."

Barb seems to muster herself for a moment, and then asks, "But you loved him, right?"

Helen nods. "Absolutely."

Barb keeps looking at her. "Yeah?"

*She knows*, thinks Helen. And while half of her wants to keep whistling a happy tune, the other half is proud of her daughter's deductive skills.

"I loved Dad," says Helen. "I loved what a good father he was to you guys. I loved that he was a kind and loyal person." She gazes at her daughter. "But . . . we weren't always in sync."

Barb nods, digesting this. Translating it to its true meaning.

"Is that hard to hear?" asks Helen.

"No. I think I always knew."

It hurts to learn that no matter how much Helen and Jim had tried to put a good face on things, Barb could see the disconnect anyway. Helen has the sense of having let her children down in some crucial way, like not teaching them to tie their shoes or cross the road safely. Not teaching them what a genuinely happy couple looks like.

"You and Cormac seem pretty synced up," she says.

Barb smiles. "Yeah." But it sounds apologetic, and Helen won't have that.

"It's wonderful, the way you two just get each other."

"We're lucky."

"It's more than luck. It takes effort. You've been through some hard days, but you always seem to turn toward each other. Some couples turn away when the going gets tough." Helen wonders, not for the first time, how Barb was able to make such a good match, when she and Jim weren't exactly Barack and Michelle. But she's never asked before. Now she says, "How do you think you learned to connect like that?"

Barb seems surprised by the question. "What do you mean, how did I learn?"

"Well, you just seem to know instinctively—"

"Mom, *you* taught me."

Helen laughs. "I did? How did I do that?"

"You connected with me. You showed me how it's supposed to feel, to be completely loved and to love completely back."

Helen is blown away. All she can manage to say is, "Oh, sweetie . . ."

Barb smiles, clearly pleased at having struck her mother dumb. "Remember when I would wake up scared in the middle of the night and crawl into bed with you? You would put your arms around me and say, 'You're my love letter, and I'm your envelope.'"

Helen remembers. She remembers how tired she was taking care of three demanding kids. (Well, two, but she tried to give Sam extra attention so years later he wouldn't complain to a therapist about how overlooked he was.) She remembers countless nights of herding them to bed and attempting to pull the house back from the brink of being designated an EPA Superfund site.

After washing the spaghetti sauce and bike grease and glitter glue off her body, she'd crawl under the covers. She'd be snug in the arms of Morpheus (because most days, the god of sleep was the only guy in her bed), and in would toddle a weepy kid. So she'd tuck whoever it was into the curve of her body, wrap her arms around them, and hope they'd calm down quick.

She doesn't remember how she came up with the envelope thing. It's possible she was thinking how nice it would be to just mail the wailer to Jim. But soon it became a sort of whispered lullaby, reminding herself and the child that they were both exactly where they were supposed to be, and that everything would be okay.

"I loved when you said that," says Barb. "Sometimes I wasn't really scared, and I could have gone back to sleep on my own, but I just wanted to hear it. I wanted to be reminded that I was someone's love letter. It was the safest, most adored I ever felt in my life until I met Cormac."

Helen hadn't realized the words packed quite so much power. But now that she thinks of it, there was magic in them. In fact, there were days when the kids were *her* envelope, unwittingly holding her together when life felt hard and long and pointless.

Barb gets a funny little smile on her face.

"What?" says Helen.

"I probably shouldn't tell you this."

"You know you're going to tell me," Helen teases. Barb has never, not once, kept something to herself after saying, "I probably shouldn't tell you this."

Barb thinks for a minute. "Oh, what the hell." She sighs and her smile fades. "Okay, remember the night of Dad's funeral? We were at the house, just you, me, and the boys, because it was Covid, and we couldn't give him the blowout funeral he deserved. We were all so wrecked, and everything was so bleak and sad. You finally went to bed, but we stayed up."

"You did? I thought we all went to bed around the same time."

"No, we were going to, and then we just didn't get off the couch. At one point we were talking about how empty the world felt without Dad in it. And Sam says—of course, Sam, the defender of all things Mom—says, 'We're lucky we have Mom.' And Danny—complainer of all things Mom—says—and I swear to God I'm not making this up—he says, 'Mom makes it safe.'"

"Safe? *Me?*"

"Yeah, and he says that when he was little, and school was so hard, and he was crawling out of his skin, and Dad wasn't around, he'd climb into bed with you, and you'd give him the envelope line."

"It wasn't a line, Barb."

"No, of course it wasn't. I knew you meant it—and apparently so did Danny, because sometimes when he's in a jam, like he's lost in some backcountry area and he's starting to freak out, he remembers your envelope, and it helps him calm down and figure out what to do."

"He *said* that?"

"That is pretty much a direct quote." Barb points at her. "You. You're the one he thinks of when he's imperiled himself six times before breakfast."

"Danny." Helen needs confirmation that they're still talking about the same person.

"Yes, Danny! But here's the best part." Barb shakes her head. "Oh my God, this was so awesome. Sam freaked out! He was *sputtering* he was so mad."

"What?"

"Yeah, I know, right? It was crazy. I wish I'd been filming just for proof. He gets all outraged and says, 'She said that to *me*. That was *mine*! That was *our thing*.'"

"Then I raised my hand and nodded, and Sam turned on me—he actually *turned* on me, Mom—and he yells, 'YOU TOO?' Danny high-fives me and says to Sam, 'Yeah, shithead, Mom loves us, too.'

"Sam starts to laugh. 'She played us,' he says. '*Mom played us.*' Then we all start, and we're howling with laughter, tears coming down our cheeks, and I swear to God, our father was dead, and I have never laughed so hard with my brothers in all my life."

THE NEXT MORNING, when Helen wakes up in her sunny bedroom, she's still smiling. When she goes for her run, through a carpet of red and orange and gold leaves in Jansen Woods, she's grinning like the Cheshire Cat. And when she showers and heads to Cormac's Confectionery to start crunching the week's numbers, she forgets that this is not the plan.

The plan was to avoid Cal fucking Crosby.

She has stayed out of Jansen Woods since the previous week when Logan's fall cast them, literally, into each other's paths. She's even stayed away from the bakery. But not today. Today she's mentally swimming in the warm waters of having done something right as a mother, and having her children actually acknowledge it. This is the one-two punch that leaves her dazed and dunderheaded with joy.

She's sitting at her usual back table clicking away at her calculator when she hears a man's voice say, "Hey, Helen."

She looks up, and that's when she remembers the plan.

"Hey, Cal."

# Chapter 14

## 1979–1981

*He just needs time.*

That's what Francie said, and all through the winter, that's what Helen told herself. There were occasional Cal sightings, but she had no classes or extracurriculars with him, so that's all they were. Sightings. No jokes, pep talks, or heart-to-hearts.

No Match and Wheels.

Once in March, she saw him across the parking lot with some kids she didn't immediately recognize and wondered if he had found a new group. Well, not a new one. Like her, he'd had a few friends but no cohesive "crowd" he ran with. But now he seemed to have one. And they seemed to be on the shorter side, because his head was about midrange among all the other heads.

Helen waited for track and field to start, figuring that Cal had needed a season off from her and her heartbreaking ways, and he would return now that a new season was beginning. But once again, he was a no-show.

"He's doing baseball," said Francie as she painstakingly applied glaze to a square-sided vase she had twisted and bent in the middle to give it a sort of Salvador Dalí drippy-clock feel. Helen suspected flower holding was not in its future.

"How do you know?"

"Ricky told me. He was surprised when Cal showed up for tryouts."

"Ricky's still into baseball, huh?"

"Yep. He's a slugger," said Francie wanly, baseball having no real meaning for her. "He says he loves smashing the cover off the ball."

"Well, *that* makes a lot of sense."

Francie smiled. "It's a good outlet."

"And Cal made the team?" Helen was half hoping that he'd get cut and do track. But that was selfish. Cal didn't need anything else to be bummed out about, she told herself. But there was no amount of telling herself that could get her to hope that he'd do anything other than track.

"Yeah, he made it. Ricky says he's a terrible hitter, but he's so fast that if he can somehow get himself to first base, he can steal the rest."

Helen slammed her hand on the glazing table. "Are you *kidding* me?"

Francie startled at the noise and grabbed her piece. "Hey—"

"I taught him to run like that! *I* did! Coach Costarellis gave him *nothing*! He was too busy with that snotty bitch, Wendy Moriarty, and now because of *my* efforts Cal is stealing bases on the goddamned baseball team!"

"Wow," said Francie.

"Wow what," snarled Helen.

"It's like that olden days story where the wife sells her long locks of hair to buy her husband a watch chain while he's out selling his watch to get her a barrette or something."

"Yeah, except Cal didn't give up anything he cared about for *me*, did he? I'm just standing here like a loser, stupidly hoping we can be friends again, and he's living it up playing *baseball*!"

Weirdly, as upset as she was, there was some relief in it, too. Helen stopped feeling bad about breaking Cal's heart. He was fine. He was a *baseball player*.

She still missed him. There was no one quite like him, after all. But he'd clearly moved on, and it was time for her to do the same. Helen now channeled her energies into running, and she was getting good. Really good. Other kids noticed not only her winning mentality, but her growing self-confidence. She was no longer a scared little tenth grader, a little fish in a big pond, hanging out with another, even littler fish. She was setting her sights, bearing down, paying less attention to what people thought, and running her ass off. And, as it has been from time immemorial, the less you cared what other kids thought, the more they liked you.

One teammate in particular showed heretofore unexpressed interest. Mark O'Malley started hanging around, sprinting alongside her at practice even though he was slightly faster than she was. Sometimes Jerry Klimper would sidle up and say, "Hey, Mal, wanna go . . . ?" and hook a thumb over his shoulder toward the bleachers, under which unenthusiastic team members would huddle, avoiding Coach Walker, who never seemed to be looking for them anyway.

"Nah," Mark would say. "I'm gonna keep practicing."

The best part was, he never asked her out. He was too busy getting himself into her good graces to risk a negative response from her. He was a nice guy—smart and friendly and not bad-looking, with his scruffy blond hair and freckled nose and green eyes that seemed to go almost emerald when he looked at her. Helen didn't mind him at all.

Cal could just go play *baseball*.

In June, Francie's parents gave her older brother, John, a Chrysler LeBaron for his college graduation present. John in turn gave Francie, who had just hit sixteen and a half, his green Ford Pinto. The name of the paint color was actually "Ivy Glow" and it sparkled. At least it did in the spots that John hadn't dinged up and patched with housepaint or duct tape.

This gave Francie, and by extension Helen, an unprecedented amount of freedom. Of course, Annabella was apoplectic about the thought of the girls "driving around for no good reason," and Luigi practically had seizures over the state of the paint job. But eventually they relented when they saw that most nights, the car was parked in their driveway, and the girls generally used it for nothing more nefarious than ice cream runs.

"Let's go to the Baskin-Robbins in Velmont," Helen said one night in August.

"It's too far, and it's too hot." Francie's air-conditioning was on the fritz again.

"We'll roll down the windows."

Helen changed her T-shirt, put her hair up in a ponytail, then took it down again.

"Okay, Marie Osmond, what's with the wardrobe changes?" asked Francie.

"What are you talking about?"

"I'm saying, you're a little bit country."

Helen sang into her hairbrush, "And you're a little bit rock and roll!"

They danced around singing the *Donny & Marie* theme song for a minute until they started bungling the lyrics and then headed out to Velmont.

When they pulled into the Baskin-Robbins parking lot, Helen could feel her pulse rev a little. *Relax*, she told her pulse, *it's just Cal.* But it kept cantering along anyway.

The place was small: an ice cream case, a counter, and a couple of café tables with narrow metal chairs. She would've seen him right away. But maybe he was in back.

"Is Cal Crosby working today?" she inquired in the most casual possible way of the guy with greasy hair behind the counter. She could feel Francie's eyes on her.

"Oh, um, Cal?"

"Yeah, Cal. You know, red hair?"

"Uh, I don't know."

"You don't know if he's here?" Helen's powers of casual were beginning to strain.

"No, he's definitely not here. But also, I think he mighta quit."

"Oh."

"Is he a friend of yours?"

"Yes." *Sort of. At least he used to be.*

"But you don't know if he quit? Because that would be helpful to know. For me, I mean. So I don't, like, ask him to cover a shift. My friend's sister's birthday is coming up and I—"

"Yeah, I don't know," said Helen.

The guy deflated, presumably at the thought of missing his friend's sister's birthday, but Helen didn't care about that. In fact, she was nearly at the point of wringing the guy's neck. He let out a mournful little sigh. "I guess football takes up a lot of time."

"Football?"

"Yeah, there's a lot of practices. I mean, I guess. I've never been on a team."

Helen was incredulous. "Cal Crosby joined the *football* team?"

Mournful Scooper Guy was suddenly suspicious. "You said he's your friend."

Francie hooked her arm through Helen's and said, "Just make sure you wash those scoops carefully, okay? Because this place is

slightly more, since she didn't want to give up her lunches in the ceramics room with Francie entirely), and she saw Cal eating with the football guys, cracking them up like he'd once cracked her up. Surreptitiously, she liked watching him laugh. But it was a new person she was seeing. She caught snatches of conversation; his voice was lower. Even his face had changed: a jawline had emerged out of nowhere; cheekbones were wider and more prominent; skin looked less delicate and pale, speckled as it was now with whiskers.

*So that's how you turned out*, she'd think. And she was happy for him. But she still missed her little friend, a boy who was only a memory now.

HELEN WAS NO Felicity Manning, with her six feet and legs up to her neck. But Felicity had graduated and headed off to Indiana University on a full scholarship, so she was no longer there to dampen the hopes of shorter, slower, but just as hardworking girls. Helen was making her way up the varsity ladder, not hanging precariously off the bottom rung anymore. It also helped that Wendy Moriarty had joined the cheerleading squad. One less girl to beat.

Mark, too, had found a way to add a little rocket fuel to his stride; he and Helen encouraged each other and kept up on each other's times. He even took a book out of the library on how to increase speed and endurance. Helen was impressed by his industriousness.

Mark was friendly—if not exactly friends—with Ricky Zugravescu, and both of them enjoyed watching the high school football games. Francie and Helen had never been interested in going. The stands were a mosh pit of yelling and flirting and spilling stuff on one another. "Not my cup of Earl Grey," Francie would say when Ricky wanted her to come.

"I don't see Ricky as a football fan," Helen said to Francie one night while their boyfriends were at the game, and they were at the Bijoux waiting for *The Black Stallion* to start.

"He didn't go last year."

"Why is he so interested this year?"

"Honestly, I think it's Cal. Ricky has an underdog thing. He always roots for the weird kids who can't get a leg up."

"Like Cal."

"Yeah, except I think he's a little . . . conflicted."

"About what?"

"Well, Cal isn't exactly a loser anymore, is he? He's a football star. And he's not a moron. 'Smart Athlete' is about as high up on the pecking order as you can get in high school."

"He's not really a star."

"He kind of is."

"Seriously?"

"Yeah, Ricky says he runs like the cops are chasing him, and he's pretty tall, so he can reach up and grab the ball before the other guys get it. He's made a lot of goals."

"I think they're called touch-ins."

"Whatever."

Helen pondered this for a moment. It might be interesting to see little Cal Crosby—now big Cal Crosby—make touch-ins. "Maybe we should go sometime."

"You just want to watch Cal run."

The lights dimmed and the previews started up.

"Of course I do," Helen whispered. "I taught him, didn't I?"

HELEN WENT TO only one game.

She did enjoy watching number thirty-two run—he was fast and agile as he zigged and zagged down the field to keep away from opponents, then leaping up to snatch the ball out of the air. At one point he jumped completely over a guy trying to tackle him. *He would've been a good hurdler*, she thought. *And he made a lot of—*

"What do you call goals, again?" she asked Mark.

"Helen, they're touchdowns. Touch. Downs." He looked past her to Ricky and shook his head but with a grin on his face that said, *Isn't she adorable?*

"Jesus, Helen. Catch up, wouldya?" said Ricky, and not in a way that implied any adorableness whatsoever. He said it like she was an idiot.

He just didn't like her. *Maybe if I had a limp*, she thought, *or a lazy eye.* She missed several plays amusing herself with all the ways she could be more of an underdog so Ricky would like her. That is, if she cared about Ricky liking her. Which she did not.

The guy who kept running down the field and catching the ball could have been anyone. He didn't take his helmet off when he went to the sidelines, because Coach Dombrowski generally sent him back again pretty quickly. He had shoulder pads and the same uniform as everyone else. For all Helen knew, it was her dad out there.

The only tip-off was that when he got the ball, people in the stands would make a strange howling sound. "Hoooooooon! Hoooooooon!"

"Hoon?" Helen asked Mark.

"It's a nickname," Mark explained patiently. "Calhooooooun!"

She remembered Cal telling her once that Calhoun was his mother's maiden name and that giving it to her firstborn only proved that she'd changed her mind about it and maybe didn't want to be a Crosby. "Like, at *all*," he'd said. Helen missed the first half of the fourth quarter ruminating on that.

In the last play of the game, number thirty-two (who was supposedly Cal) caught the ball and ran into the end thingy, and Corden County Regional High School won the game. That's when he took his helmet off, red hair spilling to his shoulders, pink sweaty face grinning that Cal grin. The whole team rushed him, slamming into him and thumping him silly. Joyful screams of "Hoooooon!" filled the stadium.

When he headed toward the sidelines, a couple of the cheerleaders came up and kissed him on his sweaty cheeks. Helen felt her blood pause in her veins. Because until this particular moment in the fall of 1979 in her junior year of high school, she had never, not once, seen another girl give Cal Crosby the time of day. Much less kiss him.

"Can we go now?" she said to Mark.

"Oh," he said. "Sure, if you want to. I mean, usually kids hang out for a while, and then there'll be a party somewhere—"

"I'm ready to go home." Helen stood and headed for the parking lot.

MARK O'MALLEY WAS a really good boyfriend. Adoring, loyal, supportive, amenable to . . . well, anything, really. Whatever Helen wanted was fine with him. As she had told Cal while they lay on their backs in a meadow at Paddow Mountain State Park, Mark was an adjacent kind of guy. And as long as he was adjacent to her, things went quite smoothly.

He also didn't pressure her for anything sexually. They kissed a lot. At first it had been kind of messy and weird for Helen to be touching her tongue to someone else's. When you thought about it, why was this something humans wanted to do? But they did, and Helen did, too, especially as she and Mark got used to each other, and got better at it.

They touched each other in various places. It was all a learning process, and Mark was good to learn with because he was patient, truly interested in knowing how to please her, and never pushed things too far. He was a good Catholic boy. He was honorable.

Francie was not having as much luck with Ricky, who sometimes "lost his head."

"What does *that* mean?" demanded Helen.

"He just gets all hot and excited and kind of desperate."

"For what?"

"Well, sex," said Francie, "but a hand job will do in a pinch."

"He doesn't pressure you, does he?"

"Depends on what you mean by pressure."

"Francie, you know what I mean by pressure!"

"He's never forced me to do anything I didn't want to do, but . . ."

"But what?"

"We've had discussions."

"Oh God."

"You don't even know about what."

"Of course I do! You discuss"—Helen made little quote marks with her fingers—"whether he's going to have his way with you."

"Jesus, Helen, you're like a 1950s housewife. It's not 'his way.' I want to, too. But I just need him to slow down a little."

"He is *not* a good boyfriend."

"Just because I don't have him completely wrapped around my finger like you do Mark—which, by the way, I wouldn't want to—does not mean he's not a good boyfriend. He's a guy, Helen. He just needs his dick rubbed sometimes."

Helen started to giggle. "Seriously, those things are so high maintenance."

"I know! Can you imagine walking around with one? 'Rub me, rub me, rub me!' It'd be like having your mother yelling at you to clean your room every minute of the day."

IN THE SPRING of junior year, Francie and Ricky had sex. Francie told Helen all about it.

"Did it hurt?" Helen asked.

"Not really. Just like a pinch. And by the time he's in there, you're worked up enough that you don't really care."

"Worked up?"

"It feels so awesome to be naked together, skin to skin, hugging and stroking and stuff. Then your brain gets a little melty and you can't wait."

Helen wasn't sure her brain had ever gotten that melty. She was definitely interested in trying sex, but more as a fun science experiment than something she was passionately hungry for. Besides, Mark never brought it up, so why rush?

BY JANUARY OF their senior year, he still hadn't brought it up.

"At least I don't have to worry about birth control," Helen said.

"Yeah, condoms are expensive."

Helen looked at Francie.

"What? I'm agreeing with you."

"You are and you aren't."

"Do you *want* to have sex with Mark?"

"Well, yeah, wouldn't it be weird if I didn't?"

"Ummmmmm . . ."

"Oh, shut up."

"Why don't you ask him?"

Helen shrugged. "I could, I guess."

"You don't seem that into it."

"No, I am. I definitely want to try it."

"With Mark."

Helen thought about this.

"Tick tock," said Francie. "You took too long to respond."

ON VALENTINE'S DAY, Helen was sitting on the toilet in the lav when a group of girls spilled in laughing and talking in high-toned voices.

"So romantic!"

"He brought her an ice cream cake from Baskin-Robbins."

The hair stood up on Helen's arms.

"What did it say?"

"It said *Prom* with two question marks on either side. The first one was upside down like the Spanish do it because they have Spanish class together and that's where he gave it to her!"

"That is *so cute!*"

"*So totally cute!*"

"God, he's hot."

There was a silence, and then a screech of laughter so loud and so perfectly in unison it sounded like a car crash.

"I'd eat that whole cake!"

"I'd eat it off his chest!"

"Cal fucking Crosby is so fucking hot!" one of them moaned, and they all screeched again and sailed back out.

"MARK," SAID HELEN that night as they sat in his car in the parking lot behind the Bijoux. They had gone to see *Chariots of Fire*, which was about running, of course, and Helen had thought it would "heighten emotions," as she later told Francie.

"Mark, I think we should have sex."

He looked as if she'd offered him a lollipop and then smacked him in the eye with it.

"What?" he said. "I mean . . . what?"

In that moment, she knew something was very wrong. This was not the response of your typical teenage boy with your typical teenage penis. But much like Cal when he asked her to Homecoming, Helen chose to forge ahead anyway.

"Mark."

"Yeah?" A little sweat had broken out on his lip, and it did not look like passion-induced sweat. Also, it was fourteen degrees out.

"We've been dating for a year and a half."

"Yes, but that doesn't mean anything," he said. "I don't want you to feel any pressure."

"I don't. I want to. I'm actually *asking* you."

"Oh, um." His face flushed. "That's really sweet."

"Mark, what is happening right now?"

He squeezed the back of his neck, then rubbed his whole face, then punched his thigh. "Helen, I think I want to be a priest."

"A PRIEST!" FRANCIE was choking with laughter. "You asked a guy to have sex with you and he said he's saving himself for THE PRIESTHOOD?"

Helen had told Mark to take her home. She had called Francie before she even got her coat off. Francie had skittered her sparkly car into the driveway two and a half minutes later, and Helen had gotten in and slammed the door so hard it nearly came off its hinges.

"IT'S NOT FUNNY!" Helen yelled, but she was laughing, too. "I AM SUCH A LOSER!"

HELEN WAS GOING to break up with Mark, but he beat her to it.

"I've been up all night," he told her the next day.

*You look it*, she thought. His pallor was ashen, and the rims of his eyes were inflamed.

"I just can't continue this ruse," he went on. "I care for you deeply."

*Care for me deeply?* thought Helen. *What teenager says "care for you deeply"?*

"But I've been called."

Helen was Catholic, too (though her family went to church on Sundays and let it go at that). She knew what "called" meant. But what popped into her head was Jesus on the phone. *Yeah, suit up,* He was saying to Mark. *You're going in.*

IT ONLY GOT worse from there. It turned out that Cal hadn't asked just any student of the Spanish language to prom. He had asked Wendy Moriarty.

HELEN HAD FRANKLY given up on everything—sex, prom, Cal— everything but running. She ran like it was her last best hope for survival, as she prepped for the spring track-and-field season. By mid-March she was ready to kick some 400-meter ass.

When she showed up that first day, she didn't even look around to survey the competition. She knew there was no competition. Then two surprising things happened.

Coach Costarellis came out of the field house and spoke to the runners. "Coach Walker has a little medical situation, but don't worry, he's cool. He's good. He's just taking this season off for some R and R, and he'll be back at it in no time. Meanwhile, you're stuck with me!" (Within a week the scuttlebutt was that Coach Walker was in rehab.)

The second surprising thing occurred while Helen was listening to Coach Costarellis wax poetic about *Chariots of Fire*, the mere mention of which made her skin crawl. Someone stepped up beside her.

"Wheels," he murmured.

She turned and looked up at him.

"Match."

# Chapter 15

## 2021

"Mind if I join you?" says Cal, indicating the chair across from her.

He's wearing a gray V-neck sweater over a white T-shirt, and jeans. He's freshly shaven, and Helen suspects he's recently gotten a haircut. It looked longer a week and a half ago when they bumped into each other by the river in Jansen Woods. Or maybe it was just messy then, and now it's combed. His hair is slightly darker than it was in high school, and there are threads of gray at the temple.

She really doesn't want him to sit down. Doesn't want to open what she knows is a tightly locked little box in the back of her brain, guarded by small but vicious dogs and venomous snakes and attack birds. It does no good to call off these weird and highly trained protectors and open that box now. She's too old for this shit.

But there he is with his blue eyes, waiting. And she can see the sweet, scrawny, funny friend she once had. She can't spurn that boy.

"Not at all," she says, and slides the spreadsheets to the side of the table nearest the window.

"My daughter told me you work here."

"Janel."

He nods, clearly pleased that Helen remembers his daughter's name. "She's a twin," he says. "The other is Bonnie."

"After your mother."

"Good memory!"

*I remember everything*, she almost says.

There is a stretch of four, maybe five seconds where neither of them speaks. It's excruciating, but Helen knows she has to pace herself. Much as she wants to, it's not time to sprint, yet.

Cal lobs what should be an easy one. "How long have you been working for Cormac?"

*How long have you been here in this tiny town with me?* she translates. *How many times have we almost bumped into each other, but one went out the back entrance as the other came in the front; one was looking at the sky while the other was noticing a flower; one was talking to a friend while the other was checking his phone?*

"Actually we're co-owners."

She never tells anyone this! Cormac did everything humanly possible to keep this wonderful place afloat during the pandemic. No one could have worked harder, "pivoted" more. But people started making coffee at home, and baking—dear God, wasn't Facebook exploding with people's goddamned sourdough? Millions of collective pounds were gained by people trying to create at home what they no longer felt safe going out to buy.

Helen had the money. She all but forced it on him. "You're going to be a father one day, God willing. And your child is going to need something, and that child is, for whatever reason, going to make it hard for you to give. And it's going to make you absolutely barking mad, because there is no earthly reason for you not to help—other than pride, which let's just admit right now is in the hall of fame of stupid, useless, dangerous emotions." She put her hand on his arm. "You are like a son to me. It's time to stop being a prideful idiot and take the damn money." Cormac agreed, but only if she came on as a partner.

And yet isn't it her pride that now incites her to tell Cal something she never feels the need to mention to anyone else? It's that word, a word she will never say to Cal, a word she's never been ashamed of before now. That word is *bookkeeper*.

"That's fantastic," Cal says now. "I've always loved this place."

"It was a very solid investment," she says.

Cal gazes at her a beat too long. "Tough times the last eighteen months, though."

Helen nods. "It was touch-and-go, but we decided to expand instead of contract. Got the space next door for a song, started doing take-out meals along with the scones, put in a drive-through in back. We were lucky it worked."

He laughs. "Wish you'd been working for me. My company went under."

"Oh," says Helen, caught off guard by his honesty. As always. "I'm so sorry."

"Nah," he says. "In a weird way it's probably for the best. Ever hear of a place called Night Cap?"

"There was a bar by that name in Charlotte. We used to go sometimes on special occasions. My husband loved it."

She sees a flicker of something cross his face at the word *husband*. But then it's gone. "That was one of ours," he says.

"*One* of yours?"

"Yeah, it was a chain. We were in thirty-two cities." He shakes his head. "And counting, till 2020. Turns out a high-end whiskey bar where the draw is the experience"—he makes little quote marks in the air—"doesn't fly so well when most people are only willing to leave their homes to buy toilet paper."

Helen remembers "the experience," as Cal calls it, and that's an apt term. Dark and richly decorated, designed to impress. They'd retrofitted a hundred-year-old building, retaining the charm, amping it up with high-end fixtures. Jim told her a lot of multimillion-dollar deals were handshaken into existence there. He pointed out how the bar had just one TV with the sound off for games like tennis and golf—not football or basketball or, God forbid, soccer. Not games where people cheered. Not "beer" games. In fact, Night Cap didn't sell beer, only top-shelf liquor and very expensive wine. There were glasses of whiskey that cost upward of three hundred dollars. Jim would be so disappointed it's gone.

"Wow," says Helen. "It was a great place. Sorry to hear it."

Cal smirks—and damned if it isn't his fifteen-year-old smirk!— and says, "Yeah, doesn't help when the CFO sees the bomb dropping and detonates first. He took the liquid assets with him to Maldives. And by liquid assets, I don't mean booze. Last year at this time we were filing for bankruptcy and trying to sell off a lot of high-cost inventory."

She studies him. "You seem pretty calm about all this."

"Oh, trust me, I was very not-calm at the time. But it turns out there were some good lessons."

"Like keep an eye on the CFO?"

He chuckles. "For starters."

Cormac suddenly comes around the corner with some papers in his hand. "Helen, I just found these—" He stops when he sees she's not alone. "Oh, hey, sorry. I didn't know . . ."

*He is going to call Barb the minute he goes back to the office,* thinks Helen. But what can she do? That little box is creaking open in ways she never meant it to.

"Cormac, this is someone I knew from high school. Cal Crosby."

Cormac pulls down his mask momentarily and gives a nod, which he's adopted in place of a handshake. "Nice to meet you." He tugs the mask back up. "Are you in town for long?"

"For the duration," says Cal. "I live here."

"No kidding! And you two went to high school together." Cormac shakes his head. "What are the odds?"

"Very slim," says Helen. Microscopic. But here they are.

Cormac gives her a look. He's no dummy. "Well, I'll let you two—" and he starts to move away.

"Cormac," says Helen.

"Yeah?"

She reaches out, and he looks down at his hand, still holding the timesheets. "Ah," he says, and hands them over.

"Seems like a good guy," Cal says when Cormac is gone.

"The best," she says with a smile, because Cormac being your son-in-law is something you can only be grateful for.

They sit there for a moment. Helen notices Cal's hands on the table. They're a middle-aged man's hands, not a boy's, and somehow—somehow—this is surprising to her. How is she still so caught off guard by Cal having grown up?

"Someone you knew from high school?" he says.

She looks up at him. "It's the truth."

"It's a small fraction of the truth."

*Yes, but it's the other part that caused all the trouble*, she thinks.

"There's a conversation we need to have," he says.

*No, we actually don't!* she wants to scream. *I'm the one who got the shitty end of the stick—I'm the one who gets to decide if we talk about it!*

"I forgive you," she says quickly.

He gives her a sad smile. "Thanks, but—"

"You're welcome."

"—there's more to it than that."

Francie's words come back to her: "Maybe *you* have something to say about it."

*The stupid box is already open*, she thinks.

"Fine. But not here."

# *Chapter 16*

*1981*

Approximately one half hour into that first practice in the spring of senior year, Helen and Cal established themselves as the fastest girl and boy at Corden County Regional High School. Approximately one hour into practice, Mark O'Malley quit the team.

"Hey, *Felicity*," Cal teased, after Helen annihilated the 400, her favorite event.

"Felicity can shove it," panted Helen, hands on her knees.

Cal burst out laughing. "Jesus, who *are* you?"

Helen stood up and smiled, still breathing hard. "No, who are *you*, Mr. Football Star, Mr. Homecoming King."

"Hey, I couldn't help that Homecoming thing."

"Like you would've wanted to."

"It was a little weird."

"You think?" said Helen.

"All I'm saying is I wasn't looking for it, and it happened, and I went with it, but it's not, you know—"

"If you say it's not you, I'm walking away right now."

"Wheels, you know me. You really think I was born to be Homecoming King?"

*You know me.* The sound of that filled her like nothing had, maybe ever. She smiled. "Unlikely."

"Thank you."

"I still can't figure out why you're here, though, when you could be Cal Crosby, Almighty Base Stealer." She headed for the grassy sideline of the football field to sit and stretch her hamstrings.

Cal followed and sat down next to her. "Ninety feet, that's why."

"What's ninety feet?"

"Distance between the bases."

"What's wrong with that?"

"It's too short. I'm playing football in the fall, and I need to be able to keep my speed up for more like ninety yards. The 100-meter is perfect training." He had a little grin that said, *There's an ocean of happy back here, and I'm just trying to keep it from spilling out of my face.*

Helen stopped stretching. "Where'd you get in?"

"University of Washington."

"What? Oh my God!" She reached out and squeezed his shoulder. "That's amazing!"

"Yeah, I just found out. No one knows."

*Not even Wendy?* she wanted to ask, because of course once he asked Wendy to prom, they were a couple. But Helen didn't want to know if he'd told Wendy. She wanted a few minutes to think that maybe she really was the first.

"They had some other guy on the roster, and he decided to go into the marines instead, so the spot opened up."

"You're going to college." Helen couldn't stop smiling. "You made it happen."

"You knew I would."

"If I recall, I was pretty sure it would *not* be for sports."

"Yeah, you were maybe a little bit wrong on that. But that's okay. You get partial credit."

She was so unbelievably happy for him! Maybe a little too happy . . .

*Dial it back*, Helen told herself and rose to stretch her quads, standing on one foot, bending her other knee, foot in her hand behind her. "Good thing you scooped all that ice cream, huh?"

Cal stood and did the same. "What do you mean?"

"College is expensive."

That grin again. She waited. "Full scholarship, Wheels. *Full fucking scholarship.*"

She let out a squeal and launched herself at him, nearly knocking him over. He recovered quickly and grabbed her, lifting her off the ground for a minute. He was strong; she felt like a puppy in his arms.

He put her down a moment later, and they were both suddenly aware that her happy shriek had attracted the attention of their teammates. But Helen didn't care. She was over-the-moon thrilled for him! He had wanted so much to go to college, and now he was going for free! "So proud of you, Match!" she said.

"Thanks," he said, and she could feel the heat of his gratitude. He knew *she* knew the full force of this revelation. But he soon moved away, toward a random assortment of students, most of whom were still wondering what that was all about.

EVERY DAY, HELEN looked forward to two things: proving yet again that she was the fastest girl on the track team and being with Cal. But it wasn't like when they were tenth graders, generally ignored as they ran all those long cross-country practices together. Cal was a bit of a rock star now, especially once his full ride to University of Washington got out. Adoring/envious eyes seemed to follow his every move.

He, in turn, seemed always to be gauging how much he could hang around Helen without arousing suspicion that there was anything remotely disloyal going on. Even the vague appearance of interest in another girl would set the gossip mill to churning, which would no doubt send Wendy Moriarty, now generally accepted queen of CCRHS, into orbit. She was not the type you wanted to piss off. Helen understood this. She was just glad she got to spend a little time with Cal, even if they couldn't really talk about anything substantial.

She couldn't remember ever being this happy.

AT THE END of April, Coach Costarellis gathered the team for one of his talks. "Our next meet is a biggie."

"Hackford," Cal murmured ominously to Helen. "The Death Star to Coach C's Millennium Falcon."

"Han Solo, he is not."

"Wendy begs to differ. She says if she'd known he was coaching, she would have joined the team."

That seemed like a pretty weird thing to say to your boyfriend, unless of course you were making the point that he wasn't the only guy you had eyes for—that rock star or no, he should watch his back. But Helen reminded herself that it wasn't her business. Instead, she played along. "Jealous?"

Cal squinted. "I mean, should I be? Look at him." Coach was blathering on so enthusiastically about how they were going to beat Hackford—finally! for once!—he was practically doing an interpretive dance.

"I think your place as the king of Wendy's heart is safe for now."

"More like the pawn."

Helen glanced up.

"Or knight." He affected a jaunty air. "The knight's a pretty suave guy."

"All that armor."

"And a trusty steed."

"You realize we're talking about an inanimate object that's like two inches tall, right?"

Coach's voice rose to a fever pitch. "We've got some super A-plus power this year! Helen Iannucci is an absolute stick of dynamite, and Cal Crosby is with us for the first time since he was a tiny little sophomore who couldn't even think about a race without throwing up!"

The team clapped. Cal flushed pink as a tutu.

"Feeling pretty suave right now?" Helen whispered.

"So, *so* suave," he murmured back.

"Tom Selleck's suaver younger brother."

Cal snort-laughed and Coach gave him a confused look, which made Helen laugh, and the whole team stared at them until they had to walk away from each other to gain control of themselves.

IT REALLY MADE no sense to take the track-and-field team to Paddow Mountain State Park "for inspiration." They weren't cross-country—they didn't need hill work.

"It's Coach C's thing," Helen told Cal. "Coach Walker wouldn't have taken us to the caf to win a meet."

No one cared. It was spring, and warm weather was around the corner (although on that particular day, winter was hanging on pretty tightly). They were all just happy to get out of town. Most of the team was on the bus, but the seniors were allowed to go in cars. When the musical chairs of who would ride with whom was over, Helen and Cal ended up in Jerry Klimper's Oldsmobile Cutlass listening to him endlessly extol the virtues of the Aeroback design. Cal sat up front and nodded politely from time to time. At one point he reached behind his head, grabbed a hunk of his own voluminous hair, and surreptitiously pretended to tear it out. Helen had to cover her mouth with her mittened hand to keep from laughing out loud.

When they arrived, kids didn't really know what to do; they milled around for a while. Several of them started jogging the perimeter of the parking lot.

"Guys! Guys!" yelled Coach C when the confusion became apparent. "You're supposed to run in the woods!"

"Why?" asked one brave girl.

"For inspiration! It's nature!"

"But what if we trip?" asked another.

"Trip?" Coach C was beside himself. "*Trip?* You're athletes! You're nimble! Just look where you're going!"

It was pretty entertaining.

Cal made a little exploding sound. "Han Solo just crashed the Millennium Falcon into I Don't Get It Land."

"And Princess Wendy's not here to rescue him," said Helen. She regretted it as soon as she said it. Cal probably did not want to be teased about his girlfriend having a crush on groovy old Coach C. But when she glanced at him, he was chuckling. He didn't seem to mind.

"Hey, Cal," said Jerry, loping over to them from a group of guys who could barely keep their shoelaces tied, much less win a race. "Can you drive my car back?"

"Um, sure," said Cal. "Why?"

"'Cause I might be under the weather." Jerry cut his eyes back to the little crowd. There was definitely a bottle of something under one guy's jacket. "Just leave it in the parking lot at school with the keys on the tire." He dropped them in Cal's hand and strolled back to his boys.

Cal and Helen looked at each other. "It's got an Aeroback," said Cal.

"How could you say no?"

As they zipped up their jackets and tugged down their hats, Cal said, "Want to see my bridge?"

"The one you did to earn Eagle Scout? Of course."

He gave her a sly smile. "See if you can keep up this time," and he took off for the trail.

Helen could tell Cal wasn't really putting the throttle down because she actually could keep up with him, sprinting along behind him at a quick yet comfortable pace. The sky was a cloudless blue, and buds were starting to burst on branches. It had rained hard the day before, and the smell of rich soil and growing things wafted around them as they headed deeper into the woods. The trail widened into an old cart path, and he slowed for her to come up beside him. There wasn't anything to say; they just ran. Helen had the feeling that if she could run next to Cal in the forest for the rest of her life, she'd never have a moment's unhappiness.

After a while they came to a wooden boardwalk that began in a swampy area, crossed a stream, then hopscotched around boulders on the far side.

"This is it," he said.

"Wow," she said. "A lot of sneakers aren't getting wet and muddy because of you."

"Yeah, it feels good to know it's out here."

She looked up at him. "Like you did something helpful and worthy, and the proof is just sitting here in the world."

He gazed back. "Exactly."

"Who knows about this? Back home, I mean."

"Well, the guys in the troop. But I don't really go to meetings anymore."

"Anyone you're friends with now?"

"Not really. Except you."

"You should take people here. It's cool."

"I seem to remember someone saying that *cool Boy Scout* is an oxymoron. I had to go look up that word afterward, by the way."

"I was just teasing. I didn't really mean it."

"You did, a little."

"Okay, a little. But what was I supposed to do in the face of—"
She held up three fingers. "Besides, there should be a word for
things that are both nerdy and cool at the same time."

"I think the word is Helen."

"The word is definitely Cal."

He laughed. "The cool nerd twins."

She loved him so much in that moment. It was hard to contain
all the love in her body. She felt it pulsing around, trying to sneak
out of her eyes and her lips and her chest. But it wasn't allowed
out. There were rules. The only thing she was allowed to do
was run.

"I'm cooling down," she said. "Try to keep up." And she took off.

SHE'D BEEN RUNNING for a while, following trails to the left or
right without much thought, reassured by the steady beat of Cal's
footfalls behind her. She was tired and wanted to stop, but when
she checked on the love in her body it was still throbbing loudly,
and she had to keep going.

There was a stream ahead and Helen slowed to hop from rock
to rock across it. Suddenly there was a splash behind her.

"Shit," he muttered.

She turned around. He was ankle deep.

"Are you okay?" she asked as he trudged out of the stream.

"Fine," he said, shaking his head in self-disgust. His sneakers
squeaked with every step as water seeped out of them. He sat
down on a fallen log to take them off and squeeze out his socks.
"So dumb," he muttered.

"Could have happened to anyone," she said.

"Didn't happen to you."

"Not today, but we all fall in the creek sometimes."

He looked at her. Holy God, that look. So full of . . . It was dangerous. Rules could shatter into a million pieces on a look like that.

"Do you have a watch?" she said. "We should probably get back."

"I thought you had the watch."

"Oh, that one broke a long time ago."

"You never got a new one?"

"My parents got me a fancy one for Christmas, but it's metal and clinky. It's not good for exercise."

"A grown-up-lady watch."

"I guess that's the goal. To be a grown-up lady. Someday. Maybe."

He stared down at the wet socks in his hands.

"So I guess we should head back." She pointed up the trail. "Is it this way?"

He looked around. "Not sure. I think we might have crossed into the Adirondacks."

"What? No!"

"Yeah, Adirondack Park is just north of Paddow."

"We couldn't have gone that far."

"You were running for a long time."

"Are we lost?"

He considered this, scanning around him for any clues as to their location. Finally he said, "I think maybe we are."

Lost! With Cal! Helen was thrilled.

He looked down at his bare feet. "I don't know whether to put the socks back on or not. Probably doesn't matter. My feet are freezing either way."

"I'll give you my socks. Then at least you'll have one layer of warmth."

"That's very gallant."

"You're not the only knight around here," she joked.

He smiled. "I think right now I qualify as the damsel in distress."

Helen sat back down to take off her socks.

"Hey, no," he said. "Thanks but—"

"I don't mind."

"It's really sweet, but it won't work. Your socks will just get wet when I put my sneakers on. Besides, my feet are a lot bigger than yours. They probably won't even fit."

"What should we do?"

He thumped down beside her. "What I'd really like to do is build a fire, but that'll get us back late."

A fire in the woods with Cal? How could this possibly be happening? How could she be so lucky? It wasn't breaking any rules. They would just warm up and find their way out. Nothing bad would happen. And they would finally get some time alone. Match and Wheels time. Probably the only chance they'd have, maybe ever.

"We have Jerry's car," Helen said, trying not to sound too eager.

"Yeah, but won't your parents be looking for you?"

"On Wednesdays the shop's open late. My mother brings dinner, and they eat there. I usually go to Francie's."

"Francie won't alert the media when you don't show up?"

She might eventually. But Francie wasn't the type to go off half-cocked. Helen would be home before anyone really missed her.

"She's going a little nutty trying to decide what should go in her art portfolio to send to Bennington. And Ricky's always a distraction."

"They're pretty in love, huh?"

"Yeah. You know, in sort of a Francie-and-Ricky way."

"What way is that?"

"It's . . . I mean, they really do love each other. But it's very—" Helen waved her hand around.

"Emotional."

"Yeah. They fight a lot. But also, I don't know—it's not what I would want, I guess, but they really have each other. They're connected."

That last word seemed to ricochet around the woods, and Helen could feel the pulsing in her body again. She jumped up. "We should gather wood, right?"

Cal started to put his wet sneakers on. "You're sure you're not going to get in trouble?"

"Positively. But what about you?"

"Bud and Bonnie don't really track me. I'm practically out the door, anyway, and there's five other kids who need watching more than I do. Besides, my father is so tickled about me playing college ball, I think he'd let me hitchhike across the country if I felt like it."

They set about collecting wood, and Cal found a spot up against a high rock ledge that he said was perfect. "See, there's not a lot of brush around, so we don't have to worry so much about sparks, and the fire will reflect against the rock and warm us up on both sides." Most of the fallen logs on the ground were wet, but he showed her how to knock over the small dead trees that would be dry on the inside. Standing deadwood, he called it. They pulled down some pine boughs to sit on, and after a while they had a tidy little campsite. He gathered up the dry leaves that had been sheltered by the rock ledge and pulled some matches out of his jacket pocket.

"Oh, no way!" said Helen.

"What?"

"You have to do it with the two rocks like in the movies. You're a Boy Scout, aren't you? No, you're an Eagle!"

Cal laughed. "It's not as easy as it looks."

"Can't we try?"

They searched for stones to use as flint and ended up clacking a growing pile of rocks together without much success. They got a spark here and there, which only made them want to try harder, but they were never able to ignite the leaves. The light was dimming, and finally Cal said, "Sorry to disappoint you, Sacajawea, but I'm getting cold," and pulled out the matches. Soon enough he had a nice fire going.

"This is the best!" said Helen. "I always wanted to do this. I was in Girl Scouts for a while, and I was really hoping we would go camping, but our leader was more of a crafts-and-cookies type, not a tents-and-fires type."

"You've never camped out, ever?"

"Nope. Francie and I tried to do s'mores over her parents' hibachi once, but the charcoal briquettes kept going out, and we got hungry and just ate everything cold."

"That is not remotely like camping."

"That's what I'm saying!"

"Well, let's get 'er really ripping, then!" He pulled over another of the small trees they knocked down and laid it across the flames. He sank some sticks in the ground to hang his socks on and leaned his sneakers against some rocks facing the fire. The two of them sat back against the rock ledge, and he stuck his big feet out toward the flames. It was getting cold, but by the fire it felt cozy and exciting all at once.

"So you and Mark broke up," he said out of the blue.

"Way back in February."

"Yeah?"

She let out a little snort. "Valentine's Day, if you can believe it."

They were sitting close enough that she could feel him startle slightly. "*Valentine's* Day?"

"Yup."

"You don't seem too torn up about it. Was it your call?"

"Um . . ." Was it okay to tell Cal? She figured it wasn't really a secret, and if it was, he wouldn't tell anyone. Also, it felt like they were the only two people in the world, so the whole concept of secrets didn't really exist. "He's going to be a priest, so he didn't want things to go any further."

"Are you kidding me?"

"About what?"

"About all of it!"

"You think I would make any of it up? I mean, how embarrassing is that, getting turned down by a guy for Jesus!"

"Turned down for what?"

Helen hesitated. "Well . . . anything."

"Sex."

"Pardon me?"

"You wanted to have sex, and that was too far for him."

How could he read her so well? Helen got defensive. "We'd been going out for a year and a half, for godsake, I'm not some loose woman!"

"No, of course you're not."

"And I had no idea—he never even mentioned it! We went to Mass together a couple of times, and it's not like he was taking extra sips out of the Communion cup or gazing longingly at the crucifix."

"Were you heartbroken?"

The word brought her up short. *Not like you were*, she thought.

"I was more pissed off, I guess."

"He lied to you."

"He wasted my time."

"So you weren't in love."

Helen thought about this for a moment. Mark had said "I care for you deeply," and she'd thought that was a ridiculous way to put it, but maybe it was a little more on the nose than she'd given him credit for.

"I cared for him. A lot. I wouldn't have wanted to go all the way if I didn't."

She didn't want to talk about Mark. Sitting by a roaring fire with Cal out here in the middle of nowhere, she could barely remember Mark. *Subject change*, she thought.

"I heard what you did with the cake when you asked Wendy to the prom. Pretty clever."

"That was Marybeth's idea."

"You asked her for suggestions?"

"No, she just told me what to do. Except I decided to do an ice cream cake, just to, you know, make it a little bit from me. But it was kind of a mess, as it turns out."

"But Wendy liked it anyway?"

"Yeah, it went over pretty big. She said it was very romantic, and she was a good sport about it melting on her."

*She makes everything look good*, Helen thought bitterly, *even warm ice cream.*

"Are you in love with her?" she asked.

Cal cut his eyes toward Helen, then stared hard at the fire. "No."

Helen was surprised at how definitive—and honest—he was about it. No beating around the bush about caring deeply. "Sounds like you're pretty clear on that."

He shrugged.

"How come you're going out with her then?"

He didn't say anything for a minute. Then he exhaled. "Because I can."

"Oh."

"Yeah."

"You were a geek who got made fun of, and now you're so popular you can date Wendy."

"I'm kind of a dick, I guess."

"I can understand wanting to in the first place, but if you don't really like her, why not break it off? You proved your point."

"I would, except I asked her to prom, and I'd be an even bigger dick if I bailed now. Good guys don't dump their dates with two weeks to go."

He was absolutely right about that—not to mention the blow-back would be like a category five hurricane. The whole school would side with her. She was Wendy.

"Are you going?" he asked.

"No."

"No one asked you?"

Clearly no one had asked her, or she'd be going, wouldn't she? It was an embarrassing question to have to answer twice. "No."

"I guess they all thought you'd be going with Mark."

"'*They all*'?" Helen chuckled. "Who is this vast army of guys you think want to take me to prom?"

"I could get you a date in ten seconds flat."

"You could?"

"Of course I could."

"No, I meant it, like, why do you suddenly want to get me a date for prom?"

"Don't you want to go?"

"Well, I wouldn't mind going. It's the kind of thing people talk about later in life. But my parents didn't go to any prom, and it doesn't seem to have crushed their spirits or anything."

"I think you should go." He was looking at her, and there was something else going on. Something he wasn't saying. Then he took a breath and said, "I want you to go."

*So I can watch you dance with Wendy?* thought Helen. *No thanks.*

He was still looking at her. It felt like rules might be starting to break. Just little chips and cracks, but . . . He seemed to sense it, too, because suddenly he got up to get more wood for the fire. "I want to see you dance," he said offhandedly as he put another log on and poked at the embers with a stick. "Ever since you told me how you let loose when you dance at home."

She smiled. "You just want to make fun of me."

"It sounds pretty make-fun-able."

"I'm not ashamed," said Helen, sticking her chin out. "I'm a proud crazy dancer."

Cal was still standing over the fire. Now he crossed his arms. "All right, let's see it."

"I'm just supposed to stand up and make a spectacle of myself?"

"Spectacle to who—the owls?"

"There's no music."

"I'll sing."

"You'll sing," she scoffed.

"Yeah, why not? You'll be making a fool of yourself dancing, so the owls won't pay any attention to me."

She remembered how he used to sing on their training runs, and it seemed important somehow to hear him do that one more time. This whole thing felt like one more time. One last chance.

She started to get up. "Fine. I get to choose the song."

"Nope." He shook his head. "I'm the one singing it."

"I'm the one—"

Cal held an imaginary microphone to his mouth and sang out, "Do, do, do, da, do, da, do, dum! Oh, yeah baby!" Helen recognized the opening bars of Stevie Wonder's "Signed, Sealed, Delivered."

"Like a fool, I went and stayed too long," he belted out loud enough to scare all the owls on Paddow.

*Oh, what the hell,* she thought, and started snapping her fingers and bouncing around, throwing her arms out even farther than she normally would. She knew she looked ridiculous, but it was absolutely worth that big grin on his face. She joined him in the "Ooooh, baby," then singing out the song title.

"I'm yours" was the last line. And, God, she wished she were.

The song was short and over too soon. He clapped for her, and she took a bow. "No wonder you didn't make it in ballet class!" he teased, and she loved that he remembered that little detail.

And there it was. That feeling again. She could have said, *Okay, it's getting dark, time to try and find our way out of here.* But she just wanted a few more minutes. She sat down. So did he.

"What are you going to study at the University of Washington?"

"Business."

"So you can have your own ice cream shop someday?" she teased.

He snorted in disgust at that suggestion. "So I can rule the world someday."

"Way to start small."

Cal gave a self-conscious shrug. "I just don't want to work at a lumber store."

"There's nothing wrong with lumber stores," Helen said, thinking of her own parents, her dad with his cuticles permanently tattooed with grease.

"No, but look at your dad. He owns his own shop. He's in charge; he's making the money. And it's something he loves to do. I mean, that is the American dream right there. That would be my dream, except it wouldn't be cars."

"What would it be?"

"I don't know. Something, you know, like a product or experience that makes people feel good. And like relaxed. Maybe I would own a bunch of cabins somewhere and they'd be nice, but not too nice. You'd be in nature, but if you were Helen Iannucci, and you never went camping before—except with a hibachi that you can't even work right—you'd feel safe. Maybe I'd have people working for me that would show you how to do things."

"And take me on hikes where we don't get lost?"

"No, I'd be leading all the hikes, so everyone would get lost all the time."

She smiled. "Maybe they wouldn't mind."

They sat there for a moment watching the smoke curl into the clear night air.

"Where are you going to school?" he asked.

"Depends on who you ask."

"I'm asking you."

"Well, I got into a couple of places, and one of them is Colorado College."

"Colorado! There's some mountains for you."

"Yeah, it seems like a really beautiful place."

"But."

She affected her mother's accent. "But Colorado is-a too far away for Annabella and Luigi Iannucci."

"Your parents' names are Annabella and Luigi."

"Were you doubting my Italian heritage?"

"No, it's just those are some great names. Beats the hell out of Bud and Bonnie. Where do they want you to go?"

"Colgate."

"That's closer."

"They could take me out for lunch and be home for dinner. That's my father's idea of a perfect college for his one and only child. My mother thinks I should go to SUNY Schenectady and live at home, but I told them I would get a better job if I went to a better school."

"*Better job* being the magic words."

"Bingo."

"Will you run at college?"

"Yeah, I mean, I'd run anywhere. But Colorado gave me some really good merit money."

"No sports scholarship?"

She chuckled. "Track isn't like football. The alumni don't dump cash from the sky for track stars."

"What did Colgate give you?"

"A little less. But my number-crunching mother is factoring in flights if I go to Colorado. She's got the meal plans dissected to the nickel. We're still in negotiations—about that and majors. She wants me to do accounting, of course."

"Accounting? Has she met you? How are you supposed to sit behind a desk and punch a calculator all day long? You'd end up in the loony bin."

It had been years since they'd talked like this, and he still knew her so well.

*He gets me*, she thought, and it almost made her cry it felt so good.

"I think you should be a teacher," he went on. "You'd be walking around the classroom—you could even take your students outside on nice days. Then you could coach after school. You'd be the best coach! And you'd help the slow kids, even if they were useless at meets."

"I'd love that," she said wistfully.

"Do it," he said. "Wheels, seriously. You're not made to be a bookkeeper."

IT WAS ALMOST dark now. Helen was hungry, and she could hear Cal's stomach growling. It really was time to go. But neither of them moved. *One more little conversation*, she thought. *Just a few more minutes.*

"What's your favorite song?" she asked.

"Are you kidding me?"

Maybe this last conversation would be shorter than expected, which was probably for the best. She could barely see into the woods at this point.

"I have hundreds of them!" he went on. "I mean, you can't just say you love 'Piano Man' and leave it at that. That would only cover a very specific kind of ballad. There are a lot of categories, and my favorites change a lot."

She laughed. "You should be a DJ."

"Oh, man, I could do that with my eyes closed, except it would drive me crazy to have to choose, knowing other great tunes weren't getting played."

"Okay, name one song that has stayed on the top of one of your lists for a while."

He thought for a minute, and he didn't actually seem to be deciding which song so much as deciding whether to say it.

"'Maybe I'm Amazed' by Paul McCartney. Best love song ever written."

"What makes that one head and shoulders above any other?"

"The honesty. The pure unvarnished, unsweetened truth. He's saying he doesn't really know what he's doing, he doesn't know how he got here. Paul McCartney—he was in the fucking Beatles! One of the most successful bands in the history of the world! But he's also kind of a dumb kid from Liverpool. His head is spinning. He doesn't know if he deserves it. 'Maybe I'm amazed at the way you're with me all the time,'" Cal sings softly. "She's there for him, even when he screws up. She helps him do what he loves to do, be the real him, but she also kicks his ass when he needs it. I'm sorry, but that is just . . . No one's ever going to beat that."

"That sounds like you, a little. You know, the whole star athlete thing."

"Maybe. But it's not that, really. I worked hard for that. I ran my ass off and practiced like a madman. I know I deserved it. It's all the other shit."

"Popularity."

"Let me tell you, Wheels, it is a weird fucking thing."

"Is Wendy sort of an ambassador to all that? Is that why you stay with her?"

He looked away. "Yeah, maybe. In the beginning, anyway. She's a true pro, I'm not kidding. I'm just not a good student. I go to these parties, and I think, *What am I doing here?* And she can't help me because she doesn't understand what I don't feel. I mean the girl came out of the womb popular. The nurses probably wanted her autograph. I never would've asked her if—"

He stopped short. Neither of them said anything. The fire crackled.

Cal turned to face her. "I never would have asked her if I'd known you were going to break up with Mark. God*damn* it, Helen. On Valentine's Day? You couldn't have broken up a week sooner? Hell, a *day* sooner?"

Helen was stunned.

"Would you have said yes if I'd asked you?" He shook his head, shocked at his own boldness. "Whatever. I just need to know."

"Cal, I . . . I thought you were mad at me because I said—"

"You said you weren't into me. In tenth grade, two and a half years ago, before I hit puberty. Yeah, that was not entirely hard to fathom, Helen. You were fully grown. I was a tadpole."

"But you never talked to me! You'd walk right by me in the hallways. You didn't show up at track—I waited for you! And you chose *baseball*!"

"I was so embarrassed that I'd even had the balls to ask you to Homecoming! I just needed to get over that and grow a little. I was so happy in the summer when I really sprouted, and I made first string. So then I'm all proud and ready to go back and ask again—and you're dating Mark fucking O'Malley, *who is a one-hundred-percent douchebag no matter who he's adjacent to!*"

They glared at each other. Then Helen started to smile. "He really is kind of an a-hole."

"Yes! He is!" Cal was still breathing hard from the little speech he'd made.

"He knew he wanted to be a priest. He was just taking me for a joy ride before he got locked behind the seminary door."

"Exactly!"

She gazed at Cal. He was so beautiful to her. Just every part of him, inside and out. "I missed you so much," she whispered.

"Even when you were with Mark?"

She smirked. "That douchebag?"

Cal tipped his head up and laughed at the stars. Pure, un-varnished, unsweetened joy. Then he looked back down at her. "Helen," he whispered. "I love you."

# Chapter 17

## 2021

"Hey, Francie, it's Helen. Am I catching you at a bad time?" Helen leans against her kitchen counter later that afternoon.

"No, not at all. It's great to hear your voice. What's up?"

"Well, something happened."

"Cal Crosby found you."

"How did you know?"

"I knew the minute I saw your name on the caller ID."

Helen laughs. "Seriously?"

"He's owed you an apology for forty years, and he's not too much of an asshole to know it. I mean, he's an asshole. But he's not a sociopath. The daughter's in on it."

"Janel," said Helen.

"Janel?"

"That's his daughter's name. And why would she be so invested in her father talking to me? That can't possibly be something you'd tell your kids about."

"Mmmmmm," hums Francie. "No, I suppose not. But I come from a family where you could have a whole secret life, and no one would politely ask you why you've been gone for weeks at a time, so I might not be the world's foremost authority."

"I still can't believe that about your dad."

"Yeah, I never saw it until I saw it. He was always the kind of guy to put himself first. Lucky for him, my mother was the kind who drank to avoid thinking about it too hard."

Helen shakes her head. "I just wish I'd been there for you."

"You know, in a funny way, you were. You and Annabella and Luigi. I knew what a loving, honest, not-supremely-fucked-up family was supposed to look like; that helped me figure out what to try and fix, and what was beyond fixing. The Iannuccis have always been a bit of a North Star for me, even when we weren't on speaking terms."

"You always gave me the best advice," says Helen. "Sometimes I'd think of you when things got hard. You have no idea how often."

There is a moment of silence for the thirty-five years of friendship they lost. Then Francie says, "Where'd he track you down—the bakery?"

"Yep."

"Did he apologize finally?"

"No, he just said there's a conversation we need to have."

Francie chuckles. "It's funny hearing the 'We need to talk' line coming from a guy. Props to him for rewording it, anyway."

"I forgave him."

"Right there on the spot?"

"Yeah, but he didn't really accept it. He said, 'There's more to it than that.'"

"Huh."

"What."

"Why did you forgive him so fast if he didn't apologize yet?"

Helen sighs. "I just wanted it to be over."

"How does forgiving him when he didn't even ask make it over?"

"I thought he'd be satisfied and go away."

Francie doesn't respond.

"I guess that's probably pretty chicken of me."

"What he did was really awful, Helen. I can understand why you wouldn't want to revisit it."

"But . . ."

"But what?"

"You were going to say *but*. I could hear it."

"I didn't say it out loud, though. I can't be held responsible for things I may or may not have thought."

"Did you think it?"

Francie is quiet. Then she says, "I love you, Helen."

Helen looks at the phone for a second. "I love you, too," she says.

"I really want to stay in your life this time. Like, till the end. I don't want any stupid guys getting in the way again."

"Agreed."

"Weighing in on this seems a little dangerous right now. I don't want to say the wrong thing."

"Francie, I'm asking you. How can it be dangerous if I specifically request your opinion?"

Helen can hear Francie breathing, but that's all she hears.

"Francie."

"Don't you have any other friends you can ask?"

Helen has Megan and Julie and Karen in North Carolina. She's remained friends with them and continues to Zoom in to their monthly get-togethers. They all knew and liked Jim, while also knowing that he and Helen weren't the best fit. She certainly never told them about Cal or Kesia Neep. She's never told anyone about Kesia. Helen honestly sometimes can't even believe it herself. A couple of times in the year and a half since Jim died, she's had the urge to call Kesia and say, *Did I dream that? Was that real?* But of course she hasn't.

And Helen hasn't made any new friends in Belham. It was a pandemic. You weren't exactly inviting people over for coffee to get to know them better. You were wearing your mask and crossing to the other side of the road. She once saw a mask printed with the words SIX FEET, MOTHERFUCKER, and she kind of wanted one, even though she would never have worn it.

Besides, she has her hands full trying to keep the confectionery afloat and being a new grandmother. Barb and Cormac serve as her limited social life, and the three of them are there for one another in many ways. But they are not her friends.

"I don't think I've ever had a friend who understood me the way that you did—do. But I respect that you don't want to endanger what we have at this point. It's precious. It's truly precious to me, Francie. So that's fine, and no hard feelings."

They chat a little more and talk about Francie coming down to Belham when she can break away from the farm. Probably in a week or two. They hang up.

Helen's phone buzzes almost immediately, and she answers without looking at the caller ID, hoping it's Francie and that she's changed her mind about the "but." Helen is beginning to realize that forgiving Cal—if it can even be categorized as such, given that it was to an apology that he never offered—was a bad move. *A chickenshit move*, Francie would probably say. But Helen would feel better if she could hear Francie say it in real life.

"Hi," she says.

"That was a fast pickup. Waiting to hear from your drug dealer?"

"No," she says. "I was waiting to hear from my handler at the CIA."

"You're a spy," he scoffs.

"No one would know."

"Oh, they'd know."

"I can be stealthy." This is the way she talks to her third child, the one who never gives her a break.

"You suburban moms are so inconspicuous."

*Business owner*, she wants to say. *Grandmother, runner, friend.*

"Okay, smarty," she says, "what is it? You're hang gliding in the Andes and wanted to say *hola*?" She expects Danny to ask for money. They have an unspoken agreement that if he needs money for safety equipment—and it's almost all safety equipment— she'll help out. She wants him to live. In this way (as is the way of all children) he has her over a barrel.

"No, smarty," he says, "I wanted to see about Thanksgiving."

"Thanksgiving, like next month Thanksgiving?"

"No, I'm planning ahead for 2022."

Helen laughs. Danny generally plans about twenty-four hours in advance, if that. But he's nothing if not surprising.

"A Danny sighting!" she says.

"Brief but magnificent. Like an asteroid."

"Asteroids generally crash to the ground or burn up in a fiery inferno, so I'd prefer a different analogy."

"I'll text you the flights when I know them."

She puts the phone on the counter, and it buzzes again. This time she looks; this time it's a call she's been expecting.

"Hi, sweetie."

"Hi," says Barb. "What's new?"

Seriously, her children are hilarious.

"Yeah, it was someone I knew in high school."

"Cormac said it seemed charged."

"Charged?"

"That was the word he used. 'Charged.'"

"Like a battery?"

"Mom, you know what *charged* means."

"It was perfectly calm."

"Cormac said he was nicely dressed. Nice shoes."

"I didn't notice the shoes."

"Cormac didn't either at first, but I asked him, and he said they were nice."

"You specifically asked Cormac about the shoes?"

"You can tell a lot from footwear."

Helen glances down at her runners. She tips her foot up and studies the tread, which is worn smooth. She hadn't noticed. "I guess you can."

"Boyfriend?" says Barb.

"You know I only ever dated Mark O'Malley in high school, and he's a priest now." Annabella had kept Helen apprised. Mark's dad came to the shop to get a fender dent pounded out, and he was very proud about Mark. "Studying one old book," Annabella scoffed. "That will only get you so far."

"But this wasn't Mark," says Barb.

*Not by a long shot*, thought Helen. "Nope."

"You're being very secretive."

"What would you like to know?"

"Who's the guy?"

"His name is Cal Crosby, and we were friends. We had a falling-out, and he wants to clear things up."

"It must have been some falling-out if he got decked out in his nice shoes and tracked you down after all this time. What's it been, like, fifty years?"

"Forty, but thanks for that."

"I'm just kidding. Did he clear things up?"

"Not yet."

"All right, I'm getting the distinct impression that you don't want to tell me."

*I don't want to tell anyone*, thinks Helen. *I don't even want to tell myself.*

"Maybe someday," she says to Barb. "But it's on a need-to-know basis for now."

THAT NIGHT, HELEN checks her email before shutting down her laptop. There's a new one from Fran Hydecker. The subject line is: *This is not from Francie.*

*This is not Francie*, it begins.

> This is not Francie. It's from someone else entirely, and Francie is not responsible for the content.
>
> If a person named Annabella Iannucci (a person I have never met) were in a situation wherein a man from her past who had hurt her and let her down terribly and indirectly caused her to think things that didn't turn out to be true wanted to "have a conversation" (i.e., "we need to talk" *gag*), this Annabella person would give him a massive piece of her fiery Italian mind. She would unload on this guy like there has never been an unloading in the known history of unloadings.
>
> She would also listen to him. Annabella was a fair person (so they say), and she would hear him out. She would recognize that there are enough burdens in this life, and when you get a chance to put one down, you should not squander that opportunity. And if this guy's apology was thorough and sincere—like seriously fucking thorough and sincere (apparently Annabella had a real eye for bullshit)—she would accept his apology, and she might even make

him some pasta fagioli. Maybe not. She'd have to see how she felt. There would be absolutely no obligation for her ever to see this guy again, much less bestow upon him her magical soup. It would be entirely up to her.

Conversely, if a woman named Georgette Hydecker (of whom I have no knowledge) were to be confronted with this same situation, she would probably turn off the lights, pretend she wasn't home, and pour herself another cocktail in the dark.

Just some thoughts mixed liberally with love from a non-Francie friend.

# *Chapter 18*

## *1981*

All the love that had been ricocheting around Helen's body all afternoon and into the evening that cold April day paused.

"I love you," he'd said.

*Surf's up!* replied Helen's love, and there was nothing she could do anymore to contain it. She put a hand on his shoulder, leaned up, and kissed him.

It was the best kiss she'd ever had. After recovering from the surprise of it, Cal responded with the kind of gentle-but-ardent passion that is the hallmark of best kisses everywhere. His lips were soft and warm and responsive. He put his hands to her ribs, caressing them, then pulled her gently onto his lap. He whispered in her ear, "I've wanted this since the day I met you."

"I've loved you so long," said Helen. She slid her hand behind his head, into his hair, her fingers deliciously tickled by the silky strands.

He pulled back a little to look her in the eye. "But not that long, though," he murmured.

"Yeah," she said, "that long." She tapped him on the chest. "This is what I loved." She waved her finger around. "All this other stuff is an added bonus."

"You are the most beautiful thing to me," he said. "I see you and I just . . ." He shook his head.

Helen slid her fingers inside Cal's jacket and pressed them against his chest and felt his heart thumping. He took her face in his hands and kissed her cheeks and her nose and her mouth. Her body flooded with the feel of him, and with the desire to discover more of it, to have every single inch of her in contact with every single inch of him. She unzipped his jacket and nearly climbed in. He unzipped hers and pushed it off, enveloping her in the warmth of his arms.

Shirts came off. The fire glowed against their skin, warming the spots that were not warmed by each other. She could feel his erection beneath her thigh and slid her fingers inside the waistband of his track pants.

He let out a little moan, but then put his hand on her wrist. "We don't have to," he whispered.

"I want to."

"But it's your first time. I don't want you to feel like—"

"I love you," she said. "I want it to be you."

"I don't have any protection."

Helen thought fast. It had been almost a month since her last period. "It's okay, I'm in a good place in my cycle."

"Are you sure?"

"Are you?"

"Yes," he breathed. "I'm really sure." He slid her off his lap and turned to arrange their jackets over the ground. Helen took off her bra, and when he turned back to her, he sighed at the sight of her breasts.

"They're not that big," she said.

"They're perfect," he said and laid his warm hands on them.

They took off their pants and underwear, and she marveled at his body. Lean and muscular, rosy skin sprinkled with fine red hairs. He lay down on the jackets and put his hand out for her to join him. She lay beside him, pressed against his broad chest, wrapped in his strong arms, and her brain went utterly melty.

"We don't have to," he whispered. "We can just lie here."

"Can I be completely honest?"

"Of course!"

"I'm going to be really disappointed if we don't."

She felt the rumble of his laughter against her.

He went slowly, positioning her carefully, stroking her first before gently sliding inside. There was a bit of a poking feeling, and then she just felt full of him.

Full of Cal, whom she loved.

"Are you okay?" he murmured.

"Yes, keep going."

"You can tell me to stop anytime."

"I'm not telling you to stop."

"Does it feel good, though?"

"Cal, it's amazing. Please stop talking and kiss me."

She started to feel like she was falling into an abyss, or levitating, or both, and she moaned as he went faster. They went on for a while, hovering weightless together in a state of slowly crescendoing bliss. She didn't fully climax, didn't hit that highest possible note . . . but it felt very, very good, and she knew that was more than most girls got on their first try.

He let out a long moan, his body quivering slightly, and then he slowed and gently rolled off her. He tugged her tight up next to him, and said, "Helen."

"Yes?"

"Nothing. Just Helen."

SHE WASN'T SURE how long they lay there; she may have even dozed off for a moment or two. The wind had picked up, and they decided they'd better put their clothes on.

"Should we lie back down?" said Helen, tugging on her hat and mittens. "Just for a few minutes?"

"Okay, but it's getting colder, and I don't want to put any more wood on the fire. We have to make sure it's out completely before we leave."

"Just a minute or two," she assured him, longing to extend any possible time in his arms. "My parents will start to worry soon."

They dressed fully and lay back down. The wind whistled around them, but Helen felt safe and warm and loved. She never wanted to leave.

"This is the best night of my life," he whispered.

"Mine too."

HELEN WOKE SHIVERING in the dark. The fire still had some embers, but they were almost completely buried beneath ash.

"Cal," she said. "Cal, it's late."

"Mmm?" He blinked his eyes.

She pulled out from the cave of his arms and a gust of wind hit her hard. One of her legs had fallen asleep and she had to wait for the pins and needles to pass. Her body quaked with cold.

"Cal, seriously. We have to go."

He sat up, shivered, and rubbed his face. "Jesus, it's freezing."

She stood gingerly. "Come on, get up. If we head downhill, we'll eventually hit the road at least, right?"

Cal pushed himself up, tried to rise, then thunked back down. "My feet are asleep."

"Give them a minute."

He waited. Nothing happened. He looked up at her.

"No pins and needles?"

"Nothing." A look of alarm came over him. "Oh, shit," he said, pulling off one of his sneakers and socks. "Oh, no . . ." He wrapped his hands around his foot, then his toes. "They're freezing. I can't feel a thing."

"Are your socks still wet?"

"Yeah, and the sneakers, too. They were warm when I put them on so I didn't think . . ."

"Can you walk? Should we build another fire?"

He thought for a minute. "I think we should try to make it out. The movement will help with circulation."

Helen helped him up, and Cal steadied himself on her shoulder as he took a step. "Jesus, it's like walking on stilts."

She wrapped an arm around his waist. "Put your arm over my shoulder and we'll go slowly till the circulation comes back."

They made their way at a snail's pace down the path. It was dark, and though the sky was clear and they could see stars prickling through the trees, there was no moon, so they couldn't have gone too much faster anyway.

"Any better yet?" Helen asked every so often until he snapped, "Stop asking. Trust me, I'll let you know."

On any other day, she would have snapped back. On this night, the best night of their lives till now, she felt as if he'd slapped her across the face. She tried to reassure herself that he was just freaked out, he'd apologize when his feet felt better . . . but he'd never, ever spoken to her like that before.

They continued on for what seemed like hours in silence. His feet never seemed to get any better. In fact, they seemed to get worse. He began to make the tiniest little noises, as if he were doing everything in his power to swallow pain.

THERE WAS A sound way up ahead of them. Or maybe several sounds. As they inched closer, Helen thought she could almost hear voices. Who could be out here in the woods in the middle of the night? Whoever it was, they weren't up to any good, she was sure of that. Thieves, rapists . . . Her imagination spun. She wanted to say something to Cal, but he had said not one word in all the time they'd been walking, his arm still over her shoulder, leaning on her—her back was starting to ache, and she would have liked to lean him up against a tree and take a break for a minute. But she didn't dare ask.

The voices got louder. Not the raucous voices of a pillaging biker gang . . . It seemed to be some sort of emergency. There was a quick streak of light. Then another. There was a faint glow in the distance. Was it the sun? It couldn't possibly be that late. Did the sky seem lighter, or had her eyes adjusted?

"What is that?" he said.

"A party in the woods?" But it was a Wednesday night. Who partied in the middle of the week?

The trees thinned, the voices rose, and they emerged at the end of the trail above the parking lot. There were a bunch of vehicles—including police cars with the lights spinning. Officers were shining flashlights into Jerry's car, searching for something. Silhouettes of people shifted like wraiths.

"Mom?" said Cal suddenly.

"Cal? Cal?" screamed a woman's voice.

All the silhouettes turned toward them.

"Helen!" bellowed Luigi.

Suddenly there was a rush like a flock of crows across the parking lot.

A girl's voice cried out, "Cal, oh my God!"

Wendy Moriarty, fleet-footed as she was, got to them first. Cal let go of Helen.

"What happened?" Wendy demanded as she wrapped her arms around him. *"What happened, Cal?"*

"Nothing," he said. "We just got lost."

Wendy's head spun toward Helen, eyes boring into her, suspicion flaring.

"Wendy," said Cal, "nothing happened."

# *Chapter 19*

## 2021

Helen doesn't sleep well that night. The damn box is open now, and the memories come flooding back. Her parents' haggard faces, Annabella clutching her and muttering in Italian, *"Mi vita, mi vita . . ."*

The police officer calling for an ambulance for Cal. "Frostbite," he says into the radio. "Temps dropped like a stone up here, windchill's bad, and they were out a long time." Another officer takes Cal's statement as they wait.

"We got lost," Cal says, his voice sounding butchered. "I fell in a stream, and I lit a fire to get warm. We must have fallen asleep."

This is all true.

*But what about the rest of it?* wonders Helen.

Wendy never leaves his side. She takes possession of him. Even Cal's parents are sidelined by the force of Wendy's Wendiness.

Helen can't catch Cal's eye. She wants to go to the hospital with him, but everyone objects to that. "You need rest," they say. Wendy stares at her, as if she can see that Helen is no longer the same girl who went into those woods. As if she knows.

ANNABELLA AND LUIGI are silent in the car. Everyone is so tired. Helen realizes she got more sleep than they did. When they get home, Helen knows she needs a shower, but she can still smell Cal on her, and she's not ready to let that go. But Annabella is looking at her.

"What happened?" she says.

"We got lost," Helen says. Because that's what happened.

"And then what happened?" says Annabella.

HELEN GOES TO the hospital the next day. She sees Wendy through the glass in the door and waits down the hall till she leaves.

Cal's feet are all bandaged up.

"Hey," she says, and goes to sit on the bed. He doesn't look at her. "Hey," she insists.

"Probably going to lose a toe." His voice is dead. "Maybe a couple."

"Oh, no. That's awful. When will they know if—"

"I'm going to lose my scholarship."

"I'm sure there's—"

He glances up at her and the avalanche of regret on his face stops her cold.

"I cheated," he says. "And now I'm losing everything."

*Not me*, she thinks. *You'll never lose me.*

But it's clear that's not what he wants to hear. Last night it was all he wanted to hear, and today everything's different.

His eyes start to leak, and he mutters, "Worst night of my life."

THE REST OF it is more of a blur. Kids staring at her in school. The word *bitch* scrawled across her locker. Cal coming to school on crutches the next week, avoiding her. Losing races she should have won; almost quitting the team in despair. Marybeth Guchel calling her a whore in the lunchroom. Ricky Zugravescu telling Marybeth to "Fuck off, parasite!"

Helen sits up in bed and turns on the light.

In all the times she's thought of that horrible series of events, the part about Ricky has never surfaced before. Ricky defended her! And now she knows why she buried that little bit of medieval history extra deep: he must have finally seen her as an underdog. Ricky Zugravescu, of all people, felt sorry for her.

Helen shakes her head and wishes hard—so hard!—she'd apologized to him before he died. This is when she knows she has to go to the damn parking lot in Jansen Woods in the morning: to give Cal the opportunity she lost.

At the bakery yesterday, she and Cal discussed where they would have their "conversation." He made suggestions and she shot them down. She didn't want to be in a public place like a restaurant with him, and she didn't want to be in either of their houses. Finally he'd suggested a walk, and because Helen was at her limit with the whole thing, she agreed.

An hour later she was ready to kick herself. A *walk* in the fucking *woods*? Isn't that what got them into this mess in the first place? What was she thinking?! That's when she had called Francie.

Cal would never know it, but he had Francie's quirky email and Ricky's takedown of Marybeth Guchel all those years ago to thank for Helen showing up at all.

THEY HAD AGREED to meet at seven A.M. Helen suggested it because there was almost no one in Jansen Woods at that hour on a Saturday morning. She didn't want to run into the odd acquaintance or a regular from the confectionery and be forced to introduce Cal.

Cal said, "Great. I'm up at the crack of dawn anyway."

At 6:45 A.M. the sky opens up like the wrath of God, and Helen thinks smugly, *Oh, well. Another time then!*

But she was the one who declined to give him her mobile number in case there was a change in plans. She's going to have to put on seven layers of foul-weather gear and go to the Jansen Woods parking lot, anyway, and tell him it's off.

*I could just not go.* But then she thinks of Ricky and Francie. And the fact that Cal will probably track her down eventually anyway.

Helen takes another sip of her coffee and tries to tell herself she's being a baby, there's nothing to be afraid of.

But that's not true. If she looks too closely at that perfect night and all the hell that followed—gives new life to a monster she's been trying to kill for forty years—she might fall in a hole she'll never be able to crawl out of. And that is legitimately terrifying.

THERE IS ONE car in the parking lot: a Honda Pilot. Helen pulls her RAV4 up next to it. Cal rolls down the window. "Nice day!" he says, and smiles.

"I'm just here to reschedule."

"Helen."

"What."

"How about if you get in my car, and we talk right here?"

*Nooooooo!* she wants to wail. But then she thinks, *Oh, just get it over with.*

His car smells good. Not like a new car, but not an old one, either. Not strong, but still faintly noticeable. She can't place the smell, but it's pleasant. And then she realizes it's Cal.

He turns toward her, his back angled slightly toward the window. "So I'm not really sure where to start," he says.

*Well, don't look at me,* she thinks.

"I guess maybe I should begin by saying I'm sorry. I acted like complete trash, and you didn't deserve it. Not one ounce of it. I've regretted it all my life."

Those last few words ring in the air. *Regretted it all my life.* Helen knows a little something about that.

"There's no excuse for the way I behaved, Helen." He takes a breath and lets it out. "I was freaked out about my toes and my scholarship and cheating on my girlfriend, but I handled it in a really shitty way. I took it out on you, when that was the last thing I should've done."

She's braced herself against these memories for so long, but what he's saying, and even more, the humility with which he's saying it, makes her let down her guard a little, and she nods.

"Um," he says, "do you want to . . . maybe say anything?"

She's not sure what he means. Is she supposed to apologize, too?

"I mean, let me have it," he says. "Take my head off. Please!"

"It was just hard," she says. "I didn't expect it . . . after . . ."

His face colors. "Yeah," he says.

"It made me question . . . And I didn't really trust myself after that."

They stare at the windshield, the rain sliding down in sheets.

Cal clears his throat uncomfortably and says quietly, "A while back someone asked me when I decided I wasn't a good guy. At the time I didn't really give a straight answer, but I knew. It was that morning in the parking lot."

"Who?"

He glances over at her. "Who?"

"Who asked you that? It's kind of an unusual thing to ask."

"Marriage counselor."

"Oh."

"Yeah, so . . ."

"Is that why you're here? Is this a marriage therapy assignment?"

"No! Absolutely not. We're not even seeing the guy anymore."

"Oh."

The rain rattles on the roof like a little tin drum that Sam had when he was about six. Helen wonders what Sam is doing right now.

"One time a marriage counselor gave us the assignment to look at each other for three minutes straight," she says. "But Jim's allergies were acting up and he kept sneezing."

Cal seems almost confused by this at first, but then he smiles. Helen shrugs. "He wasn't good about taking his allergy medicine."

Cal's smile fades. "Wasn't?"

"Oh." Helen hadn't planned on talking about this. "Um, he died about eighteen months ago. Heart condition."

"Jesus, I'm sorry."

"Yeah, thanks."

"Are you . . . ? How are you doing?"

She's learned to say a few words about how it's hard, but as a family they're getting by. People generally want to know that the deceased is missed, but his loved ones are managing. But sitting here in Cal Crosby's car, with the rain coming down like they might have to build an ark soon, she just says, "I'm okay."

"Yeah?"

"Yeah." She nods. "I'm good."

"You have a daughter," he prompts.

"Barb. She's thirty-five, the mother of the baby you saw me with."

"You started young!"

"Ah, well. Not by design."

His eyebrows go up, but not in a judgmental way. She knows he wouldn't get high-minded about that.

"And two boys," Helen goes on. "Men, I should say."

Cal wants to know more about them, and she finds herself talking about how funny and exhausting they were when they were little. A little bit about what they're up to now. He keeps asking questions, and she keeps answering. He seems genuinely interested in every detail.

"Was it hard to leave North Carolina?" he asks.

"I miss some of my friends, but . . . I guess I've really come to like it here, taking care of my granddaughter, and I love working with Cormac—"

"Janel said you said you were the bookkeeper."

"Yeah . . . I don't generally tell people I'm a co-owner. It was hard enough to get him to take the money. Better to keep that on the down low."

"But you told me."

She levels a gaze at him. "I didn't want to say *bookkeeper*."

He knows what she's referring to. "Hey, who am I to judge? I'm just interested in how that came to be."

*Jesus, he's asking for it*, she thinks. But this whole clambake is about honesty and facing the past, so she gives him the truth. "I felt really guilty about scaring my parents like that. And I was just . . . not feeling solid about my decision making, so I let them make the call. I went to Colgate and studied accounting."

He takes the hit. He *wants* the hit, Helen realizes. "Thanks for telling me," he says.

"You asked."

"How'd you manage all that sitting?"

"Oh, I got creative. I was probably the first person in the world with a standing desk. And I took lots of dance breaks. Drove my roommates a little crazy."

Cal's eyes lose focus for a moment, and she knows he's remembering.

"What about you?" she says. "Did you study business?"

"Yep. SUNY Schenectady for a year and then I transferred to the University of Washington."

"Wow, that's a jump."

"I needed to get out of Dodge."

"You must have worked very hard."

That seems to settle on him in a funny way, not as the compliment she intends, but she's not sure what to do about it now.

"I . . . um . . . It turns out I sometimes have a tough time knowing when to take my foot off the accelerator."

"Workaholic?"

"Yeah, but don't worry, Covid fixed that."

She gives him a nod. "The job market's tight."

"Oh, it's not that. I'm a known quantity. Everyone wants the guy who works fourteen-hour days."

"So . . ."

"I was spending most of my time on the road. I was head of operations, and it's important to show up in person. We had a very specific product we were promoting, and at that level, patrons notice when a cocktail napkin's out of place. I'd land at a site, throw on an apron, and tend bar just to see things from the ground level."

"You were a company exec mixing drinks and washing out glasses?"

Cal chuckles. "Yeah, it freaked out some of the workers, but it gave me a lot of cred in the boardroom. Then Covid hit."

"Suddenly you're working from home."

He laughs, but there's no humor in it. "Not for long. Lance took the money and ran in May. So then I'm grounded without a job, holed up in the house with my wife and girls. And I start to realize that I'm not really part of the family. Like, I am, but not on a day-to-day basis. I'm kind of . . . in their way."

"How old are your girls?"

"Twenty-nine. Bonnie was in Brooklyn—she's in PR—but she lived in a high-rise, so she moved home. Janel and her husband, Eli, and Logan were in a triple-decker in Somerville. The other two floors were college kids who were still throwing parties, so they moved back in, too."

"Must be a decent-size place."

"Yeah. Bigger than we need." He shrugs. "Suze likes nice things."

"Your wife."

He nods.

"So you were off tending bar in thirty-two places all those years, and they sort of formed a little family without you." She almost says, *My husband, too,* but she's not throwing Jim under the bus. Not to this guy, of all guys. She can tell he's uncomfortable, that he's forcing himself to fess up. But why to her? This isn't part of their history. Is she supposed to feel sorry for him now? For the record, she's Team Suze on this one.

"It just became really apparent, all locked up together like that," he says. "The ways I had let them down. I was so focused on providing, making sure they had everything they wanted—the best schools, every lesson imaginable, interesting travel—I didn't realize how much I didn't actually show up for most of it."

"You were trying to give them what your father didn't give you."

Cal smiles sadly. "Thank you, Dr. Iannucci. Sorry, I mean . . ."

"Spencer."

"Thanks for that kind interpretation, but at the end of the day, kids don't care what your baggage is. They just want you in the room."

Helen nods. "True."

"I, um . . ." He glances over at her. "I mean, not that this is anything to do with you, but in a weird way it is . . . I wanted us to go into family counseling, and they shot me down. Suze said, 'You're the one with the issues. You do the work.' So I did. I ended up with this great older lady, Dorothy, and she kind of sweetly beat the shit out of me. She told me she thought my life was ruled by shame, and that I needed to face it."

"How were you supposed to do that?"

"I went back to Paddow Mountain."

# Chapter 20

## 2021

*S*weet *Jesus*, thinks Helen. *The belly of the beast.* She wonders if she could ever in a million years go back there and not crumble into pieces. She has to give him points for bravery, anyway. "To that big rock where we built the fire?" she asks.

He nods.

"How'd you find it?"

Cal doesn't say anything for a moment, as if bracing himself. "I knew where it was."

"But we were lost."

"Um, not actually. My Scout Troop camped in those woods a lot."

"You're not . . . You can't be telling me you knew where we were that whole time."

He doesn't answer.

"Oh my God. You *knew*?"

His steady gaze continues, and she can see it costs him a lot, facing her like that.

"You lied to me."

"Yes, I did."

"Why in the hell would you do that?!"

"Because I wanted to be alone with you. I wanted some time . . . to just . . . be together and talk. To be Wheels and Match. It was my last chance."

Helen almost flinches at the nicknames. Their names for each other. "You could have talked to me anytime you wanted—we were in school together every day!"

"No, I could not do that. Wendy would've flipped right out and made my life a misery."

"But that happened anyway! Except she made *my* life a misery!"

"Which only proves I was right."

"What did you think would happen when we spent all that time in the woods alone together? That she wouldn't notice? That the whole damn town wouldn't notice?"

"Yeah, um, I wasn't planning on that. I only wanted a little time to talk. At least that's what I told myself. To take a break and be real for a few minutes. All that big-man-on-campus shit—it was surreal, and not in a fantasy way. In a *Twilight Zone* kind of way. But you knew me, and it just felt good. The more I was with you, the more I didn't want to go back, like, ever." Cal pauses and then adds carefully, "You didn't seem to mind."

This is absolutely true. Helen could have stayed there for years.

"We scared the hell out of people."

"And I knew you'd do the responsible thing. So I built the fire instead of leading us out."

This was starting to come together in her mind. Once they left that rock, Cal knew exactly where he was going. A couple of times she had moved to go down one path, and he'd tugged her toward another. But she didn't pay attention at the time. All she could focus on was his silence.

"You don't seem to regret that in the least. The fact that you basically held me hostage."

"I wasn't holding you hostage, Helen. You and I both know that. In fact . . ."

He trails off, but she knows what he's thinking: that she was the one who kissed him first, and wanted to have sex, and suggested that they hold each other for one more minute, which then became hours. If she hadn't done any of these things, would he have initiated them? She thinks he would. She's damn sure he didn't mind.

He started over. "If I'd told you that I could get us back to that parking lot in under an hour . . . You were a good girl. You loved your parents."

"They were terrified!"

"Yeah, honestly that's the only thing that made me hesitate. Your parents. Everyone else could go screw."

"You thought it wouldn't come back to bite you. It wouldn't be our fault if we were lost."

"It's what I told myself, yeah."

"Boy, did that not work out."

He looks away, and she can still see the pain of it. The cost had been so high.

"So you went back there."

"Yeah."

"Returning to the scene of the crime."

He nods.

"What was it like?"

He turns back to her. "You really want to know?"

"Why wouldn't I?"

"Because I just told you I lied to you and made you do something you wouldn't have wanted to do that ended up really badly for both of us."

"I didn't say I wouldn't have wanted to do it. You didn't exactly have to tie me to a tree. But you're right, I was a good daughter. If

I'd known we could have gotten out that easily, I probably would have gone back sooner. But Monday-morning quarterbacking is cheap. We didn't know what a mess it would make at the time."

"Thanks for that."

"For what?"

"For admitting you wanted to be there, and that we couldn't have foreseen the consequences. That means a lot to me." He sighs. "I've spent forty years trying to believe those two things so I wouldn't hate myself so much about it."

"Oh, Cal." Helen shakes her head. "We were young and stupid. You don't have to keep paying for it."

"Yeah, but, see, I did keep paying for it. I lost my scholarship. So I had to give up University of Washington and go to a school I didn't want to go to and work my ass off to pay for it. And I married someone . . . You know I love my wife, and I'm committed to her. But I think I married her because she would help me get past all that. She's strong in all the right ways. But sometimes . . . I don't know.

"And I just kept working so hard. It became a drug, the only thing that made the shame go away. So I basically missed my kids' childhoods, and one of them is actively pissed at me and the other one got an offer in Australia and took off as soon as she was vaccinated. The ripple effect from that one mistake, Helen. Jesus, it's a like a tsunami that won't recede."

Helen suddenly feels so sad. Because she was part of it, this thing that keeps crashing on him over and over—and her, too, it turns out. And she did want to be there. Very much. With all her heart. She was thrilled that they were "lost."

"How did it feel?" she asks. "At Paddow."

"'How did it feel?' You know, not everyone would ask that, or put it like that."

"How would they put it?"

"I don't know, but they'd probably avoid it. Like, why go there?"

"Because you actually went there. And you did it to feel something, so what did you feel?"

Cal smiles, and she can sense his gratitude. "Well, honestly it was surprising. I, um, well, as I said, I went there to face my shame. I hope that doesn't offend you."

"I'm not offended."

"No?"

"Should I be?"

"Absolutely not. It's my shame and you have no part in that. You didn't do anything wrong."

"Everything that happened—it's compounded by the fact that it didn't have to happen, right? That you could have put a stop to it and gotten us out of there?"

"One thousand percent."

"So what did your shame look like?"

"It, uh"—he laughs—"it didn't look that bad."

"No?"

"It just looked like two kids who really . . . Okay, maybe this is presumptuous, but I'll say it anyway because it was a long time ago. I was staring at that big rock ledge where we stayed . . . and it looked like two kids who loved each other and just wanted some time."

Tears are suddenly stinging behind Helen's eyes. She won't cry to Cal Crosby, no matter how apologetic he is. She bites down on her molars, willing her emotions back to composure. But he sees something change in her.

"Hey," he says gently. "Did I say the wrong thing?"

"No. I think what you saw—" Why lie? She can be brave, too. "It's . . . it's exactly right."

"Really?"

"One thousand percent."

# *Chapter 21*

## *2021*

The rain finally lets up, but they stay in the car watching the woods come clear in front of them. *Two kids who just wanted some time*, Helen can't stop thinking. *That's all it was.*

Cal knew when he woke up next to the dead fire that he was in trouble. He was a Boy Scout; he knew about frostbite and the damage it could do. And he knew how it could alter the trajectory—this new, magical, free-ride arc—of his life. He also knew that he wasn't going to be able to hide the fact that he'd spent the night alone with a girl who wasn't Wendy. "I cheated and I lost everything," he told Helen in the hospital that next day.

He had not been honorable. And he would pay for it for the rest of his life.

She could have compassion for that. It wasn't an excuse for his abominable behavior toward her—which was no behavior at all, really. He simply ignored her like he had after she'd told him she wouldn't go to Homecoming with him. He was in pain, and to his eighteen-year-old, not-fully-developed brain, shutting down was the only way to survive. The kids would say he ghosted her. But he also ghosted himself.

Helen is thinking something she never thought she'd think. That she's glad he tracked her down. That it does relieve a burden, as Francie predicted. Maybe it's a chance to change her own trajectory now . . .

And then Cal says, "So . . . just to be thorough . . ."

God, is there something else he hasn't told her? "Yes?" she says.

"I have a tiny little mouse-size bone to pick with you."

She can't imagine what it is, but this morning has been nothing if not pleasantly surprising, so she says, "Shoot."

"That note you mailed to my house."

Helen freezes.

"You remember that?" he asks.

Oh, she remembers. She can practically recite it from memory. *Merry Christmas. You gave me chlamydia. Get checked out before you give it to someone else.* No salutation. No signature. He'd know who it was from.

"I do," she says.

"Kinda harsh, don't you think?"

Helen can suddenly feel her blood sluice a little faster in her veins. "Harsh?"

"Yeah, it was a little kick-in-the-teeth-y."

"How do you figure?"

"It was the one thing I had no control over. I didn't know Wendy had given it to me, and I sure as hell didn't know I was giving it to you. I'd just finished my first semester at the wrong school, and I was pretty depressed. That note sent me even deeper. I mean, obviously you had to notify me, but . . ."

Helen blinks at him, stunned. Then she inhales. "You're saying that I should have told you in a nicer way."

"It could have been a little less—"

"Harsh."

"Well—"

"So, just to be perfectly clear, I should have sent you a nicer note about how you gave me an STD."

It's starting to dawn on Cal that he may have made a bit of a gaffe. "It's not a big deal, but I figured while we're airing things out, I'm just suggesting the note didn't have to be so—"

Helen nods. "No, I get it," she says.

"Okay, great."

"You're saying that after lying to me about being lost, telling me you loved me, deflowering me, then punishing me for the fact that you had cheated on your girlfriend and gotten frostbite, I should have been nicer about the fact that you had *infected me with a disease* in the process."

His face drops like a failed soufflé. "Helen."

Oh, but that box is open now, isn't it? The small but vicious dogs and poisonous snakes and attack birds are sitting back, having a smoke, and enjoying the show.

"You came here to apologize, Cal, and I know you meant it, but all we talked about is you and your lost scholarship, and your big house from working so hard, and your shame. You think you're the only one whose life changed? You think studying *accounting* is the only thing what went sideways for me?"

He stares at her, dumbfounded. He has no response, and that's a lucky thing because Helen thinks she may actually punch him if he opens his yap and says one more word. She who is generally known for her composure and rational thinking and good goddamned judgment—she is now a person who could inflict violence if further provoked.

"Let's really air it out, huh, Cal? Okay by you? Let's start with the fact that because of your actions and your choices, it became the worst night of my life, too. You say you were depressed? Well, so was I. My tender little heart was smashed into a thousand shards in that parking lot—in front of everyone. But the public humiliation didn't end there. Wendy Moriarty launched a full-scale campaign to show me I couldn't sleep with her boyfriend and get away with it. I was ostracized. No one would run with me. No one would look at me. Someone scrawled *bitch* across my locker. Wendy actually mailed me a picture of the two of you at prom, all gussied up, smiling like all was right with the world and if it weren't for the crutches, you'd be dancing a jig."

"I had no idea—"

"Oh, for chrissake, Cal. You had no idea? You had *no idea* she had marshaled the entire student body against me, a dork who had the unmitigated gall to try and steal the star football player away from her? Please don't tell me you didn't know. Everyone knew."

"I didn't know all of that. And what little I did know, I figured"—he's running blind now, and they both know it—"I guess I thought it would only make things worse for you if I tried to intervene."

"*Are you fucking kidding me right now?!*" The sound of her own exploding fury makes Helen feel like she's going to faint. She opens the passenger door, gets out, and slams it so hard the bang echoes like a gunshot through the trees.

She can't get in her own car, can't be confined. Her feet move toward the old trail. In a second she hears the other door slam, and his footfalls behind her.

"Helen. Helen!"

"Fuck you, Cal. Fuck you *so* much."

He's hurrying along beside her. The trail is wide here, but his big feet still hit the brush, and he almost trips on a root. "I'm sorry!"

Helen turns on him then. "Sorry for what? You don't even know the half of it." Is she going to say it all out loud for the first time in her life? She moves back and forth, unable to keep still.

"My parents never got over the night they thought their one and only beloved daughter was kidnapped or lying dead in a ditch somewhere. They took over my life. They wanted me close. And I let them because I didn't trust myself. I Did. Not. *Trust myself.* Can you get how . . . disorienting and just . . . nightmarish that is for a person like me? Little Miss Good Judgment miscalculates so wildly about who to love and who to trust that she can barely decide what to eat for *lunch*, much less where to go and what to do.

"I hated Colgate and I hated accounting, but I didn't dare deviate from the plan. And then in the middle of first semester exams, weird goo starts coming out of my vagina. It's like my body is possessed by some kind of alien. I go to the infirmary, and this ancient doctor from like the Spanish Inquisition wants to know all about my sex life and treats me like a dirty girl, and before he hands over the antibiotics, he tells me that since the infection has gone undetected for eight months, I'm *probably infertile* now."

At this point she wants to grab him by the lapels of his jacket, but at the same time the thought of touching him seems unthinkable, so she squeezes her fists tight and howls, "INFERTILE!"

"Oh my God, Helen," he breathes.

"All I hear is that one word! And I'm so stupid I don't do any research or anything because the goddamned internet hasn't been invented yet, and I'm too mortified to ask anyone, and I'm *paralyzed* by the thought that my poor parents will never have any grandchildren. Do you have any idea of how long they waited and prayed for *me* to be born? Any idea at all?"

He shakes his head, still wide-eyed at her ongoing tirade.

"THIRTEEN YEARS!" she yells. "They waited thirteen long, sad, heartbreaking years for yours truly, the girl who scared the living shit out of them by staying out all night with *you*!" She jams her finger in his direction.

"So you think you were a little depressed that Christmas, Cal? Well, you weren't alone. Trust me. And THEN—"

It's all coming out now. All of it. Helen can't stop the firehose she has become. And she doesn't care. Fuck him if he can't take it.

"—THEN I finally get up the courage to date again, this nice guy that somebody sets me up with, and he takes me golfing. Golfing, for godsake! Well, being outside is nice, though like you, I'm terrible at hitting a ball with a stick. But whatever. He's a good guy. The type who talks about honor and doing the right thing. And he's the last guy on the planet who'd screw me and leave me for the goddamned vultures. You know how I know? Because he *did* screw me, and when I got pregnant—because we weren't always perfect with the birth control since I was *probably infertile* and all—he married me."

Helen shakes her head ruefully. "Francie warned me, God love her. She said, 'He's not the guy for you.' We had a horrific fight about it and didn't speak for the next thirty-five years. I lost my very best friend because I couldn't admit she was right. But I knew. I just thought, I don't *care* if he's the guy for me. He won't abandon me. He won't hurt me. In fact, it's *better* that he's not the guy for me because I won't ever be disappointed or heartbroken again.

"But that's not how it works, is it, Cal? If you marry someone who could never break your heart, you live in a state of low-level heartbreak because you gave up your chance for real happiness. And I not only gave it up for me, I ruined it for him!"

Poor Jim. Poor loyal, old Jim. Poor Kesia Neep.

Helen starts to cry. But who cares? Let Cal see it. Let him feel it.

"Because he was in love with someone else." The words almost break in her throat, rising as they are for the first time. "I didn't find out until after he died. But he was. And he never acted on it. He didn't cheat and he wouldn't divorce me. That's what she told me. He wouldn't take a mulligan on our marriage. You know what a mulligan is, Cal?" She doesn't wait for his answer. "It's a do-over. And you know what I want right now, for *all* of us? *A FUCKING MULLIGAN!*"

She's sobbing now, but she can still see him drop to his knees in the fallen leaves.

"Helen," he chokes out through his own tears. "Jesus—"

Suddenly, two teenage girls jog toward them, and one says, "Awww," as if Cal is on his knees proposing or something. But as they get closer it's clear something entirely different is happening. The other girl says, "Uh-oh," and they pick up their speed and hurry by.

"Helen, I am so sorry . . . I am *so sorry*."

Helen is breathing hard, exhausted from this half-rabid rant, this torrential spewing of toxic memory from her body. But her crying starts to abate.

Cal sits back on his heels, hands to his face in shame.

Shame.

Which rightly takes its place in the hall of fame of stupid, useless, dangerous emotions.

# Chapter 22

2021

They're by a field, and as Helen's body starts to recover from this volcanic eruption, she runs a sleeve over her face and looks out over the still-dripping bramble. It smells slightly dank, but also clean at the same time, the wet soil and rot embracing the growing things now sleeping beneath the surface. She sucks a load of misty air into her lungs and lets it out. And then another. And another. She realizes she's starving.

"Cal," she says. He's still on his knees, but his hands have fallen onto his thighs. "Cal, get up."

He looks up at her, his face so spent she feels like she now knows what he'll look like at ninety. He rises slowly and stands before her. Whatever happens next is her call. She could hike farther down the trail to the river. Or she could turn and head back to her car. She could walk away from him, and he would not follow.

But there's something unexpected happening. She can't really put her finger on it. Maybe it's simply relief at finally having busted open that old rusted-shut release valve. Or maybe it's more than that. She realizes that over the years she's wanted to tell him all this, and not only to punish him with it. Just to tell him. To share these strange turns her life has taken since that one night forty years ago. To look piece by piece at all the dominoes that fell . . . and continue to fall.

"I'm starving," she says wearily. "I was too nervous to eat."

"Helen, I'm sorry," he says one last time.

"I know. You gave a thorough and sincere apology, and I accept it."

He slumps a little. "Yeah?"

"Yep. I do."

"That's really generous."

"You were brave to track me down and open such a huge can of worms."

He scrubs his hand back through his hair. "I sure as hell didn't know what I was in for."

"Do you wish you hadn't?"

"Nah," he says. "The worms kept escaping anyway."

"I need food."

"I'll take you out for breakfast."

"I'm still too—" She waves her hand around. "I need to go home. You can come if you want. I'm going to scramble some eggs."

He's studying her as if testing for the subtlest fluctuations in the air currents around her. "You sure?"

"Yeah. I think it's a good idea, actually. This is a weird way to leave things."

"I love scrambled eggs."

She knows he'd say he loves mashed toads if that's what she offered. They walk back to the cars. "Follow me," she says as she opens her driver's-side door.

"Lead on."

# Chapter 23

## 2021

The kitchen at 2 Barley Spring Lane is small, but it opens onto the living room and dining area across a wide countertop, adding space and light. Two stools are tucked under the living room side facing into the kitchen. The stovetop is on the opposite side of the counter.

"How can I help?" says Cal, and Helen indicates the stools and gives him a red pepper and half a Vidalia onion to chop. She pulls some bacon out of the fridge but pauses.

"You're not a vegetarian, are you?"

"Highly carnivorous."

Cal Crosby is dicing a pepper at her kitchen counter. If someone had told Helen two weeks ago . . .

"What," he says.

"No, it's just"—she shrugs as she peels a slice of bacon away from its greasy brethren and lays it in the frying pan—"funny."

"Yeah." He chuckles. "In all the times I've thought about seeing you again, it never started with quite such a galactic ass-kicking, and it definitely never ended with cooking breakfast together."

Helen shakes her head in wonder. "I have never spoken to anyone like that in my life."

"Come on. Not even your husband?"

"I mean, I'd get frustrated with him and raise my voice occasionally, but . . ."

"Suze and I have had some real ripsnorters."

"We followed a pretty strict live-and-let-live policy. Or maybe run-and-let-golf."

His head tips slightly, and she knows he's adding another piece to the puzzle of her marriage. That's certainly not what she wants to talk about.

"Tell me about your family," she says. And as long as she's asking, she might as well begin with the thing she wants to know most. "What's your wife like?"

He starts on the onion. "Suzanne Bell-Crosby is a force of nature. Pretty sure every newspaper article ever written about her says that."

Helen raises an eyebrow. "Hopefully the articles aren't about her criminal activity."

He smiles. "Oh, I wouldn't put it past her, but if she's broken the law, she's never been caught. She's the chair of the Massachusetts Domestic Violence Action Committee."

"Oh my gosh, I've read about her in the *Globe*. She's doing great things." Occasionally there have been pictures of her testifying before the legislature or speaking at conferences. Helen seems to remember a woman with short, fashionably messy blond hair.

Cal nods, a little smile, and Helen can see his pride. "She's crushing it."

"Sounds like you two have dedication to your work in common."

"She's making up for lost time. I was gone a lot, and someone had to hold down the fort. She fundraised for her causes, but she was always itching for more."

"She's a doer."

"With a capital *D*. But not the kind that runs around like a squirrel on crack. She has this . . . I don't know . . . evenness. She's unflappable. I mean, I've made her flap plenty, but generally she's like one of those birds that sails along on the wind currents."

"How did you meet?"

"Senior year of college. I was the head of the Businessmen's Club, and she was the head of the Social Justice Club. She wanted to collaborate on a program to train us filthy capitalists on how the private sector can support worthy causes."

"Wait, Business*men's* Club?"

He laughs. "Yeah, you picked up on that one. First thing she did was get me to change the name. Like, on our first date. She just calmly said something along the lines of 'That's not going to work anymore.' I was like a baby looking at a butterfly and just said, 'Uh, okay. I'll get on it.'"

"She was a good feminist at an early age!"

"Yup."

"How did you two end up in Belham?"

"She's from here. Waltham." It's a mostly working-class city not far from Belham. Cal slides the cutting board piled with neatly diced pepper and onion across the counter to her.

"So her family's nearby." The bacon is starting to sizzle, and Helen turns it with a fork.

"Yeah, her parents are gone, but her brother took over the family landscaping business. Their dad built it into a real empire. And her mother was a state rep for years."

"A power family." Helen can see how the son of a lumber store worker from a tiny town in Upstate New York would have to pedal hard to keep up with all that.

He gives her a knowing look. "If you're guessing I was intimidated, I can confirm that definitively."

She smiles. "But you kept your hat in the ring."

Cal nods. "She was what I needed."

It sounds more like a prescription for some unspecified malady than love, but people get together for all kinds of reasons. (Doesn't Helen know that for a fact.) She respects that he's proud of Suze, and he's been nothing but complimentary. So many spouses are willing to spill their complaints at the drop of a hat.

"And I met Janel, of course," Helen says as she cracks eggs into a bowl.

At the mention of his daughter, a light goes on deep inside him. He adores this girl. "She's a pip," he says.

"She's beautiful. And persistent."

"Oh?"

"Once she put two and two together that I was the one in the woods with Logan that day, she went all investigative reporter on me."

He colors. "Anything else you want me to chop?"

Helen slides the box of mushrooms over to him. "I guess you told her about me."

"A little." He focuses on the fungus. "Not much."

"How much?"

"Logan was talking about the lady who picked him up when he fell, so Janel went all investigative reporter on *me*, and I had to fess up that he got away from me. I mentioned you were someone I knew, more to get her off the fact that a stranger was holding her kid. The story came out after that."

Helen stops beating the eggs and waits.

"No, not the whole story," he says.

"What portion of it?"

Cal puts the knife down. "I told her you were a good friend, but I wasn't there for you when you needed me, and I've always regretted it."

"That's all you said."

"Hey, she's a kindergarten teacher."

"Apropos of?"

"She spends all day with people who can't always tell her what's up. She's good at interpreting."

"And she interpreted there was more to it than that."

Cal gives her a look. "Do your kids get you more than you want to be gotten some days?"

Helen laughs. "Yes, they do."

"That one has my number all day long."

"With mine, the one who puts me on a pedestal doesn't always get me like the one who can't wait to knock me off." She sautés the veggies while recounting the story about Sam getting so upset that he wasn't the only love letter in her envelope.

Cal slaps his hand on the edge of the counter and laughs. "'Mom loves us, too, shithead.' I've gotta meet that one."

*That's unlikely*, thinks Helen. First because Danny is a rare bird—both in type and location. Second because how long is this supposed to go on, this little reunion? Are she and Cal becoming friends, now? That is not at all what she signed up for when she invited him for eggs. She'd only thought it would be sad and unsettling to have her last sight of him be on his knees after she'd verbally eviscerated him.

"Why does Sam put you on a pedestal?" he asks.

"Oh, I don't know. I guess we're the most alike. We were the quieter ones. Not a lot of demands—more likely to suffer in silence than the others."

His face goes wide with surprise, and Helen lets out a laugh. "Yeah, not so much with the silence today, though, huh?" she says.

They are actually laughing about the way she unloaded on him! And now she's feeding him. Won't not-Francie be not-surprised.

Helen turns back to the pan and adds the beaten eggs. They're just beginning to bubble when Cal says, "That thing about your husband . . ."

She pushes the eggs around in the pan. After a minute she murmurs, "I've never told anyone."

"Not even Francie?"

"Especially not Francie."

Cal is quiet. Helen turns the eggs over and over, making sure they're fully cooked. She hates finding a little gelatinous pocket of uncooked whites when she's eating. She goes to the fridge and takes out some shredded cheddar and sprinkles it over the top, covers it with a lid, and sets the heat to low so the cheese melts.

"I don't know why I didn't tell her. I guess I thought it would prove her right that I shouldn't have married him." Helen crosses her arms and leans back against the far counter. "Not like she would've been I-told-you-so about it."

Cal nods.

"I just feel bad."

"For Jim."

Helen shrugs. She turns off the gas under the eggs, but she doesn't serve them. She doesn't know why, but she has this strange urge to talk about it. Maybe because it's Cal, and he's got busloads of shame, so she's in good company. Or maybe it's like telling a stranger, someone you'll never see again, and your secret's safe.

"He didn't want kids," she says.

"No?"

"Yeah, that came out pretty early when we were dating. He wanted to travel and come and go as he pleased. The word he used was *unencumbered*. I remember thinking how it was one of those expressions people usually only use in the negative. I mean, is *cumbered* even a word?"

Cal seems to know this isn't a question he should answer.

"But, you know, I thought I was . . ."

"Unable to."

"Yeah, so it was a relief, really. You have to be careful not to lead someone on. If they think they're heading toward a family, and you're probably not . . . I mean you can adopt, and that's a wonderful thing to do, but a lot of people don't have that as their first choice."

"How old were you when you got pregnant?"

"Twenty-three. I was studying for my CPA and Jim had just gotten an entry position with a golf course design and management firm. He went golfing one day and lucked into an empty spot with a threesome that included the CEO of the company." Helen smiles. "He spent eighteen holes charming the argyle socks off the guy."

"Were you in love with him?"

The air comes out of her, and she whispers, "Dammit, Cal."

"I'm not trying to make you feel bad."

"You don't have to try. No one has to say a word for me to feel bad about this."

"You were twenty-three. My girls could barely figure out how to get car insurance at that age, never mind how to wade through the major life issues you were dealing with."

He's right, and on a rational level she knows this, but something inside her just can't help but feel like she was selfish. Especially now, knowing . . .

"I wasn't in love with him, but I really liked him. I loved him, but . . . you know, not to the point of . . . And I think he felt the same. He had a similar problem, after all. Most women want kids. Being together was a comfortable, easy thing. But I don't think either one of us thought it would be long term." She sighs. "Then my dad died."

"Oh, Helen, I'm sorry."

She smiles up at him. "It was a long time ago."

"Still. Your dad."

"Yeah. He was a good guy. He liked Jim. Wasn't jumping up and down for me to marry him, or anything, but they got along." She puts the cutting board in the sink. "I found out I was pregnant about a month after he passed."

"So you were grieving your dad, thinking you'd never have kids, dating a guy you kinda loved"—he tilted his hand back and forth—"and boom."

"Boom."

"How'd he handle it?"

"He was polite—Jim was the most courteous guy you ever met. But he wasn't happy. We were at this golf course his company was constructing—he took me there to show me all the features they were putting in. He was so excited about it. For him it was like watching a cathedral being built."

"The religion of golf," says Cal.

"Tiger Woods as Jesus."

"Second coming and all."

Helen glances at the pan. "The eggs are getting cold."

"Finish the story. What did he say?"

"He didn't say anything for a long time. He just stared out at the course. Then he said, 'Let's get married.' And I went through the whole 'You don't have to' and 'I know this isn't what you wanted.' But there was no way in hell I wasn't having that kid."

"For all you knew, it was your only chance."

"And Jim understood that. He launched into this metaphor about how it's like when you're laying out a course, and there's an enormous boulder in the way. You want to blast it, but it might disturb the aquifer, and the conservation nuts threaten a lawsuit. You stop trying to get rid of it and you make it a feature. Suddenly it's that course with the giant rock that's such an interesting challenge to play around."

"That's a hell of a take."

"He said, 'Helen, everyone shanks a shot now and then. It doesn't mean you can't still birdie the hole.'"

"I have to admire his attitude, even if it is a little . . ."

"Golfy. Seriously, living with him was like listening to a never-ending podcast about Jack Nicklaus."

"How'd he take to fatherhood? You did end up with three, after all."

"He was great. Loving and kind. But yeah, three. It was more than he wanted."

"More birth control failures?" Cal asks wryly.

"Tell me how those little pill cases work again?" She laughs. "No. I just needed more. They were ridiculously cute. And it made my mother so, so happy."

"He was okay with that."

"You know, we didn't really talk about it. There was just an understanding. We each got what we wanted. I got children and he got freedom. I never complained about his being gone for work all the time or playing golf with his buddies. He was around just enough to connect with the kids and show up for the really important stuff."

"That was the deal."

Helen nods. "That was the deal."

"You were cumbered."

"Fully."

"And he was in love with someone else."

"Jesus, Cal, can we just eat?" she whines. "I'm starving."

"Sure, serve it up. But don't think you're getting away without telling me. I'm hooked on this story now."

# Chapter 24

## 2010

"Kesia Neep's in town," said Jim. "I thought we might have her over for dinner."

"Here?" said Helen.

"Yeah, do you mind? I already kind of invited her."

"Jim."

"I know."

"I was just going to do takeout tonight."

"Sorry. I thought you might want to meet her."

"One of your clients?" Helen occasionally attended dinners where the spouses were involved, but she didn't enjoy it. So. Much. Golf. And she'd tried—taken lessons and everything. But she just couldn't make herself care if the ball went in the hole. Golf courses were overmanicured; she liked the woods. Games were interminable and cost a lot in babysitting. In her mind it was like paying for the privilege of watching towels tumble in an unnecessarily expensive dryer. "You never bring clients home."

"Kesia's great, though. You'll like her."

Jim talked about Kesia more than any of his other clients. She impressed him, as a Black woman running a course in Georgia mostly patronized by white guys, and the praise sounded well-earned. "Being secretary of state would be a day in a hammock compared to that," Jim told Helen. He would often recount some sticky situation Kesia had faced and how she'd solved it, or some funny quip she'd made. These generally tended to be golf-related, however, so Helen would smile and nod as if she understood. Which she did not.

She was glad Jim had someone he regularly talked to who was different from him (other than the fact that they were obsessed with the same thing). Helen was friendly with Daphne and Martha Kelley-Cates, who had a daughter Barb's age, Celia. Daphne had an outlandish sense of humor and Martha was an amazing artist; they certainly were not the standard Pinehurst wives. Helen never quite felt like one herself, so she always gravitated toward the couple at social events. But by middle school, Barb and Celia were in different girl groups, and then Martha got a coveted job as a curator in Raleigh, and they moved. Pinehurst felt a little empty without them.

"You don't have to cook," said Jim. "Kesia's not picky. How about Thai—she's a big fan of peanut sauce."

"Sam won't eat Thai." The kid did not like flavor. Make the mistake of putting ketchup on his burger, and you'd be eating that burger yourself.

"He can have a grilled cheese. Come on, I'll help with the house. Looks like Dick's Sporting Goods picked a fight with Joann's Fabric in here."

That's when she should have known. Jim was a slob. He never cared a whit about the muddy clumps of grass he tracked through the house; never "saw" the quilting squares and wet bathing suits and board game pieces that littered the floor, the tangled yarn and dirty golf tees on the coffee table, or the half-done homework and uncapped pens scattered on the couch. He just blithely dodged it all and kept going.

But Kesia was coming, so for once he picked up.

THE DOORBELL RANG while Jim was out getting the Thai food.

"Sorry I'm a few minutes early," Kesia said in a soft southern lilt. She wore a sleeveless pink button-down blouse and tan pants. She was tall—as tall as Jim—with remarkably toned upper arms and big brown eyes.

And she was a full twenty minutes early. Helen would later wonder if that was on purpose, in order to see the family (or more likely Helen) as they were before they were ready for company.

"No worries at all," Helen said warmly. "I was just blowtorching the last of the hardened jelly off the doorknobs."

Kesia's face went a little flat, and Helen thought she didn't get the joke. Later Helen would understand that Kesia hadn't wanted to like her, and the jelly thing was funny and self-effacing and kind of cute in the way that you really hoped the wife of the man you were in love with couldn't pull off.

It was May of 2010 and twenty-four-year-old Barb was once again in between living arrangements that had gone awry for one reason or another. Sam, age eighteen, was heading off to college in the fall and quietly perseverating to an alarming degree about whether he should major in biology and go to veterinary school or history and become an antiquities professor (because who didn't love a good Greek myth?). At thirteen, Danny was at the height of his back-talking, risk-taking, principal's-office phase before hitting puberty when he often didn't utter a word for days.

Kesia had brought gifts to this skittish and/or surly crowd: a funky, multihued, gauzy scarf for Barb, which immediately became her signature accessory; *The Library of Greek Mythology*, a book written in the first century by a guy named Apollodorus for Sam, who leafed through it for the entirety of dinner while trying to keep melted cheese from dripping onto it; and a minitrampoline for Danny, who missed dinner altogether after setting it up under his basketball hoop so he could dunk. They occasionally heard a thump and an "Ow!" from the driveway, which turned out to be his head hitting the rim, but this was the price you paid for suddenly being able to slam a basketball into a net at five feet, three inches tall.

Kesia did not bring the more traditional hostess gift for Helen. She didn't bring anything for Helen. Helen didn't care. She wasn't the type to really enjoy yet another pretty dish towel or teak cooking spoon. She didn't even notice. At the time.

Throughout dinner, Kesia asked Sam and Barb about themselves and their activities, charming them—and Helen—with the genuineness of her interest. Occasionally one of them would say something particularly astute or funny or endearing, and Kesia would cast the quickest of glances over at Jim, who beamed with pride in his offspring. Well, he was beaming at something, anyway.

Kesia did not cast these glances at Helen. Nor did she inquire about Helen's work or interests. In fact, when Helen tried to ask Kesia a polite question or two, Kesia ignored it and turned her attention back to the kids. After dinner she went out and admired Danny's new slam dunk skills and got him some Neosporin and a Band-Aid when he gashed his knee on the driveway.

Then Jim said, "I thought I'd take Kesia over to check out the Pinehurst Resort and the village. She's a fan of Olmsted." Legendary landscape architect Frederick Law Olmsted had been hired in the late 1800s to plan the village, which had been recently designated a National Historic Landmark. Helen and Jim always took visitors there for a drive or a stroll. But not usually at night.

Helen was home washing the dishes and breaking up fights. She didn't think too hard about any of this, or the fact that Jim certainly knew a lot about what Kesia Neep was a fan of, and Kesia certainly knew a lot about what his kids were into.

Not until a decade later, when suddenly it was all she could think about.

# Chapter 25

## 2020

Helen had just returned from Hestia, New York, in April of 2020, where she had buried her beloved mother's "scorched" ashes, briefly seen the best friend she'd ever had for the first time in thirty-five years, and anxiously spent a night in a hotel room she had spritzed liberally with an internet-prescribed concoction of water, alcohol, and white vinegar, and subsequently dreamt she was drowning in hard cider. She was not at her best.

Neither was Jim. He looked ghostly pale and said he felt pressure in his chest. "Just a little, barely noticeable." But she knew she had to multiply anything he said by a factor of three.

"Did you take your heart medicine?"

"Yes, I took it, okay? I took it! But it's not working!"

"When did you take it?"

"About ten minutes ago."

"You have to take it consistently! It's not an as-needed thing!"

It did no good to point this out now, obviously. That ship had sailed so long ago, it was probably in Tahiti by now.

"We're going to the emergency room."

"And get Covid?" Jim snorted. "I don't think so."

Helen narrowed her eyes. "You get your ass in the car right now or I'll kill you myself!"

Boy, would she come to regret that one.

On the way, Jim started to press on his chest.

"Is the pain getting worse?" Helen asked.

He didn't answer her, only muttered to himself, "This is not fair."

*Not fair?* she thought. *You didn't do the very thing that was supposed to keep this from happening. How is that "not fair"?* Later she would thank whatever spousal gods were listening that she had not said this out loud, too.

His head was turned toward the window, and he murmured so softly she almost didn't hear it. "I've been a good guy."

At this, her own heart seemed to miss about ten beats. She pulled up in front of the Moore Hospital Emergency Department.

He turned to her then, hand spread like a starfish across his chest. "Promise me, if anything—"

"Jim, it's going to be okay." She wasn't sure about this, but she didn't want him to be any more scared than he already was. Her own fear was now rising like a geyser.

"Promise me you'll tell the kids I love them. And give my clubs to Kesia. Her number's in my contacts." And he got out of the car.

Jim hadn't talked about Kesia Neep in many years, nor had he made any trips to Georgia that Helen knew of, and she booked all his flights. In the surreal swirl of the current crisis, it took a minute for Helen to remember who the woman even was. But apparently Jim still had her number.

A week later, Helen would find that Kesia Neep was not only still in Jim's contacts . . . she was in his favorites.

THE FUNERAL HOME wanted to get Jim in the ground quickly, since he'd been in an emergency room, possibly exposed. There was no real reason to wait, other than tracking down Danny. No one was getting grand sendoffs during a pandemic. Helen notified friends and family via the family Christmas card list. She was the bookkeeper for his consulting business, so she sent a delicately worded notice to his clients. The kids posted beautiful, heart-breaking pictures of him on their social media accounts. (Helen herself had never been interested in social media. It seemed like a lot of work just to keep up with people's dinner plates and flower deliveries and toes on beaches.)

It was a wretched and sorrow-filled week. Helen focused on comforting her distraught children. "It was the last thing he said," she repeated over and over. "'Tell the kids I love them.'" That thing about the golf clubs was just too strange to contemplate, much less repeat.

Eventually Barb and Cormac went back to Massachusetts, and Sam went back to Seattle. Danny and his new tattoo went off to heal in the great wide wherever. Helen was left to figure out what to do with all that Jim had left behind.

Including her.

THE HOSPITAL HAD given Helen a bag of Jim's clothes and belong-ings, which she'd immediately tossed in his closet and actively avoided, even when she'd occasionally heard the phone buzz. It was too much to look at, these things that had been on his body when he'd taken his last breath, surrounded by strangers, no doubt terrified. He was always such an upbeat, can-do, all-is-well kind of guy. But that's not how he went out. Helen hated to think of it. *Unfair* suddenly seemed the perfect description.

The house was quiet now that the kids were gone, and in a weird way, everything had almost gone back to normal. It was as if Jim were just on a long business trip. His phone battery died eventually. The person she really missed was her mother.

People kept saying it was a blessing that Annabella had died before she got Covid, that it would have been such a terrible way to go. At least she died at home with people around her.

*It's not a blessing!* Helen always felt like screaming when these well-intentioned yet dense comments were made. *I needed her. She would have helped me with all this. She would have cooked and made sure my bills were paid and told me to toughen up when I wallowed, and I would have gotten through it. Now I'm just stuck!*

Jim's Jeep Grand Cherokee was still in the garage, of course, and every time Helen passed it on her way to her own RAV4, her eye would catch the glint off his meticulously polished golf club heads.

The clubs, a set of expensive, highly curated TaylorMades and Titleists and Callaways, lived in the back of the Jeep. "In case you're out picking up the dry cleaning and someone suddenly asks you to play a round," Helen would tease him. "Always be prepared," he'd say. He'd been a Boy Scout, though he'd quit before he'd made Eagle, busy as he was with the high school golf team.

When Jim traveled for work, those clubs were by his side. He would rather have left his laptop or entire suitcase at home. "I can pick up clothes and toiletries, I can work from my phone." The clubs were critical, though. He felt borrowing a set from whatever course he was working with would show him up as a hack. They were, in fact, his most prized possessions and constant companions.

*"Give my clubs to Kesia"? What the actual fuck was that about?*

WHATEVER. IT CERTAINLY didn't matter now, though Danny might have something to say about it someday. It was Jim's final request—Helen had to honor it. He'd been honorable to her in some very life-altering ways. The least she could do was track down old Kesia Neep. Helen guessed it was some sort of bet they'd made long ago, and he was making good.

She tugged the hospital bag out of his closet and charged the phone. As soon as she powered it up, a string of buzzes erupted and went on for so long it seemed like the phone itself might be angry with her for failing to release it from solitary confinement sooner.

He didn't have a security code. Unlike for Helen, numbers were a foreign language in which Jim had been only casually fluent. He would set up a code for himself and immediately forget it, calling from an airport or car rental agency, flipping out because he couldn't access important information.

"I thought you used Barb's birthday," she'd remind him.

"Oh. Was she born on the sixth or the seventh?"

"The twelfth."

Now Helen scrolled through a torrent of text messages, older ones from friends or clients who hadn't yet gotten word of his passing. Most were from someone whose only identifier was *Quiche*.

Jim loved quiche. If there was quiche on the menu, that's what he ordered.

The text messages ran from *Hey where are you? Locked out of your phone again?* to *Did I do something wrong? Pls just tell me.* To *Jim what is happening? Ur scaring me.*

Helen clicked on Quiche's contact. It was the nickname for Kesia Neep. From the call history it was clear that they talked or texted late at night. Every single night. She was in his favorites along with his family, for godsake!

Helen froze. An affair? Jim?

She slumped onto the bed, mind spinning to put pieces together, remember any clues that had gone unnoticed—remnant perfume in his laundry, unaccountable business trips, coolness toward her.

Nope. Nothing. Helen managed so much of his coming and going (and laundry—God knew Jim could barely get his clothes into the hamper), and there had been nothing out of the ordinary or that lacked explanation. Jim was as Jim had always been. Even in bed.

They had never, even in their dating days, had the frenzied kind of lovemaking that you saw in movies. They didn't sigh and coo I-love-yous afterward. It was reasonably reliable, mutually satisfying, and it got the job done. Like most couples, frequency had fallen off when the kids were little. Come to think of it, it hadn't really picked back up again since. She'd read the occasional magazine article about renewed passion after children got older, but, well, Jim was gone a lot. And when he was home, they didn't always get around to it.

But it wasn't like her husband was actively avoiding her in the bedroom. And he was affectionate with her, always giving a hug or a kiss on the cheek when he came or went, a shoulder squeeze as he went by. He did that with the kids, too, though.

*Jesus*, thought Helen. It was like wearing smudged glasses for years and finally wiping them clean.

She dropped the phone on the carpet and flopped back on the bed, legs dangling off into air. She stared up at the ceiling and thought for the first time—but not for the last; in fact, it would become a familiar refrain—*How the hell did I get here?*

She was furious with Jim!

She tried that on, and it didn't really track.

*Get mad, for godsake!* she told herself. *Your husband cheated on you! You've been—* What was that word again? It was kind of funny sounding, and no one used it anymore . . . *Cuckolded!*

She wondered for a brief moment about the word's origin and decided to look it up later.

*Am I mad?* Yes, she was mad. She'd certainly never cheated on *him.* In fact, any outside observer would say she'd been a damned good wife, supporting his work and interests, running a well-functioning home, never asking too much.

That last one. That was the cornerstone. And its quarry of origin was Paddow Mountain.

If Helen hadn't slept with Cal and been a willing accomplice (*very* willing) to his cheating, she would never had gotten chlamydia, nor thought she was infertile, and her birth control efforts would have been flawless. She would never have gotten pregnant and married Jim. In fact, she probably wouldn't have dated him for very long. He didn't want kids. That alone would have nipped things in the bud.

But she had slept with Cal—in fact, she'd instigated it and urged things along.

*I want it to be you.*

Cheating had gotten her into this mess in the first place—the "mess" being the vast majority of her life. And Jim's. Not asking too much seemed the least she could do. How much right did she have to be self-righteous? She had been the Kesia in that scenario; she was the Wendy now. And both roles sucked.

Jim's phone buzzed. Helen leaned off the bed and picked it up off the carpet.

*Jim, please.* The text was from Quiche.

*Poor thing,* Helen thought instinctively.

"Are you crazy?!" she castigated herself out loud. "She's your husband's mistress!"

*Still. Just get it over with.*

Helen hit the call button on the text.

Quiche answered before the end of the first ring. "Oh, thank God! You had me so worried!"

"This isn't Jim. It's Helen."

Silence. But she was there. Helen could hear her breathing.

"I'm very sorry to tell you this, but Jim had a massive heart attack nine days ago. He didn't make it."

"What?"

Helen understood that one syllable so well. *It can't be true, please tell me it's not true, my mind won't make it true.*

"He died."

A howl erupted on the phone. The primal agonizing wail of a heart imploding.

Then the line went dead.

THAT NIGHT AT eleven o'clock on the dot—Helen later figured out that's when they talked. She was always in bed by then and she was a deep sleeper—Jim's phone buzzed. It was on the floor on his side of the bed where she'd dropped it that afternoon.

Tonight she wasn't out like a light, as she usually was. She was all stirred up thinking about the secret life Jim had led. And wishing, in the dark privacy of her own thoughts, that she had a secret life, too.

She knew who it was even before she looked at the caller ID. If she were that achingly in love with someone, she would need to process his death somehow. With anyone—even his wife.

"Hello," she said.

"It's Kesia." Her soft southern lilt had gone even softer. "It's" came out as "Iz."

"Yes, I know."

"Oh, you know, do you? You *know*. Well, lemme tell you something. You don't know *anything*." The words leaked into one another like wet paint colors.

*My God, she's drunk!* thought Helen.

"You think you know 'bout me?"

"I'm pretty sure I don't know anything about you, Kesia. I only met you once about ten years ago."

"That's right, you don't. And you don't know Jim, either."

"Um, not so sure about that."

"You *don't*! He's a *good man*! He's the best man there is! And you don't 'preciate that. You don't have any idea how good he is to you!"

*Well, he cheated on me for over a decade, but sure, he's awesome*, thought Helen, rolling her eyes. This woman had some nerve. "All right, why don't you educate me."

"He was loyal! He was so loyal to you and those kids! That's why he flew me up there that time—to see his family. Put faces on the people he was true to."

Helen looked at the phone for a minute then put it back to her ear. "You're telling me you and Jim weren't having an affair all this time? Because that is pretty hard to be—"

"NO WE WERE NOT! I am a Christian and a moral person. How dare you accuse me of such a thing?!"

"Uh, okay, but I saw the call records. You talked every night. You're telling me you two weren't—"

"Yes, of *course* we were."

This was getting confusing, but then talking to someone who was bombed often was. "Having an affair?"

"IN LOVE!" bellowed Kesia.

Oh. That.

"And we never, ever . . ." She started to cry. "We talked about it. I'm against divorce, generally, but I was just so desperate to be free to . . . And he was, too. But he never even took a mulligan on the golf course. *Never. Not once.* And he said he wasn't going to start now with his marriage." Kesia started to weep. "Jim," she keened. "*Jim . . .*"

Helen hung up.

Honestly, she wasn't sure which was worse: Jim having a normal extramarital affair, or Jim nurturing a deeply emotional bond for years while denying himself any physical consummation.

*The latter,* she thought. The latter was way worse for everyone, even Helen. She knows that if he had come to her and said, *I'm in love with someone else, and I haven't done anything about it, but I'd like to be free to do so,* she would've given him an amicable divorce. He had done his part: he had been a good father and an adequate husband.

He could have had one mulligan in his life. It would have been fair.

# Chapter 26

**2021**

"Did you ever send her the clubs?" asks Cal.

"I texted her the next day for her address. She had them within a week."

They're sitting on opposite ends of the couch in the living room now, and it's almost lunchtime. At eleven, Helen toasted some of Cormac's famous muffins she keeps on hand in the freezer and made another pot of coffee. The knees of Cal's jeans slowly dry as she talks, leaving two rings where they'd pressed into the wet leaves at Jansen Woods.

Helen doesn't tell him every detail (certainly nothing about her tepid sex life), but she gives a fairly thorough accounting of the Jim and Kesia story. It feels good to unburden herself. She's never told anyone any of this. Cal is a good listener, offering little nods or expressions of surprise, prompting with a question here or there. But mostly he just lets her talk.

"That is one hell of a story."

"It's still hard for me to believe. My husband was madly in love with another woman, and I was absolutely clueless. I mean, what planet was I on?"

"Planet Helen."

"I'm so self-involved that I'm incapable of noticing my own husband's emotional state?"

"Well, we're all pretty self-involved. Also . . ."

"What."

"No, I don't mean to . . ."

"Just say it."

"You weren't in love with him."

"You have to be in love to pay attention to someone?"

He laughs. "Helen . . ."

She rolls her eyes in self-annoyance. "Fine. We were in a massive matrimonial rut, and to me it just looked like Jim, doing his Jim stuff, as my mother would say."

"Also, you weren't really that jealous when you found out. You were kinda mad, but you weren't fit to be tied. I was out of my—"

He stops short.

Helen waits. She gives him an *Is there more?* eyebrow raise.

He shakes his head.

Oh, there's more. Clearly there's more. But he doesn't want to talk about it. He stretches his arms out in front of him.

Helen gets up and takes the muffin plates back to the kitchen. Cal follows with the coffee mugs and stands there as she rinses things and loads the dishwasher.

"I want to tell you something," he says.

She wipes her hands on a dish towel and turns to him.

"You were an amazing friend to me back in tenth grade. I was in kind of a shitty place, disconnected from my family and feeling very . . . unknown."

She remembers that boy, gawky and slightly miserable, trying desperately to find a patch of blue sky in the downpour of adolescence.

"You took me as I was," he goes on. "You didn't feel sorry for me, or think I was weird. You listened and laughed at my jokes and gave me the occasional much-needed pants kick."

Helen smiles. "Actually I did think you were weird."

He laughs. "I'm crushed! All this time, I thought you thought I was cool."

"Come on, Cal, neither one of us was cool. We were both pretty dorky."

"Me more than you."

She lets out a chuckle. "I'll grant you that. But you were earnest and sweet and smart. And you were really good company. I, um . . ."

"Yeah?"

She shrugs. "Sometimes I miss that little nerd."

Cal's smile downshifts to something slightly more bittersweet. "I've always wanted to thank you for how kind you were."

Helen gazes back at him. And there he is. Her little nerd. "Thank *you*."

*This is how it ends*, she thinks. It's a surprisingly satisfying epilogue to something that was so painful—and continued to hurt all these years, even though she never let herself admit it. She had relegated him to Cal fucking Crosby, that asshole back then, having no bearing on now. A necessary numbness had settled in, she realizes, and maybe a bit of that emotional anesthesia had leaked into other areas of her life, too. Maybe that's why she never noticed that her husband of thirty-four years had given his heart (if not his body) to someone else.

Appreciating the kindness—it's the perfect ending. She's ready to say goodbye and wish him well.

But then he says, "So . . ."

"So?"

"I'm wondering if we can be friends again."

# *Chapter 27*

*2021*

W ondering,' like not sure if it's possible?" Francie asks later. "No, wondering like hoping."

AFTER CAL LEFT on Saturday, Helen went back to bed. She was exhausted. Beyond exhausted. She remembered feeling similarly wiped out after childbirth. Kid's fine, count his fingers and toes, nurse him, kiss him, and hand him off to Jim. Then sleep so deep the hospital could evacuate for a five-alarm fire and they'd have to wheel her out still snoring on a gurney.

She woke feeling refreshed, lighter. She woke smiling. She called Francie.

"Hello?" said Francie.

"The spirit of Annabella Iannucci lives!"

Francie let out a triumphant yelp. But she did not want to hear anything about it, not over the phone. "I have to see your face when you tell me!" she said.

"We could Zoom."

Francie groaned. "Fucking Zoom. It's like a trigger word these days. I'm getting a facial tic just thinking about it."

"Then we'll just have to get together."

SIX DAYS LATER, it's Friday morning and Helen takes Francie to meet Barb and Lana. The two artists quickly spin off into a conversation about authenticity and derivativeness that Helen can barely follow. She doesn't care. She loves watching two of her favorite women connect so quickly.

"She is so cool!" Barb whispers to Helen as they're leaving. "Are you sure she's your friend?"

Helen bats her on the arm and murmurs, "Meanie. Don't worry, I'll share."

Then they swing by the bakery to meet Cormac and pick up sandwiches. Cormac is his usual self-effacing yet gregarious self, and says things like, "Helen's the mad scientist of the operation. I'm just Frankenstein." Helen feels so proud to show off her old friend and her family and her work. It's the first time in a long time that everything in her life feels just right.

They take the sandwiches back to Helen's so she can tell Francie everything without interruptions. Lunch is long gone; Francie is now stretched out on the couch, and Helen is sitting on the floor, occasionally throwing logs on the fire she's built.

"So, 'friends' with Cal," says Francie. "That's a little complicated, isn't it?"

"Not really. Not so far."

"What do you mean, 'so far'?"

"We got together at a playground with the grandkids for about an hour yesterday. Logan's in preschool, but there were no openings on Thursdays, so Cal's got them both."

"He's basically a stay-at-home grandpa with the baby?"

"Yeah, I get the impression he's trying to make up for lost time. He's dropped a few offhanded comments about Janel not liking him and getting back in her good graces."

"How was it?"

"Nice."

"'Nice'? I come all the way down here, and you give me '*Nice*'?"

Helen laughs. "Okay, how about weirdly easy. I'm not going to say it was like picking up where we left off in tenth grade, but . . . I don't know. He's still that kid in some ways. I mean, he's Match. That's still him."

"You call him that?"

"Oh, God, no! That would be so—"

"Good. You can't start getting cute like that."

"Absolutely not."

"Married people do not have cute pet names for nonspouse adults unless they're—"

Helen gives her a look. In the course of recounting her Saturday morning with Cal, she told Francie about Jim and Kesia—aka Quiche. The subject no longer seems to require the code word security clearance it once did.

"Shit," says Francie. "I forgot."

Helen shrugs it off.

"No, seriously, Hellie, I have a lot more respect for Jim now that I know the whole story. A *lot* more."

"Turns out you were a little bit right, though."

"Yeah, okay, but being a little bit right is a dangerous thing if it makes you think you know more than you do. I really wasn't seeing the big picture when you came to me that day."

Helen sighs. It's so good to have her friend back!

"What did you talk about during your grandparent playdate?" asks Francie.

"You, mainly."

"Me?"

"You and Ricky. I had told him about the whole . . . thing that happened after college, and he wanted to know what it was like seeing you again. He was sad to hear about Ricky. Said he always liked him. 'He used to call me Archie,' he said."

"I forgot about that! You were sure he would hate it."

"Apparently he liked it. Boys are so weird." Helen puts a hand on Francie's knee. "He wanted me to tell you he's happy for you about the farm, and sorry about Ricky and that he had a good heart."

Francie smiles and her eyes get a little shiny. "Very sweet." Helen thinks about good hearts and how sometimes they're hidden. Francie located Ricky's and never lost sight of it.

"Soooooooo," Francie says, "sounds like you two are really patching it up."

"I mean, sort of. It's just the occasional playdate." Helen hears the defensiveness in her voice. *It's no big thing,* she wants to say. *There's no danger here.*

"What does Cal's wife think about it?"

"I don't really know."

"Do you want to know?"

"Isn't that their business? And if I bring it up, doesn't it imply that I think there's something going on that a wife might object to?"

"I'm just asking if you want to know," says Francie. "I'm not making any recommendations at the moment."

Helen shrugs. "I guess I'd like to know that she's okay with it."

"Yeah, but would you like to know if she's *not*?" Francie sits up and swings her feet down to the floor. "See, this is what I mean by complicated."

Helen thinks for a moment. She's not Kesia Neep, having a chaste but still very intense and intimate relationship with someone else's husband. Not by a long shot. But still . . . "I'd want to know either way. If his wife is bothered by us being friends again, I don't want to be a part of that. It's just bad . . ."

"Karma."

"I was going to say *juju*, but yeah."

"Tomato, tomahto."

"Potato, potahto."

"If you call the whole thing off, how will you feel?"

Helen pokes at the fire. A log shifts and glowing red embers fly out onto the slate hearth. She flicks them back in with the poker. "I guess I'll feel sad."

"Because . . ."

"I don't really have any friends here. First it was the pandemic, and then I was so busy with the bakery and the new baby. I got kind of dug into my own little world. My default has never really been set to friend-making. Sometimes I think I have a short somewhere in my relationship circuit."

"Don't get fancy. You're just an introvert."

"Well, whatever I am, it doesn't mean I don't want people in my life. It's really nice to have someone in town to hang out with. And it's not like making a new friend. There's all this stuff I don't have to tell him or explain about who I am. He knows me."

Francie frowns. "You definitely have to ask him."

"Yeah?"

"Absolutely. Because if she's not cool with it, you have to get out now before you're any more attached." She gives a pointed look. "And for godsake, override that default and make some damn girlfriends, would you?"

HELEN GOES TO bed that night practically giggling. She can't stop thinking about how lucky she is. How in her whole adult life she has never felt this . . . right. Unburdened from the past. Enjoying the present. Excited about the future. She has Francie back!

Cormac and Helen have been toying with the idea of opening a second site—it's just in the wouldn't-that-be-something phase, but if the numbers keep going in the right direction, it could happen. Danny's coming home for Thanksgiving! She hasn't seen him in the year and a half since Jim's funeral, and she has that motherly ache to just . . . get her hands on him. Hug him and pat his face and maybe cut his hair if he wants a trim. (Danny is famously opposed to barbershops and hair salons. He had a man bun way before they were popular, and he was a little pissed off to find himself suddenly in fashion.)

A new family moved in down the street. Helen waves occasionally as she runs by. The wife spends a lot of time in the garden doing battle with the weed-clogged beds. The kids are high school or college-ish, Helen guesses. Their mom is younger than Helen, but in striking distance of friend potential. Helen decides to bring them a dozen fresh muffins from the bakery this weekend and introduce herself.

And Cal. My God, Helen thinks in wonder, didn't she just scream her bloody brains out at him! And he took it—even wanted it in some strange way. They both got exactly what they'd needed for forty long years, and now they're friends again.

*Everything's perfect.*

# *Chapter 28*

## *2021*

On Saturday, after her run, Helen showers and puts on her cleanest jeans and her least pilly sweater. She hasn't dressed to meet new people in a long time, and the state of her wardrobe—to which she has paid zero attention since March 2020—is concerning. But cleaning out her closet and replacing the stuff that's past due for textile recycling is a job for another day. Today she's got some muffins to deliver.

Helen swings by Cormac's Confectionery and picks out her favorites: pistachio with the little nut on top, banana almond with the sprinkle of brown sugar on the crust, and lemon bomb, which tastes like lemonade in cake form. She also grabs a couple of standard-issue blueberry and plain old chocolate chip muffins in case the new neighbor kids are picky, and some gluten-free cinnamon walnut, too. Half the world is gluten sensitive these days, and Cormac is nothing if not conscientious about his customers' dietary needs.

When Helen arrives with her basket of goodies, the wife is at her usual post, sitting on a little stool, digging in the overgrown garden, her back to the street. Her shiny black hair is pulled into a high ponytail, and Helen can see earbuds in her ears. As Helen nears, she realizes the woman's back and shoulders are shifting back and forth. She's chair dancing! Helen smiles.

"Hello," she says, but the woman doesn't respond. "Hi there!" she calls a little louder.

The woman startles and a shovelful of dirt goes flying into the air, landing in little clods around the woman's hair and shoulders. She turns quickly to see what's snuck up on her, wiping her eyes with the backs of her gardening gloves and spitting.

"Oh, no!" Helen says. "Are you okay?"

"No, it's—" The woman tries to blow a few last pieces of dirt from her mouth as delicately as possible, making a *thooo, thooo* sound. "I did not hear you—" Now she's fumbling to pull off her gloves and hit the pause button on her phone. "Sorry . . . sorry . . ."

"No, I'm sorry for scaring you. I should have come around so you could see me first."

"Not your fault," says the woman, raking dirt from her thick black ponytail. "I am in my own world out here." She has light brown skin and enormous brown eyes.

"It's a lovely world," says Helen pleasantly, though in truth, there are piles of weeds and swaths of naked earth and a few decrepit-looking plants that seem like they haven't been pruned in years. "I'm Helen Spencer from number two down the street. I know I'm late to welcome you to the neighborhood, but I thought I'd bring you some muffins . . ." She attempts to hand over the basket, but the woman is brushing her hands on her pants and the belly of her shirt, and Helen thinks better of it. "I'll just put it on your front step."

"I'm Prisha O'Connell. Very nice to meet you, Helen. You are very kind to bring us treats!" She smiles warmly but Helen can tell she's uncomfortable at having been caught in such an unkempt state. She keeps running her fingers back against the tendrils of hair that have come loose around her ears.

They chat for a moment, exchanging basic information. Prisha has two teenage children and a husband. They lived on Long Island in her husband's hometown before moving to Belham for his new job in Boston. The delicacy with which Prisha describes the increased distance from his parents leads Helen to suspect that Prisha doesn't mind that one bit.

They end with vague intentions to get together for coffee sometime, but Helen suspects they'll just return to waving as they pass. At least she can report to Francie that she tried to make a friend.

ARE YOU VOTING? Cal texts on Tuesday. Helen's glad he isn't the kind of middle-aged adult who uses *R* and *U*. It always feels juvenile to her. How hard is it to text *Are you*, anyway?

*Yes I'm civically dutiful.*

*I figured.* And then: *For who?*

*You want a list?*

*Look I vote for pres, congress, and state. I don't know town pols.*

*Suddenly interested?*

*Trying to be a good community doobie.*

*Janel*, texts Helen.

*Bingo.*

*Where's her list?*

*Told me I should do the research myself and make up my own mind.* He adds, *Brat.*

*I'm your research then.*

Smiley face emoji.

Helen's "research" consisted of asking Cormac. He grew up in Belham, so he personally knows half the people who run. The other half he serves coffee and crullers. He knows who's reasonable—and more importantly who's not: Joe Mikus who's running for Conservation Commission, against whom he's brought four suits (and counting) for trying to protect the wetlands that border his property; Clarise Delacroix who's running for Select Board because she wants to cut taxes by 50 percent *just cuz* (Cormac's words); and kookie Marty Spannox who'll run for anything because he likes to pull stunts at candidates' night, such as reciting derogatory haikus about his opponents.

*Hey want to meet me at town building?* texts Cal.

*Sure just slip me your ballot and I'll fill it in for you.*

*That's a joke right?*

Smiley face emoji.

NOVEMBER CAME IN so cold yesterday it seems like glaciers might appear on the horizon at any moment. Helen bundles Lana up to her eyes and drives over to the town building, a big brick affair with Grecian columns that seem like overreach in a quiet little New England town. It was the old Belham High School until they built a sprawling new campus about a mile away.

Cal's Honda Pilot is running in the parking lot, exhaust freezing in the icy sunlight. Helen pulls up next to him, and they extract the kids from their safety apparatus. Cal totes McKenzie in her car seat, Helen balances Lana on her hip, and they make their way toward the gym to vote.

Helen hands Cal a hastily written list of candidates.

"I feel like we're cheating before an Am Lit test," he says.

"Old Mrs. Gilcrest is in there now, waiting to haul us off to the principal's office."

"Geez, remember her?" Cal holds the door open, and they step into a blast of warmth. "She had that warbly voice."

"Ricky was in my section. Her voice got a whole lot more warbly when he clumped in with his big black boots and that sneer on his face." They join the line waiting to be checked in.

"Poor guy."

"Poor guy?" says Helen. "He scared the bejesus out of her!"

"Yeah, but you could tell he was working that bad-to-the-bone angle a little too hard."

Helen looks up at Cal. "I wish I'd understood him like you did. I never really got him."

"Well, he was hard on you."

"Me specifically?"

"Yeah," says Cal. He leans over to unzip McKenzie's snowsuit and pull off her hat. "We had words once or twice."

"About me."

He chuckles. "Yeah, about you. Who else are we talking about?"

"What did he say?"

Cal squints in thought. "I think it was along the lines of you being a tight-ass good girl, and why Francie was so devoted to you he had no idea. He just didn't like sharing her with you."

"And what did you say?"

He laughs and shakes his head.

"Tell me!"

"I don't know, I'm sure it was like 'Helen's awesome and don't talk about her like that,' and maybe I punched him."

Helen's face goes wide with delight. "*Maybe* you punched him?"

"No, I definitely punched him."

She's laughing now. "What did he do?"

"Uh, I believe he decked me."

"You never told me that!"

"Of course I didn't! It was embarrassing."

"Did you get hurt?"

"Nah, the whole thing was pretty half-hearted." He shrugs. "We liked each other. We didn't want to tussle over girls."

Helen's face falls. "You're ruining it."

"How am I doing that?"

"No one's ever fought for my honor before. I'd prefer if it wasn't half-hearted."

"Well, don't feel too bad. If I recall, I was pretty damn whole-hearted about you."

Whoops. Too far. They both look away. The man ahead of them finishes checking in and heads to a voting stall with a big white ballot. Seated behind the table is an elderly woman with ELEANOR on her name tag, who says, "Oh, my, look at that beautiful child!" She squinches her face at Lana and says in a singsong voice, "Are Nana and Papa taking you to do your civic duty?"

That goes right up Helen's spine at the very moment she senses Cal's flinch.

"Nonna," says Lana.

"No-na?" says Eleanor.

"It's Italian for grandmother," says Helen with a smile. "She's correcting you."

The woman laughs. "Well, I stand corrected!"

"I'm Helen Spencer, 2 Barley Spring Lane." She nods at the thick pages of the voter rolls, hoping to end the conversation there.

Eleanor flips to the correct page and checks Helen off with a red felt-tip pen. She turns to Cal. "Are you registered? I only have one name at this address."

"That's because I don't live there," he says patiently. "Calhoun Crosby, 110 Wetherby."

Eleanor is starting to grasp that she may have stepped in it. Luckily, she has no idea how deep. "Certainly," she says, getting back to business.

Helen takes her ballot to one of the little pop-up voting booths and sits Lana on the shelf, bracing the child from falling with her own body. She fills in the circles next to the names Cormac suggested and looks over to see if Cal is done. He's donned a pair of readers and is studying her list, comparing it to the names on the ballot, carefully filling in circles.

Calhoun Crosby. She can hear the howls of *Hoooooon!* in her memory. He doesn't look like a sports star anymore, with his glasses and threads of gray in his hair shining under the fluorescent glare. But he's still reasonably fit. And handsome.

He looks up, finds her gazing at him, and smiles.

As THEY WALK back out to the parking lot Cal says, "Want to come over for lunch? I've got a nice big piece of salmon in the fridge from last night's dinner, and I can whip up some salads."

*No!* thinks Helen. *Wait, salmon?* She loves cold salmon in her salad. But what if Suze is there? *Absolutely not.* Then again, she's curious about this big house . . .

"No worries if you have to get back," he says quickly. "Or if you don't have a bottle. I mean, we have formula if you need it. Or milk. And baby food. But it's fine if—"

"I'd love to," Helen says, saving Cal from his mounting embarrassment. Besides, is there any reason she shouldn't?

She follows him north on Route 47, and they turn down Wetherby, a road so narrow and winding you can practically see the settlers who made the first tracks with their wooden carts. He puts on a blinker and turns down a driveway that passes through a stand of pines to a flat open yard. The house is a Tudor with a brick first floor, white stucco and brown vertical stripes of timber on the second. There's a big bay window and four gable windows above. The landscaping is tidy but unimaginative.

One of the garage doors goes up, and Cal drives in. Helen pulls up and peers in to see if there is a car on the other side; the bay is empty, and she releases a little sigh of relief. She wants to meet Suze, she tells herself—why wouldn't she? Her friend's spouse—but maybe not today.

By the time Helen unbuckles Lana from her car seat and tugs out the diaper bag, Cal is opening the front door for her.

The house is beautifully decorated, and Helen thinks some of the art must be expensive. There's a print in the hallway of a woman done in blue shades, and she does not look happy. In fact, she looks terrified. Helen gets the sense that domestic violence is somehow more personal than just a good cause to support. She stops to study it a little more closely.

"Not my favorite," Cal says. "Suze bought it at a fundraiser. She says it keeps her focused. I never met her father—he keeled over when she was a teenager—but apparently he was a real bastard. Got physical with her mother sometimes."

"What a thing to witness. I'm surprised it didn't make her wary of relationships."

"Oh, it did. In fact, she purposely provoked me once when we were dating."

"Provoked you? How?"

"She picked a fight with me about something, I can't even remember what, and kept escalating until she called me a moron who was bad in bed. It was so unlike her; I should've known something was up. But you know, bad in bed. That's a bullet at point-blank range for a guy. I could barely see straight, much less analyze her motivations."

"What did you do?"

"I walked away. I believe I got very drunk that night—still a little sketchy on those particular details—and she called me in the morning to tell me I'd passed the test."

"You didn't resent what she'd put you through?"

He chuckles. "Well, she had some 'splainin' to do. But the makeup was pretty great. And you know, I'm twice her size. She had to be sure. I understood that. Part of why she married me was to keep her safe."

As they continue on to the kitchen, a picture of this union is coming into focus for Helen. Clearly there's love, but like most people, each also had an agenda. It makes sense why they fit.

The kitchen is done in a dark cherry, and there are a lot of expensive appliances lining the yards of black granite countertop. A huge KitchenAid stand mixer, an espresso maker that's not as big as those at Cormac's Confectionery, but close. A food processor with so many attachments it looks like it could fold your laundry while it chops your carrots.

"Someone loves to cook," says Helen.

"Yeah, not as much as you'd think. We just like shiny stuff." He makes a little face that indicates that *we* is a term that doesn't really include him.

There's a heaviness to the room with its dark decor and many pounds of machinery. Cal leads them to a little kitchen nook with white painted seats built into the walls and a light maple tabletop. Sunny windows look out to raised beds on the side of the house.

"This is my favorite spot," he says. "I can watch my vegetables come up."

"You're a gardener!"

"I am now. It's a good activity with Logan. He appreciates the magic of it."

McKenzie is snuggled in the crook of his arm, and Helen has Lana on her hip. They look out the window at the straw-covered beds, tucked in for the winter. It's strangely calming. Helen feels like she could stand there for a long time and not be bored or unhappy in any way.

Lana's small hand finds its way to Helen's face. "Nonna," she says in her soft voice.

"She's hungry," says Helen.

"You got that from 'Nonna'?"

"She only has three words: *Nonna*, *Mama*, and *Dada*. But she makes excellent use of them."

Cal gazes down at Lana. "Smart girl, learning the names first," he tells her. "Janel's was 'hi' and Bonnie's was 'book.' That tells you a lot about them."

"A communicator and a scholar."

Cal smiles. "Yours was probably *go*."

"Yours was probably *crank up the tunes, daddio*."

McKenzie lets out a squawk, Lana's hand comes up to Helen's face again, and it's time to feed the hungry. Helen situates Lana in Logan's booster seat, adjusting the straps to her fourteen-month-old body, and spreads some Cheerios on the table. Cal heats up a bottle for six-month-old McKenzie and Helen holds her while she slurps at it. On Helen's suggestion, Cal makes a peanut butter and jelly sandwich, which he pulls into small pieces for Lana, and fills a sippy cup with milk. Then he sets about making their salads.

"Tell me about Janel," says Helen.

"What do you want to know?"

"Whatever you feel like telling me."

He glances over from portioning spinach into two bowls. "You want to know why she's mad at me."

"Well, yes, but you don't have to start with that. You could start small. Like . . . I don't know . . ."

"Yeah, you can't even think of anything."

"All right, why's she mad at you?"

"Because I was never home."

"So she's been pissed off at you her whole life."

"Oh, no, not at all. She adored me until a couple of years ago when Logan was born. That's when she started picking fights with her husband because it set off her daddy issues."

"Daddy issues?"

"Yeah, you know."

"Not really." Helen can tell it pains him to go into it, but also, in some small way there's a desire to confess. She wonders if he's talked to any of his friends about this thing with Janel. She also wonders who his friends are.

"Just . . . abandonment. I chose work over being with her. Which I didn't really mean to—you know, I love my kids, and I love being with them. But the work thing was always so . . ."

"Urgent." Jim was like that. Work was something he *had* to do.

"Yeah, I guess, although in retrospect what's more urgent than your kids' well-being. Apparently she thought marrying a guy whose job kept him local was the solution, but when Eli became the daddy, it all got stirred up again."

"So therapy."

Cal laughs. "Barrels of it."

"It's good she figured it out, at least."

"And stopped taking it out on Eli," he adds.

"And aimed her anger at the true culprit?"

Cal sighs. "Guilty."

"Okay, you made some mistakes." Helen wipes a dribble on McKenzie's chin. "You didn't beat her."

"No, but apparently I abandoned her."

Helen considers this. Did her children ever feel abandoned by Jim? Danny was always the one who took it hardest when Jim was gone, but she wonders if Barb and Sam have residual feelings about it, too. Hard to do anything about it now—they can't confront him, and he can't try to make it up to them. She also thinks about how Cal is so open to discussing his failures. Jim would've been hard-pressed even to understand the concept of abandonment, much less cop to it.

"How's her marriage now?" asks Helen.

"Very solid. Eli's a great guy—a do-gooder like her. He works at St. Francis House shelter downtown."

"Wow, impressive. So they got through it?"

"Yep. They're very connected."

"Jim and I weren't terribly connected, and I always felt like I let the kids down by not showing them what a couple in love looks like."

"How do I let thee down, let me count the ways," he murmurs as he slices cucumber into the bowls.

"Hey, the Virgin Mary was perfect, and her kid couldn't stay out of trouble."

Cal laughs. "She was a tiger mom." He wags a finger. *"Jesus, stop playing video games and turn that water into wine!"*

He brings the salads, each topped with a lovely pink piece of salmon, over to the table, then goes back for dressing, napkins, and forks. McKenzie's no longer drinking, just chewing on the nipple, so Helen tips her up to burp her.

"Here, I can do that," says Cal.

"I've got her. You start."

"Nonna." Lana holds out a piece of sandwich in her little fingers.

"Thank you, lovey!" says Helen and lets Lana tuck it in her mouth.

"See, she knows you're hungry," says Cal. "Even a baby is a better host than I am."

"Cal," she says. "I'll let you know if I'm not getting what I need. I promise."

# Chapter 29

## 2021

The girls should be sleepy after lunch, but they both seem wide awake.

"Kenzie's an eye rubber," says Cal. "I wait for that before I try to put her down."

"Barb says Lana went down early last night and slept late this morning."

When Lana doesn't nap, Helen often feels a little annoyed. By one or two in the afternoon, she's ready for a break to check email and get a bit of work done. But today she's grateful for the excuse to stay. Childcare can be lonely. She never realized how lonely until she had a friend to share it with.

They take the girls into the family room off the kitchen, with its plush carpet and a wall of cabinets that hide the television and toy bins. Cal takes out one with baby toys and spreads them on the floor. Lana's eyes light up as she crawls around exploring new treasures. McKenzie chews on a rubber rattle, sitting on Cal's lap, his back against one of the pale green slip-covered couches, long legs stretched out in front of him.

"When you told me about Night Cap folding," says Helen, "you said there were some 'good lessons.' Janel and her feelings about you were one of those lessons?"

"Well, you know, nobody around here was particularly happy with me, and I had to face that. But Bonnie and Suze are . . . They just have this self-contained quality. Like, okay, Dad's gone a lot. That's how it is. Plan accordingly. Janel's more . . ."

"Permeable."

Cal snorts in agreement. "Jesus, that's the word for it. Things permeate. They get to her."

"Speaking as someone who's starting to realize things should have gotten to me a lot more than they did, it's not the worst way to be."

"Yeah, but it hurts her sometimes. And it hurts to be the source of that hurt."

"So what did you do?"

"I didn't look for another job, which was like having an itch I couldn't scratch. I mean, not work? It was like trying not to breathe. But I was trapped here with her and her daddy issues, and I couldn't not see it. I was the daddy. I had to step up and try to fix it."

"Did she let you?"

He chuckles. "She told me to shove off so many times and in so many ways, I was practically expecting her to branch out to foreign languages. Like, *Dad, go jump in* el lago."

"She had to punish you for a while."

"Honestly, I think she was just trying to get through the pandemic like the rest of us, and dealing with her issues with me felt like one thing too many. She was Zooming with a bunch of five-year-olds, and Eli's shelter job isn't exactly Zoom-able so he was gone every day, and Logan—the kid was all over the place and into everything!"

Helen smiles, remembering how Logan played a "trick" on Cal and set this whole reunion in motion. "The pandemic and Dennis the Menace conspired to give you an opening."

"Big enough to drive a truck through! I just started taking him, playing with him, digging up the garden, feeding him, changing him. It was pretty hilarious watching Janel squirm, dying to shut me out, but desperate for help. And then"—he grins widely—"*then* she got pregnant!"

"Jackpot!"

"She was pukey and exhausted, and I swooped in for the save!"

Helen laughs. "Opportunist."

He shrugs. "Hey, that's business. You see a chance to grab market share, you take it."

"Where was Suze through all this?"

His grin decelerates slightly. "Well, you know, she's got this big job now, and she has a life. She helps out, but she can't really commit like I can."

*A life?* Helen's life is full of Lana, and she's never wanted it any other way. She knows not all grandparents want to be boots-on-the-ground like her. Or Cal. But what is this life Suze has?

Helen is about to ask a follow-up when Cal says quietly, almost reverently, "I was Janel's labor coach."

"Hold on. You went from persona non grata to *labor coach*? That's one heck of a comeback."

"She was two weeks early. And fast. I mean it was like three minutes apart from the get-go. Eli didn't realize his phone had died. I finally got through to the shelter, but then his crappy car broke down on the Pike. Suze was away . . ."

"And you were hanging around, ready to increase your market share."

He feigns outrage. "Hey, that's my kid we're talking about."

"What was it like?"

He grins. "Well, to be perfectly honest, at first it was pretty awkward. I was like, 'Do you want me here?' and she was like, 'Do you want to be here?' Let's face it, that's a lot more up close and personal than most fathers and daughters ever want to get. But she was alone and in pain, and I couldn't leave her. So I just said, 'I'm going to stay till you kick me out, okay?'"

"I take it she didn't kick you out. How was it, seeing all that?"

"Amazing. Life altering. Holding my baby's hand while she's having a baby?" He shakes his head in wonder. "Unbeatable."

"Were you there when she and Bonnie were born?"

"Yeah, but it was different. Twins. Suze is tiny, so she ended up with a C-section. It was complicated and stressful . . . I don't know. I couldn't just be there and enjoy it. Of course, being there"—he makes little quote marks with his fingers—"wasn't my strong suit."

Helen gives him a commiserating smile. "It is now, though, boy."

"Honestly, I don't even recognize myself."

Lana crawls over and climbs in Helen's lap. Cal wipes the drool off McKenzie's fist.

"I recognize you," says Helen.

He looks up at her. "I recognize you, too."

It doesn't feel awkward this time to admit that they know each other on some deeper level. That they're starting to get each other again. It's friendship. It feels good.

"Ah, shit!" says Cal, glancing at the wall clock with the numbers that look like different types of pressed leaves. "I'm gonna be late. Damn it."

"For?"

"Pickup."

"Logan?"

"Yeah." He scans the space. "What did I do with that snowsuit?"

"Just give her to me and go."

"No, that's okay." He rises with the baby in one arm. "It's like a half-hour round trip by the time we collect all his art projects and say goodbye to the trucks and blocks and dress-ups."

"Right, and I have so many things to rush off and do."

He looks down at her. "You've got your hands full."

She scooches Lana to one leg and holds out an arm.

"Seriously?"

"Unless you don't trust me."

He snorts a laugh. "I trust you."

She tips her head at him.

He relents, placing the baby in her other arm. "You need the bathroom or anything?"

"Cal, just go."

As Helen listens to the garage door go up and the Pilot accelerate down the driveway, McKenzie jams a fist into her little eye. Lana lays her head against Helen's chest and watches McKenzie rub herself pink.

"Nonna."

"That's a baby. You see the baby?"

"Bay. Be."

Another word! It's all Helen can do not to shriek!

"That's right," she whispers. "Baby."

Lana sighs. "Nonna." She turns her face into Helen's chest. McKenzie gives her eye one last frantic rub and then her little fist slowly descends and drops into her lap. Lana's breathing slows. Two sleeping girls.

Helen suddenly has an urge to laugh. Here she is, fifty-eight years old, in Cal Crosby's house of all places, holding their two granddaughters. What would Francie say?

*Life is some weird shit.* That's what she'd say.

A few minutes later, Helen hears a car pull up.

*That was fast*, she thinks. *Too fast. Probably a delivery truck.*

A door opens.

"Hi!" a woman's voice calls out. "Whose car is in the driveway? Do we have company?"

# Chapter 30

**2021**

Helen holds her breath. She has a strange urge to hide, though this would be tough, pinned as she is by snoring babies.

*You didn't break in, for godsake*, she chides herself. *Calm down.*

"Hello?"

Helen can't respond without waking the girls, so she waits for whoever it is to find her.

*Please, not Suze*, she prays. She's not ready for Suze. And she's damn sure Suze isn't ready for her, a woman from Cal's past suddenly appearing on the floor of the family room with Suze's granddaughter sleeping on her.

"Dad?"

Oh, thank God. Janel she can handle. She thinks.

Janel comes around the corner from the kitchen and stands there looking down at a woman she met once briefly, now piled high with babies, and takes a beat or two to try and make sense of it. She's wearing a big soft blue sweater the color of her eyes, black leggings, and socks with numbers on them. Her strawberry blond hair is down around her shoulders, thick and silky like Cal's used to be. She's a strikingly beautiful young woman, and she reminds Helen of a young Cal so much it practically hurts.

"Oh. Wow. Hi."

Helen wiggles her fingers in hello and smiles as warmly and nonthreateningly as she can. *Nothing to worry about*, she wants that smile to say. *I come in peace.*

Janel's eyes go half lidded. "Dad got you to tell him who to vote for, didn't he?"

Helen nods and gives the tiniest little shrug.

"That stinker."

Helen whispers, "At least he voted," enunciating so Janel can read her lips.

Janel rolls her eyes and says, "I suppose." She comes and sits next to Helen on the floor. "Here, I can take her." They carefully transfer the sleeping child, and Helen can smell Janel's scent. It's very light and lilac-y, and Helen thinks kindergartners must flock to her like bees.

"How'd you get stuck with her?" Janel whispers.

*Your dad was late for pickup? Nope.* There's no way Helen is fueling the daddy issue fire. "I offered so he didn't have to take her out in the cold. I don't think he knew you were coming home this early."

"There's usually an all-staff meeting after school on Tuesdays, but the principal was having one of his many personal crises—the guy lives to wring his hands. I texted Dad that I could pick up Logan, but he didn't respond."

"I don't think he got it."

"He forgets to take his phone out of his coat sometimes, now that—" Janel stops herself, but Helen can guess the end of that sentence is something like *now that he doesn't have it hot-glued to his palm at all times for work.*

Janel is an intriguing creature, with her nice smell and silky hair and frank talk about the principal's penchant for drama. Helen has half a thought to hang around and see what comes

out of her next but doesn't want to press her luck. Best to have a
nice friendly little interaction and scram before anything tricky
happens. She's about to say something like *Well, I'll let you get
on with your day*, when Janel says, "So you guys voted together."

Helen nods.

"And then you came back here."

"The girls were hungry, and we thought it might be nice for
them to have a little playdate."

Janel looks at Helen in a way that is strangely reminiscent
of . . . Helen can't quite put her finger on it, and then it occurs
to her. Annabella. This is a babies-don't-have-playdates-for-no-
good-reason look. The skill level for this conversation just jumped
about five notches, and it's too late to scram now.

"You and Dad are friends again," says Janel, the subtext being
*So let's cut the bullshit.*

"Yup. We are."

"You cleared up . . ." She gives a little head wag, prompting
Helen to finish the sentence.

"We did."

Janel recalibrates her strategy. "Were you guys together in high
school?"

*Boy, this kid doesn't fool around.* Helen wishes she'd had a
second cup of coffee this morning. "Uh, well . . ."

"So, yes?"

It's tempting to lie. But Helen senses that sweet-smelling,
straight-talking Janel will make more out of a fib than the actual
thing you're fibbing about. Besides, why lie? Helen reminds herself that there's no shame in the truth and says, "For a very brief
time."

"Because he screwed it up."

*Okay, enough. You're not conscripting me into your little anti-
Cal army.*

"You know, if your dad wants to tell you what happened, that's fine with me. But I'm not going to spill his personal life to anyone." Helen smiles sweetly but pointedly. "Even you."

"You must have meant a lot to him," says Janel, still fishing.

"We meant a lot to each other."

"And now you're . . ."

"Friends again. Which is the most important thing we ever were."

Janel sighs. "I'm really glad."

Helen's mouth practically falls open. "You are?"

"Yeah, of course. He could use some real friends. At least better than that asshole Lance Bixby from Night Cap. He was Dad's best friend and he screwed him."

"The CFO who bolted with the money?"

"Yeah," Janel says, then mutters, "asshole."

"Wow."

"That's what happens when the only people you spend time with are your business contacts," she grumbles.

*Permeable*, thinks Helen. *Let's pour something sweet in those holes.*

"Your dad was telling me how amazing it was to be with you when McKenzie was born."

Janel's face loses its bite. "He was?"

"He called it life altering, holding his baby's hand while she had a baby."

Janel's cheeks go pink. "He said that?"

Helen nods.

"She's practically his kid," murmurs Janel. "He spends more time with her than I do."

"He adores her, just like he adores you."

Janel's lip makes the tiniest little tremble. Helen reaches out, squeezes Janel's arm, and thinks, *Score one for the old lady.*

The sound of a car pulling into the driveway curtails Helen's moment of glory. *Please, not Suze*, she thinks. *I've got no more rabbits to pull out of my hat.*

A door opens and a little boy's voice calls out, "Mom! I was da line leader. I was first!"

Logan spins around the corner and bombs toward them, but Janel holds her hand out like a stop sign and stage-whispers, "Hi, hi, hi! The girls are sleeping! We have to be—"

"Dat's my friend," says Logan, stopping to take in Helen. "And her baby."

Janel tips her hand flat and lowers it to the ground. "Quick! Crisscross applesauce!"

Logan drops to the carpet and folds his little legs in front of him.

Janel gives him a big smile and a thumbs-up and whispers, "Good listening!"

Helen is wildly impressed by this. If only she'd had such skills when Danny was little!

Cal finally comes into view, a tiny backpack over his adult-size shoulder, eyeing the two of them like the situation might call for a hostage negotiation.

"Dad, you have to be better about checking your phone."

He pats his pants pocket, where his phone clearly is not, and says, "Oh."

"I texted you that I could pick him up."

"I'll try to be better about that."

Apparently satisfied with the obedience of both the males in the room, Janel offers her father a smile, and says to Logan, "Helen's a baby whisperer! They both fell asleep on her lap!"

"Together?" says Logan.

"Yes! At the same time! And you know who's not asleep now, but will be soon?"

"Me?"

"Yes! You! Let's go upstairs and you can pick out any book you want!"

"Even da dinosaur book?"

"Oh, sorry, that one's too long." Janel stands carefully so as not to jostle the still-sleeping McKenzie. "How about *Goodnight Moon*?"

Logan frowns. "Dat's for babies."

Cal leans over and gently pulls Logan to a standing position. "Sleep tight, kiddo. See you when you wake up."

When they leave, he sits on the floor next to Helen. "How'd it go?"

"You, sir, have some strong women in your life."

His grin is tinged with pride. "Don't I know it."

"Glad you're happy, because that girl could interrogate a charging rhinoceros."

"Ah, geez, Helen, I'm sorry."

"Nothing I couldn't handle. But she wants to know what happened between us, and I said that was up to you."

"Don't worry, she couldn't waterboard it out of me."

"Actually . . . I don't think it's the worst idea to tell her. I mean, she's making up all kinds of things in her head, anyway. It's probably better if she knows."

"You don't mind?"

"It's ancient history, Cal."

"Is it, though?"

"It is now." She levels her gaze at him. "Right?"

"Right."

Helen tightens her grip on Lana and stands up. Cal helps her reassemble the diaper bag, drapes her coat over her, and walks her out to her car.

"By the way," says Helen, flicking a look up to the second floor of the house, "she loves you and she wants you to be happy."

His eyebrows go up. "She said that?"

"Not in so many words, but it's clear. The third degree was more about vetting me than digging up further reasons to be mad at you. She's worried you don't have many friends. That's probably what the voting thing was about—making you get involved in the community."

"I thought it was just garden-variety chops busting."

"She told me about Lance."

"My supposed best bud," mutters Cal. "Asshole."

"Anyway, maybe stop tippytoeing around her quite so much and just let her love you."

"YOU'RE IN A good mood," Barb says later that night.

Helen pauses for the briefest moment, then recommences serving the reheated lasagna. Cormac often brings home dishes from the bakery that he deems to be "on the verge," as he calls it. "If anyone's getting food poisoning," he says, "it's gonna be us." None of them have ever gotten even mild indigestion. So far, anyway.

"We had a nice day, didn't we, Lana?"

The baby gives her nonna an applesauce-y grin. Barb scoops the drips up around her mouth with the rubber-coated spoon.

"What did you do that was so nice? Wasn't it about forty below?" Barb knows that Helen's favorite activities with Lana are outside: playgrounds, farms, and the like.

"Well, we voted."

"Not for kookie Marty Spannox, I hope," says Cormac, pouring seltzer into everyone's glasses. "The guy is entertaining and all, but he shouldn't be put in charge of a yard sale."

"Nope, Marty did not get my vote."

"On behalf of the entire population of Belham, I thank you."

"Oh!" says Helen. "I forgot to tell you. Lana said 'baby.'"

Barb inhales a happy little gasp and turns to Lana. "Did you say 'baby'?"

Lana studies her mother. "Ba-by," Barb enunciates. "Bayyy-beee."

"Bay. Be."

The three adults send up a cheer, and Lana grins and claps for herself.

"Yay!" Barb beams at her daughter. "Yay for Lana! Ba-by!"

Lana picks up the spoon Barb dropped on her high chair tray and bangs it into a little puddle of applesauce, which then spatters all over Barb's shirt, and she has to go and change.

Later, about halfway through their meal, Barb says, "What made her say it?"

"Sorry?" says Helen. The lasagna is delicious, but it's one of those very thick slices that you have to stab deep with your fork to hack off a bite-size piece.

"Baby. What was the inspiration?"

Helen is about to launch into the whole thing about being at Cal's house with the girls on her lap . . . but of course she'd first have to explain everything. Until a couple of weeks ago, Barb and Cormac knew every detail of her days. They even found out about Cal tracking her down at the confectionery. But since then she's been leading a bit of a secret life, and she realizes now, with a forkful of lasagna halfway to her mouth, she's not quite ready to go public.

She was fine with the idea of Cal telling Janel. Clearly Janel wanted things sorted out between them. Maybe she thought it would help her own issues with Cal to have him unburdened from a past mistake.

But for some reason Helen balks at telling her daughter, even though she knows there's nothing about it worth hiding. She's fairly certain Barb and Cormac would be happy for her.

"Oh, there was a baby at the polling station who was smiling at us, and I said, 'See the baby?' and that's when she said it."

THAT NIGHT IN bed, Helen ponders this. Why did she fib?

*Because Cal is a married man, and we were in love once.*

Helen could simply have said she reconnected with an old friend and, as she truthfully told Janel, that's the most important thing they ever were to each other. But that in-love part. That's not nothing. That's a cogent detail.

Helen would never have a romantic relationship with a married man, and Cal gives no indication that he's interested in heading in that direction, either. He talks about his wife with pride. (Sometimes a little cryptically, but he never complains about her, like the stereotypical guy looking to have an affair.) Helen and Cal never touch. Not a hug. Not so much as a pat on the arm. They are 150 percent platonic.

But if she's honest with Barb about their past, and reveals that they've been getting together fairly regularly since Cal's apology (and Helen's fusillade of rage) in Jansen Woods a week and a half ago, she knows that Barb will eventually ask a question that Helen doesn't have an answer for:

*What does Cal's wife think?*

# Chapter 31

*2021*

Helen wakes up the next morning, Wednesday, and wonders how things went after she left the Crosby house. Did Cal and Janel talk after her visit? Helen hopes so, and that her words may have softened the daughter a little and given the father more confidence. They are clearly so important to each other, but they seem to communicate mostly through childcare.

She starts to text Cal and ask him, but she realizes that she's never texted him first before. Up till now, he's done all the reaching out. She puts her phone down.

*What is your problem?*

She knows, but it's not a pretty thing to admit. She's covering her ass.

If Suze is hurt or angry that her husband is suddenly spending time with another woman—whom he once loved and slept with—Helen doesn't want to have been the instigator. She wants to be able to reassure herself that she never chased him.

Helen doesn't hear from Cal for days, and she knows she hasn't missed a text or a call. She keeps her phone with her at all times and checks. A lot.

"Hey, Farmer Fran."

"Hello yourself, Helen Reddy."

This of course requires Helen to croon, "Delta-a Dawn, what's that flower you have on?"

Francie cracks up. "Forget the bakery. You should impersonate stars from the seventies."

Helen belts out an off-key, "I am woman!"

"Okay, maybe not."

Helen laughs. "That's a relief. So what's the latest?"

Francie tells her about a boy with debilitating social phobia who just joined their equine-assisted therapy program. The horse is someone he has to "meet" and get to know, but because horses are nonjudgmental and at the same time so responsive, it's a non-threatening way to practice connecting. "It feels good to help a kid like him," says Francie. "He's so lonely."

"That's really beautiful," says Helen. "You're doing great things, my friend."

"Ah, well," Francie sighs, but Helen can hear the satisfaction in it. "What's the news in Belham-shire-town-berg? And by that I mean Cal Crosby."

"He's not the only thing going on in my life, Francie. I do have other subjects to discuss."

"Okay, let's start with those then. Fire away."

"Danny's coming home for Thanksgiving!"

"I think you mentioned that—it's so nice that you'll have all three of them home."

Helen silently deflates. She had a paragraph or two to say on the subject, and Francie just summarized all of it. "Lana has a new word."

"Nice! What is it?"

"*Baby.*"

"Very cool. Is she around babies much?"

"Not usually."

"So just something she saw on TV?"

"She doesn't watch TV."

"Okay." Francie waits. Helen can feel her waiting.

Finally Helen says, "It was Cal's granddaughter."

Francie says nothing. Then she snort-laughs into the phone.

"It's not funny!" says Helen.

"What's not funny about it?" says Francie, still tittering.

"Okay, it's kind of funny, but that doesn't mean I'm some boring old lady who has nothing going on but an occasional visit here and there with a guy she knew a long time ago."

"Absolutely not. You're neither boring nor old. But can we just agree that your most interesting thing at the moment is more interesting than most people's most interesting thing—and talk about it?"

When Helen finishes bringing Francie up to speed on all things Crosby, Francie says, "Wow, the daughter. She's a dynamo."

"I'm sure every preschool mother in Waltham prays her kid gets Ms. Crosby."

"Kinda funny how she's trying to keep the fury with Cal going, when it's clearly losing steam."

"Sometimes mentally you feel like you should be angry at someone but emotionally you just aren't anymore."

"Do you feel that way about him?"

Helen thinks for a moment and chuckles. "When you scream so long and loud that you practically give yourself an aneurysm, it's a lot easier to let your fury evaporate."

"So you two are in a good place."

"Yeah. I think we are."

"Except about his wife."

Helen sighs. "Oh, that."

"Yeah," says Francie. "That."

HELEN DECIDES SHE'LL text Cal on the following Tuesday, when she has Lana again, and suggest an outing with the kids. This time she'll ask him about Suze.

But she doesn't have to wait until Tuesday. On Saturday morning around ten he texts, *What's on your docket for the day?*

*No big plans. Just got back from a run.*

*Still running.*

*Every day. You?*

He doesn't respond for a few minutes, so Helen jumps in the shower. When she's done, she wraps a towel around herself and checks her phone.

*I bike and lift.*

*Where do you bike?*

*Basement mostly.*

*Please do not tell me you have a Peloton.*

*Ok I won't tell you.*

*Seriously?*

*I don't use most of the features. Basically it's a really cool-looking stationary bike. Birthday present.*

Helen translates this as *Not what I would have picked out for myself.* This is dangerously close to my-wife-doesn't-get-me territory. Helen decides the time is now.

*What's on your docket?*

*Grandpa-ing. It's Janel and Eli's anniversary. They're at an Airbnb on the Cape for the weekend. Want to come for lunch? I have leftover steak tips this time.*

Helen hopes Suze is there, so she can finally see for herself what's what.

# Chapter 32

*2021*

Helen pulls into the driveway, walks up to the house, and peeks through the garage windows. Cal's Pilot is there. The bay on the right is empty. Does this woman even exist?

She rings the doorbell and immediately hears a high little voice yell, "She's here! She's here!" Footsteps *tap, tap, tap,* then the doorknob shakes like it's being tugged from the inside.

"Hold on, I got it!" Cal's voice and his footsteps *thump, thump, thump.*

The door opens and Logan throws himself at Helen's legs, and she has to grab the doorjamb to keep from falling backward. Cal grabs her other hand to stabilize her but drops it as soon as it's clear she's not going to tumble back down the front steps. "Whoa, buddy! Let's not tackle our guest before she even gets in the door." He gives Helen an apologetic smile. "We're a little excited for fresh faces," he says.

"Where's da baby?" says Logan, little arms still wrapped around Helen's legs, looking up her torso.

"She's home with her mommy and daddy."

Logan points up at her. "Dat's *your* baby."

"She's my granddaughter. Just like you're Grandpa's grandson."

Logan gives her a blank look and says, "Want to see da trains?"

"Absolutely."

They walk back to the family room where McKenzie is bouncing in an activity center with more lights and sounds than a planetarium laser show. Spread out on the floor is a vast and intricate maze of wooden train tracks with bridges and underpasses, depots and roundhouses, splits, curves, and straightaways.

"I like trains," admits Cal.

"Grandpa likes trains," says Logan.

"I can see that." She turns to Logan. "Do you like them, too?"

"I like bridges."

"Bridges are the best. Show me how you make the trains go."

Cal goes off to make lunch, and Helen soon learns that her role is not to touch the trains, but to rebuild bridges and straighten tracks when he nudges them out of place with a line of coupled cars longer than his arm. Also, she must comment approvingly on his engineering skill every time he makes it successfully around a curve or under an overpass.

"See dat?" he regularly prompts her.

"Nice job!" she says, or, "Good driving!"

Cal calls from the kitchen, "A-plus for self-esteem building, kiddo!"

McKenzie's squawks take a turn from engaged to annoyed with her activity center, and Helen moves to pull her out.

"She's okay," says Logan. "She just yells. See dat?"

"Great work!" Helen tugs McKenzie out and gives her a kiss on her round little cheek. The baby grabs a handful of Helen's hair and tries to put it in her mouth.

"Dat's not okay, Kenzie! No eating hair," scolds Logan.

"Lunchtime!" calls Cal.

Helen unwinds her hair from McKenzie's fist and the three of them head for the nook. "Grandpa for the save," she murmurs to Cal.

"Got your back," he says, and helps Logan into his booster seat.

Helen straps McKenzie into the high chair, and Cal brings out the food: an almond butter and honey sandwich ("The kid has preferences," says Cal) and some apple slices; salad and steak tips for the grown-ups; and cereal mush for McKenzie. ("She's wildly ambivalent.")

Cal is good at managing his family's nutritive needs: a spoonful of mush for McKenzie, a bite of salad for him, an admonition to Logan to stop steering the sandwich around his plate and take a bite.

"Are you dating?" he says to Helen in the middle of all this.

Helen almost chokes. "Sorry, what?"

"Seeing people."

"Like romantically?"

"Yeah, like romantically. Isn't that sort of central to dating?"

"Oh. I, um . . . Not really." As in not at all. Barb has brought it up several times. *You know, we'd all be fine with it, in case you're worried about that. Well, Sam will probably cry and suck his thumb, and Danny will accuse you of betraying Dad, but they'd get over it eventually.*

"Why not?" Cal asks.

Helen takes an extra moment to chew while her brain scrambles for an answer. "A pandemic isn't the greatest time to do dinner and play who's-your-favorite-band with strangers."

Cal slides a spoonful of cereal into McKenzie's mouth. "I hope you're not worried that someone wouldn't swipe right, or whatever they're doing these days, because they would."

"Dating apps," Helen groans. "Yikes."

"Or you could meet someone through friends."

"Did you have someone in mind?" she teases. "I hear Lance Bixby's come into some money recently."

"Actually, he'd be a lot of fun. Too bad he's a little hard to find. Also he's a"—Cal mouths the word *douchebag*—"but other than that."

"Ah, well. If I can't have a thieving backstabber, I guess it's the nunnery for me."

McKenzie bats the spoon away and rubs a cereal-smeared fist in her eye. Logan lays his head on his arm and drives a crust at eye level across the table.

"Naptime." Cal gets a wet cloth to wipe the kids' faces while Helen clears the table.

"Read me a book?" Logan asks her as he crawls down from his booster seat.

"Sure."

"Da dinosaur book?"

"Five pages," says Cal.

"To the pterodactyl?"

"No way, smarty. The *Elasmosaurus*." To Helen, he says, "Don't let him con you. He's like Ponzi with that book." He gives McKenzie a sniff and makes a face. "This may require a hazmat suit and a call to the EPA hotline."

They all go upstairs and head down a hallway to the left. Helen brings up the rear and looks to the right. At the end of the hall she sees a bedroom door open, and beyond it a king-size bed with the sheets all askew. She looks away quickly before her mind conjures Cal and his blond wife in that bed.

They pass a couple of closed doors, and then a little suite of rooms with a bathroom. Logan is in one small room, and McKenzie is next door in what Helen suspects is a converted walk-in closet. She snuggles Logan in his toddler bed and reads till *Gallimimus*, while listening to Cal murmur to the baby. "Kenzie girl, you are pooptastic. Yes, ma'am, you're a poopadillo."

Finally they head downstairs, and he says, "Tea? Coffee? Shot of tequila?"

Helen acquired a taste for an afternoon coffee when she was working the counter at the confectionery, so she asks for that. She sits in the nook while Cal fills the pot, measures the grounds, and asks, "So no dating?"

"Nope."

"Any particular reason?"

She shrugs. "I guess over the years I got used to managing on my own most of the time. Also, pandemic obviously. Then moving up here, and working every day to keep Cormac's afloat. Then the baby. I'm not opposed to dating, but . . ."

He brings mugs, spoons, and a container of half-and-half over to the nook and sits down. "I'm just surprised."

"Why?"

"You're . . . you know, smart and kind and funny and attractive. I would have thought that even if you weren't out there trolling for guys, someone would've snapped you up."

"No snapping has occurred thus far, but hey, tomorrow's another day."

"Maybe reconsider on the apps? I hear that's how it's done these days."

Helen picks up the spoon and puts it down again. "Why do you care if I date?"

"I just want you to be happy."

"And you think I'm not?"

"Oh, it's just . . . No, I, uh . . . If you're happy, that's great."

"It's just what?"

Cal gets up and checks the coffeepot, which has only about an inch of coffee in it so far. Helen can see that from the nook. "I don't want to stick my foot in it," he says.

"Well, your foot's halfway in, so . . ."

"You didn't have, like, an overly huge amount of love in your marriage, and I would just want you to have that at some point. You deserve that."

"Well, thanks. Really. I know you mean it—"

"I do."

"—but not everyone gets that kind of love, Cal. A lot of people don't. And if you have that with Suze, that's great. But I didn't, and I might not ever, and I can still have a perfectly happy life."

"Of course you can. I'm sorry if I—"

"And by the way, where *is* Suze?"

"Oh, um, she's at a friend's for the weekend."

"You don't sound sure."

"Believe me, I'm sure."

"Okay, because I was starting to wonder if she's like the crazy wife from *Jane Eyre*, stashed in the attic, or Norman Bates's mother from *Psycho*."

Cal gets up to check the coffee again, which has at last fully perked. "You're suggesting that my wife is insane or dead, and I'm just carrying on like everything's copacetic?"

"I think it's reasonable at this point to ask for proof of life."

Cal pours the coffee. "She's definitely alive, she's just not around a lot."

Helen takes a sip. "Have you ever told her about me?"

"Yes." He puts the pot back and sits down.

"Yes? That's your final answer?"

"You asked a yes-or-no question."

"What did you tell her?"

"All of it."

"Every single thing."

"Pretty much."

"When?"

"When did I tell her?"

"Cal."

"When we were dating. She asked about my toes. I gave her the whole nine yards." He sips his coffee. "Did you ever tell Jim?"

Helen looks out the window at the straw-covered garden beds. "Not the whole nine yards. Maybe about five yards." She turns back to his gaze. "I told him how I got chlamydia and why I thought I was infertile."

"So basically what a great guy I was."

"I was still pretty upset about it."

"I'm sure you were, since you were still pretty upset about it a couple of weeks ago."

Helen gives him a warning look. "I hope you're not suggesting—"

Cal raises his hands in surrender. "I had it coming and then some. Actually, there's this little part of me that thinks now that we're friends again, I got off easy."

"You didn't. You took it on the chin, and you apologized. That's why I forgave you."

"Did you, though? I mean, completely? Because you were holding on to that for decades—and not like you shouldn't have—that's totally on me. I should've fixed this shit a long time ago. But when you've got something like that in your heart for forty years, it's a little hard to let go."

"Cal, what would I be doing spending time with you, talking to you about deep, heartbreaking stuff, things I can't say to other people. Why would I *ever* do that if I was still holding something against you? Maybe the person who can't let go of it is you. Maybe you're the one still carrying that burden."

"Yeah, okay, it's me." He shifts uncomfortably in his seat. "Because I was not a good guy to you, Helen. I was a dick. And that's never gonna not be true."

"Jesus, we're all dicks sometimes! We're all stupid and scared and just trying to get out alive. And sometimes we're even willing to throw other people's happiness into the line of fire. And yes, that's a total dick move. But that doesn't make you a permanent dick for all time, Cal. If it did, there'd be no hope for any of us."

He shakes his head a little and looks out the window. She knows he's trying to believe her, but he can't quite get there.

"You're a good friend to me, Cal. And you're trying so hard to fix everything. With everyone. And that's all you can do. That's what makes you a good man."

His eyes come back to hers. So much regret.

She knows about that. Regret has been her constant companion since Jim died. Regret about marrying him, about not listening to the people who loved her, about not believing that she could have something better. And regret on Jim's behalf, because he chose her and their lukewarm marriage over real love. She's carrying two people's regret now.

Cal nods. "Thank you," he murmurs.

"So there's something on my mind. Something I don't want to regret in the future, and that is causing your wife any pain. I need to know if she's okay with us hanging out together."

There, she said it. *Finally*, Francie would say.

Cal's face goes wide with surprise and then he lets out a little laugh. He's laughing, for godsake!

"Goddamn it, Cal, if you haven't told her—" Helen starts to slide out of the booth.

"Of course I told her!"

"Then what was that weird laugh?"

"Because she's fine with it."

"Oh, come on."

"It's true."

"You're telling me your wife is *fine* with you spending time with someone you once slept with."

His face goes a little hard when he says, "Yes."

"I don't get it."

"You wouldn't."

"Because I've never experienced such a great love as you two have? And this is some sort of . . . I don't know . . . She's so devoted that anything that makes you happy is fine by her?"

He's avoiding her gaze. "No."

Helen's about done with this game. "What the fuck, Cal?"

Still not looking at her. "She's seeing someone."

"A therapist?"

"No."

Helen thinks for a moment. *"An affair?"*

"Yes."

"Will you look at me, please?"

Cal wrenches his gaze from the window, and suddenly there's a kaleidoscope of emotion coming at her: rage, sadness, shame, hurt, helplessness, and more rage.

"Tell me," Helen says.

"I just told you."

"Give me the whole nine yards."

# Chapter 33

## 2021

In May of 2020, Cal was frantically trying to keep Night Cap afloat in the Northeast and in Washington State, where Covid-19 had hit quickly and with a vengeance. Takeout, the main thing keeping restaurants limping along, was not an option, and the Reston Group, Night Cap's corporate parent company, had shut down all business travel.

"It was a one-two punch," he tells Helen. "Venues were struggling, and I couldn't get there to help."

He was also trying to figure out what the hell was going on with Lance Bixby, who was suddenly not responding to calls or texts or threats to track him down at his home in Montauk, Long Island. "Fucker," mutters Cal.

By June it was all falling apart. Reston Group preemptively closed up shop on all thirty-two venues, leaving Cal and the CEO, an older guy whose wife had just left him, to clean up the mess and salvage what they could. "In short, I was out of my fucking mind. I do not like failure. I mean, okay, no one likes failure, but I'm a little . . ."

"Obsessive?" says Helen.

"Well—"

"Controlling?"

"Hey—"

"Deluded about the extent of your power over people and events?"

Cal sits back in the booth and crosses his arms. "Look, working harder always worked."

"Except occasionally it doesn't."

"Do you want to life-coach me right now, or hear the rest of it?"

"Oh, I definitely want to hear the rest of it."

He was working out of a corner of the basement. "Suze had taken over my office on the main floor years before, and she wasn't giving it back." He would come upstairs after banging his head against a corporate wall all day long, and no one was particularly sympathetic. Bonnie, running her media trainings and managing her clients' TikTok gaffes, had her own fires to put out. "We're all working our tails off now, Dad," she said to him at one point. "Not just you."

Janel, still wrestling with her abandonment issues, was actively hostile. "Why should I care?" was her general attitude. Cal was nonplussed by this. One day he said, "How about because I'm trying to keep a roof over your family's heads!"

Janel had her bags packed and Logan in the car within an hour.

Suze stalked into his corner in the basement and said, "What did you do?"

Cal got up to the driveway just in time to stand in front of her car and beg her not to go back to the three-decker with all the partying, Covid-spreading college kids.

"You're going to therapy with me," she hissed at him. "This time you don't have anyplace to jet off to. There's nowhere to hide."

"Did you go?" asks Helen.

He sighs. "I sure did."

"And you learned a few things."

He smiles sadly. "Yep."

The response that really surprised him was Suze's. She'd complained about his peripatetic work life for years—they'd been in marriage therapy over it. But a few years before, she'd stopped fighting and had seemed suddenly to be fine with his being gone so much. Now she encouraged him to find another job.

"Like pronto," says Cal.

"Was she worried about money?"

"No. I've always been very careful to save and pay things off early. Never bought boats or second homes. She wasn't making nearly as much as I did, but I was on her insurance, and she could cover the bills without too much trouble. She just wanted me out of her hair."

"So she didn't have to hide what she was up to."

"Oh, she wasn't hiding it."

Suze, with her razor-sharp intelligence, even-keeled manner, and eye for style, was a hit everywhere she went. If she was planning a fundraiser for the local food pantry, battered women's shelter, or open space protection effort, everyone wanted to be on the committee. Suze was popular without caring about popularity, which made her the coolest of the cool.

While her outer circle was wide, her inner circle was very tight. She had two or three close friends, but none closer than Noni Feldman, who was now the assistant secretary of the Massachusetts Department of Health and Human Services. Noni was divorced with no kids, content to be an honorary auntie to her friends' children, including the Crosby girls.

"Oh God," says Helen. "Suze didn't start up with her best friend's ex-husband, did she?"

"Nope." He waits.

Helen blinks a few times. "Hold on . . ."

"Yep."

"Holy shit. Were you . . . ?"

"Shocked? Sure. My wife's having an affair. Just stop there and that's a mindfuck. But with a woman, and someone I've known for years?"

"Was there ever any indication . . . ?"

"Actually, yeah. Suze told me when we were dating that she'd had a relationship with a woman in college. But she was clearly into men, so I guess I thought she was college-bi but not, you know, *bi*-bi."

"How did you find out?"

"Well, I was pretty distracted with my career going up in a mushroom cloud, and my kids clearly not happy with me. Suze seemed pleasant by comparison, other than bugging me to get a job. At first I didn't think anything about the fact that she spent so much time at Noni's in Wellesley. And that Noni never, ever came here."

"You didn't notice that she wasn't sleeping with you anymore?"

Cal doesn't say anything.

"She was sleeping with you, too?"

He shrugs. "Apparently it worked for her."

"Did Noni know?"

"I guess."

"And she wasn't upset about that?"

Cal's face flares with disbelief. "Was *Noni* upset? That's what you're worried about?"

"No, I—"

"Tell you what," he snarls. "*Fuck* Noni and her feelings."

"Cal, I'm sorry. I'm just trying to understand—"

"Yeah, well, join the club."

Helen waits for him to calm down a little and asks, "So how did you find out?"

Cal had been to therapy with Janel a couple of times, and it was really starting to sink in how deep in the doghouse he was. He asked for family therapy, and they unanimously turned him down. "Said they were all too busy with work," he says dryly.

"Oh, the irony."

"Exactly. And, hey, it was my bad. I had to make it right. So I started on my own with Dorothy, this sweet granny type who was not having it with my workaholic provider bullshit."

"She's the one who sent you to Paddow Mountain."

He nods. "Yep."

Dorothy listened to all his woes and got down to business. Her constant refrain was "How can you express your fatherly love in ways that feel genuine to them—not you—them?" Cal started cooking dinner and whipping up lunches, which he'd never done before. He'd perk coffee in the morning and make sure Bonnie was topped off when her mug was low. He talked with her about her work and gave helpful advice when she renegotiated her contract.

Janel was angrier, but in some ways easier. Just taking Logan off her hands while Eli was at work made a world of difference for her, even though she retained her prerogative to regularly vent her spleen. When Cal whined to Dorothy about it, she'd say things like, "Where do you think that comes from?" and "How are children shaped by their environments?"

"Oof," says Helen. "Right in the teeth."

"You're not kidding."

When Dorothy asked about Suze, Cal told her things were better than they'd been in a long time. Suze had stopped complaining about Cal's absence years before and was delighted with his better-late-than-never attention to their daughters.

"How did she make peace with you being gone so much?" Dorothy wanted to know. Cal wasn't really sure. He thought it just happened. "Magically?" asked Dorothy.

"Jesus, I'm dumb," Cal tells Helen.

"There were a lot of plates spinning," she says. "You focused on the wobbly ones."

"Yeah, but . . . that question. I didn't like it. It struck a nerve that I didn't even know was there. Like, down deep I knew something was up, but as long as I wasn't getting called out anymore, I was a little too happy to let sleeping dogs lie."

Dorothy suggested Cal simply ask Suze what had changed for her. Instead he set about trying to prove his stated hypothesis that everything was fine. He took Suze on bike rides and made romantic dinners that he served in the backyard under twinkle lights he'd strung up. He helped her strategize about partnerships with companies who could support her domestic violence work. They enjoyed each other's company.

"All systems were go," says Cal.

"All systems?" says Helen.

"A hundred percent go," he replies.

But in listening to Cal describe how he spent his days, Dorothy noticed that Suze was gone a lot. "Noni's in our bubble," Cal told her. "It's safe." Dorothy wanted to know why, if it was so safe, Noni never came to the Crosby home. And why, other than occasional bike trips and date nights with Cal, Suze was spending far more of her free time with Noni.

"It's interesting that Dorothy wouldn't let it go," says Helen. "I mean, if you were happy and things seemed to be working, why upset the apple cart?"

"I asked her that very thing."

"And?"

"She said that I was very 'defended.' That I had become a pro at papering things over so I didn't have to look at them. And maybe everything was fine with Suze, and she'd simply come to terms with the reality of our marriage. But the fact that I wouldn't ask was a red flag."

"Wow, that's some serious x-ray vision."

"Yeah, it sucked."

Helen laughs. "At least you kept going. I would have run twenty miles in the opposite direction if anyone had asked me to look at my marriage that closely. Maybe if I had . . ."

Cal nods sympathetically. "As a wise woman once said, 'We're all stupid and scared and just trying to get out alive.'"

"Yeah, but sometimes a little bravery stops an avalanche of remorse."

They both think on that a minute. Then Cal says, "I wish I'd been braver in high school."

Helen sighs. "I wish I'd been brave enough to go to you and say, 'What the fuck?'"

He gazes at her, his chest rising and falling, hands clasped in front of him, and she sees that boy. And she knows he's seeing that girl. Helen has never let herself envision what might have happened if either one of them had been brave enough to alter the course of events. But for a brief moment in Cal Crosby's kitchen nook, she can see that boy and girl and how happy they could have been. It's heartbreaking.

"So you asked her," Helen says.

"Yeah."

"What did she say?"

"She said, 'I found other ways to meet my needs.' And I said, 'All your needs?' And she said, 'Yeah, Cal. All of them.'"

# Chapter 34

## 2020

"You're cheating on me?"

"I'm trying to save our marriage," said Suze.

"*By cheating on me?!*"

She got that look, that calm, steely, *I am not to be fucked with* look. "By not leaving you."

Cal was about to boil over, but she brought him up short with that answer. He glared at her. "And those are the choices."

"Yes. And if you think I haven't racked my brain to come up with others, then you are very sadly mistaken."

"So I'm just supposed to sit tight, waiting for you to come home from your lover, and be happy that you come home at all? Or no, wait, I'm *not* supposed to sit here—I'm supposed to get on the road again, so you can have your freedom and a nice chunk of change to spend. Is that all you want out of me? A penis and a paycheck?"

"That's not all I wanted out of you, but for years now it's all you wanted to be. And it would be really great if you just fucking admitted it."

Cal batted the antique alarm clock Suze bought at a charity auction off their dresser. It disassembled itself against the wall, the pieces scattering across the Persian rug. "Fine! You want me to admit it! I do! Officially! I'm to blame!"

"Don't come at me with your victim shit," Suze said coolly. "The universe is not conspiring against you. You didn't get swept out to sea on a raft. You made choices. And maybe it all goes back to your own daddy issues, but that's what therapy is for, Cal, and it's wonderful that you're finally coming around to that. Wish you'd picked up on it a little sooner, like when I dragged you into marriage counseling, but better late than never. Except the terms of the deal have changed since then. I'm no longer asking for more attention. I'm content with less. And now you have to be, too."

"And if I'm not?"

She shrugged. "Then you're not."

"You're basically daring me to divorce you."

Suze sighed wearily. "I'm not daring you to do anything. To be honest, I like this arrangement. The whole world is in a nose-dive, and we're all relatively safe and sound together. I don't want to do anything to jeopardize the girls' comfort here—I certainly don't want them scurrying back to less-safe living arrangements because our marriage is imploding."

She had a point, he realized. His bruised feelings were not as important as his daughters' comfort and safety. Not with a deadly disease raging.

"Fine," he snarled. "We'll act like everything's hunky-dory." He narrowed his eyes and made one last bid. "But I want you to leave her."

"No."

"I'm your husband and I love you. That counts for something!"

"Of course it does. And I love you, too, which is why I didn't leave. But you relied on me to be chill about everything for too long. I can't help the fact that I'm not the type to throw tantrums, but I'm not, and you benefited. Now I'm the love of someone's life, her top priority. I earned it. I deserve it. And it's fair, Cal. You have to admit it's fair."

## 2021

Helen doesn't know how to respond to this part of the story. She's Cal's friend, and it's utterly ridiculous to her that Suze expects him to put up with adultery—much less welcome it as a marriage saver! Helen herself was in a similar situation, and she would never have resorted to cheating. As Ricky so eloquently put it all those years ago, she's a tight-ass good girl, and she's not ashamed of that. But Helen can't help feeling that Suze has a point.

Cal is looking at her, waiting for a reaction. Finally she says, "How do things stand now?"

"Pretty much the same."

"She's still seeing Noni, and you're still trying to get her to stop."

This hits Cal. Helen can see it land. He's hearing it from an outsider's perspective, and he does not like how it sounds. He shrugs a yes. "Besides, Janel is still at the house. I don't want her taking the kids back to that apartment with Covid-spreading college kids all over the place."

Helen knows that most if not all local universities require vaccination now. In fact, college students are one of the most highly vaccinated groups in the state. And both Janel and her husband, Eli, are working in-person jobs. Logan goes to preschool. They're all potentially exposed every day. She understands his worry, and why he initially stayed in his marriage. What she doesn't understand is why he's still in it.

"What does Dorothy say?"

Sadness clouds his face for a moment. "She said people make all kinds of adjustments to keep relationships afloat. Open marriage in some form isn't as uncommon as you'd think, apparently. People change. Hell, they change genders and still stay together."

"So she suggested you give it a try?"

"She basically told me not to make any sudden moves. And to put aside preconceived notions about what marriage is supposed to look like. To think about what it is I really want and need. She said, 'Once you figure it out, head in that direction.'"

*I guess he hasn't figured it out yet*, thinks Helen. *That's why he hasn't left.*

"That's when she zeroed in on Paddow Mountain," he adds.

"Facing your shame."

"Yeah." Cal takes a breath. He keeps his eyes on Helen's even though it seems like this isn't easy for him. "And how I don't think I deserve real love, because I had it—or the beginnings of it—and I ruined it. For both of us."

They sit with that for a moment. Because that's ground zero, isn't it? Helen is tempted to say, *It was a mistake, we both could have handled it better.* But while it's true, she senses that now is not the time to try and sand off the jagged edges of what happened. For a moment, anyway, they can remember how badly their tender young hearts got cut.

Finally she says, "I guess old Dorothy is pretty proud of you, the way you tracked me down to apologize."

He sighs. "I like to think she is."

Helen's face drops. "You quit therapy?"

"She died last March. She'd just gotten her second Covid shot, and she was talking about seeing her new great-grandson. Died of a stroke in her sleep."

"Oh, Cal." His arm is lying on the table in front of him, and Helen can't help but reach out and touch him. "I'm so sorry."

"She was a great lady. Actually, after I went to Paddow, she started gently poking at me to find you. I didn't know your married name, but, honestly, I wasn't looking too hard. Then she died, and I let it go. I didn't think I could face you without her whispering in my ear." He smiles. "Pretty sure she threw you in my path that day with Logan. If spirits can do that kind of thing, she surely would have."

"You did great, even without her."

"Except the part where I said you should've written a nicer note." He shakes his head. "Boy, she would have had my ass over that one."

Helen smiles. "She's still whispering in your ear, after all."

THE KIDS WAKE up, and Helen tells Cal she should get going. She has some errands to run. This is true—she's out of yogurt and bananas, two critical staples for her—but if she'd wanted to stay, that wouldn't have stopped her.

What she really needs is a break. It's a lot of . . . interaction, all this talking with Cal. A lot of friendship in its finest form, sharing real, at times heart-wrenching, aspects of their lives. But Helen's introversion says she needs some quiet. A little recharge. She forgets about the yogurt and bananas and goes straight home.

She builds a fire and sits on the rug in front of the hearth stretching her hamstrings, which she forgot to do when Cal called after her run. She thinks about his daughters and his marriage. But what keeps coming back to Helen is Dorothy's advice: figure out what you really want and need, and head in that direction.

*Friendship*, Helen tells herself. That soft, cottony comfort of knowing and being known. Of getting each other. And Cal is so good at it! He somehow makes her feel safe enough to talk about things she's never told anyone. Maybe this is a vestige of their friendship from all those years ago, but Helen doesn't think so, at least not entirely. It's the work he's done—and is still trying to do—to be a better man, a better person, that makes her feel like she, too, can be open. Vulnerable even.

Plus, he's fun to be with! They enjoy grandparenting together. Their humor still lines up. She smiles just thinking about it. Everything about their friendship feels good.

But peeking out from behind that is something else. Something she doesn't want to acknowledge. She knows that she, too, is a pro at papering things over, and for now she employs her mental wallpaper and paste, even though eventually it will not hold. Sooner or later it will peel, and she'll have to look at what's behind.

Friendship—that's what she really wants and needs. For now.

# *Chapter 35*

## *2021*

It's Veterans Day, and things are a little slow at Cormac's Confectionery. Barb's photography studio is closed. ("Roy doesn't get it that, since a lot of people have this day off, it's actually a good day to, you know, make portraits?") She went in that morning to work on getting photo packages out the door but is back earlier than expected in the afternoon.

When Helen and Lana come in, red-cheeked and smiling, both Barb and Cormac are home.

"Where've you two intrepid explorers been?" says Cormac, sitting on the couch with his enormous, socked feet up on the coffee table, going over inventory lists on his laptop. Barb leans in the kitchen doorway with a spoon and an open cup of peach yogurt in her hand.

"We went to Drumlin Farm, didn't we, Lana?" says Helen, untying the little girl's hat and pulling it off her head, static electricity making the silky black hair stand on end for a moment.

"We saw sheep, right?"

"Bay. Be," says Lana.

"Baby sheep?" says Cormac. "Aka lambs?"

"Well, we did see some lambs, but we also saw a baby. Actually, it was my friend Cal's granddaughter."

Helen continues to divest Lana of her snowsuit, fully cognizant of the fact that her daughter's spoon has stopped stirring yogurt, and her son-in-law's gaze has flicked to his wife several times. Helen waits.

"Well, fancy that," says Cormac, nothing if not diplomatic.

"The guy from high school," says Barb a little too casually.

"That's the one." Helen sets Lana on the rug by the coffee table, where she stands and pats her father's foot. Helen unzips her own dark teal puffy coat and pulls off her fleece headband.

Barb puts her yogurt on the counter, crosses her arms. "Seriously, you're hilarious."

"That's me," says Helen innocently. "The Sarah Silverman of Belham."

"You don't even like Sarah Silverman."

"I do sometimes. Sometimes she's a little . . ."—*crass*, Helen thinks, but decides on—"extra."

"Since when do you say *extra*?" says Barb.

Cormac, whose gaze flits between the two women in his life, says, "Should I . . . ?"

"No. She's going to tell you everything after I leave, so you might as well hear it from me." Helen sinks into the overstuffed (the stuffing is actually coming out along one of the seams) armchair. Barb goes to sit on the couch next to Cormac, who pulls Lana up onto his lap; the little girl snuggles down and in a matter of minutes is off for a snooze.

"Cal and I were really good friends in tenth grade. We had these great talks. He's a good listener, and he was the rare kind of teenage boy who was willing to dive in about real things. Next to Francie, he was my best friend."

Helen goes on with an abridged version of the story. How she and Cal reconnected senior year, but he was dating Wendy. That night in the woods, finally revealing that they loved each other. (Helen doesn't say they had sex, knowing most people prefer to think of their parents as anatomically incapable of intercourse. Barb will fill in the blanks but will appreciate not having to hear her mother say the words.) She tells them about Cal getting frostbite and losing his scholarship, and about his abandonment of her.

As Helen talks, she's surprised to find that the sting has gone out of it. She was so angry at Cal for so long. But now it's more of a sad and unfortunate thing that happened, and less the defining moment in her young life that tripped off a series of events that then defined her adulthood. It's still those things, too, but not in a way that makes her feel locked and loaded with unspent fury, sorrow, and regret.

Helen does not mention the chlamydia, nor how Barb's conception precipitated a lackluster marriage. Nor does she reveal the struggles in Cal's marriage. Nor will she ever.

"So you two have been getting together for weeks now," says Barb, and Helen sees that her daughter is a little hurt. Barb is an open book (occasionally Helen wouldn't mind if a few of those pages were closed), but Helen is not. Never has been.

"Yeah, we had a lot to process. I wasn't ready to talk about it. But now we've kind of come to a new place, and it feels more . . . settled."

"His wife is good with all this?"

"Yep. He told her everything, and she's fine with it."

"Really." Barb says this in an *imagine-that* tone while making it clear she has additional thoughts on the matter. Thoughts Helen hopes she won't share. Because honestly, she just doesn't want to hear it. So she nods and smiles.

"Are we going to meet him?" Barb asks.

"I've met him," says Cormac, and Barb shoots him a look. Cormac shrugs and says, "Nice shoes."

"Oh, um . . . I guess someday."

Barb turns to Cormac. "What's for dinner?"

"I've got these beautiful chicken breasts stuffed with spinach, prosciutto, and—"

Barb turns back to Helen. "How about tonight? Do you think Cal and his wife might be available?"

"Both of them?" Helen is immediately horrified at this idea, but desperately tries to hide just *how* horrified. "It's kind of short notice," she says with forced nonchalance.

"No harm asking, right?"

Helen laughs. "Tonight?"

"Yeah, get them in here. You've met one of *their* kids."

Cormac smiles and shakes his head.

"What," says Barb.

"This is not emergency surgery, babe," he says gently. "No one's losing a limb if you don't give this scenario the once-over in the next four hours."

"I am not giving—"

"Barbitybarb," he chides. "You're the best daughter anyone could ask for."

"True," says Helen.

"What's your point?" Barb snaps.

"My point is you can stand down and still retain the title."

Barb glares at him, and he gazes calmly back till she rolls her eyes, and the hint of a smile breaks through on her face. The situation is resolved in the look they share.

*This*, thinks Helen. *All I ever wanted for her is this.*

"You'll get your chance," she tells Barb. "Someday."

WHEN HELEN CALLS Francie that night, Francie says, "Oooh, good, my favorite Netflix series is on!"

Helen is confused. "Which one?"

"You! You're like *Bridgerton*, except without the costumes and accents and steamy sex."

Helen laughs. "So not like *Bridgerton* at all then."

"Cal could wear a waistcoat."

"I can definitely see him prancing around the playground in a satin vest."

"Why don't you suggest it before the next episode."

"Or you could ask him yourself."

"Oh?"

"I was saying it's my turn to visit you, and he mentioned very casually that he hoped he'd get a chance to see you some-day."

"I.e., he wants to come with you but doesn't want to put you on the spot for an invite."

"Basically."

"And that won't bother his wife, him traipsing off for the day with an ex-love to a romantic horse farm in Vermont."

"Is it romantic, though?" says Helen. "I mean, the smell is quite pungent."

"Doesn't seem to bother Vernon. But then it could be raining nuclear waste, and he's like, 'Wanna fool around?'"

Helen chuckles. "I was thinking maybe Sunday."

"Sunday's great. But you need to catch me up first."

"HUH," SAYS FRANCIE, after Helen finishes.

"'Huh,' as in that's pretty messed up?"

"No. I mean, it's . . . I wouldn't be into that kind of arrangement, but . . . I can see how it works for her—staying with Cal even though she's with someone else and he's hanging out with you. At some level she probably feels bad cheating on someone she obviously cares about, no matter how fair she claims to think it is. Maybe his having you in his life again makes her feel less guilty about it."

"Cal doesn't seem to think she feels guilty at all."

"Maybe not. She might sing a different tune if the two of you took up romantically."

"Well, we'll never know."

"Because you have zero interest in each other." Francie's tone is neutral, but Helen can hear the ping of skepticism.

"Because I won't sleep with a married man even with a hall pass from his wife. And he wants her back. He's not going to ruin his chances by starting up with someone else."

"So the hall pass part, that wouldn't matter to you?"

"No."

"Because it's morally wrong?"

Helen smiles. "Hmm, just how rigid and judgmental has Helen become in her old age?"

"Well?" says Francie.

"Look, other people can do whatever works for them. I take marriage vows for what they are—vows—and I would never want to sleep with a man who was sleeping with someone else."

"Even if it's his wife and she's okay with it."

"Especially if it's his wife."

"Because you don't want to share, but you *really* don't want to play second fiddle."

Helen laughs. "Yeah, screw the vows. I just want to be the main event."

"Nobody puts Baby in a corner!"

"I'm doing that *Dirty Dancing* leap thing right now—by myself!"

"Ouch. Be careful."

EARLY SUNDAY MORNING, Helen carries two travel mugs of coffee out to Cal's Honda Pilot idling in her driveway. "This one's yours," she says, handing it over. "Mine has milk."

"Thoughtful."

"Nice of you to drive." She types the address into Google Maps on her phone and props it between the gearshift and the dashboard.

As they glide through the quiet streets of Belham, they don't talk much, and Helen finds this a relief. There has been So. Much. Talking. It's nice to see that they can sit in companionable silence and not feel the need to clutter the air with chatter. She doesn't remember if they were ever happily quiet together as kids, but they certainly are now.

When they curl onto Route 2 and the engine noise gets louder, Cal turns up the music, which till now has been a pleasant hum in the background. Van Morrison's scrabbly voice sings "Into the Mystic," and Cal quietly sings along. He knows every word.

"Is this a playlist?" Helen asks.

"Yeah, it's my '70s Road Trip list."

"You are a man of many lists, aren't you?"

"Many."

"I only have one."

"Songs to Run By?"

"Mom's Playlist."

He gives a knowing smile. "One of your kids set it up."

"So?"

"No, that's great. You just wouldn't refer to yourself as 'Mom.'"

"It is a major part of my identity, after all."

"Of course. It's just . . . they're grown now. I mean, they're still a very important part of your life, but there's more to you than that."

*Is there?* she wonders. For so many years those three little beings were virtually all she cared about. But now . . .

"Maybe I should change my playlist name."

"Or start a new one."

Helen scoffs. "Now you're just talking crazy."

"Helen Spencer. Woman of two playlists." Cal makes a little exploding sound.

A new song comes on. "Gonna find my baby, gonna hold her tight . . ."

"Oh my God," says Helen. "'Afternoon Delight'? Seriously?"

He laughs. "It's a classic!"

"A classic? It's ridiculous fluff!"

"Au contraire, my snobby friend. It was a number one hit. Billboard rated it the twentieth sexiest song of all time."

"It's about as sexy as a *Hee Haw* rerun."

"Okay, them's fightin' words. Let's get Mom's Playlist going, and we'll see who's got ridiculous fluff."

Helen's phone resists syncing to the car audio system, and Cal pulls over in the breakdown lane to help. A minute later a cruiser rolls to a stop behind them, and a skinny state trooper with sunglasses and a hat that looks two sizes too big for his head struts slowly toward the Jeep. Cal rolls down the window.

"Everything okay here?" The officer affects brusqueness, as if prepared for a criminal response.

"Completely fine," says Cal.

"You don't have your hazards on."

"Oh, sorry. I guess it's just my blinker."

"Blinker's not enough. State law requires hazards."

"I'll keep that in mind," says Cal.

The officer takes off his sunglasses and peers into the car at Helen. He looks to her to be about nineteen. "Everything okay, ma'am?"

"Yes, thank you, Officer. My friend was just trying to help me connect my phone to his audio system so we can listen to music."

He looks at the dashboard screen. "You shut off the Bluetooth."

"Now how did that happen?" says Cal.

"Easy mistake," says the trooper. "Put your hazards on till it syncs."

When he leaves, they both start to laugh. "Dispatch, we have a 957 in progress," says Helen, imitating the guy's monotone. "Elders attempting technology. I may need backup."

When they pull onto Route 2, a pop-y yet deceptively deep "Beautiful Soul" comes on.

"A boy band from the nineties?" says Cal with disdain. "And you're sassing *me*?"

"It's not a boy band. It's Jesse McCartney. And it was early two thousands because Barb played it a bunch of times on the drive up here from North Carolina for her freshman year at Emerson."

"She's the beautiful soul it reminds you of."

"It was like a prayer that all these new people would see how wonderful she is."

"Okay, I retract my disgust. Parental love trumps musical taste."

"It's also a great dance tune."

"You'd dance to *Crime and Punishment* if it were set to a good beat."

"I might," said Helen. "Besides, that book could use a little pick-me-up."

Cal grins at her a moment, and she smiles back.

"I don't want my love to go to waste," sings Jesse McCartney.

*Me neither*, thinks Helen.

It's a bit colder in southern Vermont than it was in MetroWest Boston, and they can see their breath when they get out of the car. Cal looks down the hill at Seven Meadows Farm and murmurs, "Okay."

"Pretty great, huh?" says Helen.

"Very Francie."

"Completely."

They walk down the hill, and suddenly Francie dashes out the door of the gallery in an unzipped parka, the hood bouncing against her back, and whoops, "Cal Crosby!"

"Francie Hydecker, my old smoking area buddy!" he hollers back. When she reaches him, he gathers her up in a big bear hug.

Helen's smile downgrades slightly. Cal has never hugged her like this. In fact, he's never so much as fist-bumped her. As Cal and Francie grin and say how great the other looks, Helen thinks back. He grabbed her hand for a second when Logan almost knocked her over on the doorstep. She touched his arm when he told her Dorothy had died. This is the full and complete inventory of their physical contact for the last forty years.

# *Chapter 36*

## *2021*

"Hey, thanks again for last week," says Helen.

"It was wonderful to have you guys here!"

"Horseback riding was amazing. I haven't done that since I was at Hotchkiss's barn with you in high school."

"Thanks for bringing Cal. It was great to see him all grown up. And all those stories from back in the day—I haven't laughed that hard in a long time."

"I hope Vernon wasn't too bored."

"He said he really enjoyed it. It was like getting to know me in a whole new way."

"You're the you you always were."

"We all are."

"In some ways."

"In some ways we're better."

"Hope so," says Helen.

"What's up?" says Francie.

ON THE DRIVE home from Vermont, still warmed by their wonderful day together, Helen had commented on how Thanksgiving was coming up fast, only about ten days away. She had asked Cal if he was hosting anyone.

"No, not really."

"Just the family?"

"Well, Bonnie's in Australia. Doesn't make sense to come back just for a long weekend. And obviously Oz doesn't take Thanksgiving off."

"I guess I should be glad Danny's on American soil this year."

"What's his latest project?"

"Ski season's starting out west, and he's doing bio-docs for a couple of semipro snowboarders."

They got talking about that and never came back to the topic of Thanksgiving.

The following Thursday, when they took the three grandkids to an indoor tot lot in Acton, Helen suddenly remembered she hadn't ordered her turkey yet. Barb and Cormac's house is tiny, and his parents are getting on in years, so Helen had offered to host. "I guess we'll be"—she counted up guests in her head—"seven? Or eight if Sam brings a girlfriend."

"*A* girlfriend?" said Cal, pushing Lana and Logan in adjacent swings.

"Sam always has *a* girlfriend, but he hasn't found *the* girlfriend," Helen said, bouncing McKenzie on her hip. "I'm not supposed to ask too many questions, so I just try to get a name and city of origin. Like Jeannie from Boise. Or Emma from Yakima. Sometimes, if I'm not on my toes, a girlfriend comes and goes, and I never even got basic identifiers."

"Ladies' man?"

"Not really. It's serial monogamy. But he's a bit of a perfectionist. If she doesn't floss religiously or tip well enough or whatever, she's out."

Cal raised his eyebrows. "He may find marriage a challenge."

Helen chuckled. "Ya think?"

In the car on the way home, Helen returned to the turkey issue. "There's some sort of amount per guest calculation, but I can never remember what it is."

"I think it's half a pound per person," said Cal. "Plus more for leftovers."

"How big is yours this year?"

"Oh, pretty small."

Apropos of nothing, Logan suddenly sang out from the back seat, "I'm going on a plane!"

Cal said nothing for a second, almost as if he hadn't heard. Then a beat too late, he said, "That's right, buddy. Your first flight."

"I'm going to . . . Where am I going?"

"To see Grandma Gina and Grandpa Dave."

"Yeah, on a plane!"

"That's exciting, Logan," Helen said.

"Yeah," he said, "planes are exciting!"

"Poor kid's going to be so disappointed when he lands," murmured Cal. "St. Louis doesn't look much different from Boston. He asked me if there were dinosaurs."

"Eli's from Missouri?" said Helen.

Cal nodded. "With Covid and all, he hasn't been back in a year and a half. Gina and Dave are dying to see the baby."

Helen couldn't care less about Gina and Dave. "So it's just you and Suze, then."

"We haven't really talked about it. But yeah, I guess."

"Ohhhhhhh," says Francie.

"Right?"

"That sounds . . ."

"I know!"

"What about Noni?" asks Francie. "Maybe she'll be with her own family?"

"Yeah, but why haven't they talked about it?" says Helen. "It's only a week away."

"Could he go to Hestia?"

"His parents are gone. I don't even know where his siblings are. And wouldn't he have said 'I'm going to my sister's' or something?"

"Is it possible that Suze will go off with Noni, and Cal will be—"

"Alone! Alone on Thanksgiving!" Helen is outraged just thinking about it. "That marriage . . ."

"Seriously. Fish or cut bait."

"Pardon the damn turkey or shoot it already."

"Would you ever want to . . . ?" Francie says carefully.

"That's the problem." Helen sighs. "I don't."

"Not like it's your responsibility."

"I mean I would, but I just want my kids, you know? We haven't all been together since Jim died. We need time to figure out who we are now. To find the new us. I don't want to juggle that with 'Oh, and by the way, here's this random guy I used to know.' If he comes for a major holiday, there's no way they'll believe nothing's going on. It'll just be this big . . ."

"Distraction."

"Yes! An enormous, exhausting distraction."

"Cal's a grown-up. He'll be fine."

"He'll be miserable."

"Holidays are miserable sometimes. Just ask a significant portion of the population."

ON SUNDAY, HELEN is cleaning. She's generally pretty tidy, but this is the first time since moving to Massachusetts that she'll be hosting more than just Barb and Cormac. Cormac's parents are joining them for dinner, and Danny and Sam are staying with her. Helen knows they couldn't care less about the state of the grout in her bathroom. (Danny won't even notice if his sheets are washed.) But people are coming, and this sets off a cleaning urge as strong as a salmon's inexorable drive to swim upstream.

Helen's in her stained Sheryl Crow THIS AIN'T NO DISCO T-shirt, a Mother's Day joke gift from the kids because she turned the house into a disco every night after dinner. Her gray sweats are so stretched out she has a safety pin in the waistband to keep them from falling off. Hair in a ponytail, face oily with sweat, Helen is scrubbing a coffee stain out of the living room rug to the beat of Des'ree singing about all the things "You Gotta Be" (bad, bold, wiser—traits for which Helen always feels she could use a little encouragement). It's playing at such a volume that she only hears the doorbell when the song slides into its final fade.

She wipes her face on the shoulder of her T-shirt, hits the pause button on her phone, and answers the door.

"Hi," says a small blond person who looks like a cross between Kristin Chenoweth and Peter Pan. Helen almost expects her to start singing "Popular" from the musical *Wicked* and possibly fly.

"Hi," says Helen. Alarms are going off in her brain, and she knows in another second she'll figure out why, but then—

"I'm Suzanne Bell-Crosby." And though there is absolutely no need to clarify, the woman adds, "Cal's wife."

Helen tries to be cool, but she can't keep her eyebrows from going up as she says, "Oh."

"Mind if we chat for a minute?"

"Uh, no. Not at all." Helen backs up into the suds on the carpet and tries to cover by pointing to the nearest upholstered chair. "Please sit down."

"Thanks so much." Suze lowers herself into the chair and smoothly crosses one leg over the other. She's wearing jeans, but definitely not the kind you get at Old Navy. Her cropped booties are a nutty brown suede and so small that Helen wonders if she orders from the children's department at Neiman Marcus. The winter white sweater is a simple crewneck, but definitely cashmere. Over that is an unzipped short white parka with a Canada Goose label. She wears no jewelry (her perfectly heart-shaped face and aquamarine eyes provide plenty of bling) except for a beautifully cut diamond and platinum ring on her left hand.

Helen swipes a lock of unwashed hair off her sweaty face and says, "Can I get you something? Tea, a glass of water?"

"No, thanks. I'm sorry for popping in without warning."

*Are you, though?* thinks Helen.

"I just thought, I know about you from Cal, and you know about me from Cal, and maybe it's time to cut out the middleman." Suzanne Bell-Crosby smiles, and it's in this small effort that Helen gets a hint that the woman is slightly less sure of herself than she lets on.

Helen sits on the couch and crosses her own long legs. She notices a gaping hole in her sock, uncrosses, and tucks her feet under the coffee table. "What would you like to know?"

"Well, it's not so much what *I'd* like to know as what I'd like *you* to know."

*Oh, for crying out loud, now what?* thinks Helen. *You're not really Suze, you're Suze's evil twin? If someone suddenly develops amnesia in this little soap opera, I am going to lose it.*

"I love my husband," says Suze. "You may be questioning that based on our current arrangement, but I promise you, it's true."

"I'm not questioning anything. That's between you and Cal."

"Yes, it is. But you've wandered into the fray, and I want you to have the facts."

"If you're concerned that something other than friendship is happening between Cal and me, you have nothing to worry about. I would never—"

"That's the least of my concerns. In fact, theoretically, you'd have my blessing."

*Her blessing? Theoretically?* Helen can't keep her jaw from visibly dropping.

"What kind of person would I be," Suze went on, "if I enjoyed an extramarital relationship and didn't allow my husband to have his own?"

"Um . . ."

"That's not why I'm here."

"Let's get to that, then."

"To be blunt, the last time he was with you, he broke. I'd really like him not to break this time."

*The nerve of this shiny little pixie!* As if Helen could ever come up with something worse than cheating on him!

"And you blame me," she says, trying to maintain her calm.

"Not at all." Suze waves this away as if she can put a stop to this notion with her small bare hand. "Really. I know he made a mess of it. But at heart he's a good man, and he seems to be growing in some important ways. It's clear that spending time with you is—for now, at least—good for him. But I can't help but worry that—"

"I'll break him."

"That he'll get hurt."

Helen levels a gaze at the woman. "Anyone can get hurt at any time. That's the nature of relationships."

Suze glances away and mutters, "Isn't that the truth."

"*You've* been hurt."

Her eyes swing back to Helen's. "Yes, I have."

"And yet you're here to . . . what? Try to keep that from happening to him somehow?"

Suze considers for a moment before conceding, "Point taken. I suppose I want him to keep moving forward, not get mired in the past. I know enough about what happened between the two of you back then and how he bungled it to wonder if this . . . friendship . . . is entirely healthy. For either of you."

This lands for Helen. She has to admit that deep down, a little part of her wonders the same thing, despite how good it feels—or possibly precisely because of that. But Suze is not the arbiter of Helen's choices, even if she might be right.

"I appreciate your concern—I really do. But my feelings are not your responsibility. And Cal's a grown-up. Shouldn't he decide for himself what's healthy and what's not?"

"Yes, but I . . ." Suze shakes her head.

"Hurt him. Because you love someone else now. And you still love him enough to worry about what that's doing to him."

The woman's gaze goes a little steely. "I want what's best for my husband. I'm just not sure that's you."

At a loss for words, Helen studies this sparkly gem of a woman. She can see what attracted Cal to her—why any man, woman, or child would want to warm themselves in her glow. Suze emits microwaves of calm and competence. You're in good hands with a person like this.

However, it's also clear that as much as Suze acts like all is well because she's calling the shots . . . in this particular instance, she knows very well that she's not. At least not all of them, not anymore. Helen's arrival has upset the balance.

The woman has come here to ask Helen not to throw a monkey wrench. Suze's is a funny kind of love—one with unfamiliar parameters—but it's love, nonetheless. It's probably why she hasn't left Cal, Helen realizes. She knows he isn't ready. He hasn't found a direction to head in yet, as Dorothy said.

But that's Cal's problem to solve, not Suze's. And certainly not Helen's.

"All I can tell you is that I'm enjoying our friendship, and as long as he's married, that's all it will be. Beyond that, it's up to Cal to do what's best for him."

Suze eyes Helen, then lifts her small shoulder. "Fair enough."

It's not until the woman is pulling away in her Audi that Helen remembers what she really wants to know. *What about Thanksgiving?* she feels like shouting after Suze. *How about THAT, if you love him so much!*

# Chapter 37

## 2021

Helen is waiting at the curb at Logan Airport Terminal B on Wednesday afternoon when Sam emerges pulling a rolling carry-on behind him. When he takes off his airline-required mask, it hits her just how beautiful he is. Striking in a young Brad Pitt / Robert Redford kind of way, with his perennially tousled sandy-blond hair. Strong jaw, broad shoulders. It never fails to surprise her when she hasn't seen him in a while. The real Sam is a lovable geek, obsessing over whether French explorer Samuel de Champlain traveled to what would become Massachusetts in 1605 or 1606 (it was both, he would later inform her), caring just a little too much about everything to be cool. She's eternally grateful that he never became a veterinarian. Putting down an animal would have wrecked him every single time.

But his looks belie all that. He hit the physical gene pool lottery, getting the best of what both his parents had to offer. Jim's thick blond hair and broad shoulders, Helen's hazel eyes and aquiline nose, their two heights compounding to make him the tallest in the family. He never works out, but he still looks fit.

Danny and Barb hate him just a little for all this. That and the fact that he never went through the tortured adolescent phase, or if he did, he had his nose too far into a book to notice. Also, Sam loves Helen unabashedly. Danny took to sneering a line from *Bill and Ted's Excellent Adventure*—"Dude, that's your mom!"—whenever Sam hugged her a second too long.

He stands on the curb and scans the area, adjusting his glasses, buttoning his leather jacket against the Northeast chill, and Helen sees several women, from their teens to middle age, glance at him an extra moment. Then he spies her, and he smiles that perfect I-wore-my-retainer-every-single-night-after-I-got-my-braces-off smile, and one of the women nudges her friend, who makes a little swoony face, and they both laugh.

Poor Sam. He will never be up to the task of managing the desert-island fantasies that women—and probably more than a few men—have about him. Luckily, he'll probably never be fully aware of it anyway.

Helen pops the trunk and hops out of the car. "Hey, sweetie!"

"Hey, Mom," he says, and wraps her up in a hug. He smells of airplane—that slightly metallic, overcirculated, pressurized odor. But beneath that he smells of his usual Sam-ness: part library, part eyeglass cleaner, part boy. Or man, she supposes. At twenty-nine his boyhood is a decade behind him, but to Helen all her offspring contain the children they once were.

Sam slumps slightly in her arms. She has a policy of never ending a hug first with her kids. They know how long they need. After another second, he releases her.

"How was the flight?" she asks after they strap in, and she pulls into the slow crawl of vehicles carrying their prizes home for the holiday.

"Fine. I read." He holds up a book with the title *Sapiens* in an oversize font.

"How's Kiersten from New Haven?"

He mumbles something.

"Sorry?" says Helen.

"New London."

"Did she fly home, too?"

"Probably." Sam shrugs. "We broke up."

"Sorry." There isn't much more to say on the subject. Helen only knew a name, and now this Kiersten is in the rearview anyway. Helen wonders idly why she got the ax. Not into historical documentaries? (Sam says he tries to be patient about this, but if you didn't at the very least love *The Dig*, it's hopeless.) Allergic to animals? (He has a mutt named Titan who reminds Helen of that little pup from the Mighty Dog commercials.) An overexerciser? (Sam doesn't think highly of people who spend too much time at the gym to the detriment of other more worthwhile pursuits. Like watching historical documentaries.)

"She broke up with me."

"Oh." If Helen is correct, this hasn't happened in four or five girlfriends.

"She said I was stressful."

Helen doesn't know how to respond to this. Sam is generally a very kind person, but he does seem to find a way to let his romantic partners know about any lapse in his idea of perfection. Finally she comes up with, "That's a hard thing to hear."

"And too pretty, she said."

"You're too pretty?"

"Yeah. First of all, what does that even mean? I don't, you know, *do* anything. I have about three products in my bathroom, and one of them is toothpaste. I don't care what I wear or get sporty haircuts." He scowls. "I'm just me."

The traffic into the Mass Pike tunnel barely qualifies as a crawl. "Show me a picture of her," says Helen.

He flicks at his phone for a moment, then hands it to Helen. "It's from her Instagram. Her sister's wedding."

The picture is stunning: the two of them with their arms around each other on the edge of a lawn overlooking the ocean, a sunset warming their faces. Kiersten is only slightly shorter than Sam—she's either very tall or in treacherously high heels—wearing a lovely, simple midnight blue dress. She's what Helen would call ample without being heavy. Her face is round and plain, her dark hair cropped at the shoulder. Her eyes, though. Big and brown and positively glowing into the camera with happiness.

Sam, whose looks are pumped to dangerously high voltage by a well-cut gray suit, is gazing down at Kiersten with unabashed admiration. And love. Yes, that's love right there.

Helen is careful to glance up at the traffic every few seconds and slide a few inches forward when necessary. The funnel into the tunnel is maddening, but it gives her time to look at the comments. Kiersten's caption at the top says simply, "With Sam."

Below is an explosion of heart and wow and hand-clapping emojis interspersed with a long trail of variations on "Gorgeous couple!" and "So happy for you!" and "You look great!"

These are the comments of people who are not only happy for Kiersten, they're impressed. A little too impressed, as if a beautiful picture of her with a very handsome man is unexpected. If Kiersten is paying attention, and her self-criticism of her body is in the average (which is to say toxic) range for young American women, Sam being "too pretty" now makes a whole lot of sense.

"And she thinks *I'm* pretty," Sam mutters.

Helen glances up at him.

"Look at her," he says. "She's gorgeous."

Helen hands the phone back. "Do you tell her that?"

"All the time! She says it's stressful because it makes her feel like she has to keep up with my expectations."

*Oh, dear*, thinks Helen. *Poor girl.*

"Sounds like maybe she's a little insecure?"

"She is," he says quietly. "She admits it. I thought telling her she's beautiful would make her understand that she shouldn't feel that way. At least not with me."

"Is there anything else that might be . . . getting under her skin?"

He lets out a little snort. "Yeah, I know, okay? I'm too picky. Barb tells me all the time."

Helen is heartened to hear that he's talking to his sister about this. As emotionally generous as Sam is with most people, for some reason his romantic partners don't always get the same perks.

"I'm not like that with her," he says. "At least not anymore. Kiersten is just . . . good."

"Maybe she just needs a break, honey."

"It's not a break, Mom. She's out."

He turns toward the window, and Helen leaves him be. Once she's in the tunnel, the traffic picks up. She remembers what Francie said about the holidays being miserable for a lot of people. This year, apparently Sam is one of them.

HE IS NOT a moper, though, and when they reach the house, he takes the tour and compliments her on every room.

"I really did nothing," Helen tells him. "It was more or less like this when I moved in."

In the hallway, Sam takes a moment to gaze at a framed picture of the five of them from about a decade ago, taken by Annabella. She'd made them laugh, teasing them from behind the camera that they were almost as delicious as her anise cookies. "I could eat you up!"

"Damn," whispers Sam. "Still can't believe they're gone."

Helen puts an arm around him. "We were lucky to have them."

He turns and smiles at her. "You're sticking around, right?"

"Going absolutely nowhere."

There's a knock and the sound of the door opening. "Hey, weirdo!"

Sam and Helen come around the corner to find Barb with Lana on her hip.

"Nonna!" Lana reaches for Helen, who takes her while Sam hugs his sister.

"Boss," he says, unwinding her scarf and hanging her coat on a hook in the entryway.

"She's the boss now," Barb says, tipping her head at Lana.

"Hello, beautiful," he coos at his niece. "I'm Uncle Sam. I'm going to teach you how to smoke cigarettes and skip class, just like your mother did for me!"

"You never did either," Barb scoffs.

"I did, too! That one time I smoked with you on the way to school. I got so nauseated I had to turn back and hide in the shed all morning so Mom wouldn't know."

"Barbara Annabella Spencer!" says Helen.

"Your uncle's a tattletale, honey," Barb tells Lana.

"Wait till Uncle Danny gets here." He grins at the baby. "You're gonna learn all sorts of things! Can you say *tattoo*?"

Barb laughs. "I should probably hide her, huh?"

HELEN SLIDES INTO bed late that night, exhausted but happy. She and Sam and Barb took turns playing with Lana while the other two prepped the turkey and sides for tomorrow's big meal. They put leaves in her round maple table and pushed the couch and upholstered chairs against the walls to make room. Cormac came by with a couple of pizzas for dinner.

Little by little, Sam got incorporated into what Helen still considers their "bubble." He played peekaboo with Lana, ducking under her high chair tray and popping up again and again, making her laugh her lovely tinkling-brook laugh. He tried to get her to say "Sam," but she took it as a game and simply clapped when he repeated it over and over. All the while she studied him as if loading him onto her hard drive, pixel by pixel.

Danny was due in the next morning. Cormac had offered to pick him up, but Helen wanted to be the one waiting at the curb for her knight-errant.

The Spencers would all be together. Finally. Helen had to admit she was a little anxious about it. Jim hadn't been around all that much, but when he was, his presence generally calmed any turbulence that arose. Spats most often originated with Danny or Barb, but with Sam in a mood about Kiersten, anything was possible.

Last Thanksgiving Helen had been with only Barb and Cormac. They'd Zoomed with Sam and Danny, but it was all so foreign that Jim's and Annabella's absence had hardly seemed strange. This year, however, she misses her mother. And yes, she even misses Jim.

As her brain meanders toward sleep, one last image flickers across the fading screen of her consciousness: Cal Crosby sitting in his kitchen nook eating turkey. Alone.

# *Chapter 38*

2021

Danny's plane is late. Actually, it isn't even the right one. He'd been trying to get a little more footage for one of his bio-docs, missed the last flight out of Provo, drove to Salt Lake City, had to connect in Houston and then Newark. He texted her with updates, but Helen was on the way to the airport before she got the one about the final flight taking off late. She waits in the cell-phone lot for an hour, talking Sam through basting the turkey and where the good napkins are. Barb and Cormac opened the bakery this morning for people to pick up baked goods. It's just the two of them, Cormac having let his staff off for the day. Lana is in a backpack on his back.

Helen finally gets a text from Danny, *Landed*, and she heads to Terminal C. When he comes out and looks around for her, she can tell he's out of sorts. His long brown hair is stringy, and the wind is whipping it in hanks around his face. When he takes his mask off, she sees he's got a scruffy stubble, and the duffel hanging off his shoulder looks like it took a trip around the world in the bowels of a coal barge. In short, he looks homeless. Not only are women not checking him out, some are actively moving away from him.

Helen pops the trunk and hops out of the car. "Hi, sweetie!"

"Hey." Danny tosses his duffel in back, slumps into the passenger seat, and says, "Got any food? I'm fucking starving."

At five feet, ten inches, Danny is the shortest male in the Spencer family. Incongruously, he also has the lowest voice. He sounds a little like Harrison Ford, with that same kind of perpetually annoyed grumble. Sometimes Helen can't hear him. Sometimes she thinks this is purposeful. She asks a few innocuous questions about how the shoots are going, to which he replies with shrugs and grunts.

*You're twenty-four*, she wants to say. *Your adolescence is over.* But she does not say this, having learned in the thirty-five years since Barb was born that one of the advanced skills of parenthood is tongue-biting.

Also, things are clearly not going well. He looks bad. He smells bad. His clothes are ratty. She suspects he needs money, but if she offers before he asks, it humiliates him. There is nothing about getting funds from his mom that Danny likes other than not being forced to live naked and hungry in an abandoned cargo container.

When they arrive, Sam is in the kitchen spattering turkey juice all over the inside of the oven as he attempts to baste. He's wearing an apron to protect his clothes. Danny smiles for the first time all morning and says, "Hey, Gorgeous George."

Helen cringes. Sam has never liked this nickname, and now that his ex-girlfriend has deemed him "too pretty," it lands particularly badly. Sam gives Danny a brief hug, wrinkles his nose, and says, "Hey, Pigpen."

"It's been a long night, so fuck off," Danny growls wearily.

Sam chuckles. "Mom, you got any air freshener?"

DANNY IS STILL in the shower when Barb and Cormac arrive with Cormac's parents. Helen has always liked Charlie and Bridget McGrath. Bridget is kind and soft-spoken; Charlie is lovably cantankerous. He worked at the Belham Town Dump for fifty years before coming to work for Cormac at the bakery. In his eighties now, he doesn't get around like he used to, and the pandemic was a good excuse for retirement.

Barb comes in first with Lana and murmurs, "Charlie won't use the cane. Stubborn as a cat." She and Helen stand in the doorway to greet them as the elderly man slowly makes his way up the steps to the porch, irritably waving off Cormac's offers of help. He wobbles and Cormac grabs his elbow. "Pop, let me just—"

"Get yer mitts off!" This exclamation destabilizes the large man even more, and for a moment, Helen thinks he may tumble.

"Charlie, let him help!" Bridget urges from behind them. She's carrying something, and Helen dearly hopes it's not a Jell-O mold. Her son produces the best cakes and pies in MetroWest Boston, and Bridget still considers banana slices suspended in a jiggling gelatinous blob necessary for any festive occasion.

"Don't tell me what to—" Charlie bellows and misses a step.

"Charlie!" Bridget gasps.

"Dammit, Pop," Cormac groans as he catches the older man.

"Cormac, don't speak to your father that way!"

*Oh, boy*, thinks Helen. *Now it's a party.*

THE TURKEY IS dry. Helen is attempting to carve it while marshaling the troops to stir gravy, fill water glasses, set up Lana's high chair, find serving utensils, set out butter, salt, pepper, and the right napkins (not the slightly stained ones Sam found), and plate the sides.

"Please, let me help," says Bridget, coming to stand beside Barb at the stove. Three people in the little kitchen is one and a half too many, but the older woman's need to be part of it is palpable. She sticks a finger into the sweet potatoes, licks it, and says, "Where's the sugar?"

Barb says, "We don't usually—"

But Bridget has already unloaded half the sugar bowl into the pot. Barb shoots her own mother a dark look. Helen smiles brightly and says, "Bridget, could you transfer that to a serving bowl and take it to the table?"

When she leaves, Barb mutters, "I'm not eating that Jell-O shit. It's gruesome."

"Marriage Rule Number 457: Don't snub your mother-in-law's cooking. It's never, ever worth it."

Barb makes a gagging sound and slops mashed potatoes into a bowl.

ALL THE FOOD is on the table and all the guests are seated except Danny. Helen doesn't want to start without him, but Barb mutters, "Seriously, Mom, it's not like he'll care."

It's true. He won't. In fact, he'll probably prefer to slide in after grace has been said.

Helen clasps her hands, and the others follow suit. "We're thankful for all this wonderful food, and for the chance to be together again after so much isolation. We pray for all those who aren't able to be with their loved ones." She sighs and suddenly feels emotional. "And we say a prayer of thanks for the lives of Dad and Grandma, whom we will always love, and who are with us in our hearts."

There's a beat of silence and she glances up to see Barb wipe a tear from the corner of one eye, and Sam bite the inside of his lip, which he's done since he was a child to keep from crying.

*Mama*, thinks Helen. *I miss you. You would make this so much better.*

Danny walks in just as food is being passed. His long hair is still dripping, and he has an empty beer bottle in his hand.

"Seriously?" says Sam.

"You never had a shower beer?" says Danny defensively.

"I shoulda had three," grumbles Charlie.

"'Cause that definitely would've improved things," Cormac mutters sarcastically.

Bridget glares at her son. "That was unkind."

Cormac is one of the kindest people Helen knows, arguably kinder than any of her own children. He adores his father. But the older man has always been hardheaded, even more so now that he's losing his independence. Helen knows this is tough on Cormac.

"Let me put on some music." She rises, gets her phone, connects it to the speaker in the living room, and hits one of Spotify's random dinner music lists. A balmy instrumental piece fills the air, and Helen takes the opportunity to refill wineglasses when she returns to the table.

Neither the wine nor the music helps in the least.

ACROSS AMERICA, HOURS and hours are spent in preparation for Thanksgiving dinner: turkeys laboriously stuffed and basted, good china excavated from attic boxes, snowflake rolls kneaded and baked, yams whipped and (for some unknown reason) topped with marshmallows . . . and then the whole meal is scarfed down in twenty minutes. For once Helen is glad that the fruit of all this labor is eradicated quickly, and she's fairly certain she's not alone.

Bridget McGrath, ever polite and thoughtful, folds her napkin neatly, tucks it beside her plate, and asks, "When's the egg hunt?"

"Mom," breathes Cormac.

"Ah, Bridgie," Charlie sighs.

Helen's eyes dart to Barb's, who gives a sad little nod.

"Don't Bridgie me," says the older woman. "I don't care where she came from, the child should get to hunt for eggs."

Stunned into silence, everyone looks at Lana. The little girl's lip trembles.

"Sweetheart," coos Barb.

Lana opens her mouth and lets out a wail the likes of which Helen has never before seen from this child. Her beautiful dark eyes are immediately swamped with tears that pour in rivulets down her smooth cheeks. The little uvula in the back of her throat quivers anew with every sob.

Barb unclicks the tray and seat straps with such speed, it's as if she's saving her child from a submerged vehicle. She lifts Lana into her arms and hugs her close. "Okay, sweetie, okay," she soothes as she heads down the hall to one of the bedrooms.

"Time to go," says Charlie.

Cormac helps them back into their coats and out the door.

Helen, Sam, and Danny are left sitting at the table. Lana's sobs are still audible from down the hall. Danny takes another slug of his beer, eyes focused on the front door that has just closed behind the McGraths, and murmurs a wry, "Happy Thanksgiving."

"You always have to make it worse," says Sam.

"Sam," warns Helen as she rises and begins collecting silverware.

"The fuck is that supposed to mean?" says Danny.

"It means just clear the table and don't mouth off." Sam stands and gathers plates.

"What are you—Dad, now?"

"Danny!" says Helen.

"No, I'm a responsible adult. Try it sometime."

Danny stands up. "You're also a self-righteous prick."

Sam narrows his eyes. "At least I'm not a—"

"Boys!"

"A what?"

Helen drops a handful of utensils onto her plate with a loud crash. "That's enough!" They both turn to stare at her, and before she loses control of herself and the moment, she snarls, "Go to your rooms."

Sam's face goes wide, and Danny lets out an astonished laugh.

"*Now*, goddamn it!" she yells.

"Fine by me." Sam puts down the plates and walks down the hall. Danny, never one to follow orders, heads for the front door, grabs his coat off the hook, and leaves.

Helen surveys the detritus of the meal. She picks up a stack of plates, takes it to the sink, and tugs on a pair of rubber gloves.

She glances at Cormac's beautiful pies and the now-slumping tower of red gelatin, pulls off the rubber gloves, and slams them on the floor.

Her phone is sitting on the counter. She grabs it and stabs at it until the music goes off. Then she places a call.

"Happy Thanksgiving," he says.

"I'm drowning in pie here. Want to come over?"

"Hey, I'm fine, in case this is just you feeling sorry for me."

"Sorry for you?" she snorts. "At the moment I envy you."

He laughs. "You're sure it's okay with—"

"Just come."

# Chapter 39

## 2021

Helen is loading the dishwasher when she hears voices on the porch steps.

"—love the place." It's Cal. "You ever think about a second site?"

"Helen's brought it up a couple of times." Cormac. "I'm not sure, though."

The door opens. "Hi," Helen says to Cal. "Wearing a lead vest, I hope."

Cormac laughs. "You called in reinforcements."

Helen goes wide-eyed and innocent. "Now why would I do that?"

Cal grins warmly and shrugs. "No danger is too great as long as I'm compensated in pie."

Helen smiles back at him; she can feel her whole body relax. Her friend is here.

The two men take up the task of clearing the table as Helen mans the sink. They continue their conversation about a second Cormac's Confectionery.

"I'm there all the time. How could I handle two?"

"You hire a couple of reliable managers. Or you could think about franchising."

"How does that work?"

Helen stays quiet as she scours pots with her back to them. It's soothing just to listen. She likes the way Cal gently offers his ideas without any pressure.

"Uh, hi." Helen looks over her shoulder. Sam is in the living room on the other side of the counter eyeing Cal.

"Have you met Cal?" says Cormac. "Your mom's friend from high school?"

Sam smiles tightly. "I don't believe I have." Subtext: *Never even heard of the guy.* "I'm Sam. Middle child." He reaches out to shake Cal's hand without taking his eyes off him.

"The environmental attorney from Seattle," says Cal. "Nice to meet you."

To divert Sam's laser stare, Helen says, "Can you put the left-overs in containers?"

He aims his gaze at her. "Sure, Mom." His look says a thousand things, but Helen is too worn out to care. She pulls out plastic containers and lids and places them on the counter near him and turns back to her pots. *Let them figure it out*, she thinks.

"Hey, I heard this great story out of Seattle about composting human remains," says Cal.

"It's a company called Recompose," says Sam. "My firm's done some work with them."

"Seriously?" says Cormac. "Dead people?"

"Yeah," says Cal. "Great-uncle Homer kicks, they turn him into compost, and you spread him in your rose garden."

"Way more eco-friendly than cremation or burial," says Sam. He starts to scoop the sugary sweet potatoes into a container.

"Wait," says Helen. "Here, I'll take that." She slides them into the disposal.

Out the kitchen window, she sees Danny approach across the tiny backyard from the woods. It's something they have in common: the head-clearing, mood-lightening response to nature. He comes in the back door just as Cal is bringing in a load of dishes. Danny glances to Helen, who says, "Danny, this is my friend, Cal, from high school. We bumped into each other last month. He lives in town here."

Danny shakes his hand. "Hope your dinner was better than ours."

"Completely stress-free. It was just me." Cal smiles affably and goes back to help Cormac with the table.

Danny watches Cal a second and then murmurs to Helen, "He's your friend, and you let him do Thanksgiving by himself? That's pretty cold."

Helen sighs. *Can't get it right with this kid . . .*

She hands him a dish towel and tips her chin at the just-washed pots. "Dry, please."

"SHOULD WE WAIT for Barb?" Helen asks Cormac when the kitchen is reasonably clean, the coffee is brewing, and the table has been reset for dessert. He's bringing out the pies: bourbon pecan, apple cranberry crumble, and the traditional pumpkin. There is an unspoken agreement between them to ignore the shiny red mound that sits sad and lonely on the kitchen counter.

"They're probably napping," Cormac says. "It could be a while."

But just as they all start to tuck into their pie slices of choice, Barb comes down the hall with Lana. Their faces are sleep wrinkled and relaxed. Anxious to maintain the equanimity, everyone keeps their voices soft with "Hey, sleepyheads," and "Did you have a nice snoozer?"

Barb's eye catches on Cal, sitting closest to her. He smiles a hello, and Barb immediately sizes him up like he's a suspect and she's a polygraph test. But before Helen can make an introduction, Lana, who is also studying Cal, says, "Bay. Be."

"That's right," says Cal. "Baby McKenzie. You remember."

The little girl leans out for him to take her. Cal's eyes flick to Barb for permission, and she reluctantly hands Lana over. He snuggles her onto his lap and says, "Do you want some pie?"

Danny, sitting next to Helen, mutters, "Holy shit."

*That's right, Cal*, thinks Helen. *Surprise the hell out of them.*

"Is it me, or does your daughter have an MRI machine in her eyeballs?" Cal murmurs to Helen as they wash dishes together after everyone pushed back their chairs and declared themselves utterly stuffed. "I think I got a brain scan back there."

Helen laughs. "Don't complain. I got the same from Janel."

"How can I complain after Lana came in for the save? Pretty sure I owe that kid a fiver."

The others are clearing and taking the leaves out of the table, setting the room to rights, and Danny comes in with too many things in his hands. Before he can set down his load, a wineglass tips its last few sips onto Cal's right foot.

"Oh, shit. Sorry, man," says Danny.

"No worries." Cal pulls off his sock and says, "I'm planning to suck on this later."

But Danny isn't listening. He's staring at Cal's foot. "Whoa, what happened?"

"Frostbite."

Danny nods appreciatively. Frostbite is, of course, a professional hazard in his line of work. "Does it affect you much?"

"The toes aren't really the issue, strangely enough. You can get around pretty good without the two smallest ones. Big toe would have been far worse, so I was lucky."

*Lucky?* thinks Helen. She never thought she'd hear him express gratitude for the collateral damage of that night.

"It's more about the foot itself," Cal goes on. "You freeze a foot and you're going to have neurological damage. It affects something called proprioception—awareness of how your body is moving through space. I have a little trouble with lateral movement. It's not even noticeable unless I do something where you have to cut left and right, like tennis."

"Or football," says Helen.

He glances at her. "Yep. That too."

"How'd you do it?" Danny clearly hopes there's a cool story, like climbing K2.

"Uh, well, I fell in a stream and then I stayed out too long."

"Long enough to get frostbite? You didn't notice it happening?"

"I fell asleep."

Helen knows Cal is protecting her, making it sound like he was alone that night. He doesn't want her implicated. But it's disturbing to hear a de-Helen-ized version of the story. He's probably been telling it that way for years, she realizes, and this hits her in a strangely painful way.

Danny gives a knowing smile. "Had a few? I passed out on Joey Frattaroli's lawn once and woke up like a Popsicle. But it was North Carolina, so I was barely hypothermic."

Helen hadn't known about this, though she did know the Frattarolis were asleep at the switch when it came to their kids' parties. She'd rather talk about cold, drunken teenagers—or anything, really—instead of Cal's Helen-less night. But before she can cut in, Cal says, "No, I was sober."

Danny blinks a few times, trying to figure out how a guy who seems fairly intelligent lost toes to frostbite if he wasn't under the influence.

"He was with me," Helen says suddenly.

"With *you*?" Danny's incredulousness goes right up her spine.

"Yep," she says, "we were out in the woods, and we didn't feel like coming back, so we built a fire and then we fell asleep."

Danny's eyebrows go up so high they practically hit his hair-line. "Jesus, Mom."

Helen shrugs, as if to say, *There you have it.* Cal's gaze flicks from one to the other, wet sock still hanging from his hand.

Danny mutters, "Okay then," and leaves the kitchen.

"You enjoyed that," murmurs Cal.

She grins slyly. "*So* much."

"He underestimates you."

"Chronically. But maybe that's changing just a little . . ."

WHEN THEY FINISH the dishes and turn toward the living room, Helen sees that her children stalled out on putting the room back together. The couch is still pushed up against one wall and the two upholstered chairs against the opposite one; the rug has yet to be returned.

Barb and Cormac are on the sofa with Lana; Danny and Sam are in the chairs, sullen as two kids outside the principal's office. Can't they just lighten up a little? Would that be so hard? Helen motions for Cal to sit on the couch next to Cormac and perches on the arm next to him.

Cormac catches her eye. "Where's your phone?" Helen pulls it out of her back pocket and hands it to him. In another minute, a thumping bass rhythm starts up from the small but powerful speaker on the mantel. Helen's head starts to tip back and forth of its own accord. She recognizes the song, of course: "She Drives Me Crazy" by Fine Young Cannibals. It's on Mom's Playlist, an after-dinner dance favorite from when the kids were little. Across the room she notices her sons are also moving ever so slightly to the beat.

"Watch this," she hears Cormac whisper to Cal as he raises the volume until the high guitar riff fills the room.

Barb hands off Lana to Cormac and slowly stalks across the floor to her brothers, feet advancing to the beat, shoulders swaying slightly. "Get up, you fine young cannibals!" she dares them.

Danny rolls his eyes. Sam frowns, but Barb grabs his hand, and he lets her pull him up.

When she reaches for Danny, he growls, "No way."

"Chicken," Barb sneers.

He's having none of that, and he gets up, grabs her by the hand, and spins her till she nearly topples. "Mama!" yells Lana.

"It's okay," Cormac says. "Mama's having fun."

Barb turns to Helen and beckons, but Helen balks. Under any other circumstances, she'd need no cajoling, but with Cal sitting right there . . .

"Are you kidding me?" says Barb. "You started all this!"

Cormac raises the volume another notch. Helen gets up.

Maybe it's the wine, or maybe she's just sick of caring about everything and everyone, how they feel and what they need. What *she* needs is to dance.

And apparently so do her kids. At the bridge, just as they did when they were little, both men point at their sister and howl, "She drives me crazy! Like no one e-else!"

Only once does Helen glance over at Cal on the couch next to Cormac. The two men seem to know to stay put. Spencers gotta Spencer. But Cal is looking right at her, and she knows he's remembering her hopping around in the woods that night.

She's self-conscious for a moment, but she turns away and thinks, *Oh, who cares.*

Next up is "Lovely Day" by Bill Withers, with its sneaky little bass-player intro and cool-cat vocals that belie its danceability. But the Spencers know how it builds to an arm-spreader. "Then

I look at you, and I know it's gonna be . . ." Barb heads for the couch and pulls Cormac up. Cormac tips his head at Cal to follow, and then they're all bouncing, singing out "a lovely day!" at the chorus.

It's on to "Two Princes" by the Spin Doctors, and "September" by Earth, Wind & Fire. During "I'm a Believer" by the Monkees, Cormac sings out, "Then I saw her face, now I'm a believer" to his bride, while Danny and Sam make gagging noises. Occasionally Helen finds herself dancing with Cal, but not for long before they move away from each other.

"Too much pie," groans Danny at the end of the fifth rousing song. Somehow in the melee he's been given Lana, and he sinks down into a chair with her in his arms.

"Not enough wine," says Sam, and heads off to the kitchen.

Helen picks up her abandoned phone from the couch and chooses Al Green's sexy "Let's Stay Together." Cormac immediately pulls Barb in close, an arm around her waist, his hand holding hers against his chest. They melt into each other and sway.

"Their wedding song," Helen tells Cal as they return to the couch.

". . . whether times are good or bad, happy or sad . . ." Between the business-pummeling pandemic and their quest for parenthood, Cormac and Barb have certainly had their ups and downs. But tonight they beam nothing but gratitude as they gaze at each other.

Cal tips his chin at them and murmurs, "Must make you so happy."

"Nothing more satisfying than seeing your kid pick just the right person."

"No matter what they got from us."

"Janel seems to have found her match, too."

He nods. "One down, one to go."

"Not sure what lies in store for my other two," whispers Helen.

Sam comes in with a glass of wine in one hand and a bottle of beer in the other. He hands the beer to Danny, and they clink. Lana has a chubby little hand wrapped in Danny's hair, but he doesn't seem to mind as he whispers to her.

"They'll be all right," says Cal. "You raised good kids."

"You, too, my friend."

He smiles at her. "At least we got something right."

The song ends, and Cormac sits in the last spot on the couch and pulls Barb onto his lap.

"Excuse me, we have an announcement," Danny says suddenly, and Helen pauses the music. "Lana has something she'd like to tell you." He whispers in her ear, and she smiles.

"Da. Nee."

They all cheer—all except Sam, who feigns outrage and hisses, "You *bastard*."

Danny grins and covers Lana's ears. "Sometimes the underdog wins, shithead."

AT THE END of the evening, after more dancing, more pie, and, for those not driving, more wine, Helen walks Cal out to his car. "Thanks for braving the cannibals," she says.

"That's what friends are for."

"I should've invited you in the first place."

"My atypical family situation is not your problem. And you needed some time with them."

"If I'd known what a train wreck it would be, you and I could have ordered takeout and avoided the whole thing."

"Nah," he said. "It ended up being good. For all of us."

"It did, didn't it?" She sighs. "I may need you on backup for all family occasions."

He smiles. "I'm your man."

*I wish.*

She immediately tries to unthink this, but it can't be unthought. It's true. She does.

"Happy Thanksgiving," he says.

His gaze lingers on her in a way that makes her neurons fire and her hair tingle and her solar plexus hum. He's absolutely motionless, but it's dangerous, this look. It feels like the spark that starts the forest fire.

*Married.* The bucket of water that douses the flame.

"Yep," she says a little too brightly. "Happy Thanksgiving."

As he drives away, she thinks, *Time to build another box.*

# *Chapter 40*

## *2021*

When Helen gets up in the morning, Sam is asleep on the couch, an arm hanging off, mouth open, snoring quietly. He's still in his clothes; someone has thrown a blanket over him. The kids (should Helen stop calling them that at some point?) stayed up long after Cormac took Lana home and Helen herself went off to bed. There was something deeply comforting about hearing her offspring's muffled voices as she fell asleep.

She does remember one or two times when their conversation grew loud and intelligible.

"It's hopeless!" Sam howled at one point.

"That's when it means the most, asshole!" Danny shouted back. "That's when you try your hardest!"

*Oh*, Helen thought, lying in bed. *That's who he is now.* A man who knows his chosen profession is a long shot, grueling both physically and monetarily. But he has a goal (the romantically inclined might call it a dream, but Helen is more of a pragmatist), and he'll do what he has to do to get there. He's a fighter. Helen chuckled to herself. *Well, that I knew.*

She's putting on her running shoes when Danny comes in also dressed to run—sweats, sneakers, hair in a ponytail, and a jacket that Helen recognizes from high school.

"How far?" he whispers to her.

She holds up three fingers.

He tips his head in a *Mind if I join?* look.

Helen gives him a *suit yourself* shrug and turns back to her laces, in case her face reveals any of the fist-pumping joy that is now coursing through her body.

After she latches the back door behind them, she says, "You okay with the woods?"

"I prefer it." And they start off across the backyard.

"You're a runner now." She tries to sound casual.

"I need a lot of cardio to stay in shape for work, and I can't always get to a pool."

"I'm sure you're a lot faster than me."

"Doesn't matter. Important thing is just to get out there."

Belham is full of undeveloped land—the locals love to call it semirural, touting both its bucolic bliss and closeness to Boston—and Helen's route hopscotches from one conservation parcel to the next.

"How'd Barb get home?" she asks.

"She's in Sam's bed. We got a little sloppy."

"But no fistfights."

"Pretty mellow, actually."

They run in silence for a while. Danny is close, but not on her heels. She likes hearing his breath behind her. They hit an old cart path, and he comes up next to her.

"Sam's gonna need your car today."

"For?"

"New London."

"He's going after Kiersten?"

"Yeah, I kicked his ass pretty hard about it."

Helen smiles. "Showing your brotherly love."

"Something like that."

They slow to cross a road, but it's still early, and there aren't many cars out. From there the trail heads uphill, and they don't speak. Helen runs harder up that incline than she ever has before. She doesn't want to disappoint him.

He beats her, but not by a humiliating amount, then turns to wait, jogging in place, smiling. "Not bad," he says.

"For an old lady," she pants.

"For anyone."

They jog a little more slowly so Helen can catch her breath. The path winds through a meadow studded with hog-mown grass and runs along one of the countless old stone walls that crisscross New England.

"Thanks for your help last month," Danny says as he lopes beside her. His face is blank, but she knows what it costs him. She thinks about what she heard last night.

"You work hard, Danny. I'm happy to support that."

"Wish I didn't need it."

"We all need help sometimes."

"Sam and Barb don't."

"I've helped Barb and Cormac a lot."

"Yeah?"

"A lot."

"Fucking Covid."

"Exactly."

"But not Sam."

"Sam doesn't need money." She smiles. "He just needs his butt kicked sometimes."

He laughs. "Wuss."

"He's in love."

"Finally!"

"We all have things we're working on."

They slow to climb over a tree that's fallen across the path.

"I'm proud of you, Danny."

His eyes flick over at her. "Yeah?"

She holds his gaze a second. "Yeah."

When they make it back to Helen's backyard, they slow to a walk and stop outside the back door to stretch.

"Hey, um . . ."

Helen looks up.

"I, uh, I may have switched my flight last night," says Danny.

"Oh." He's supposed to leave tomorrow, but the apologetic look suggests it's sooner now.

"All that talk about hopeless love."

"Oh?" He never tells her about his private life, and she knows she should be glad for even this tiny tidbit, but she can't stop herself from asking, "You have a Kiersten?"

He doesn't answer for a moment, and she's sure she's pissed him off. But then he says, "Maria."

Helen nods. "Maria."

Danny shakes his head and looks away, as if he can't believe he's doing this. "She's an instructor for NOLS. It's a wilderness training school." He shrugs to hide his pride. "Actually it's the best one."

"She must be pretty good at it then."

"Total badass."

When they go inside, Sam is no longer on the couch, and the shower is running.

As she and Danny take off their shoes, Helen says, "It's Black Friday."

He smirks. "You're not going shopping."

"No, but I do like a good sale now and then. Let's go online and order you some clothes."

He gives her a warning look. "Mom."

She flicks the ragged collar of his jacket. "Just sayin'."

"You're using her against me!"

"I'm simply getting some early Christmas presents for my hardworking son."

SAM DOES INDEED ask for the car and leaves without telling her why he needs it or where he's going. He probably suspects she already knows. Later that afternoon, Helen and Danny are perusing REI.com when Sam texts, *Is it okay if I keep the car overnight?*

Helen shows it to Danny. He nods. "Promising."

*Sure*, she texts back. She waits for more, but that's all she gets.

Squinting at a highly insulated parka on the computer screen, Danny says, "Cal's a solid dude."

Helen freezes for a moment. She has half an impulse to reciprocate his revelation about Maria from NOLS, but it's a level of exposure she's not ready for. Might not ever be ready for. Not about Cal, anyway. "Yeah, he's a good friend," she says.

Danny clicks on the parka color choices. "The blue?"

Grateful for the reprieve, Helen says, "I was thinking the same thing."

After agreeing to accept quite a bit more clothing than Helen could even have hoped for, Danny gets a ride from Barb to the airport that night, carrying two turkey sandwiches and three pieces of pie Helen wrapped up for him.

Alone in the quiet house, she reheats some Thanksgiving leftovers for herself and sits at the counter with a can of seltzer. She looks down at the steaming plate and has a thought to invite Cal to join her. He doesn't have any leftovers, after all. He'd probably appreciate it. Also, she has a lot to catch him up on: Sam's quest for love in Connecticut; the run of her dreams with Danny. In fact, Cal's the first person she wants to tell.

This is disconcerting. The first person you want to tell stuff is a pretty important person in your life. Very important. Potentially *the most* important. Cal cannot be this person, not in his current marital state.

*How did this happen?* How did he morph so quickly from Cal fucking Crosby to First Person You Want to Tell status? In the beginning, being friendly with him felt good because it felt like they were fixing the past. But once that box was checked, it still felt so . . . good. Easy. In fact, there are ways Helen likes him now even more than she did in high school. He's mature and thoughtful; he's navigated some big life lessons and become a man for others. And they just have so much fun together.

*Shit*, she thinks now, *I never should've invited him over for those damn eggs.*

But she couldn't have known the trouble it would cause. And if she's completely honest with herself—which she's never been terribly good at, and Cal has nudged her to improve—she's still glad he came over and ate her eggs and became her friend again. She wouldn't give that up, even knowing how painful it would become.

Helen does not text or call Cal to tell him about Danny or anything else, because first she has to figure out how to build a box strong enough to lock away all the love she feels. She's starting to realize it could take some time.

ON SATURDAY AFTERNOON, Sam returns. When he comes in, he thanks her for the loan of the car, but says little else. Ready to throw her hands around his neck to get some news out of him

(Seriously, what is with the secrecy, anyway? It's not like he won't tell her eventually), Helen says, "You had good driving weather."

"Yeah. I like your car. Nice handling."

"I'm glad it served you well."

"It did."

Helen punches him in the shoulder.

"Ow!"

"Just tell me, you stinker!"

He looks away. "She's considering."

"Considering?"

"Getting back together."

Helen treads carefully, because this is better than a flat-out no, but it puts him in a limbo that is in some ways even harder.

Sam crosses his arms and looks away. "She says she can't take the perfectionism. That she's always worried she's going to do or say the wrong thing."

"Sam . . ."

He looks back at her. "What?"

At first she thinks it's a *back off* kind of "What?" but then she realizes he's really asking.

"You've always been so kind."

"So why am I hard on girlfriends?" He shrugs. "With any luck, you have one shot at picking the right person, right? Someone who gets you and loves you anyway, and you feel the same about them, and it . . . you know . . . *lasts*. I just don't want to look back and . . ." He glances away from her.

*Have regrets.* It hits Helen like an uppercut. *He doesn't want to end up like me.* The fact that he saw the disconnect in her relationship with Jim shouldn't surprise her. Sam always paid such close attention to her. But now, in successive attempts to avoid her fate and land the perfect partner, he's shut himself out of love entirely.

Silence looms between them until Sam says, "Hey, what's Danny's Venmo?"

"Venmo?"

"Mom, don't tell me you don't have Venmo."

"I've heard of it, but why would I need it?"

"So you can sneak-attack Danny with some cash, for one thing."

"How does it work?"

He shows her on his phone. They find Danny's username, and Sam sends him a thousand dollars with a memo that says, "Buy your girl some carabiners."

"See?" Sam grins triumphantly. "It's in his account now, and there's nothing he can do about it, the little shit."

"Can't he do the same thing and send the money back to you?"

"Well, yeah, but he won't."

"You're sure about that."

"I owe him, and he knows it. He's the one who made me go after her. Besides, if he's brave enough to dangle off a cliff with fifty pounds of camera equipment, he'd better be man enough to accept a little help from his big brother once in a while."

"And you're glad you went?"

Sam's expression goes a few degrees warmer, and he lets out a chuckle. "Yeah."

"Even though it wasn't a complete success?"

He shrugs. "I love her. And she loves me. I don't know how I know, but I know. There's something about someone who both loves you and also calls you on your shit, isn't there?" He laughs and shakes his head. "That is a fucking winning combo."

ON THE WAY to the airport on Sunday morning, Sam says, "Cal seems like a nice guy."

Helen thought she'd gotten away without this particular conversation. *So close*, she thinks as they enter the Ted Williams Tunnel.

"Barb says you two are spending a lot of time together."

"A bit."

"He's married."

Helen glances over at him. "I'm sure she also told you there's nothing going on that shouldn't, and his wife is fine with it."

"Yeah, she said that's what you told her. Though of course we all wondered why he wasn't with his family for a major holiday."

There is no way Helen is going to try to explain that one. In fact, if she defends Cal at all, it will quickly cross into lady-doth-protest-too-much territory. But she knows that, unlike Danny, Sam won't let it go.

She goes with "I'm not a hundred percent sure what happened there, but it's really not my business."

"He couldn't take his eyes off you. Is *that* your business?"

This is new information. Helen spent most of the evening trying to keep things light, not dancing with Cal too long, or looking at him too much; she had no idea he wasn't doing the same. She feels herself flush.

"Well, I can't speak to that," she says. "But for me it's only about friendship."

A lie has a distinct taste in your mouth, she notices. Foreign. Like a sip of something that's not meant for human consumption.

"I honestly couldn't care less if the poor sap has a crush on you," says Sam, "as long as you don't get hurt." They emerge from the tunnel and Helen is trying to focus on which ramp to take when he mutters, "It's better to be too picky than not picky enough."

# *Chapter 41*

*2021*

M onday night, Helen wants to call Francie. But then again, she doesn't.

Helen will tell her the whole story—she's never been good at abridging or spinning things with Francie—and Francie will see it for what it is. Unsustainable. Helen's not ready to hear that yet.

Strangely, Barb doesn't call or come over. Helen would've expected her daughter to jump at the chance to dissect every part of Thanksgiving, especially Cal. But it's radio silence from the McGrath house.

*He couldn't take his eyes off you.*

Really? Or was that just Sam being Sam, protective and a little territorial about his mother? Helen tells herself he was probably overreacting to Cal's friendly affection for her.

Except there's no word from Barb. If it were anyone else, Helen wouldn't think twice. But with Barb, it means something. There's a subject Barb is specifically avoiding.

Helen should be glad about this—Yay! No third degree!—but it's like grit in her running shoe, and she can't shake the persistent feeling that there's nothing to be glad about at all.

Cal does not text or call, either.

Helen is both relieved and devastated by this, which is worrisome. She doesn't like her emotions flying around like autumn leaves in the wind. She likes them either firmly attached to the tree or raked up and disposed of.

*Build the fucking box*, she tells herself, *or that's the end of it.*

IT'S SUPPOSED TO snow all night, and Helen lulls herself to sleep with thoughts of pulling Lana in a sled around the McGrath backyard the next day. Making snow angels. A snowman. Before bed, she digs out some old mittens and a hat and scarf. She's got a carrot for the nose but of course not the traditional coal for eyes. Can you even get coal in Massachusetts anymore? Maybe they'll use cherry tomatoes for eyes. Lana will love that.

But when she wakes there's no snow, just an unrelenting gloppy rain. On the drive to Barb and Cormac's, the weatherman on the radio explains how the projections were off due to an unexpected shift in the—

Helen pokes the power button. *For godsake, who cares?*

When she arrives, Cormac has already left, and Barb is waiting in her coat.

"Roy's got an early shoot." She hands off Lana and grabs an umbrella.

Helen and Lana watch out the window and wave as they do every Tuesday, Wednesday, and Thursday morning. Barb splashes her way to the car and gets in quickly, forgetting to wave back.

Lana points as the car pulls away. "Mama."

"Mama's in a hurry," says Helen. "Let's play!"

They do their best. They stack blocks and knock them down. They sing "Wheels on the Bus" twelve times because it's Lana's favorite. They bang on pots with wooden spoons. They even fingerpaint. By ten thirty, Helen is exhausted, and Lana, who's generally enthusiastic about whatever Helen cooks up to do, looks decidedly bored. The rain continues to pummel the tiny house and, it seems, the whole world.

"We need to get out of here," Helen tells Lana. "And Nonna needs a coffee."

"Nonna," says Lana.

"That's me!" Helen zips Lana into her snowsuit and tucks her silky hair under her cap.

Cormac's Confectionery is strangely busy for a rainy Tuesday, as if many more people than just Helen and Lana need to escape weather-induced house arrest. Cormac comes to the counter to say hello and gets them coffee and muffins, but the line is growing behind them, and he can't chat long. Helen's usual quiet spot around the corner is taken up by a teenage boy and girl hunched over the table toward each other and murmuring intensely. The coffee cups are empty, but they show no signs of leaving before *something*—Helen has no idea what—gets resolved.

Luckily, an elderly man at one of the front tables is folding his newspaper, and Helen quickly comes to stand at a respectful distance but close enough to claim the spot, should anyone else encroach. The man leaves, and Helen slides a wooden kid seat over to the table and settles Lana in, snowsuit peeled down to her waist. Helen takes off her own wet jacket and hangs it on the back of her chair. She drops her purse on the opposite chair and sits, noticing that Cormac must have loaded a new mix in the music system. She's never heard Patty Griffin's "Heavenly Day" in here before. The lyrics, full of sunny imagery, are a nice antidote to all the gray around them.

Helen sips her hot coffee and thinks, *Boy, was this a good idea.*

They've just begun to nibble at their muffins when Lana, who is facing the order counter, suddenly points and says, "Bay. Be."

Helen feels a prickle go up the back of her neck. *This place is always crawling with babies*, she tells herself, and it's true. Mid-morning, young mothers desperate for contact with the outside world swirl in hauling their babies in car seats or steering toddlers by the hand. But when Helen turns around, Cal and McKenzie are looking right at her. She smiles and gives a little wave, because what else can she do?

He smiles and waves back and heads toward them with his coffee and bag of baked goods, because what else can he do?

"Hi," he says.

"Hi."

"Nice day."

"Yeah, we were planning on making snowmen, but . . ."

"Same. I mean, when Logan gets home from day care," he adds. "Kenzie's more the snowball-fight type."

"I hear she's got a great arm."

"Scouts are calling."

He stands there an extra beat, and takes a breath to say something, but Helen has already started to say, "We've got room if you want to sit." She reaches over and grabs her purse off the other chair.

"Um. Sure. Yeah. That'd be nice."

He's juggling the baby, coffee, take-out sack, and diaper bag, so Helen says, "Here, give her to me." She unties McKenzie's cap and pulls it off, unzips her jacket, and Lana says, "Bay. Be. Bay. Be!" McKenzie grins and slaps her little hand on the table.

"How did the rest of the visit go?" Cal asks as he gets himself organized.

Helen smiles. "Much better than it started, I'll say that."

He takes the baby and hands her a bottle. "The boys stopped jabbing at each other?"

"Yeah, in fact . . ."

Helen tells him about Sam going to New London, and her run with Danny. About REI and Venmo. She also tells him about Cormac's parents, and how sad she feels about seeing such a lovely couple in decline. She can tell him every detail; he's hungry to hear it.

"They've been married over fifty years," she says. "They were happy and active and sharp as tacks when I met them."

"I guess if you live that long, you're bound to hit some hard times," he says. "But if you have fifty happy years before that, it seems like a bargain to me."

She smiles. "Good point."

Helen's still gazing at Cal when a new song comes on, gentle percussion, rich acoustic guitar. She recognizes the low rumbling voice of Marc Cohn as he begins a cover of "Maybe I'm Amazed." And in her head, she can hear an eighteen-year-old Cal call it the greatest love song ever written.

Neither of them speaks. The song goes on. McCartney was in his twenties when he wrote and recorded it; Cohn's version is softer, his voice more mature. There's more life lived behind the words now, as if one can still be amazed by love at any age.

Cal's eyes never leave hers. His face silently shifts from pleasant conversation mode to an honesty that she's not sure she's seen from him before. At least not in a very long time. She can feel a tide of love pouring across the table from him, flooding her with its intensity. There's an apology in that love that has nothing to do with forty years ago, and everything to do with now.

*We are boxless.*

Without a word, Helen stands and lifts Lana out of the wooden kid seat, takes her jacket and purse off the back of her chair, and heads for the door. As she passes him, he whispers one word.

"Wheels."

# Chapter 42

*2021*

She isn't surprised when there's a knock on her front door that night. She knows he won't leave it at that. And she's glad, really. Closure is important. But she is also sad and exhausted.

It reminds her of teaching the kids to ski. As they snowplowed down the mountain at an agonizing crawl, she would follow behind in case they fell and needed help getting up or retrieving equipment. She had to snowplow, too, of course, to keep from running them over. The scenery was beautiful, and she was happy they were learning this exciting new skill. But by the end of a couple of runs her quads were burning, and all she wanted to do was fly down the mountain at her natural speed.

This thing between her and Cal, it's not her natural speed. Not by a long shot. And the constant vigilance required to keep her feelings reined in is painful and exhausting, when every cell in her body is telling her to let them fly.

She's glad she left the bakery without a word; it gave her some time to think about what she needs to say and how to say it. God knows it won't be easy. Helen takes a deep breath as she puts on her coat, opens the door, and steps out into the mist-filled rays of the porch light.

"You're not letting me in?" he says.

"It won't take that long. You won't have to take off your shoes."

"Helen."

"This isn't good for me."

Cal's face falls, and he says only, "Oh."

"We've been acting like we're just great friends, and we're not. We're what we were up on Paddow Mountain, except this time we're too scared to do anything about it."

"I'm not scared. I'm trying to do the right thing." He looks scared, though. He looks panicked.

"You're trying to do the right thing for you and Suze. You *know* this isn't the right thing for me. But you're still trying to hang on to me any way you can—like encouraging me to date other guys so things are fair." She crosses her arms. "You and Suze, you're the same. You both want to have your cake and eat it, too. Noni and I should form a support group and call it the Crosby Cake Club."

"Helen, I'm not trying to hurt you—"

"Of course you're not. But you not trying doesn't mean I'm not getting hurt."

Cal nods. None of this is news to him. He was just hoping against all evidence to the contrary that it could somehow be okay. She understands that very well. It's what she's been doing, too. In fact, it's what she did for the entirety of her marriage.

"I don't know if I'll ever have another man in my life." The thought of this makes her breath go a little ragged, but she presses on. "Honestly, I'm pretty fulfilled. I've got my kids and my grand-daughter. For the first time in my life I have work I really enjoy. I even have Francie back."

Helen takes a beat to try to get herself under control, because the next thing she needs to say is the most important part. "It has never been better than this for me. And if this is what I get, I have no complaints."

He shakes his head, as if willing all this not to be true. "Helen . . ."

"I love you, Cal." It's both a great relief and a terrible loss to say these words, finally, to him. She feels her throat going tight, but she has to finish.

"I have always loved you even when I hated you. I didn't know it until I saw you again, and I'm really glad I know it now, because I can make peace with that. I can accept it for what it is—love that's never going to be allowed to fully grow. It'll just stay a teenager. But I'm not a teenager anymore. If I ever have romantic love again, it has to be grown-up love."

"You deserve it." Regret stains his features. "I want that for you."

"I know." She nods. "I know you do."

"Can I . . . Would it be okay if . . . I just want to give you a hug. Would that be . . . ?"

It will only make it harder to feel Cal's arms around her again after all these years, but she can't seem to stop herself from stepping forward, into the warmth of his body. To let herself be his, just for a moment. He holds her gently, and she feels uniquely precious to this man, whom she's loved for so long—and will hopefully never see again.

Then she steps back, and he lets her go. She goes into the house and sits on the couch. He's still out there. She can feel him nearby, and she wonders if she'll have this excruciating awareness of his nearness for the rest of her life. If they happen to be in different sections of the same store, or walking down trails in the same woods, will she feel him as she does now?

Finally she hears the boards creak on the steps, and she knows he's gone.

# Chapter 43

**2021**

I ended it with Cal," Helen says the next morning, before Barb can scurry off to work or an emergency spa day or Mars.

"Oh, Mom." Barb drops her purse and puts her arms around Helen. "I'm so sorry, but I'm so relieved! It was never going to work, with the wife and all." The hug continues for a while, and Helen doesn't let go because of the no-ending-the-hug-first policy she has with her kids. But then she starts to realize Barb is following the same policy this time.

"I'm okay," she whispers and pats Barb on the shoulder.

"You guys were so in love," says Barb.

Helen untangles from the hug to look at Barb. "Is that why you've been avoiding me?"

"You kept insisting it was only friendship, and I didn't know how to respond to that."

"It *was* only friendship."

Barb rolls her eyes. "Yeah, okay. You're doing it again."

"Barbara Annabella Spencer. Nothing happened." Helen cannot abide the thought of her daughter thinking she participated in adultery.

"Jesus, Mom, *everything* happened! You were in love, and he was crazy about you! I have never seen you that happy before! *Everything important happened!*"

Helen didn't cry all night. She didn't sleep much, of course, but she was comforted by the fact that she had done the right thing—for everyone in this little drama—but mostly for herself. She had faced the unsustainability of her relationship with Cal, and no one even had to tell her to. She congratulated herself on not drifting along with a man who didn't fit. She was awake and in charge and demanding more for herself, which she should have done a long time ago.

But now she bursts into tears. Barb is right. Everything important *did* happen. Her children got to see her completely happy and adored for the first time in their lives, and now it's over. Helen puts her hands to her face and sobs. She hears Lana's little voice from the floor, where she's been sitting and chewing on a board book. "Nonna!"

Barb picks her up. "It's okay, sweetie. Nonna's just sad. Sometimes the wheels on the bus don't take you where you need to go, and you have to sit by the side of the road for a while until another bus comes along. Or call an Uber."

A snort of laughter comes out of Helen, and she looks through her wet fingers at them.

"Know what?" Barb says suddenly to Lana. "Mama's going to play hooky! And we're going to go have fun!"

Helen wipes her face on her sleeve. "You don't have to do that. I'll be fine."

"Yeah, keep telling yourself that. And while you're pretending to be brave, poor me, I'll be carrying around all that sadness for you. So I am definitely calling in sick."

THEY GO INTO Boston to the Museum of Fine Arts. "You need a dose of beauty," Barb says. And she's right. There is something relentlessly uplifting about being surrounded by masterful works of art, no matter how bereft and loveless you feel.

At one point, Barb goes to the ladies' room to change Lana's diaper, and Helen wanders into the Ancient Egypt exhibit, full of wondrously well-preserved artifacts. There is an almost life-size statue of a man and woman carved in smooth black stone. KING MENKAURA AND QUEEN, 2490–2472 B.C., the description says. He stands tall and broad shouldered, left foot advancing confidently forward. His unnamed queen is by his side, one arm around his waist, the other on his forearm, supporting him. Loving him.

Helen doesn't want to be anyone's nameless girlfriend, not even Cal Crosby's. But she wouldn't mind being part of a pair as sturdy and long-standing as these two. Maybe someday she'll have that. Maybe not. She thinks about what she said to Cal: "If this is what I get . . ."

Well, apparently this *is* what she gets, isn't it? A day at an art museum with her daughter and her granddaughter. Two months ago, before she bumped into Cal fucking Crosby, she would have reveled in the chance to be with her two favorite females surrounded by all this history and culture and creativity.

She feels as if she's carrying around two people inside her—the grateful lucky one and the miserable broken one—and they tag team back and forth. *Look at this amazing sculpture that someone poured their soul into, and here I am admiring it thousands of years later!* And then, *I wish I could share this with Cal, but I can't, and I never will, and I will die without ever admiring art with someone I love as much as him . . .*

She's not used to feeling so much, she realizes. Such highs and lows, up and down and around and around. She wishes she could take her emotions off like a pair of dirty socks and throw them in the wash.

They get back to the house late in the afternoon with Lana

conked out in the back of the car. Barb is carrying her upstairs to her crib when Cormac comes in.

"Hey, just the financial genius I wanted to talk to!" he says to Helen.

"Uh-oh. Is there a crisis?"

"No, no, it's more of a hypothetical."

Barb comes back down the stairs and gives her husband a kiss. "Hey, pie guy. Who's watching the store?"

"Well, funny you should bring that up. I've been thinking about what Cal said about hiring a manager—" He stops. "What."

Helen looks over at Barb, who is now watching her intently.

"What's going on?" says Cormac. "Is this some sort of mother-daughter mind meld that I'm not supposed to know about?"

Barb sighs. "Mom gave Cal the boot."

Cormac looks alarmed. "Oh. Wow. Helen, that's . . . Are you okay?"

"I'm fine."

"Did he . . . ? I mean, if he needs a beating, I am completely prepared to kick his ass."

Helen smiles and wonders if her sweet, affable son-in-law has ever hit anyone in his entire life. "At the moment I'm going the pacifist route," she says, "but if I have need of your knuckle-breaking services in the future, I'll be sure to let you know."

"Good. Do that. I'm on standby. Meanwhile, can I make you some toast or something?"

"Babe," says Barb. "She's heartbroken. It's not really a carbo-loading situation."

Helen was planning to head home and possibly cry in the shower, but here's Cormac, so anxious to help. "Cup of tea?" she says.

"On it."

She ends up staying for dinner, even though Barb is right, Helen doesn't have much of an appetite. And when she gets home, she does head straight for the shower for a good shoulder-shaking cry. But once she's all sobbed out and in her jammies, she feels sad but not quite so much as if she's fallen down the shaft of an abandoned mine in Siberia.

*It's going to be like this*, she tells herself. *Up and down. Around and around.*

At least there are no boxes to build.

"HEY, I'VE BEEN thinking about you!" says Francie on Thursday night. "How was Thanksgiving?"

"We took the nickel tour of hell for a while but then it was pretty great. How was yours?"

"We went to Vernon's daughter's in New Hampshire. She's a terrible cook—like Popsicles-for-dessert-level bad. But she's a sweet kid, and we love her, so it was fine. Now let's get back to that nickel tour of hell—does it involve our favorite redhead?"

"Maybe I should start with the visit his wife paid me."

"No freaking way!"

"Yeah, you may want to pop popcorn for this episode."

"Oh, crap, Hellie. I've got a class starting up in the pottery building in like fifteen minutes. But I'm dying to hear everything. How late can I call you back?"

"Actually . . . I was thinking about maybe coming up this weekend?"

"Shoot, I'm swamped. In fact, I'm desperate to hire more staff. People got all artsy during the pandemic and business is booming."

"Could I . . . ? I mean, it's probably beyond my skill level—you know I don't have a creative hair on my head—but if there's anything I can do to help? I could clean out the barn or whatever you need."

"Wow. If Helen Iannucci is offering to shovel shit, something is very much up."

"Kinda."

"Is it bad?"

"Not bad. Just very . . ." Helen sighs.

"Come."

"Are you sure?"

"You need me."

"I do."

"You also need nose plugs. My horses have very healthy digestive tracts."

FRIDAY FEELS LIKE the longest day of Helen's life.

*Oh, for godsake, stop being such a drama queen!* she chides herself. During the quarter century when she was herding three headstrong children mostly by herself, there were plenty of longer days. But none of them felt quite so . . . pointless.

Barb doesn't work on Fridays, and she invited Helen to hang out with her and Lana, but Helen has always felt it's important for Barb to have alone time with her daughter. Besides, Helen has her own work to do managing the confectionery finances. She usually takes that little back table with her laptop, but she's not ready to return to the scene of the musically induced crime. So she sits at her dining room table, distracted by everything other than what she's supposed to be concentrating on. The sound of the boiler cycling on and off. The leaves blowing around the yard. That weed-pulling neighbor walking by.

*It's just going to go on like this*, she thinks. *Forever.*

THE PLAN IS for Helen to arrive at Seven Meadows Farm for lunch on Saturday, so Francie gets some time with her. But when she wakes up that morning, it's hard to get out of bed.

The thought of driving all the way up there by herself is exhausting. Only three weeks before she made the trip with Cal, and it was pure fun. Now it feels like a forced march with a bag of rocks.

*Maybe I should just stay here.* Francie's got enough to do. She doesn't need a pathetic friend moping around. The car should probably have an oil change before any more long trips. The yard needs raking. There are chores to do. Not that Helen plans to do any of them.

She's about to roll over when there's a knock on the door.

*Go away.*

But no one knocks on her door unless it's a delivery, and she hasn't ordered anything.

Helen hops out of bed, tugs on the jeans and sweatshirt she dropped on the floor last night, and runs to the door. When she opens it, someone is walking away. The hood is up on their black parka, so she has no idea if it's even male or female.

"Hello?" says Helen.

The person turns around. It's that neighbor from down the street.

*You knew it wasn't Cal!* she wants to scream at herself. *You knew it!* But the disappointment slams into her body like a rogue wave anyway.

"Oh, no!" says the woman. "I didn't mean to wake you up! I always see you running so early, I didn't think—"

*Prisha,* Helen remembers vaguely. They'd talked about getting together for coffee, but Helen completely forgot about it. She wasn't feeling the need for friends because she had one who filled up a lot of her time and brain space (and heart, it turns out). But that's not an issue these days, is it? Nope. Plenty of time and space now. Fucking gobs of it.

"Not at all," says Helen. "I was awake."

Prisha approaches. She has Helen's basket in her hands with an unfamiliar cloth in it. "But you were still in bed."

"No, I—" Helen glances at the little mirror in her entryway. Her hair looks like she may have electrocuted herself recently.

"I was dropping off your basket, and my mother taught me never to return things empty."

"Please come in." Helen runs her fingers through her hair a couple of times.

"You don't want to go back to sleep?"

*I want to go back to sleep for about a year*, thinks Helen. *But that's probably inadvisable.*

"I was about to make coffee. Want to come in for a cup?"

Prisha casts a quick glance up the street toward her house. "I'd love to."

While the coffee perks, they chat and Prisha fills in some details about her life: she's a website designer, married to Hal, and the mother of Ben, age nineteen, and Mira, fifteen. When Helen gives the same general intel, Prisha says, "My gosh. You must be a very strong person."

"Strong? Why?"

"What you've been through, with your husband passing, and moving up here to a new town, helping your son-in-law with his business. Not to mention surviving your children's adolescence." Prisha exhales in a way that makes it clear that she very much does want to mention that and find out how it can possibly be accomplished.

Helen pours the coffee. Prisha opens the tea towel over the basket to reveal a bowl with little round pastries in a syrupy sauce. "Have you ever had gulab jamun? It's a traditional Indian dessert. If I make too much, my husband and kids will eat it until they vomit."

Helen laughs. "Can't wait to try it."

# Chapter 44

## 2021

Helen gets a late start to Vermont. Coffee with Prisha took a turn when she eventually revealed that both her children had struggled with anxiety and depression during the pandemic. "The isolation really got to them. They're back to school now, of course, but I don't think my daughter has truly recovered yet. She's in a very dark place sometimes."

Helen remembers the dark places her children have been. "They take you with them."

Later when Prisha gets up to go, she says, "Thanks for listening. I don't always feel I can be honest with other mothers. It's a small town and everyone knows everyone—things get out and people judge."

"Well, I don't know anyone, so your worries are safe with me."

"I know you're a runner," says Prisha, "but maybe we could take a walk sometime?"

"Sure," says Helen, trying to sound more enthusiastic than she feels. She doesn't want to hear about other people's problems right now—she's having a hard enough time lugging around her own. But there's a vulnerability to Prisha that's hard to say no to.

Besides—the occasional walk—it's not exactly a huge commitment of time. Which Helen now has plenty of.

WHEN HELEN ARRIVES at the farm a half hour late, Francie is in a mad scramble to make sure all the various functions of her multifunctional enterprise are . . . functioning.

"What do you need?" says Helen. "I'm all yours."

"Are you comfortable with a register? I don't have anyone to cover the gallery."

"Easy peasy."

"Sweet *Jesus*, I'm glad you're here!"

The register is completely different from the one at Cormac's, but Helen figures it out soon enough. She puts on her customer service smile, sells a surprising amount of art, and gets a nice little vacation from the inside of her head for the next four hours. Francie and Vernon come to check on her occasionally, but she waves them away to go put out other fires. Helen's in charge; the gallery is under control.

At five, it's dark out and things are winding down. Francie comes to clear the cash out of the register and close up shop. "You saved my plant-based bacon!"

"I was glad to help, Francie. Honestly, it was just what I needed."

Later, after a dinner of vegetarian chili and gluten-free cornbread in the farmhouse, Vernon loads up the woodstove, refills their wineglasses, and leaves them to each other.

"The dancing," Francie says after Helen tells her everything. "That's what did it. Of course he couldn't take his eyes off that."

Helen shrugs and lets her eyes leak. "Barb thinks we're in love."

"It did look pretty cozy when you two were here."

"I don't *want* to be in love!" says Helen. "I want my life back!"

"Do you, though?"

"*Yes, I really fucking do!*" she yells.

"I'm just saying that all this stuff that happened—all those talks you had, all that offloading the past—that was important. That was healthy. You don't want to go back to a time when you were secretly hauling all that crap around with you."

"Yeah, except now I'm hauling around a shattered heart, aren't I?"

"True. But you can face that. You *did* face it, Hellie. You saw the situation for what it was, and you made the right call. I'm proud of you."

"You are?"

"Of course!"

"Thanks," says Helen and bursts into tears again.

SHE STAYS WITH Francie and Vernon till Monday afternoon, helping out wherever she can. And, yes, she even mucks out stalls. She can't speak to whether Francie's horses' digestive tracts are healthier than most, but she can attest to the fact that they are excellent producers.

It feels good to be busy and needed and away from Belham. To stop thinking about her own unhappiness and focus on helping.

On Monday morning Francie says, "Can you do an escort for me?"

Helen raises her eyebrows. "I didn't know Seven Meadows had such an extensive array of services."

"Ha ha," says Francie. "Though that could be a real cash cow: hot mature ladies on horseback."

"Lady Godivas?"

Francie boosts up her boobs and purrs sultrily, "Lady *Bad*-ivas!" and Helen laughs harder than she'd have thought possible in her current emotional state.

It turns out being an escort is simply going along with a rider who is experienced enough not to need a lesson but shouldn't be out on trails alone. "They've all proved themselves," Francie explains, "but they've got some stuff."

"Any particular stuff I should know about?" asks Helen. "And by the way, you remember I'm a beginner myself, right?"

"We like to keep the diagnoses on the down low. All I need you to do is be able to text me if anything comes up. Which it won't. They'll probably be the ones helping you."

Helen escorts six kids for a half hour each over the course of the morning. A few seem like typically developing kids, and she doesn't notice any "stuff."

One asks her not to talk to him. "I'm listening," he explains.

"To?"

"Anything that's not you or my mom."

*So you're basically Danny until the age of . . . last week*, she thinks.

Another tells Helen an elaborate story about all the witches who live in the forest: their jealousies, their interpersonal misunderstandings, the stealing of potion recipes, and calling one another out. It's like an episode of *Real Housewives of the Vermont Woods*.

The last one is a little girl who seems very unsteady on her feet. She falls for no apparent reason as she walks across the barn floor, and she needs a lot of help mounting the horse. Helen suspects it's some sort of muscular disorder. But the girl has a sunny disposition, and she tells Helen all about her school. "I only have one friend," she says. "Kids think I'm weird because I fall down a lot. My older brother says wait till they get to college and go to parties. Then they'll fall down, too. Anyway, I just keep getting up. That's my motto. Just keep getting up."

"What's your friend's name?"

The girl smiles. "Franny."

HELEN REALLY DOESN'T want to leave on Monday afternoon, and when she waves to Francie as she pulls out of the parking lot, she feels her spirits sinking. *Now what?* she thinks.

The week goes by slowly. Anytime she's not fully engaged in some activity like playing with Lana or working on the confectionery's books or having dinner with Barb and Cormac, Helen has the feeling that she's been dropped off in some foreign land with no GPS. She didn't realize how much of a focal point Cal had become in her life. Now all the scenery seems to be made up solely of background.

She's been running three miles a day since college, but now she goes farther, longer. The motion settles her, gives her purpose, pulls her out of the quicksand of her sadness. It's when she feels the best, so she does it more and more.

Prisha texts her on Friday night. *Are you up for walking tomorrow?*

*Ugh*, thinks Helen. *People.*

She's planning a six-miler and almost says no. But then she realizes it will take under an hour, and what is she supposed to do for the other twenty-three hours?

*Sure*, she texts back, and they set it up for three in the afternoon.

"DID I SEE you run by this morning?" asks Prisha.

"Yes. Six miles. I haven't done that in a long time."

"That's impressive! What inspired you?"

"Um . . . I guess I just felt like it."

Prisha says nothing. No one suddenly runs six miles for no reason.

*Oh, what the hell.* Prisha told her all about her kid problems. "I've been a little down lately."

"Anything in particular?"

"I was kind of . . . involved with someone, but it wasn't going in a good direction, so I ended it."

"How did he react?"

"He wasn't happy, but he understood."

"So not a bad guy."

"No. Not a bad guy."

"Just not a good direction."

"For me, no."

"That was brave."

"I don't know that it was brave so much as it was self-preservation."

"I should take lessons," Prisha mutters.

Helen looks over at her in surprise.

"No, it's not my husband, he's wonderful. I just . . . I think maybe I care too much about acting like everything's fine. I'm too eager to get a gold star for being a go-along girl."

*So familiar*, thinks Helen. The trap of going along . . . until it's forty years later.

She tells Prisha, "My parents were immigrants, and they always cared so deeply about fitting in and making America proud of them. But sticking to some script you imagine others want you to follow . . . I don't know. I guess I'm starting to get it that life is more complicated than that. I'm trying to be a good person instead of a good girl."

Prisha smiles. "I knew I would like you."

Helen laughs. "It was the hair, wasn't it?"

TOWARD THE END of the walk Prisha says, "I'm sure you're probably not ready for this . . ."

"For?"

"Getting back in the pool again."

"Sorry?"

"The dating pool."

"Oh. Um . . ."

"Hal has a friend. He's the nicest man. Divorced a couple of years ago. He's a real catch."

*Not on your life.* Helen smiles indulgently. "I'm sure he's a lot younger than I am."

"Early fifties."

"I'm fifty-eight."

"Really? Good for you! That's in the ballpark."

"Aren't guys dating much younger women these days?"

"Well, yes, I suppose so, but Leif is an old soul."

Helen chuckles. "Leif? Like Leif Garrett?"

"Who?"

"Nineteen seventies heartthrob? 'I Was Made for Dancin''? Oh, never mind. You're a baby."

"I'll google it when I get home. Meanwhile, our Leif is a gym teacher in Natick. And he's a runner."

"I'm sure he's great, but I'm going to sit by the side of the pool for a while. Not ready to dive in just yet."

"I understand," says Prisha. "But, not to beat a dead analogy, don't get sunburned while you're waiting."

"I'll apply sunscreen. Trust me, I'll be fine."

ON SUNDAY HELEN wakes up to a world blanketed in an icy frost and the warning grind of a sanding truck going by. Not a good day to run in the woods. She wasn't planning to anyway—her muscles need to recover from yesterday's six-miler—but the day seems to Go. On. For. Ever. She starts to think about texting Cal. Maybe they could be just friends after all. Maybe they could build boxes made of titanium.

Before she does anything she regrets, Helen laces up and heads out the back door, leaving her phone on the kitchen counter to keep herself from sending any dangerously pathetic texts from the trail. There is no real plan, no route she's following, but she knows all the conservation areas around her house quite well now, since she's stayed out of Jansen Woods to avoid crossing paths with Cal.

Despite the fact that her muscles are quivering a little from overuse, Helen runs hard. She runs like something is chasing her, and something is. Her desire for this man will overwhelm her if she doesn't keep ahead of it. At first she feels only despair, but then the familiar motion begins to rock her like a lullaby; the beauty of trees dusted in diamond-like frost calms her.

She's about three miles out, she figures, and turns to head back when her foot hits a rock hidden by icy leaves. Her right foot rolls off it, throwing her into the brush by the side of the trail. The pain flares like a small bomb exploding just below her anklebone, and she yelps in pain. Then she really starts to cry.

*"This is NOT FAIR!"* she sobs into the trees.

Helen sits there on the cold, wet ground, crying, self-pitying, and defeated until her butt is wet and she begins to shiver. Then she remembers the little girl with the muscle disorder from Francie's farm. *Just keep getting up. That's my motto.*

Because, really, what are the options? Sitting there, splayed out in the dirt forever?

By the time Helen crawls around and finds a decent stick to lean on, hobbles to the nearest road, and flags down a car, the ankle has swollen to the point where she has to take off her shoe. The young kid who picks her up keeps eyeing her worriedly. She's able to keep from actively weeping, but her eyes leak, and she has to keep sniffling so she can breathe. She borrows his phone to call Barb, who meets her at the house and takes her to the hospital.

Six hours, a set of x-rays, a pair of crutches, and an immobilizing boot later, Helen is discharged with a page and a half of instructions that boil down to RICE: rest, ice, compression with an ACE bandage, and elevation to control swelling.

"You'll be able to walk on it soon, but you shouldn't run for a while," the nurse tells her as he wheels her out to the curb while Barb pulls the car up.

"How long before I can run?"

"It's a bad sprain but it's not the worst I've seen. Maybe only a month."

*A month?* she wants to scream. *A MONTH?*

"Good to know," she says.

"MOM, ARE YOU sure you don't want to stay with us?"

"Oh, honey, that's nice of you, but it would be hard to get up the stairs to bed." Also, their house is very small, and she'd have to sleep in Lana's room, and she'd never have a moment to herself. She can't say any of these things, of course.

"Okay, well, do you have anyone in the neighborhood you can reach out to if you need something? Anyone at all?"

*Anyone at all*, thinks Helen. *She has so little confidence in my ability to connect with people.* Of course, Barb's doubts are not entirely baseless . . .

"I can call my friend Prisha," she says curtly.

Barb perks up at this. "Prisha?"

"She lives a couple of houses down with her husband, Hal, and her children, Ben and Mira." Helen feels the need to prove she has personal details. "She's a graphic designer. We walk together." Well, once, but that counts.

Barb nods appreciatively. "No kidding."

Helen resists the urge to throw her crutches across the room and scream, *Yeah, no kidding!* But she realizes that what's really pissing her off is her throbbing ankle and the knowledge that she won't be running anytime soon, and it's time for more ibuprofen and possibly a glass of wine.

Barb fixes her scrambled eggs and toast for dinner. After Barb leaves, Helen crutches herself to the kitchen and pours her own wine. She wants to make a fire but crouching down and stacking wood in the grate feels like a bridge too far. She sits on her sofa with her leg propped up on pillows, stares at her cold fireplace, sips her wine, and feels very, very sorry for herself.

A text to Cal is moments away . . .

But before she can poke out a message, a text comes in from Prisha. *My morning just opened up tomorrow. Want to walk?*

*Yes, I want to walk,* thinks Helen darkly. *I'd settle for walking to the fucking bathroom.*

*Really wish I could,* she texts back, *but I sprained my ankle today.*

*Oh no! You poor thing! What can I do!*

*The next time you make gulab jamun, you can bring me some!* Helen adds a little smiley face instead of the gargoyle face she really feels.

A few minutes later, there's a knock on the door. By the time Helen hoists herself from the couch and balances on her crutches, Prisha has opened it. "I shouldn't have made you get up," she says, "but I didn't know if we were on a letting-ourselves-in basis yet."

Helen forces a smile. "We are now."

Prisha holds out a Tupperware container. "I'd just made some."

"Won't your family be mad that you're giving it away?"

She smirks. "They'll live."

THEY EAT THE sweet, sticky pastry and drink wine, and Helen feels her jagged mood soften. With a little prodding she eventually gives Prisha a very condensed version of the Cal story.

"My gosh," says Prisha. "It's all very dramatic!"

"Far too dramatic for the likes of me," says Helen.

"You've handled it so well!" Prisha shakes her head in wonder. "The wife . . . my gosh."

"Yeah, well, I almost texted him tonight. All that handling it would've gone right down the drain."

"What stopped you?"

"You and your dessert—you flew in here like Wonder Woman to save me from myself."

Prisha affects a proud smile. "Perhaps I need a cape."

"I'm ordering you one tomorrow."

Prisha sips her wine. "Not to poke a sore subject, but it seems to me you need some distractions. And for a little while, anyway, exercise isn't going to be one of them."

"If you're offering to take me to Disney World, I'm in."

"No, but I am offering you something else."

It takes Helen a moment to get her meaning. "Not dating!"

"Maybe you shouldn't think of it as dating. Maybe you should think of it as practice for when you're ready to date sometime in the future."

"A day that will never come."

Prisha raises an eyebrow. "Now who's being dramatic?"

POSSIBLY IT'S THE three glasses of wine—two glasses more than Helen generally drinks—fortified with copious amounts of self-pity and iced with gulab jamun. Or it's the thought of moving on in a clear and obvious (too obvious?) way from her involvement with Cal. Or it's because the more Prisha talks about Leif Carlsson, the nicer he sounds. Whatever the inducement, by the end of the evening, Helen has allowed Prisha to text this man, describe her in what she feels are far too glowing terms, and set up a date—"Just drinks!" Prisha assures her. "One hour of your life!"—for Friday night.

# Chapter 45

*2021*

Helen regrets this immediately and resumes regretting it when she wakes up in the morning with a throbbing head as well as a throbbing ankle.

The sudden sound of the door opening makes her jump and spill coffee grounds on the kitchen counter.

"Hey, let me do that!" says Barb.

Helen winces at the volume of Barb's voice and squints at her.

"Have you been *drinking*?"

"Well, not this morning, but I'm considering it. They say a hair of the dog . . ."

"Mom!"

"Barbara, please. I'm a grown woman. I can drink if I feel like it. Especially with such a plethora of good excuses."

"And are we adding substance abuse to that list?" Barb pours water into the coffeemaker and sweeps the spilled grounds into the filter with her hand.

"Seems as good a time as any." Helen makes her way to the other side of the counter and collapses onto one of the stools. "Besides, the list seems to grow on its own anyway. I actually let Prisha set me up on a date for Friday night, so now I have to figure out how to undo *that*."

Her daughter's face goes wide with delight. "A *date*? You have *a date*? Who is this Prisha and how soon can I kiss her?"

"Oh, please. I'm not going through with it. That's the last thing I need."

"You're going through with it if I have to carry you there piggy-back!" Barb comes around and sits on the other stool. "It's perfect!"

"How on earth is it remotely perfect?"

"Because it's symbolic. You're taking action. Moving forward. Putting one foot in front of the other." They both look down at the immobilizer boot. "So to speak," Barb adds. "Just drinks, right?"

"Apparently that's how it's done. Except I'm not doing it."

"You are. You absolutely are."

"I won't enjoy myself."

"That's not the point! You could completely hate the guy. But after it's over, *you will have done it*. It's like exercise. It's no fun, but afterward you feel all accomplished."

"I actually like exercise."

"Yeah, well, you're weird."

"That's the one thing you've said that I almost slightly agree with."

"It's an hour of your life, Mom. You're going."

APPARENTLY, AN HOUR of her life is not worth much to those around her, because the phrase along with the requisite dismissive tone keeps cropping up. "It's an hour of your life," says Francie. "Who cares?"

"I care!"

"Look, go, don't go, I'll love you either way. But let's long-term this puppy. You're in kind of an excruciating holding pattern—emotionally and physically. You'll run again, but how are you going to break out emotionally? Why not throw a big-ass monkey wrench into all this misery and see what happens?"

"You're supposed to be on my side," Helen grumbles.

"Every damn day. Always."

What can she do in the face of all this love and concern and, yes, she can secretly admit, reasonable advice?

UNTIL SEVEN P.M. on Friday, Helen calms herself with the idea that she can still call it off. This Leif Carlsson guy is picking her up at eight. Barb doesn't like the idea of Helen getting in a stranger's car, but Helen can't drive herself, and she is certainly not letting her daughter drive her like some tween going to the mall. Prisha assured Helen that Leif is not a widow murderer. That was good enough for her.

But at 7:03, it sinks in that he really is going to show up, and she's really going to go on a date with him, hating every minute of it, no doubt, but it's only an hour of her life, as the entire planet seems to agree.

At 7:05 it sinks in that she has to wear something, and probably not one of the long-sleeve tees and loose-legged sweats that she's been wearing since Sunday. She did shower and wash her hair this morning, but only after Barb mentioned that "Um, no offense, but you look slightly hellish."

What to wear . . .

Helen hasn't dressed up for anything since the last time she had to go to one of Jim's client dinners. That's almost two years ago now. She can't even remember what she owns in that category. And what's the protocol, anyway? What does one wear on a first date in 2021?

She considers calling Prisha to ask, but that seems so embarrassing. Besides, Prisha's been married for over twenty years. How would she know? Calling Barb is out of the question. She's been infantilized by her daughter enough for one week. And Francie would suggest tie-dye or fringe just for giggles.

Helen heads to her closet and starts pulling things out.

Good jeans? She hasn't bought a new pair in years. She's been living in yoga pants for too long, she realizes. Black slacks—too business casual? Silk top—too sexy? Helen dresses and undresses about six times, going further and further afield. This is a little tiring because, though her ankle is feeling much better, it still hurts to stand on it for too long, and she has to balance on one foot to change.

After twenty minutes, Helen starts trying things on just to see if they still fit. The sparkly sequin dress that Jim "surprised" (more like horrified) her with to wear to a New Year's Eve party that made her wonder if he'd ever even *met* her. It was tight, but it was always tight. The long black slinky Morticia Addams dress she wore to a costume party once.

The green dress.

She walked by it on a mannequin in Nordstrom when she was buying scarves for Jim's female clients as holiday gifts (no doubt one of those scarves had gone to Kesia). The dress had called to her as if it had a voice. As if it were saying, *You and I are going to be friends.*

A rich dark green that complemented her eyes, long sleeves, hem a little shorter than she ordinarily wore, but that showed off her legs in a way she'd never noticed before: strong, and lovely, and elegant. Square neckline that gave the simple design a little oomph. It fit her like her own skin, moved the ways she wanted to move, didn't pinch when she sat down.

She'd only worn it a handful of times, saving it for occasions she really cared about, like a fancy party one of her favorite friends threw, and Barb and Cormac's rehearsal dinner. She never wore it to Jim's client events.

Helen gazed at herself in the full-length mirror, tousled her hair a little, smoothed her hand over her belly. *Someday I'm going to wear you again*, she thought. *There's going to be some wonderful event, and you and I are going to dance our seams off.*

It's at this moment that there's a knock on the door. The bedside clock says 7:45! Helen sees her face in the mirror go from happy and confident to angry and terrified in a split second.

*Shit, shit, shit.* She's reaching behind her to find the zipper, eyes frantically searching the pile of clothing on her bed for something—anything—even remotely appropriate to change into, when he knocks again. The nerve! As if he isn't a full fifteen minutes early! She's calling it off. Oh, yes, this is the perfect excuse. She's not going out with a guy who is so inconsiderate as to arrive early and knock *twice* . . .

She grabs her crutches and clomps defiantly through the living room to the door and yanks it open.

There on her porch is Cal fucking Crosby.

# Chapter 46

## 2021

The incongruity of it. Helen can only stare for a second.

As Cal takes her in, his mouth opens a little and his ears shift back. "Holy . . ." he breathes. Then his gaze drops to her boot, and he frowns.

"Cal," she says, looking over his shoulder, expecting to see Leif whatshisname climbing her porch steps any minute. "What are you doing here?"

He blinks, and she knows he's deciding what to ask about first, the dress or the boot. "Where are you going?" he asks. Apparently the dress issue was more pressing.

"I've got a—" But why should she tell him? It feels weird even to admit it to herself, much less say it out loud to Cal Crosby. "An . . . event."

"You've got 'an event'?"

Is he questioning her? Seriously?

"A date, okay? You wanted me to date, and I'm doing it."

"You need to call him."

"I'm not *calling* him!" Honestly, the nerve! As determined as Helen was to cancel a minute ago, now she's just as determined to go through with it.

"We need to talk."

Jesus, this guy and his penchant for big conversations! She does not want to rehash the whole mess, and she's now thinking she really *does* have to go through with this Leif thing just to get Cal off her porch and prove to Barb and Prisha and Francie and whoever else has an opinion that she really is in charge of her life, moving forward, step by immobilizer-booted step.

"No," she says firmly, "we do not need to talk. You chose someone else over me for the *second* time, and believe me, it's loud and clear at this point. You have every right to be with whoever you want, whether it's Wendy or Suze or the queen of the goddamned fairies. Okay? Now I have to go change my clothes while I still have a chance."

"Helen, I asked Suze for a divorce."

She drops a crutch. "What?"

Cal leans down, picks it up, and hands it back to her. "Can we sit down?"

"No, just tell me. You asked her?"

"Yes."

"What did she say?"

"She said she would give up Noni if I promised never to see you again."

The air comes out of Helen. She has to inhale her next breath really deeply to make up for all the oxygen she lost in that moment. "Okay," she says. "Well, good. You finally got what you wanted. I'm happy for you." It's not sarcasm. She's actually happy for this guy who's broken her heart twice now. She suddenly feels so tired, like she can't hang on to these stupid crutches one more minute. She backs up and leans on the back of the couch. "Is that it?"

*Can we wrap this up?* Because now she does need to call this Leif person and tell him it's off. There is no way she can go through with it now.

"No. Actually she did us both a big favor."

Helen stares at him. "How is any of this a favor to me?"

"Because I had to think about it—"

"Well, that's just dandy—"

"—and I had to feel it, Helen. I had to feel what it would be like never to see you again in order to have her back. All of her. No sharing."

"I'm really done with you and your feelings, Cal."

"I said no." He takes a step into the room. "Even if you never want to see me again, the marriage is over."

"Wait, what?"

"It was a test. So I would know—and more importantly *you* would know—that you aren't my second choice. That I chose you over her even if I could have her all to myself again."

"A test?"

"She was bluffing."

"*Bluffing?* And what if you'd said yes?"

"I asked her that. She said she knew I wouldn't."

"How could she possibly be so certain?"

He pauses a moment, and then admits, "She knew things were changing when I stopped sleeping with her."

"Which was when?"

"After that day in the woods with Logan."

"You didn't know if you'd ever even see me again!"

"Yeah, but I must have felt something, right? I stopped even though I never thought for a minute you and I might get together. Hell, I barely dared to hope you'd forgive me."

"So why did you?"

"It was weird. I just didn't want to anymore. It felt like a sham."

"But you told me you were still fighting for her."

"I think it was kind of a last-gasp thing. Subconsciously I had to give it one more push, especially with you in the picture. Like

I wasn't jumping ship on my marriage because I had a better offer."

"Except I never offered!"

"No, you definitely did not. But Suze knew the jig was up once she'd met you."

"I never gave any indication of that whatsoever—in fact, I specifically told her I would not get in the way."

"She admired that."

Helen shakes her head. "She said our friendship wasn't healthy, that it was going backward, and I wasn't good for you."

"She was worried, yeah. But that little sit-down changed her mind. She said it was almost as if she recognized you. Like she knew this person I'd been carrying around with me all these years, and meeting you finally . . . it made sense. She just wanted to be sure that if she was giving me up, it was to someone who'd be good to me and wouldn't take any crap." He chuckles. "Check and check."

"But she didn't give you up."

"No, it had to come from me. Otherwise you're left wondering if you were my consolation prize."

Helen goes still for a moment. "Oh. Right." Because it's *exactly* how she would've felt. She never thought of that. But Suze did.

"That's why she left you alone on Thanksgiving. So you'd finally dump her. Then she'd offer to leave Noni. And you'd say no."

He nods. "In fact that's when I decided—Thanksgiving night, after I spent half the day alone with Whole Foods take-out turkey and the other half having the time of my life with you. But I couldn't say anything because I had to tell her first, and it had to be in person. I didn't want to be one of those jerks who says he's divorcing his wife, but the wife has no clue. And I sure as hell wasn't going to end our marriage over the phone. She was in Montana with Noni's family until the following weekend, so I had to wait."

"But you'd already decided when I saw you in the bakery?"

"Yeah. Honestly, I'd been avoiding you because I was afraid I'd spill it. But there you were. And then that song comes on . . . Always makes me think of you." He shakes his head and murmurs, "I'm amazed, all right. No 'maybes' about it."

"On the porch that night . . ."

"You were so brave—it killed me not to tell you. I stood out there debating after you went in."

She blinks at him, trying to digest all this. Suze's bluff. Cal's decision. The song in the confectionery. His embrace on the porch. She was so certain it was the end, but now she has to rejigger the pieces—

There's a knock on the door behind Cal, and a man moves tentatively into the entryway. "Sorry, it was open. Should I close this? It's kind of cold out there." He smiles warmly, takes one look at Helen and says, "Wow." Then he looks at Cal, and his face clouds. "Um?"

Helen grabs a crutch and stands up. "Leif, I'm so sorry. I'm Helen."

"Hi, Helen. And this is . . . ?"

Helen sighs. "This is . . . a thing. Trust me, it was so *not* a thing until about a minute ago. And it has nothing to do with you, it's just a long-standing . . ." She looks at Cal.

"Thing," he says.

She turns back to Leif. "I'm so sorry. Can I call you tomorrow . . . ?"

He shakes his head. "Nope. Don't. Just go about your thing."

"I'm really sorry."

He reaches for the door. "Closed?"

"Yes, please."

Helen gazes at Cal as Leif's footfalls recede down the porch steps.

"Leif like Leif Garrett?" Cal says. "'I Was Made for Dancin''?"

She crosses her arms. "This conversation you had with Suze about ending your marriage—that was a while ago."

"Yeah, it's been a really long couple of weeks."

"Because?"

"Because I was dying to see you. But Suze and I needed time to talk about how it would go. How to move forward in the most amicable way, and then tell the girls. We had to focus on doing it right for them. And we started the process of getting lawyers and all that. It was really important to me that when I told you, I could say, 'This is a done deal. It's happening. We're all on board.'"

"How did you tell the girls?"

"Zoom. Bonnie in Australia, Janel on her laptop, and Suze and me together on the computer in the office. We wanted them to see us as united and perfectly friendly."

"How'd they take it?"

He smiles sadly. "Bonnie fell apart. Haven't seen her cry like that since she was little."

"Oh, the poor thing."

"She didn't see it coming. She's always been the type to dig into her work or interests and not pay too much attention to the chaos around her. She had no idea about Noni, and certainly no idea about you."

"And Janel?"

"Well, you know, Janel pays attention to everything and everyone, and sometimes that's hard on her. But it gave her the heads-up. She figured out about Suze and Noni not long after she moved home. And of course she's met you."

"She's the one who tracked me down in the first place."

"Yeah, I have to remember to thank her again for that."

"Is Bonnie okay?"

"I think so. Janel was wonderful—really sympathetic but also very positive about this change." He smiles. "She told Bonnie she'll like you. I believe the phrase she used was 'unwitting badass.'"

Helen raises her eyebrows. "Extremely unwitting." But she secretly likes the sound of it.

"Everyone just needs some time to get used to the idea. We'll sell the house eventually, but we agreed to hold off for a little while."

"Suze doesn't want to live there?"

"She officially moved in with Noni the minute we decided." He chuckles. "Not that it took much. She all but had her mail forwarded there years ago anyway."

"And what about you?"

He gazes at her. "I'm keeping my plans loose. Seeing what everyone needs. What everyone wants."

Helen takes a breath. "Is this real?"

"It's real. I'm sorry I didn't come to you right away, but I had to get my ducks in a row." He smiles. "So how much dating have you been doing?"

"You just saw the entirety of it." She sighs. "Poor Leif. At least he'll have a good story to tell. The worst nondate of his life."

"Hey, screw Leif." Cal takes a step toward her. "I saw the way he looked at you. That guy was going to be all over you by the end of the night." He takes another step.

"Unless I kicked him in the shin with my very sexy immobilizer."

He keeps moving toward her. "Yeah, how'd you score that nifty piece of hardware?"

"Trying to run you out of my system."

He's standing right in front of her now. "Did it work?"

"No."

"Good." He brushes a lock of hair off Helen's cheek with his finger. "Can I kiss you?"

"I wish you would."

Cal's hand is on her cheek. The other hand comes to her waist. He leans down and his kiss is gentle and strangely familiar, though it's hard to believe she can remember what his lips felt like forty years ago. But apparently her body remembers. It's just right. It's what she's been waiting for.

"You know what I've been dying to do with you since I was fifteen years old?" he murmurs.

"I've got a pretty good idea."

"Slow dance."

"Really?"

"Yeah, I had this incredibly elaborate fantasy about slow dancing with you at Homecoming. Taking you in my arms . . . I would've had to reach up, of course."

"That poor little guy."

"Hey, it's me. I am that little guy."

"Match."

He closes his eyes and smiles. "I've been waiting forty years to hear you call me that again."

"You've been waiting for a lot of things, apparently."

"What have you been waiting for?"

Helen puts her hand up and touches his hair, sliding her fingers in and around to the back of his head. "This, for one."

His arms come around her waist, gently drawing her in. He takes her loose hand and pulls it around him, holding her just tightly enough that she can keep her weight off the booted foot. He begins to sway a little, his hips against hers, guiding her to get in sync with him. "At last," he sings the Etta James classic quietly in her ear, "my love has come along . . ."

Helen giggles. "At last is right!"

They kiss, he sings, they sway, they kiss some more.

"How's your fantasy going?" she asks.

"Really satisfying," he says, still swaying. "I was so jealous of Barb and Cormac on Thanksgiving. I practically had to leave the room to keep my hands off you."

"Cal."

"Yeah?"

"You know what I'd like to try?"

"Tell me."

"Sleeping with you on something other than branches and jackets."

She can feel his smile against her temple. "I'd be open to trying that," he whispers. He slips a shoulder under her arm and helps her hobble into the bedroom. They stand next to the clothing-strewn bed, and he reaches around behind and unzips her.

"This is a knockout dress."

"It's my favorite."

"Must have been some fancy date you had planned."

"I was freaking out and yanking things out of the closet. I wasn't going to wear it. I just wanted to see myself in it again."

"I'm going to take you someplace worthy of this dress."

"Where?"

"I don't know. I'll come up with something." He kisses her and slides his hands inside the dress, caressing her back. "I'm a little distracted right now."

"Um . . ."

"Yes?"

"Probably stating the obvious here, but just to be clear, I don't look like I did when I was eighteen."

"Really? That's funny. I do. My toes grew back and everything."

"I've had children."

"Helen, I was in the best shape of my life the last time we took our clothes off."

"You were pretty godlike."

He laughs. "Well, prepare to be disappointed."

She slides her hands under his shirt and up his torso. "I don't know, this all seems pretty firm."

"I've been working out a ton the last few months. Needed to burn off a lot of frustration and self-doubt. Plus no sex."

"So once you're happy and sexually fulfilled?"

"It's all going to hell. You should probably take advantage while you can."

They help each other off with their clothes. It's slow and sensual, with none of the frenetic hurriedness of youth. He does not look quite like he did when he was eighteen, but he's still so beautiful to her with his rosy skin and muscular chest. "Helen," he whispers, "you're amazing." The feel of him against her, his hands rediscovering her body is so arousing she could practically take him standing up.

They shove the mountain of clothes off the bed and crawl in over and around each other, swirling like puppies eager to capture every bit of contact. They kiss and murmur and stroke until their craving for connection is so overpowering that she opens, and he enters, united, conjoined, dancing the most primal of dances. And it is so much better than forty years ago.

"Helen, my God," he moans as they crest the wave and surf down the other side.

She is flying and thinks for a moment she'll faint. "Oh," she sighs, "Cal . . ."

Afterward they curl up tight, arms around each other, legs entwined, bodies still reverberating. He starts to laugh. "Wheels," he breathes.

"Whoo, Match," she giggles.

"My fifteen-year-old self cannot get enough of hearing that."

"My fifty-eight-year-old self is pretty tickled, too."

He pulls back to look at her. "Can I tell you something?"

"Oh God, what is it?" she says. "Seriously, I cannot take one more revelation."

He laughs. "No, it's not—"

"You're joining a mission to colonize Jupiter."

"I just want to say . . ." He composes himself, his grin shifting into something softer, more serious. "When we first started spending time together, it was great, but I was worried it was for the wrong reasons. Like maybe being with you felt good because it assuaged my guilt. I kept telling myself I didn't have to keep coming up with reasons to see you. You'd forgiven me. It was over.

"But then I'd find myself wondering what you were doing, or think of something I wanted to tell you, or just . . ." He sighs a little chuckle. "God, I just wanted to be near you. As much as I loved you back then, it's more than that now." His smile is so warm, and she thinks it may be the happiest she's ever seen him. "You're the one, Helen. I'm stating for the record that I'll do anything to make this work."

She takes a moment to absorb his words, that blissful look on his face, all of it. Then she says, "Anything?"

He laughs. "Well, you know, within reason."

"So, not anything."

"Let's say short of joining a cult or committing a felony. Actually, depending on the felony . . ."

"Okay, I'll keep the potential willingness to end up in federal prison in mind. But at the moment, I can think of two things."

"Wow, that was fast."

"Well, I do have a fantasy life, and recently you've figured prominently."

He smiles seductively. "I'd like to hear more about that."

"You're about to."

"Man, this day just keeps getting better."

"I would like . . ."

"Yeah . . ."

". . . you to stop cutting your hair so short."

Cal falls back on the pillow, cracking up. Helen props an elbow under her head to face him. "It's too damn short! What are you, a marine?"

"It's not that short, and I'm a middle-aged man! I cannot pull off *flow* with any self-respect."

"Listen"—she taps her bare chest—"I am The One, as you said. I'm asking you to do a very easy thing, and you're already giving me lip? What's to become of us?"

He runs a finger down her cheek. "Fine. I'll grow it to my ass if you want me to."

"No need to overachieve. Just a little longer."

"You're officially in charge of my hair. What's the other thing?"

She gives him a sly smile. "You're thinking it's sexual, aren't you?"

"Hoping, anyway."

"I suppose it is, partially."

"Helen . . ."

"I want you to take me camping. I want to roast a decent marshmallow and have tent sex."

Cal looks up at her and shakes his head just a little, like he can't believe his luck. He slides an arm around her and rolls up and onto her and murmurs, "Wheels, I am going to take you on the camping trip of a lifetime."

"Well, that's accurate, since I've never been before."

He kisses her and whispers, "We are going to camp so hard."

"Mmmm," she purrs. "Don't forget the marshmallows."

# Chapter 47

## 2022

In January Helen is sitting on her couch with her feet up on the coffee table, tapping away at her laptop, when she looks up and feels a wave of utter disbelief.

*Cal Crosby is reading a book in my living room.*

She stares at him with his rumpled shirt and reading glasses, as his eyes flick back and forth across the page of a book about Teddy Roosevelt. *River of Doubt.*

He glances up, catches her, and smiles.

Oh, that smile.

He puts down the book, languidly stands, makes his way over to the couch, and sits next to her. "Sup?"

They both laugh. *Sup* is something he probably said in his twenties, but certainly never says now.

"I was just having one of those moments."

"Like?"

"Like I'm sitting here doing my usual Friday-afternoon thing and suddenly . . . Cal Crosby is reading a book in my living room."

"I have those all the time!"

"You do?"

"Absolutely. *Helen Iannucci is making me dinner.* Actually it happens the most when I sleep here. I always wake up before you do, and you're out like a light, doing that little snore thing—"

"Oh God, I snore?"

"A little. It's not like CPAP-level or anything."

"But it might be someday."

"Yeah, but I'll probably need one, too, at that point, so we can make mad passionate love and then strap in together."

She laughs. "So my snoring is one of those moments."

"No, it's you being there at all. I look at you with your little bear-cub snore, and I have this tiny nanosecond freak-out: *Helen Iannucci is sleeping next to me.*"

"You think of me as Helen Iannucci?"

"Well, no, not exactly. I mean, it's not like I wish you'd never gotten married or anything. It's just . . . in that moment, I guess I'm my pre-three-months-ago self who only knows you as your younger self, and I'm looking at my future, and it's pretty fucking great."

Helen snuggles into Cal, and he puts an arm around her. "I missed you," she says.

"I thought you were too busy hating me to miss me."

"It was both. I just didn't know it. And now I have to catch up on all that missing, but also, you're here, and I don't have to miss you at all. It's very confusing."

"What do you think would've happened if we'd come off that mountain and just told everyone we were together and if they didn't like it, they could jump in a lake?"

"I think it would have been a much better summer," she says.

"Way better. But what about after that?"

"You're asking if we would've made it."

"Yeah, would we be here today—or somewhere—happily sitting on a couch together?"

They ponder that for a moment, cozied up in a little town, many miles from where they started. She turns to face him, and he pulls her legs up onto his lap.

"I like to think we would," says Helen, "but I'm not a hundred percent sure."

"I had a lot of growing up to do."

"So did I."

"Not quite as much," he says. "You were pretty mature."

"For eighteen. But there were still a lot of lessons to learn."

"*So* many."

"We wouldn't have our kids," she says. "I mean, we'd probably have other kids, but not these ones . . ."

"Yeah, under no circumstances can I wish my kids away, even if I would've never known about them."

"Agreed. This is getting very *Wrinkle-in-Time*-y."

"Highly speculative."

"Do *you* think we would have made it?" she asks.

"I like to think we would, too. I was so in love with you . . . but, if I'm honest, that only gets you so far. Love is definitely a requirement for a good marriage, but it's not the only thing you need."

"If the choice is between *maybe* making it then—with the possibility of having those forty years together but also possibly breaking up forever—and definitely making it now, which do you choose?"

He laughs. "Are we definitely making it now?"

"Are you questioning that?"

"Not for a minute. I am one hundred percent sure about you, Helen Spencer."

She picks up Cal's hand off her thigh and holds it to her cheek. He gazes at her.

"What if there is no alternate reality?" he says.

She tucks his hand onto her lap. "And marrying other people was always going to happen?"

"And everything else . . ."

"So it all conspired to bring us to this moment now," she says. "On this couch."

"Which it did, obviously. Look, I'm not trying to be fatalistic here, and I believe in making the best decisions you can at the time and trying to fix what you broke and making amends and everything. But what if after you do all that . . . it goes the way it goes."

Helen nods. "Well, there would certainly be a whole lot of regret we could let go of."

"Poof."

"Big, giant, mushroom-cloud poof."

"And we could just—" Cal grins.

"What?"

"Enjoy it."

# Chapter 48

*2022–2026*

They'll spend the next four years almost constantly together. "I keep waiting to get annoyed by you and need some space," she'll say that first summer when they spend a week in one of the tiny rustic cabins at the Cape Cod National Seashore.

"How's that going?" he'll ask.

"Not well. Sometimes I miss you when you go out to pee."

You got a *mulligan*, Danny will text Helen out of the blue one day.

*You okay with that?* she'll respond.

*Yup.*

He'll never mention it again.

Cormac and Barb will adopt a little boy and name him Charlie after Cormac's dad. Upon hearing this, the elder man will tip over with emotion, since he still won't be willing to use his cane. Cormac will catch him before he hits the deck, muttering, "Jesus, Pop, I'm gonna have to start wearing a truss."

One night, snuggled up around her, Cal will whisper, "You're my love letter and I'm your envelope."

This will make Helen feel surprisingly emotional. "I guess I never thought of myself as anyone's love letter. Or if I was, I was sitting in a dusty drawer somewhere with the pennies and the paper clips, unmailed."

"We're going to spend the next forty years mailing ourselves to each other."

"Till we're ninety-eight? That's kind of old."

"We'll get decrepit together. It'll be fun."

"Okay, but use your cane, will you? Cormac can't keep catching stubborn old men. And don't lose your hair."

"I WANT TO meet Noni," she'll tell him.

"Oh, boy," he'll say, "this can't be good."

But he'll set it up. The four of them will have dinner at a restaurant overlooking Boston Harbor. It'll be a little awkward until Helen turns to Noni, cocks her head at Cal and Suze, and says, "So these two, huh?" and Noni laughs so hard she spills her martini.

WHEN HELEN AND Cal get married at Seven Meadows Farm, Noni and Suze will be there. Before the ceremony Suze will joke with Cal, "Should I be giving you away?"

"I think you already did."

"No, we were keeping each other safe until our Princess Charmings came along. Mine just happened to show up first."

KIERSTEN WILL AGREE to give Sam another chance, and he'll work hard not to cross the line from addressing valid concerns to just being nitpicky. In fact, things will go so well that Sam will ask Kiersten to marry him on a clear day on top of Mount Pilchuck with an arresting view of Mount Rainier. He'll propose with a love poem he'll write and carry around in his pocket as he waits for the perfect, most romantic opportunity. She will politely decline. Danny will show his brotherly love by verbally slapping Sam around by text, telling him to *Suit up and get your candy ass back in there.* On the third try, at a gas station, Kiersten will say yes.

THINGS WILL NOT work out for Danny with Maria from NOLS. But he'll start dating a special education teacher from Jackson, Wyoming, named Alice. He'll park his camper in her driveway and volunteer in her classroom when he's not on a shoot. During free time, kids will take turns braiding his hair.

CAL WILL HELP Helen and Cormac open a second confectionery site. They'll call it Annabella's. It will serve her signature anise cookies, and they'll sell out every day.

"SORRY ABOUT MY hair," Cal will say when he loses it to chemo.

"There is nothing that could happen to you that would make you less beautiful to me," Helen will tell him.

"I could get a Lucille Ball wig."

"Okay, maybe that."

FIVE-YEAR-OLD MCKENZIE WILL adamantly insist on seeing Cal every day after school. This will precipitate a minor transportation crisis until Janel and Eli finally agree to move out of their noisy Somerville apartment and accept some financial help from Cal and Suze. They'll buy a house on Barley Spring Lane. Eight-year-old Logan will walk his sister over in the afternoons. Six-year-old Lana will often join them.

HELEN WILL MAKE photo books of all their trips: camping in the Olympics with Sam and Kiersten; skiing in Jackson Hole with Danny and Alice; visiting Bonnie in Australia; traveling through Italy to see Helen's parents' hometowns and meet cousins for the first time; hiking in Acadia, Glacier, and Yosemite. Early on they'll set a goal of visiting every national park. It's a goal they will not meet, at least not together. Often too foggy headed to read, Cal will pore through these books over and over.

THERE WILL ALSO be a book of pictures of his life before they got together, which Helen will collect mostly from his siblings and Suze. She'll find a picture in her old senior yearbook of the track team at the beginning of the season, the two of them standing side by side, grinning. Barb will help her scan and reproduce it, circling and clarifying their happy faces. It's the picture he'll linger on the longest.

THEY'LL SLOW DANCE every night.

WHEN HIS PROGNOSIS worsens, Bonnie will move back from Australia. His siblings will visit. Francie will call or visit every week. Janel will come by at a moment's notice. Noni will keep track of the insurance and all the bills. Prisha will bring endless bowls of Cal's favorite gulab jamun when he loses his appetite for everything else. But it's Suze whom Helen will cry with.

"For someone who always had a little trouble making friends," Francie will say, "you sure are swimming in them now."

"I DON'T WANT to leave you," he'll say every day at the end.

"You're not leaving me, Match," she'll remind him. "You've been with me since the tenth grade, and that's not going to change."

"I don't want to go anywhere without you."

"The first thing I'll do when I get there is find you."

"You won't have to find me. I'll be waiting at the station."

THE LAST THING he'll say to her is "Amazed."

# *Acknowledgments*

I don't know if all writers do this, but sometimes I casually decide something about a character—for instance that Helen Iannucci Spencer can't sit still—and that one little detail leads me deep into a rabbit hole of research. If she can't sit still . . . then she likes to move. What kind of movement? Dancing? Running? I decided she would join the track team, and that's where she'd meet Cal.

Once I began writing, though, I realized I didn't know the first thing about running track—and why couldn't I have chosen an activity that I knew even a little bit about? I threw out an ask on Facebook: "Help a girl out with some writerly research? If you ran track or cross-country, what did you like/hate about it? I was a drama/music/art nerd. I know nothing, so all tidbits welcome!"

Boy, did I get some fun tidbits—many thanks to all those who commented with their stories and information. I ended up interviewing three people: Mary Kubica, Jeannie Brown, and Art Hutchinson. They gave me great intel, for instance that there's a lot of puking involved, the track team often got the other teams' cast-off shirts, Jeannie's brother used it as practice for football, a kid on Art's team would hang out in the woods till the running was over, and Mary's coach was young and enthusiastic. I can't thank them enough for providing so many details and plot points.

My brother-in-law, Dr. Paul Allen, gave me a tutorial about what exactly happens during frostbite, how many toes Cal might lose, and how his reduced proprioception (great word!) would impact his football career. My husband, Tom Fay, who knows far more about football than I would ever care to know, convinced me to make Cal a wide receiver instead of a running back. (I can't remember why, but it was important to him, so I did it.)

I borrowed Francie's "horse craziness" from my childhood friend Rhea Nowak, with whom I spent many hours cantering around her backyard. In high school we hung out in the art department—I was a potter; she was a painter. I did unload kilns because Mrs. Sullivan, the ceramics teacher, was part-time, and when she was laid off, I got her apron, which I still wear. A graduate of Bennington College, Rhea is now a printmaker and professor of art at SUNY Oneonta in New York, and her work is beautiful. I have a framed painting of a sunflower she made for my seventeenth birthday that hangs on a wall I pass every day. It always makes me smile.

Barb's photography career comes by way of my sister, Kristen Iwai, a highly regarded portrait photographer in Flagstaff, Arizona, who started out as the assistant to a guy as socially inept as Roy. I hope Barb achieves Kristen's success someday!

As always, I'm deeply indebted to the wonderful early readers who took the time to dig into that first draft and come back with great comments, suggestions, and encouragement: Megan Lucier, Cathy McCue, Kristen Iwai, Tom and Brianna Fay, Nichole Bernier, Randy Susan Meyers, Kathy Crowley, and Liz Moore.

Heartfelt thanks to the team at William Morrow: Bianca Flores, Asanté Simons, Naureen Nashid, and my wise and wonderful editor, Lucia Macro, who always makes a story that much better.

My agent, Stéphanie Abou, is there for me time and time again, in matters big and small, and always has excellent advice.

Ann-Marie Nieves and her crackerjack team at Get Red PR, including Elise Levine Cooper, Lori Edelman, and Steve Becker, are some of the best in the business. I'm grateful for their help in spreading the word about my books.

Especially during the ups and downs of the pandemic, fresh air, brisk exercise, and earnest chats with dear friends fed my soul, kept me grounded, and sparked creativity in a thousand ways. For that I thank my regular walking pals: Sally Cartwright, Barb Fletcher, Karen Kiefer, Ilene Knopping, Megan Lucier, Cheryl MacDonald, Julie Murtagh, Katherine Provost, and Karen Stack.

Writing a novel about a woman who married the wrong guy reminded me on a daily basis of how fortunate I am to have married the right one. Tom Fay, thanks for being the right guy, now and always.